CHILDREN OF THE WOODS

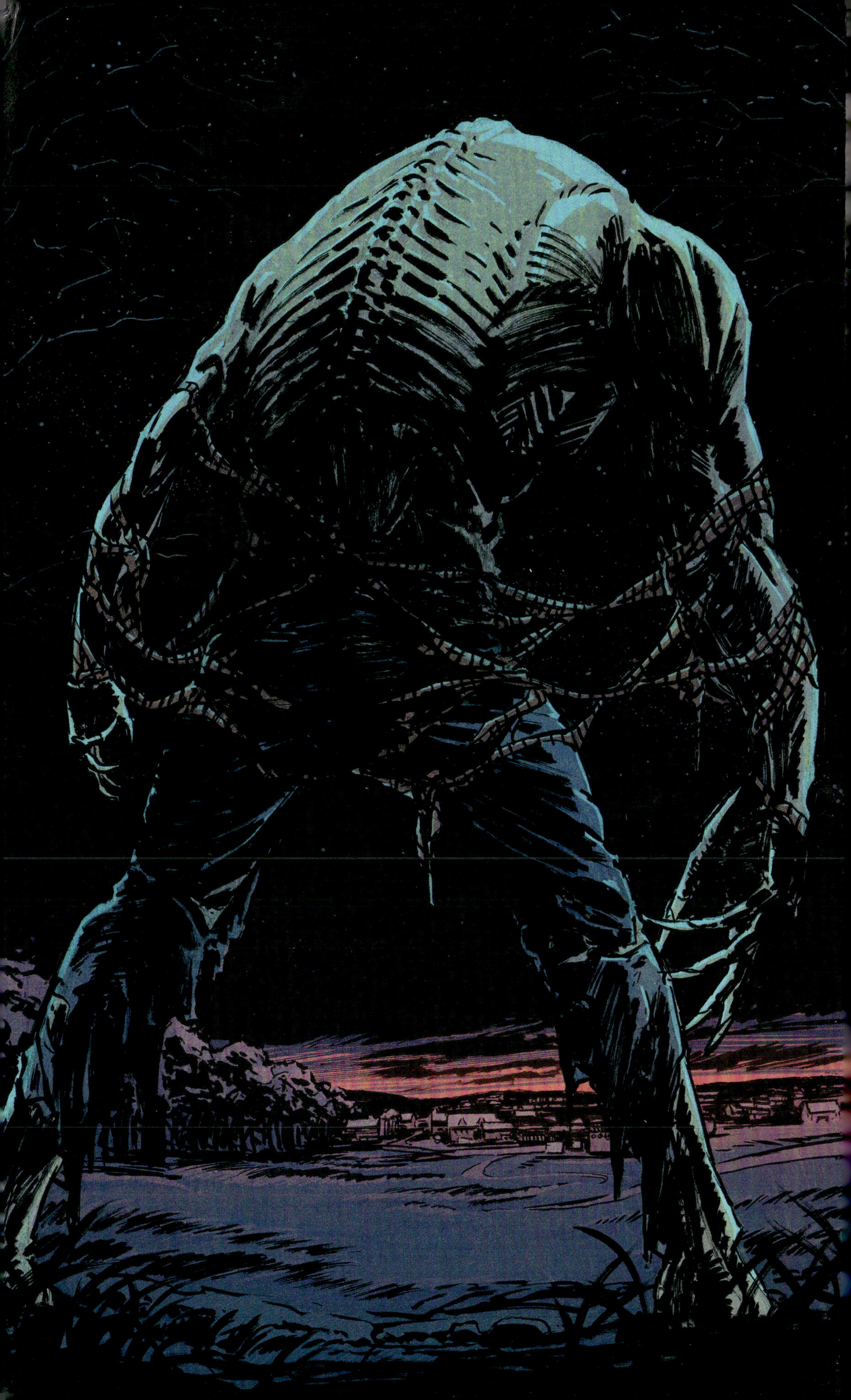

CHILDREN OF THE WOODS™

Written by
JOE CIANO

Illustrated by
JOSH HIXSON

Color Art by
ROMAN STEVENS

Letters by
HASSAN OTSMANE-ELHAOU

Title Logo Designed by
TYLER BOSS

DARK HORSE BOOKS

President and Publisher
MIKE RICHARDSON

Editor
BRETT ISRAEL

Assistant Editor
SANJAY DHARAWAT

Digital Art Technician
SAMANTHA HUMMER

Collection Designer
MAY HIJIKURO

NEIL HANKERSON Executive Vice President • TOM WEDDLE Chief Financial Officer • DALE LAFOUNTAIN Chief Information Officer • TIM WIESCH Vice President of Licensing • MATT PARKINSON Vice President of Marketing • VANESSA TODD-HOLMES Vice President of Production and Scheduling • MARK BERNARDI Vice President of Book Trade and Digital Sales • RANDY LAHRMAN Vice President of Product Development • KEN LIZZI General Counsel • DAVE MARSHALL Editor in Chief • DAVEY ESTRADA Editorial Director • CHRIS WARNER Senior Books Editor • CARY GRAZZINI Director of Specialty Projects • LIA RIBACCHI Art Director • MATT DRYER Director of Digital Art and Prepress • MICHAEL GOMBOS Senior Director of Licensed Publications • KARI YADRO Director of Custom Programs • KARI TORSON Director of International Licensing

Published by Dark Horse Books
A division of Dark Horse Comics LLC
10956 SE Main Street
Milwaukie, OR 97222

First edition: January 2022
Ebook ISBN 978-1-50672-708-0
Trade Paperback ISBN 978-1-50672-680-9

10 9 8 7 6 5 4 3 2 1
Printed in China

Comic Shop Locator Service: comicshoplocator.com

CHILDREN OF THE WOODS
Children of the Woods™ © 2022 Joe Ciano and Josh Hixson. Dark Horse Books® and the Dark Horse logo are registered trademarks of Dark Horse Comics LLC. All rights reserved. No portion of this publication may be reproduced or transmitted, in any form or by any means, without the express written permission of Dark Horse Comics LLC. Names, characters, places, and incidents featured in this publication either are the product of the author's imagination or are used fictitiously. Any resemblance to actual persons (living or dead), events, institutions, or locales, without satiric intent, is coincidental.

Library of Congress Cataloging-in-Publication Data

Names: Ciano, Joe, writer. | Hixson, Josh, illustrator. | Stevens, Roman, colourist. | Otsmane-Elhaou, Hassan, letterer.
Title: Children of the woods / written by Joe Ciano ; illustrated by Josh Hixson ; color art by Roman Stevens ; letters by Hassan Otsmane-Elhaou.
Description: First edition. | Milwaukie, OR : Dark Horse Books, 2022. | Summary: "From the minds of Joe Ciano and Josh Hixson, a tale of revenge leads to a monstrous outcome, Amber and Quinn pay the price for power and magic as they become the newest children of the Black Woods. As Amber becomes intertwined with the secrets of woods and the town they live in, Quinn learns he is not alone in the woods. And not all who reside there are welcoming"-- Provided by publisher.
Identifiers: LCCN 2021027642 | ISBN 9781506726809 (trade paperback) | ISBN 9781506727080 (ebook)
Subjects: LCGFT: Horror comics. | Graphic novels.
Classification: LCC PN6727.C4996 C47 2022 | DDC 741.5/973--dc23
LC record available at https://lccn.loc.gov/2021027642

CHAPTER 1

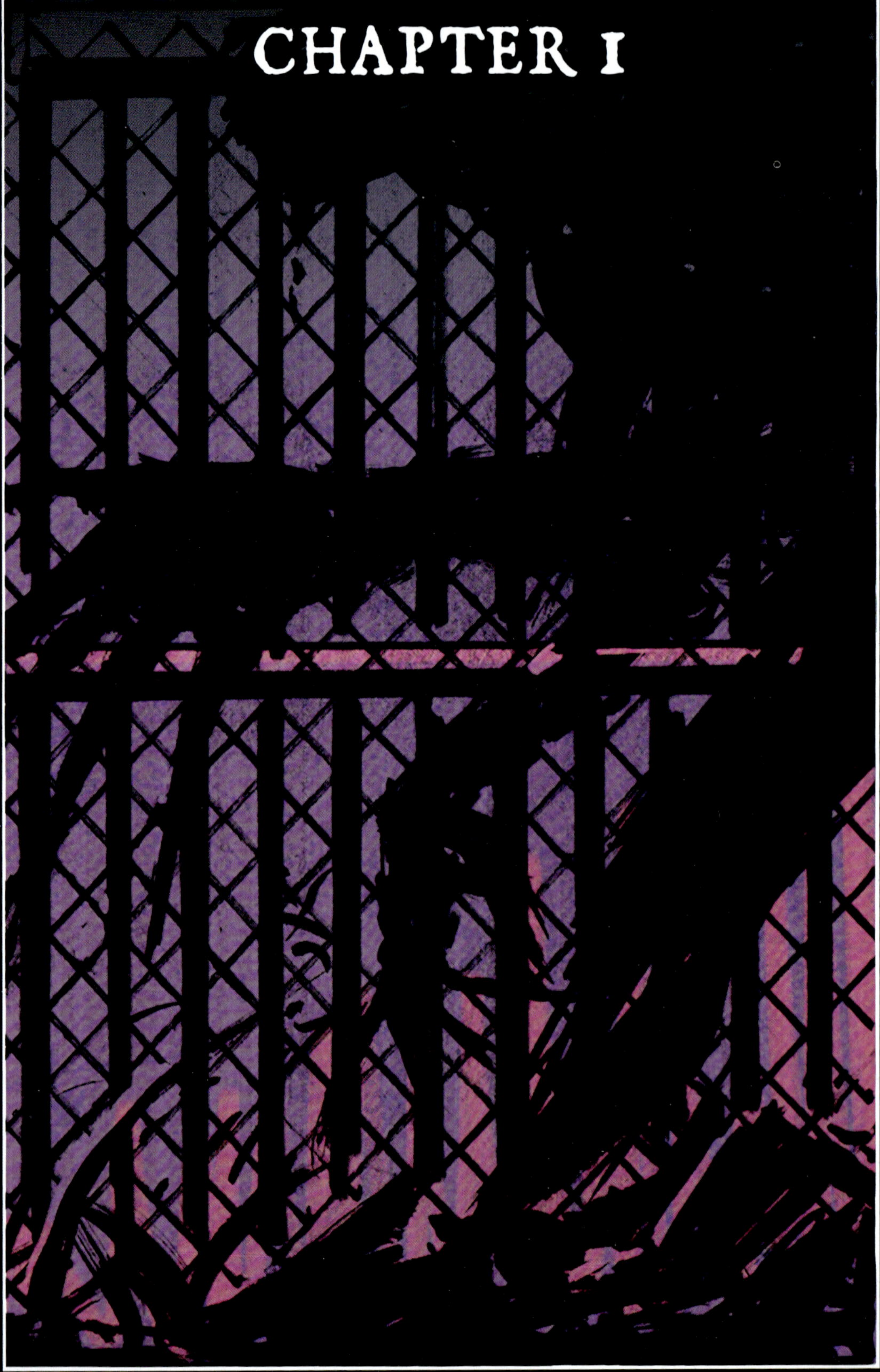

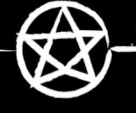

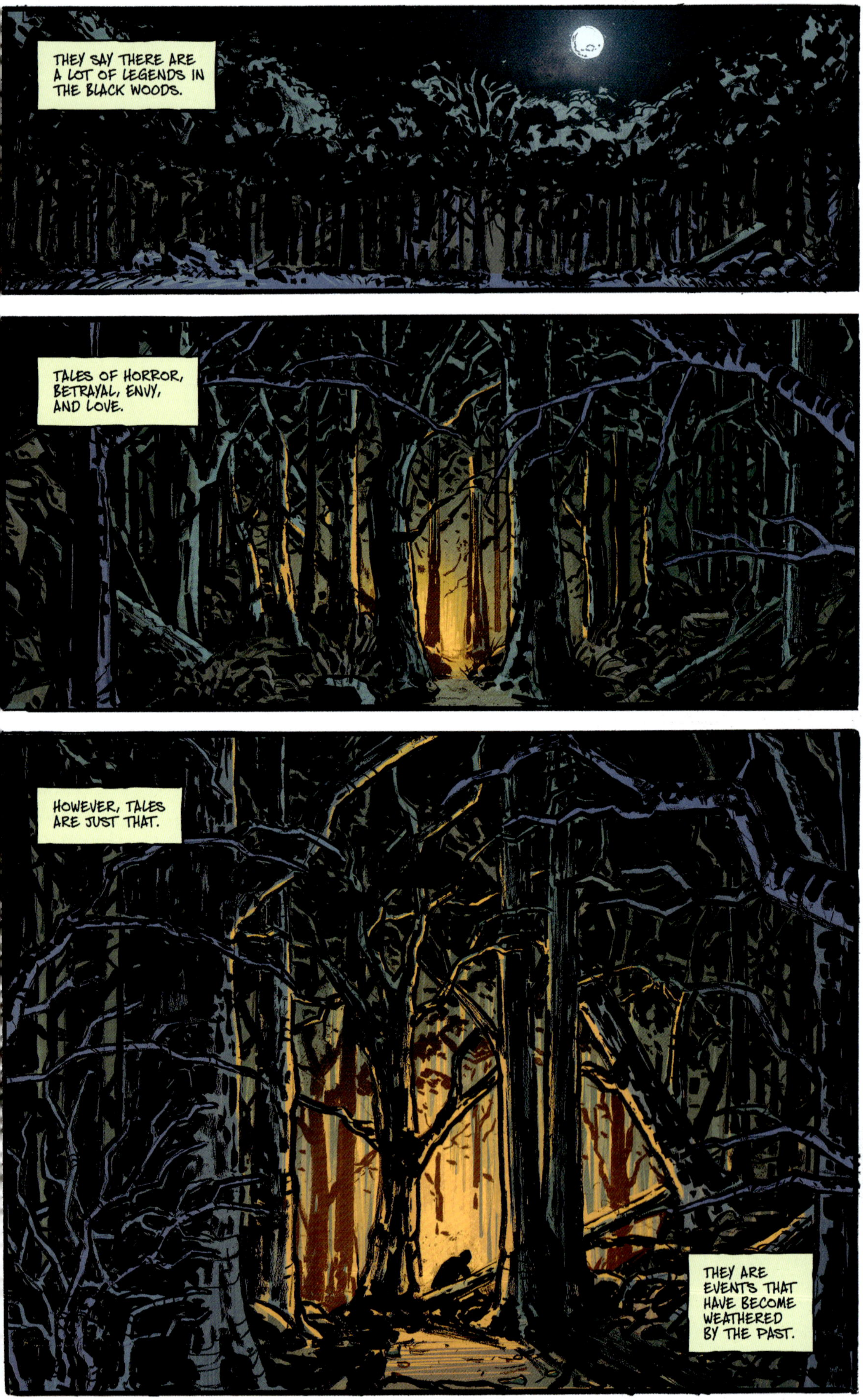
THEY SAY THERE ARE A LOT OF LEGENDS IN THE BLACK WOODS.
TALES OF HORROR, BETRAYAL, ENVY, AND LOVE.
HOWEVER, TALES ARE JUST THAT.
THEY ARE EVENTS THAT HAVE BECOME WEATHERED BY THE PAST.

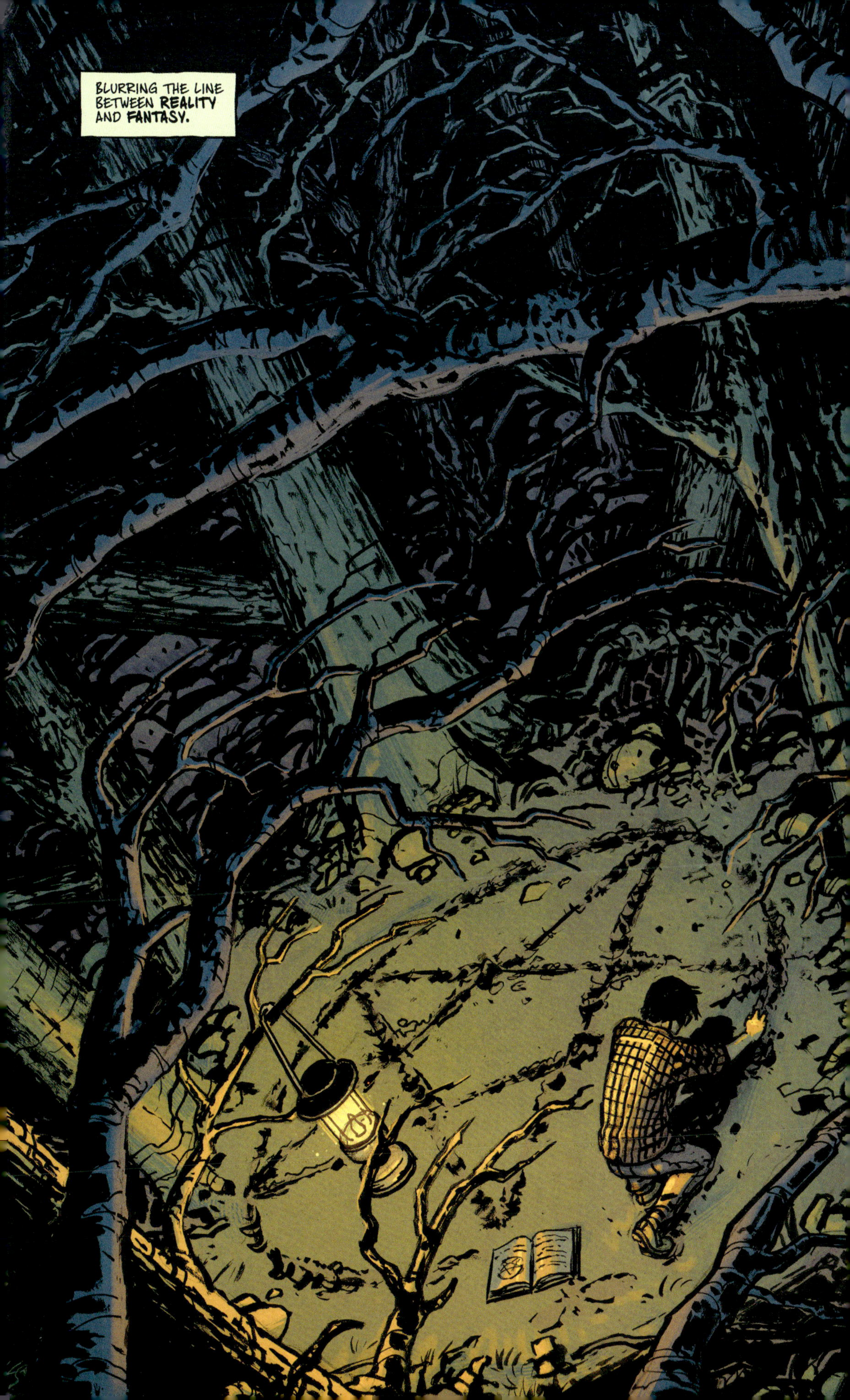
BLURRING THE LINE BETWEEN REALITY AND FANTASY.

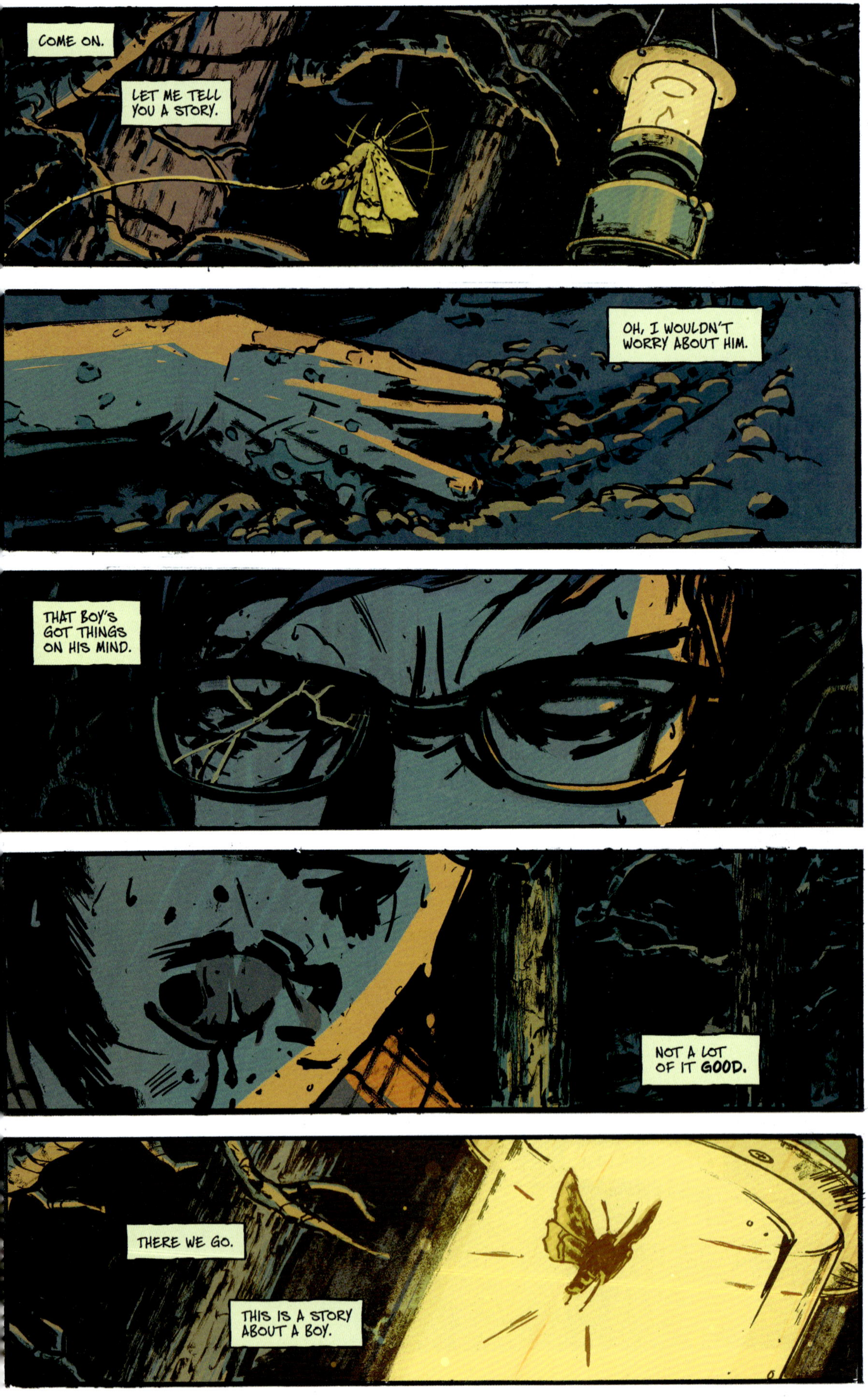
COME ON.
LET ME TELL YOU A STORY.
OH, I WOULDN'T WORRY ABOUT HIM.
THAT BOY'S GOT THINGS ON HIS MIND.
NOT A LOT OF IT **GOOD.**
THERE WE GO.
THIS IS A STORY ABOUT A BOY.

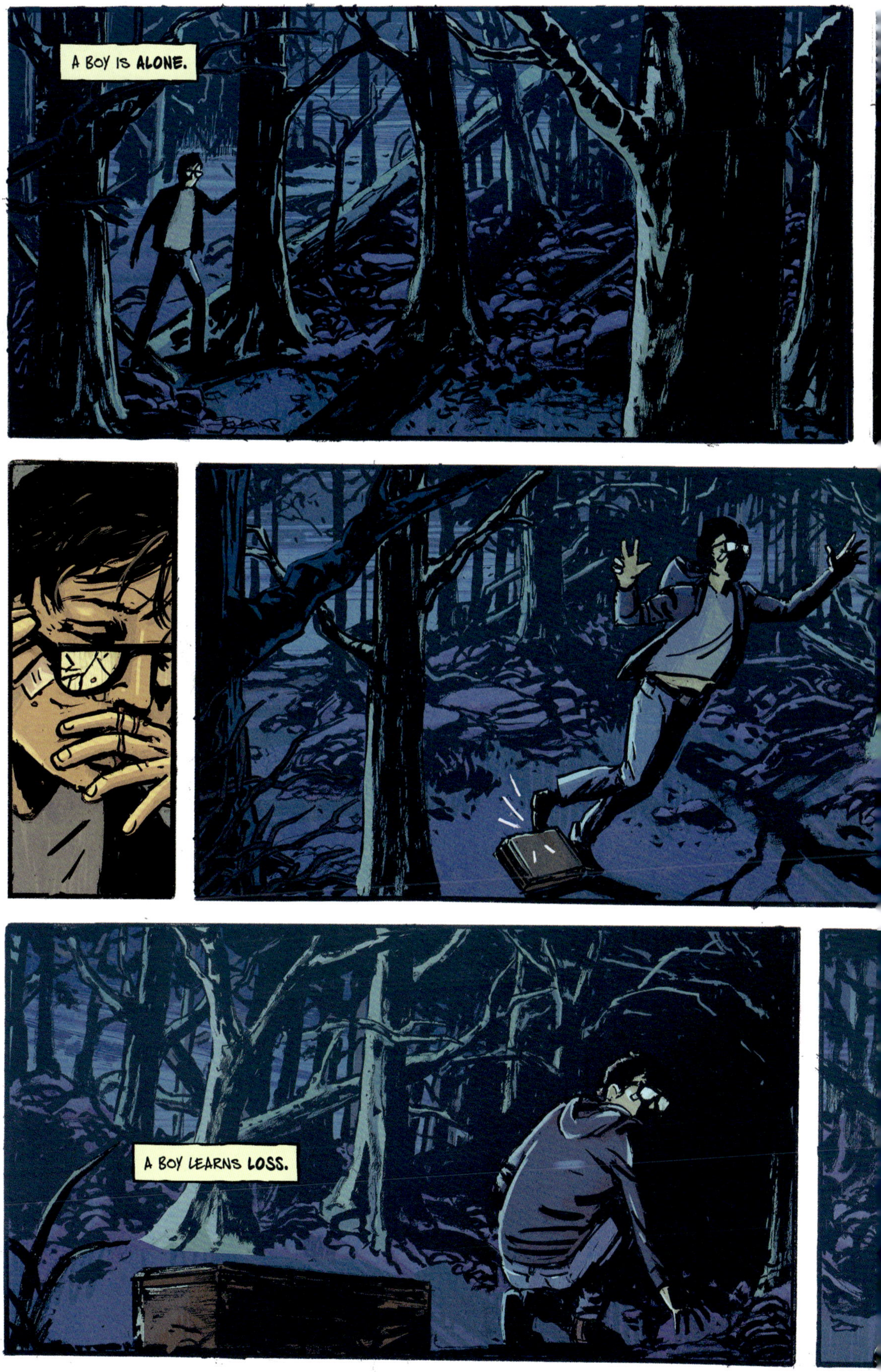
A BOY IS ALONE.
A BOY LEARNS LOSS.

A BOY KNOWS LOVE.
A BOY IS HATED.
A BOY IS LOST.
A BOY LEARNS HATRED.
A BOY NEEDS POWER.
POWER FINDS A BOY.

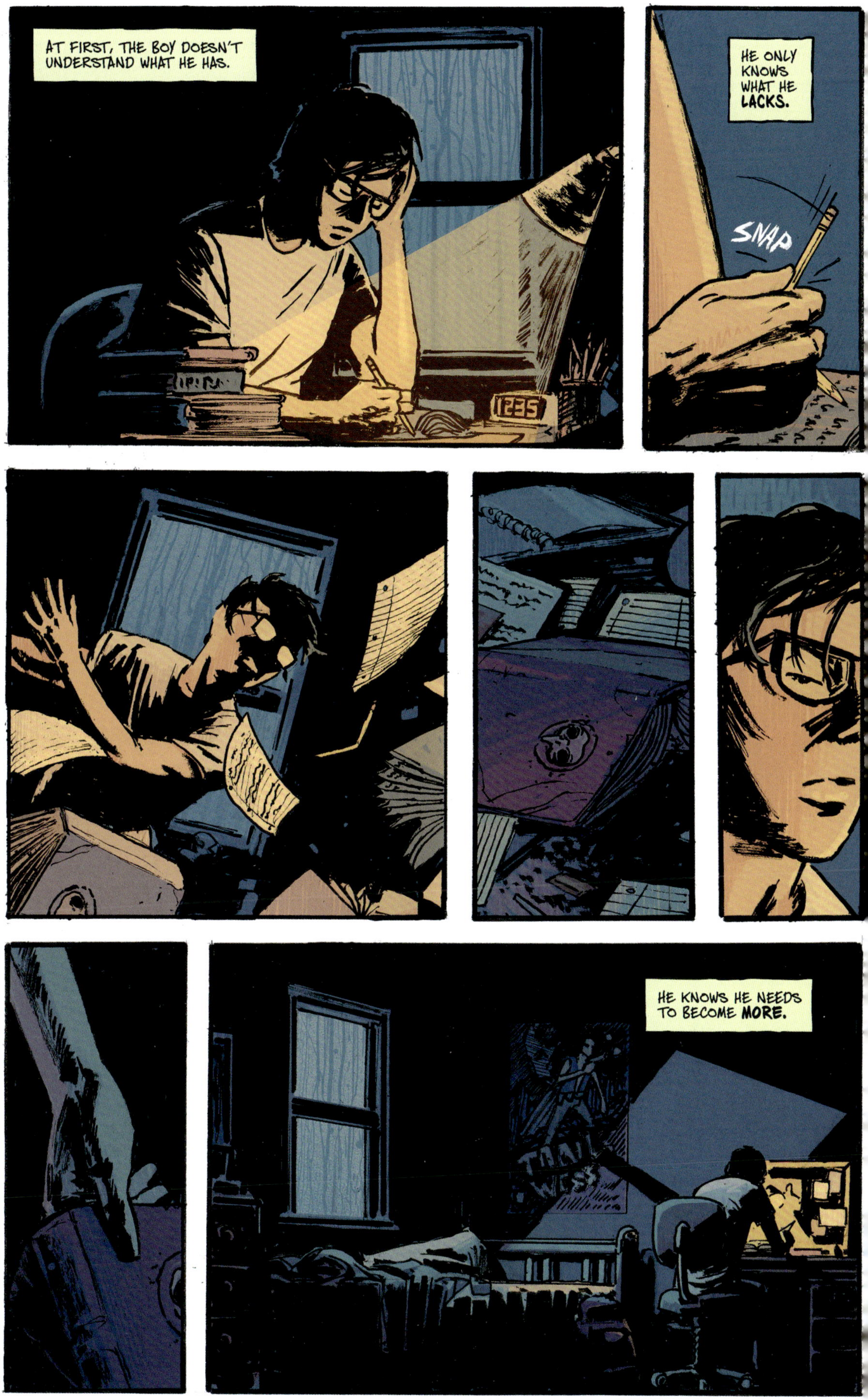
AT FIRST, THE BOY DOESN'T UNDERSTAND WHAT HE HAS.
HE ONLY KNOWS WHAT HE **LACKS.**
SNAP
HE KNOWS HE NEEDS TO BECOME **MORE.**

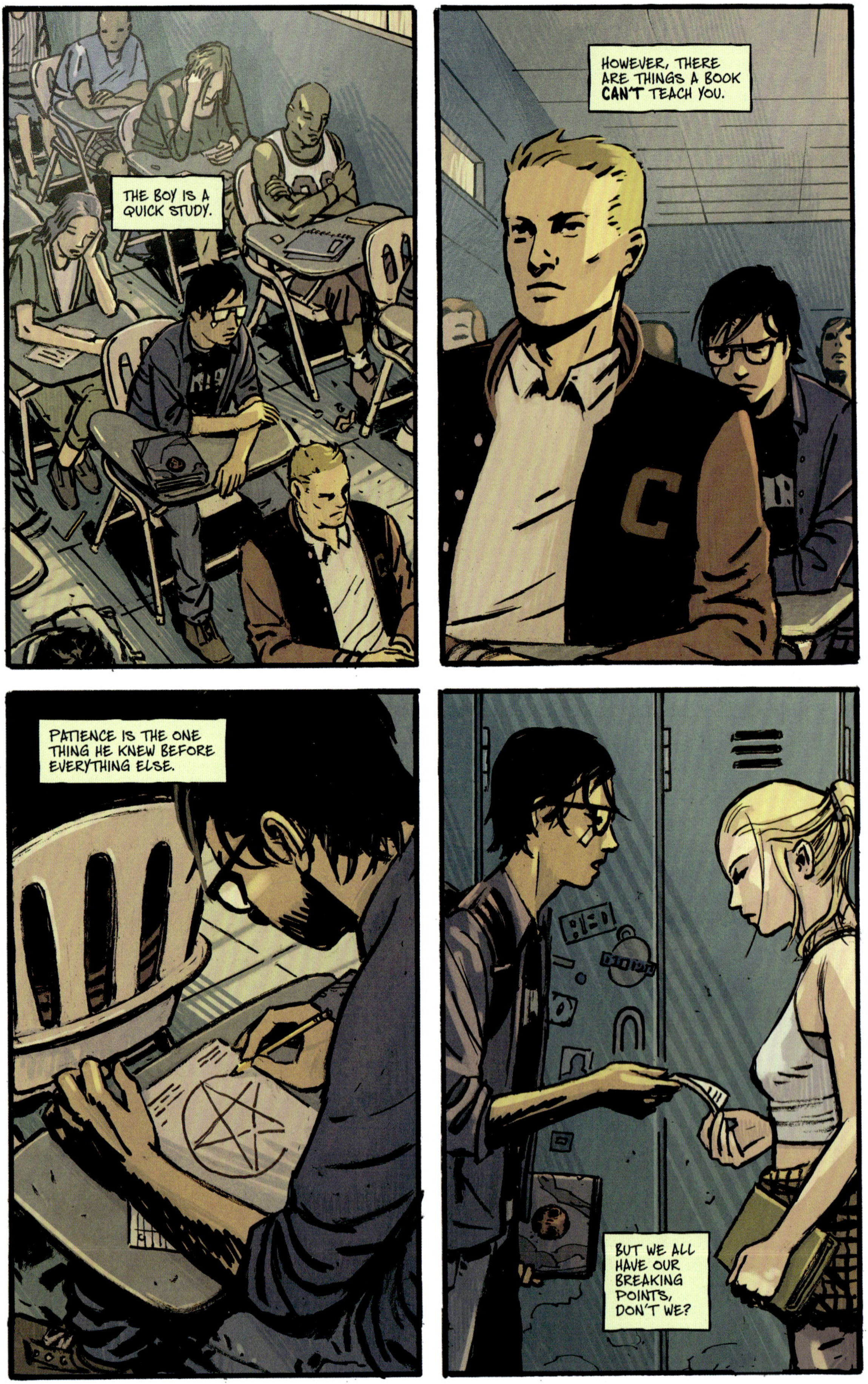
THE BOY IS A QUICK STUDY.
HOWEVER, THERE ARE THINGS A BOOK **CAN'T** TEACH YOU.
PATIENCE IS THE ONE THING HE KNEW BEFORE EVERYTHING ELSE.
BUT WE ALL HAVE OUR BREAKING POINTS, DON'T WE?

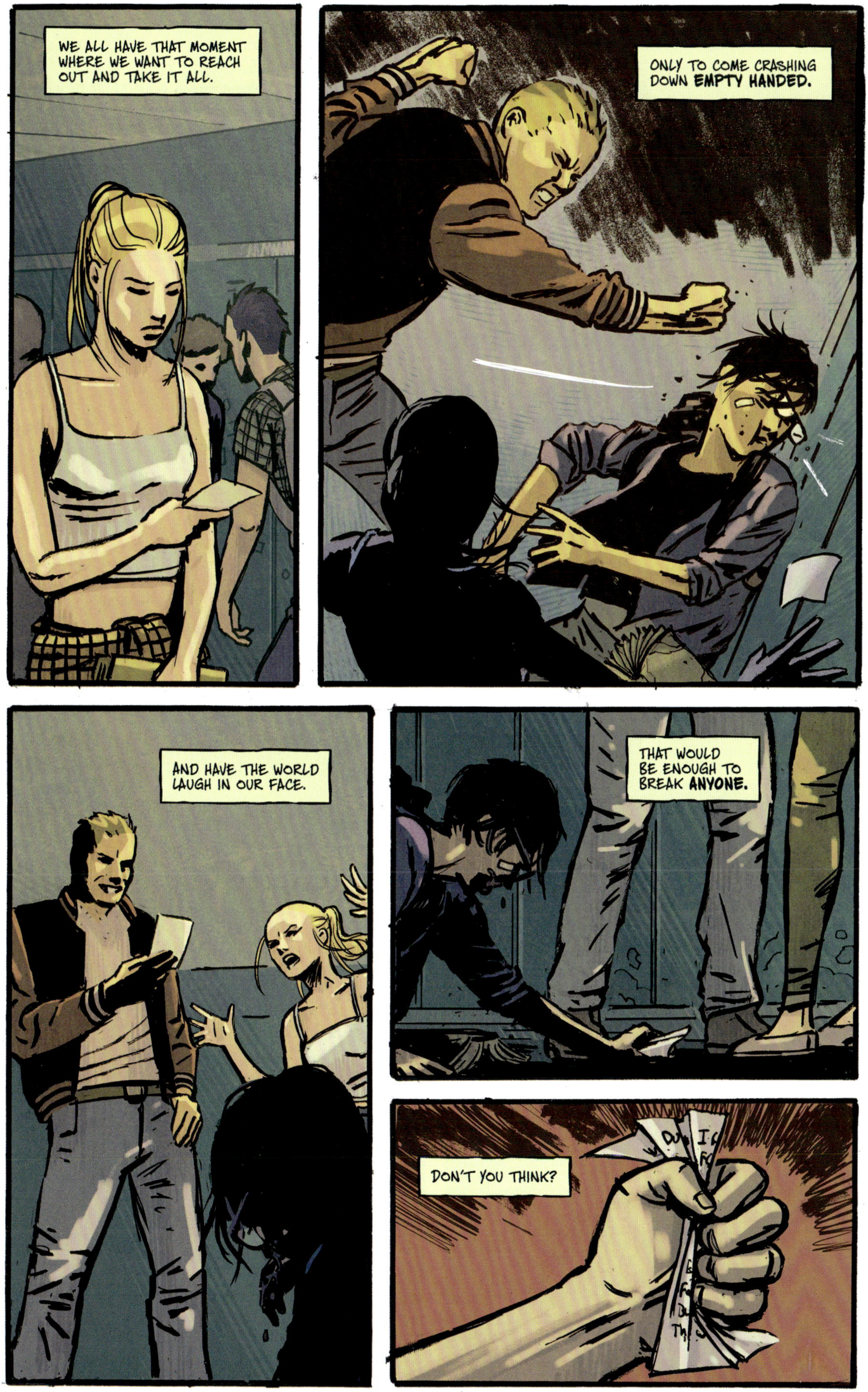
WE ALL HAVE THAT MOMENT WHERE WE WANT TO REACH OUT AND TAKE IT ALL.
ONLY TO COME CRASHING DOWN EMPTY HANDED.
AND HAVE THE WORLD LAUGH IN OUR FACE.
THAT WOULD BE ENOUGH TO BREAK ANYONE.
DON'T YOU THINK?

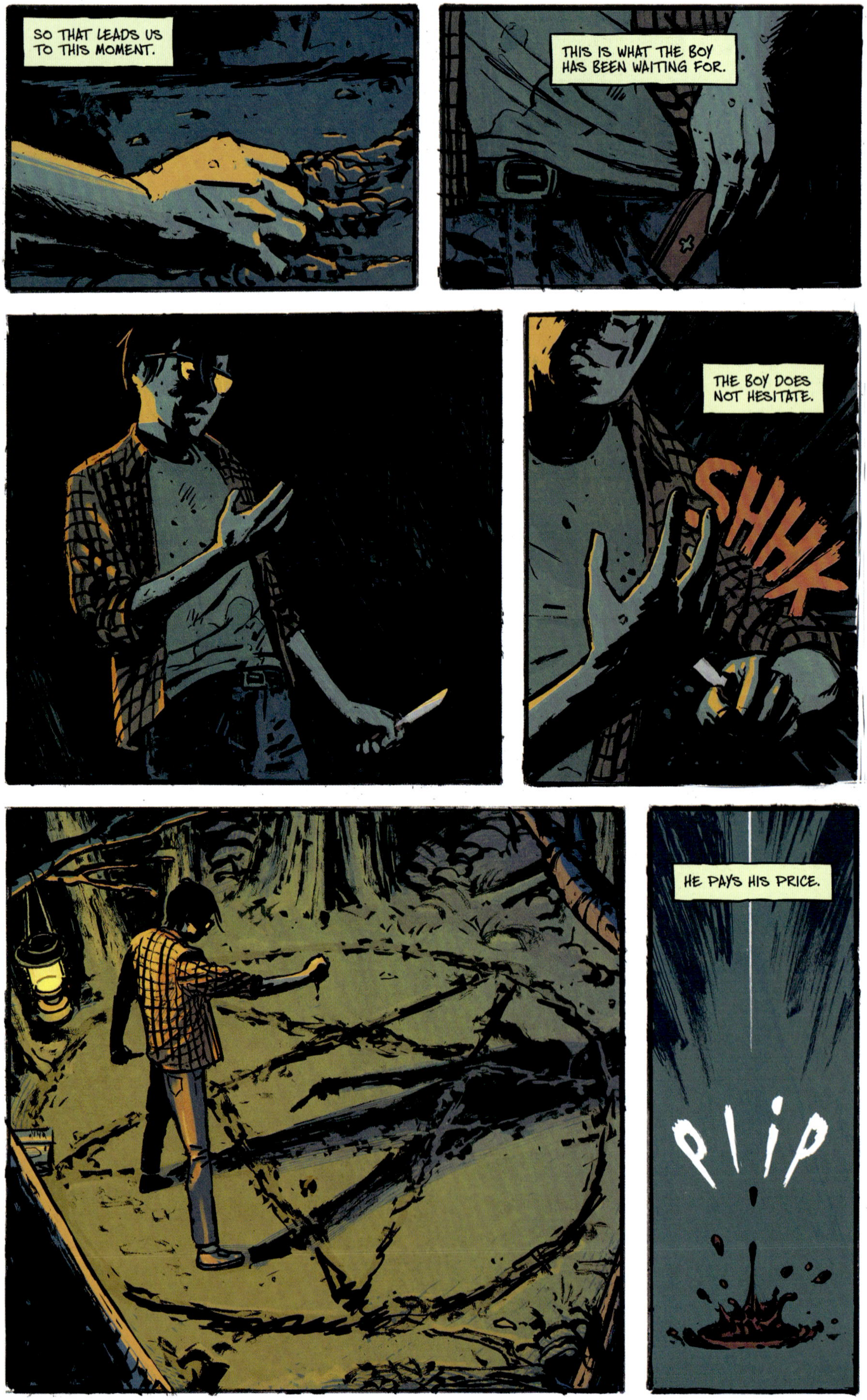
SO THAT LEADS US TO THIS MOMENT.
THIS IS WHAT THE BOY HAS BEEN WAITING FOR.
THE BOY DOES NOT HESITATE.
SHHK
HE PAYS HIS PRICE.
PLIP

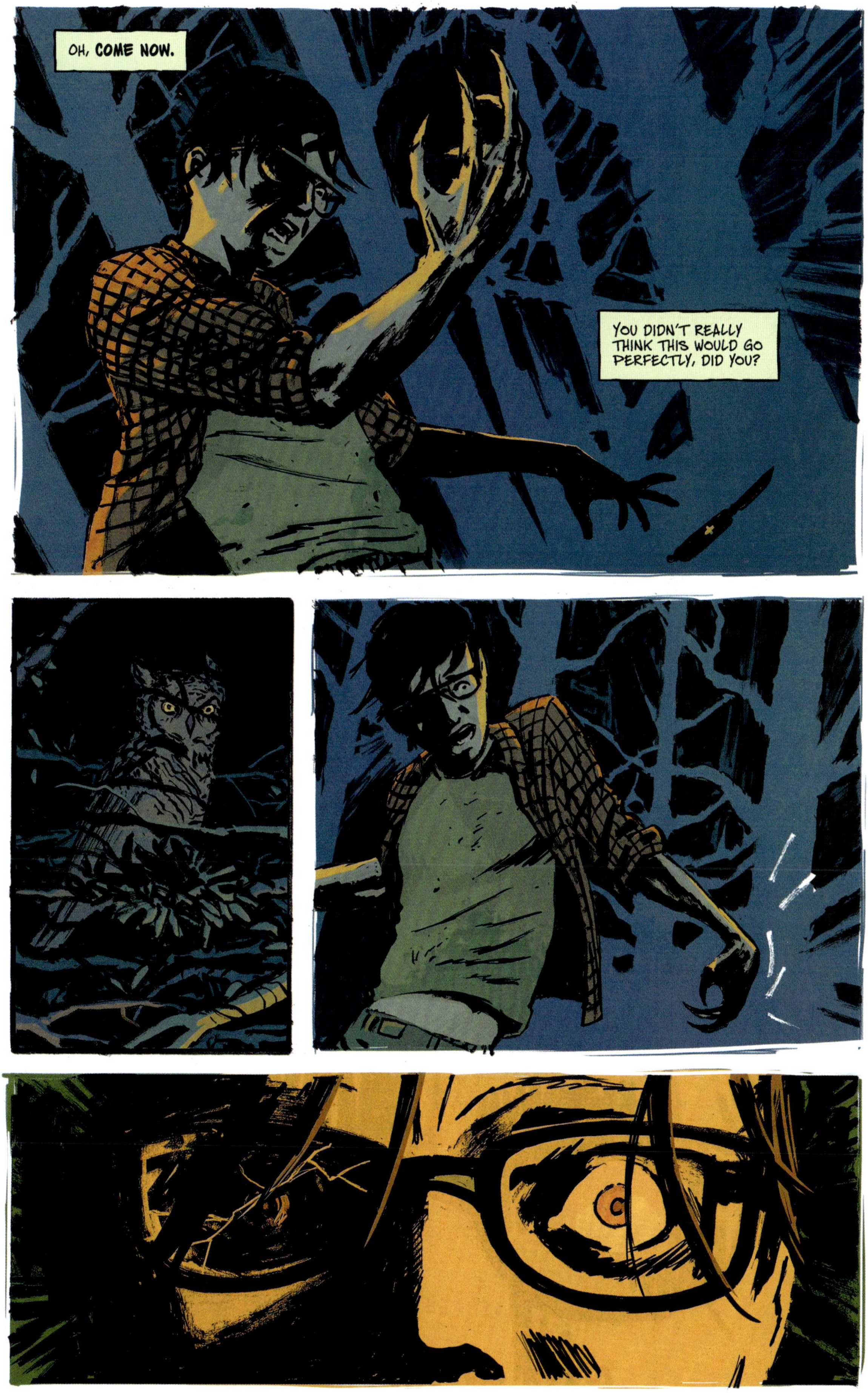
OH, COME NOW.
YOU DIDN'T REALLY THINK THIS WOULD GO PERFECTLY, DID YOU?

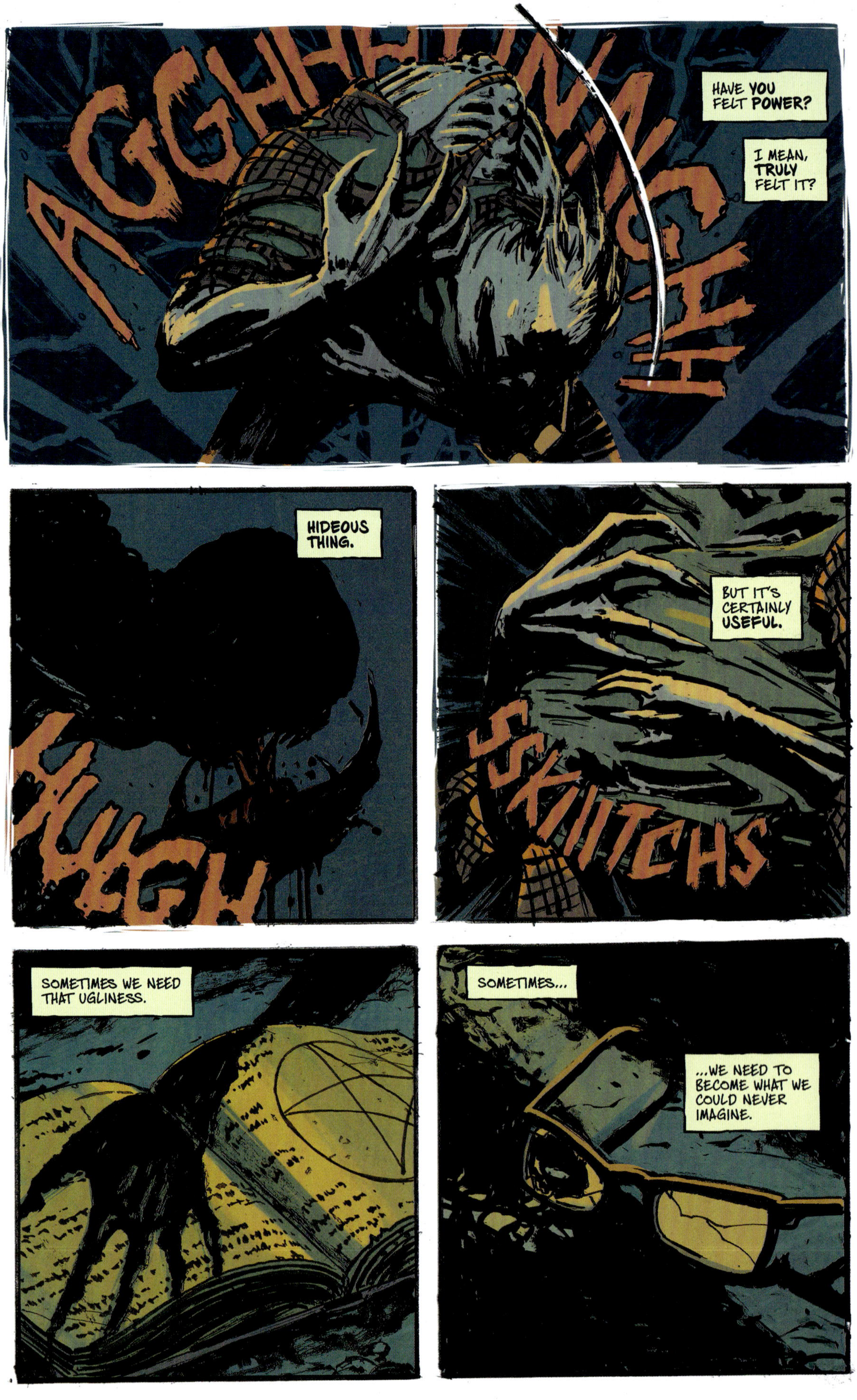
AGGHHHNNNGH
HAVE YOU FELT POWER?
I MEAN, TRULY FELT IT?
HIDEOUS THING.
HUUGH
BUT IT'S CERTAINLY USEFUL.
SSKIIITCHS
SOMETIMES WE NEED THAT UGLINESS.
SOMETIMES...
...WE NEED TO BECOME WHAT WE COULD NEVER IMAGINE.

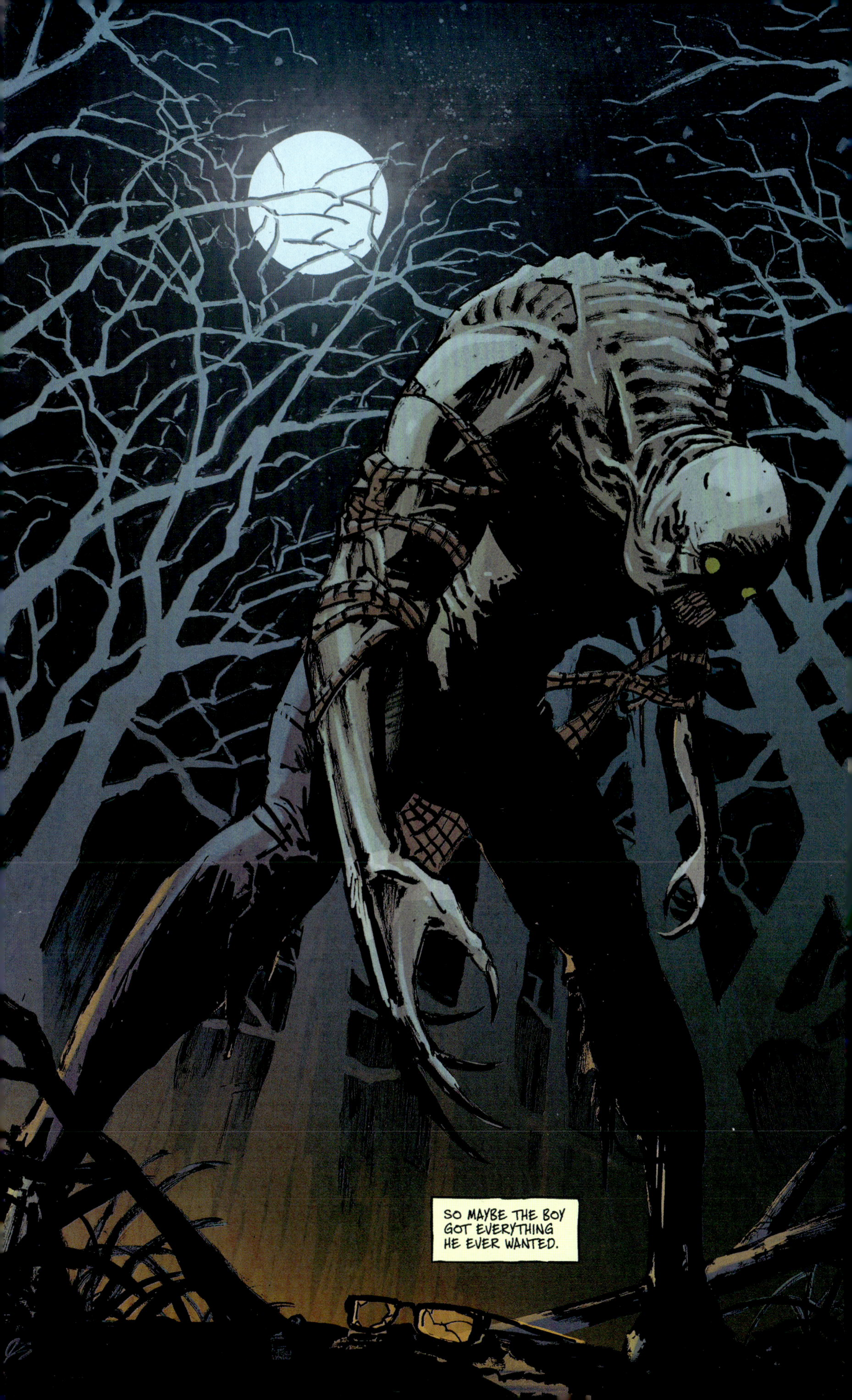
SO MAYBE THE BOY
GOT EVERYTHING
HE EVER WANTED.

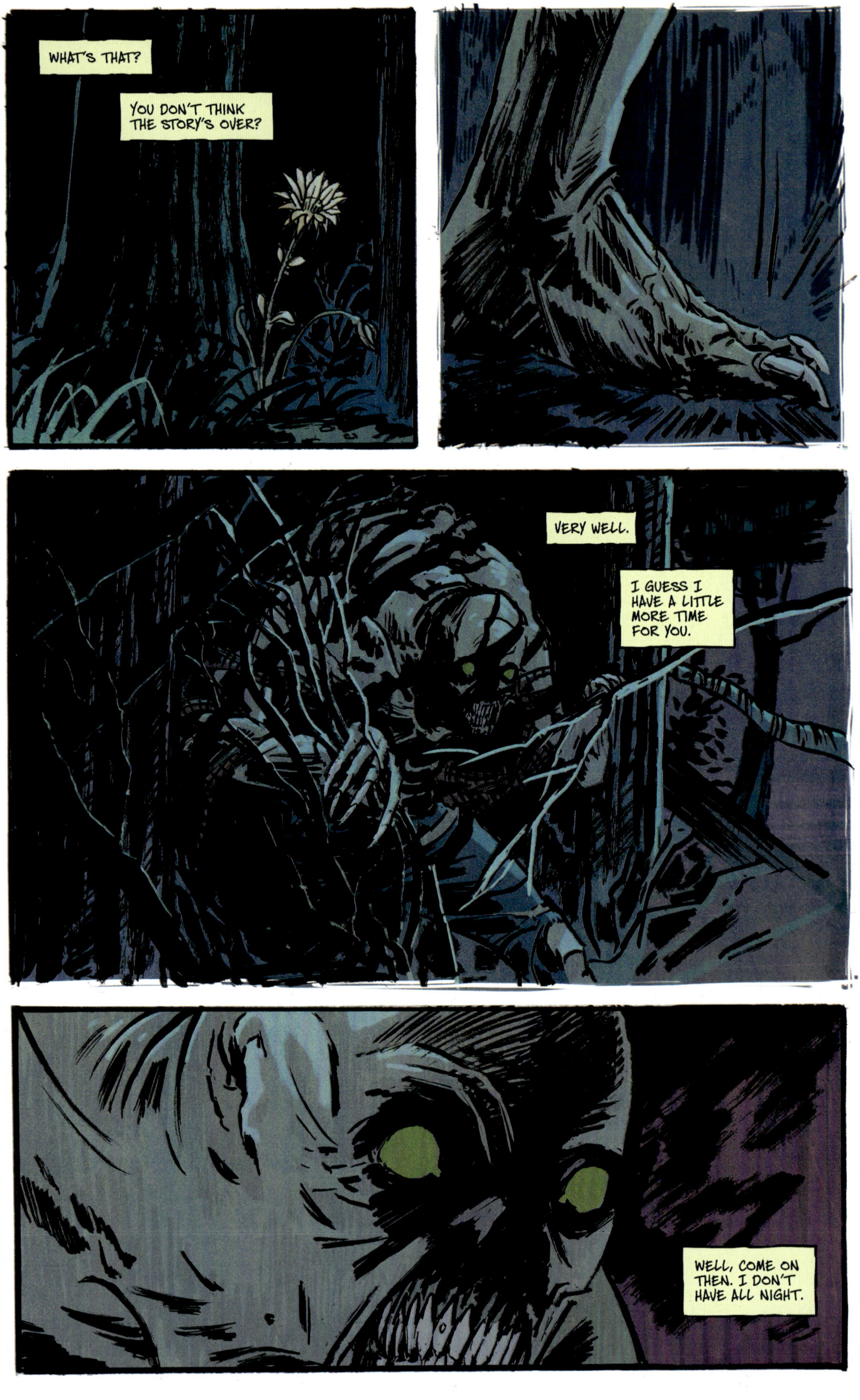
WHAT'S THAT?
YOU DON'T THINK THE STORY'S OVER?
VERY WELL.
I GUESS I HAVE A LITTLE MORE TIME FOR YOU.
WELL, COME ON THEN. I DON'T HAVE ALL NIGHT.

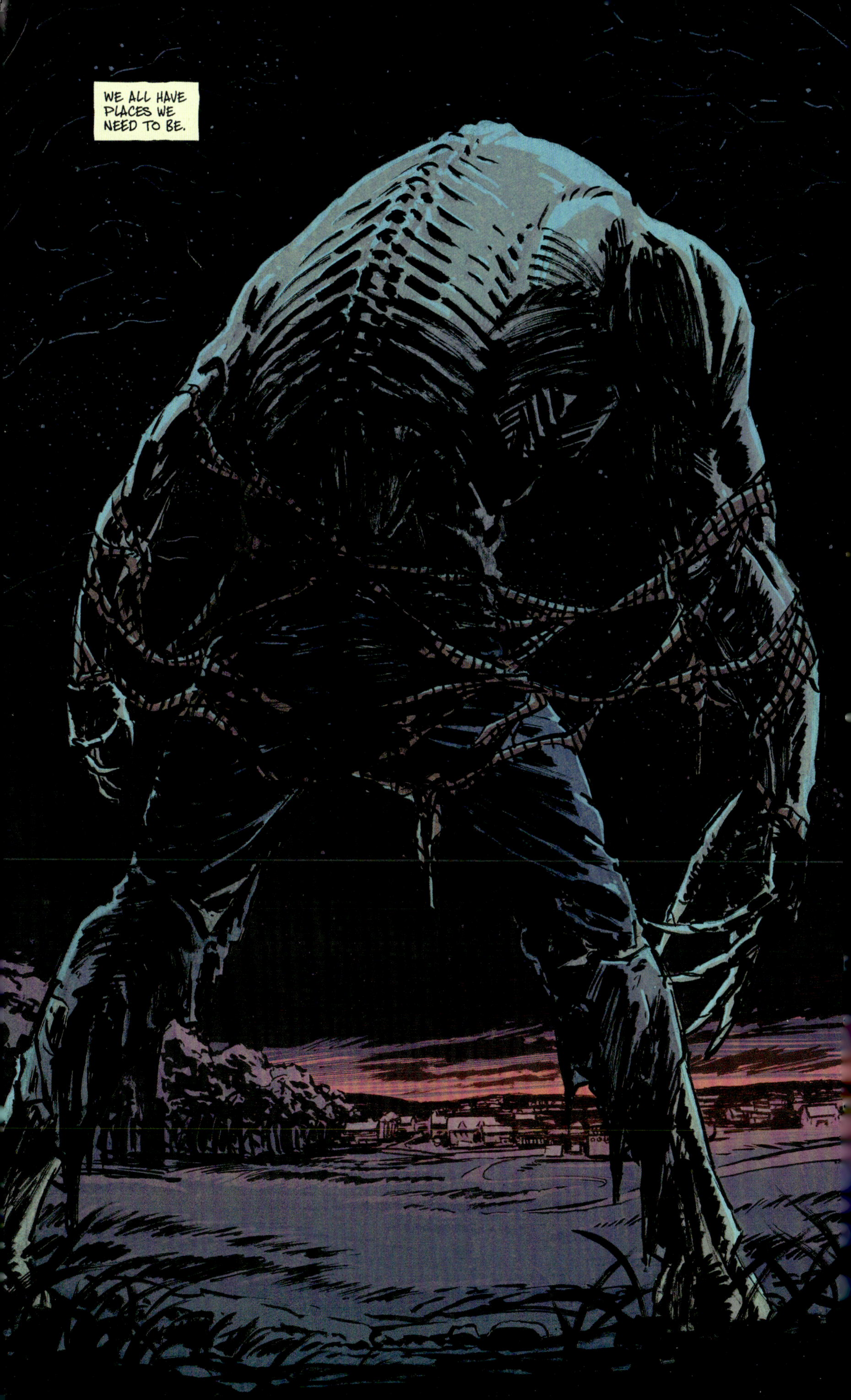
WE ALL HAVE PLACES WE NEED TO BE.

AND PEOPLE TO MEET.
AMBER!
WAIT!
AMBER!
WHAT THE HELL'S THE MATTER WITH YOU?
RONNIE'S PARTY WAS JUST GETTING STARTED.
I KNOW, TYLER. IT'S JUST...
...I'M TIRED.
YOU'RE RIGHT. LET'S GO BACK TO MY PLACE. WE CAN RELAX.
I HAVE TO TUTOR YOUR SISTER TOMORROW.
SO SPEND THE NIGHT. PLAY IT OFF LIKE YOU CAME OVER EARLY. LISA WILL COVER US. SHE LOVES YOU.
IT'LL BE FUN. COME ON.
SORRY, I'M JUST NOT IN THE MOOD.

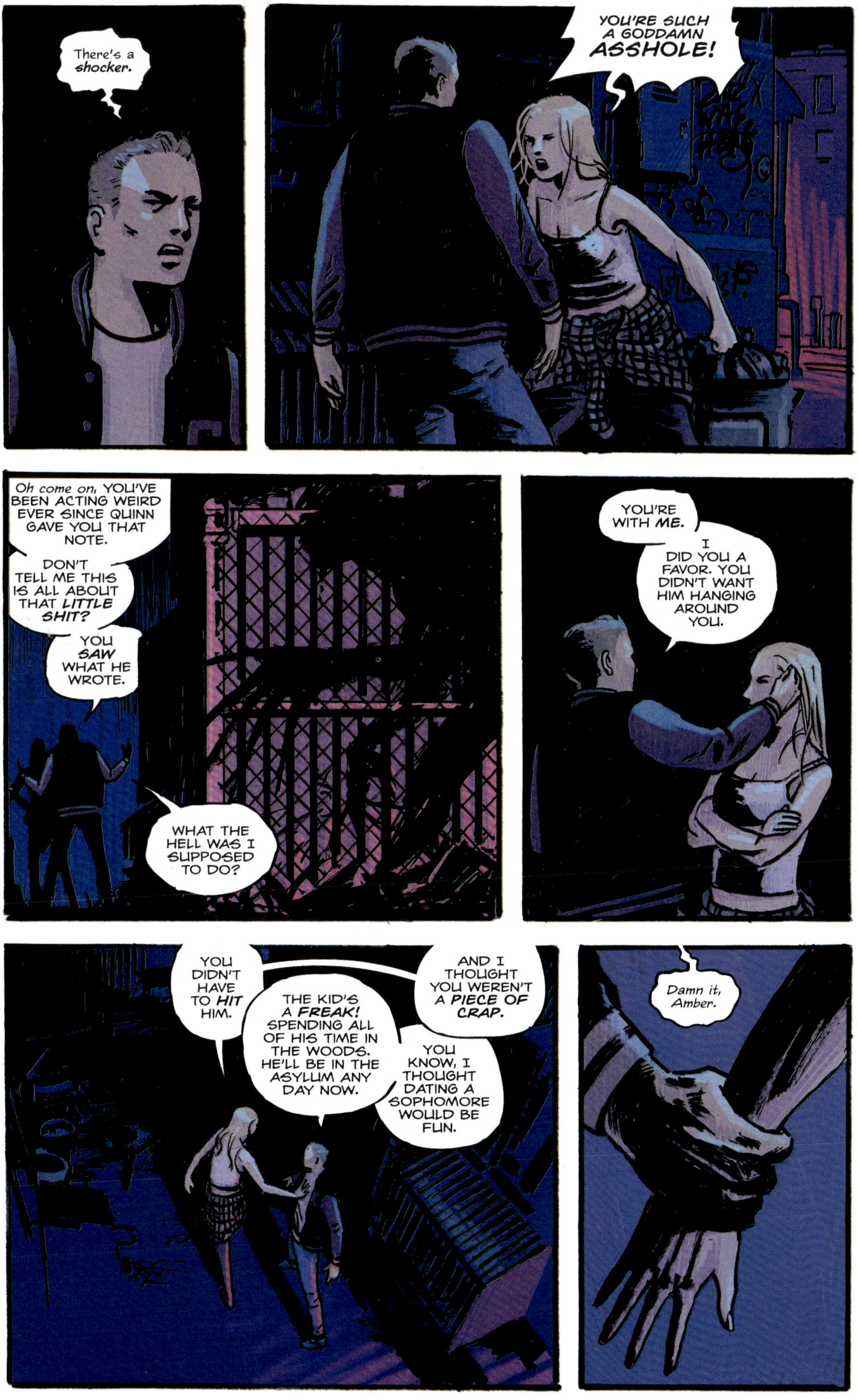
There's a *shocker.*
YOU'RE SUCH A GODDAMN **ASSHOLE!**
Oh come on, YOU'VE BEEN ACTING WEIRD EVER SINCE QUINN GAVE YOU THAT NOTE.
DON'T TELL ME THIS IS ALL ABOUT THAT ***LITTLE SHIT?***
YOU ***SAW*** WHAT HE WROTE.
WHAT THE HELL WAS I SUPPOSED TO DO?
YOU'RE WITH ***ME.***
I DID YOU A FAVOR. YOU DIDN'T WANT HIM HANGING AROUND YOU.
YOU DIDN'T HAVE TO ***HIT*** HIM.
THE KID'S A ***FREAK!*** SPENDING ALL OF HIS TIME IN THE WOODS. HE'LL BE IN THE ASYLUM ANY DAY NOW.
AND I THOUGHT YOU WEREN'T A ***PIECE OF CRAP.***
YOU KNOW, I THOUGHT DATING A SOPHOMORE WOULD BE FUN.
Damn it, Amber.

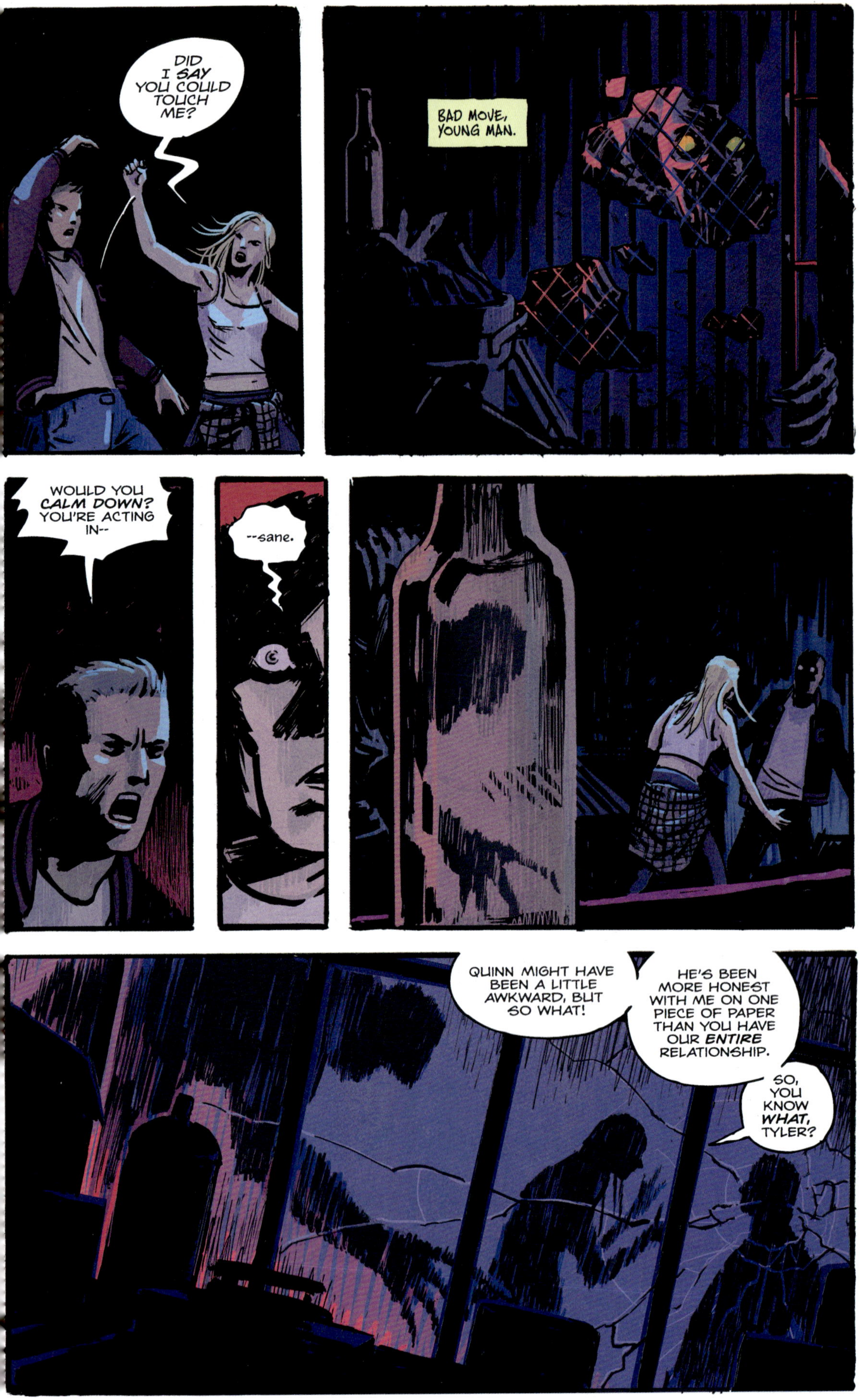
DID I SAY YOU COULD TOUCH ME?
BAD MOVE, YOUNG MAN.
WOULD YOU CALM DOWN? YOU'RE ACTING IN--
--sane.
QUINN MIGHT HAVE BEEN A LITTLE AWKWARD, BUT SO WHAT!
HE'S BEEN MORE HONEST WITH ME ON ONE PIECE OF PAPER THAN YOU HAVE OUR ENTIRE RELATIONSHIP.
SO, YOU KNOW WHAT, TYLER?

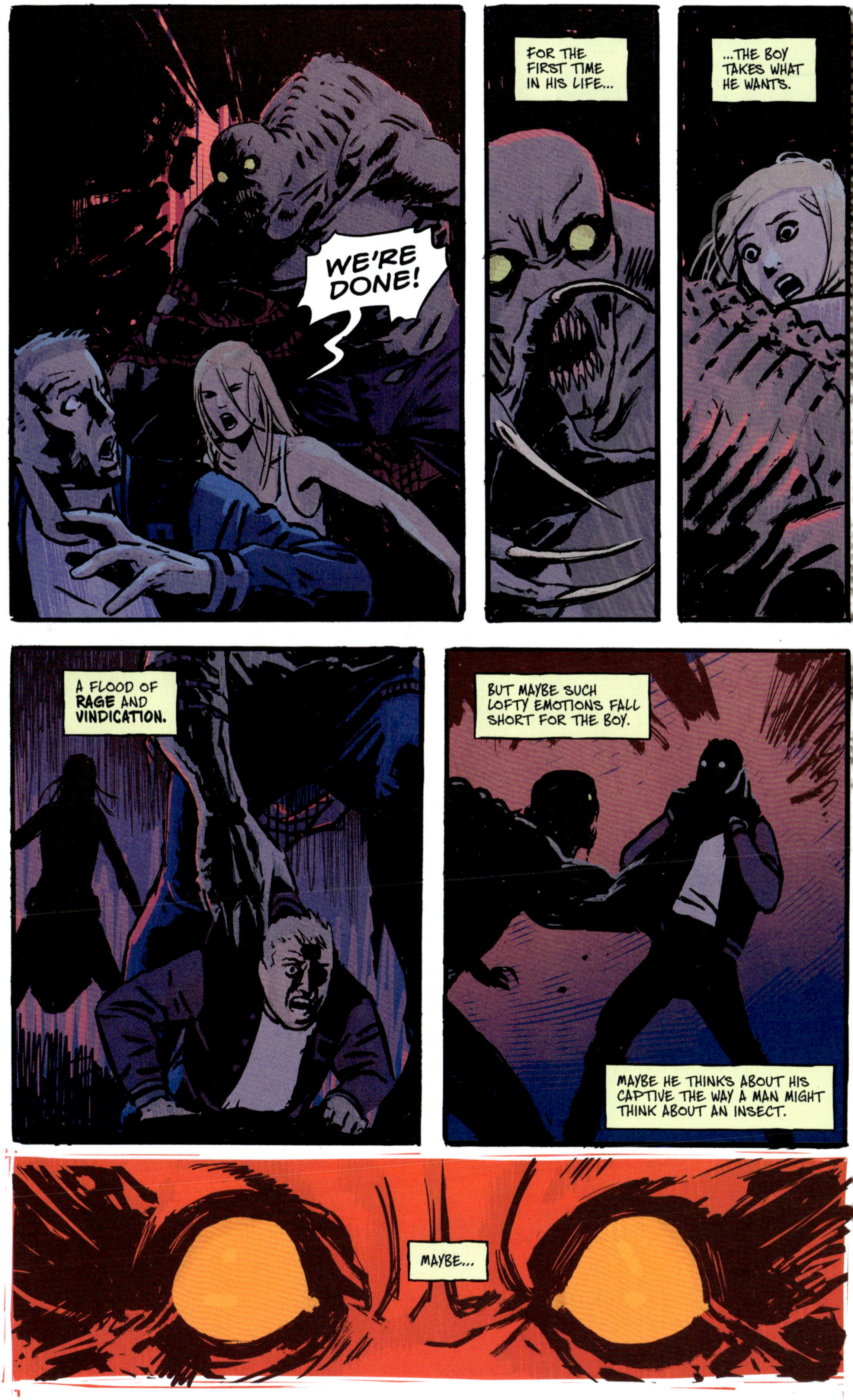
WE'RE DONE!
FOR THE FIRST TIME IN HIS LIFE...
...THE BOY TAKES WHAT HE WANTS.
A FLOOD OF RAGE AND VINDICATION.
BUT MAYBE SUCH LOFTY EMOTIONS FALL SHORT FOR THE BOY.
MAYBE HE THINKS ABOUT HIS CAPTIVE THE WAY A MAN MIGHT THINK ABOUT AN INSECT.
MAYBE...

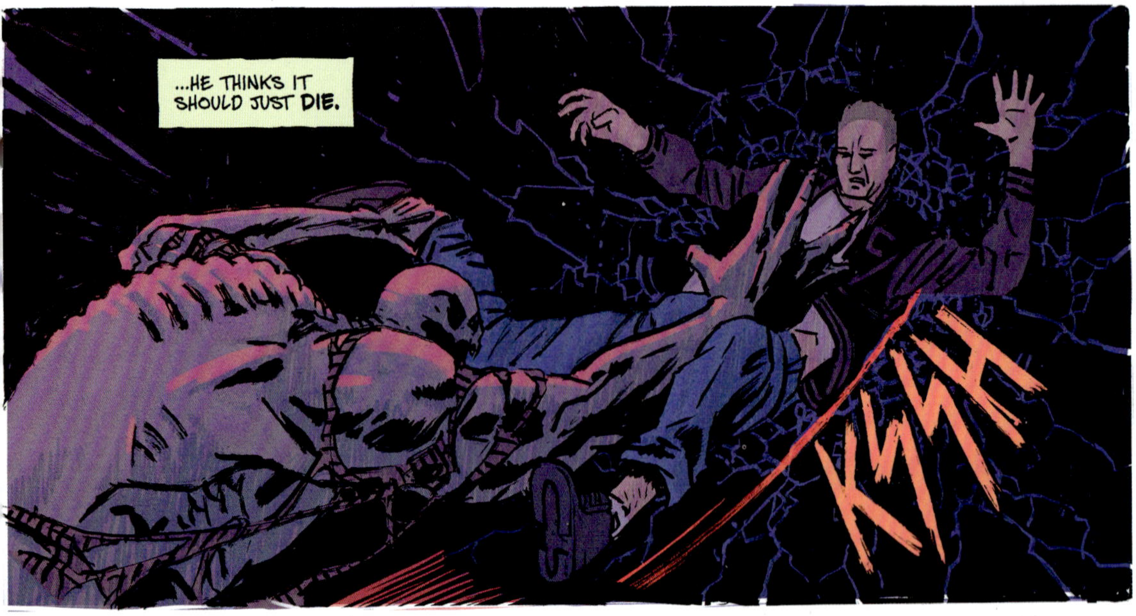
...HE THINKS IT SHOULD JUST DIE.
KSSH

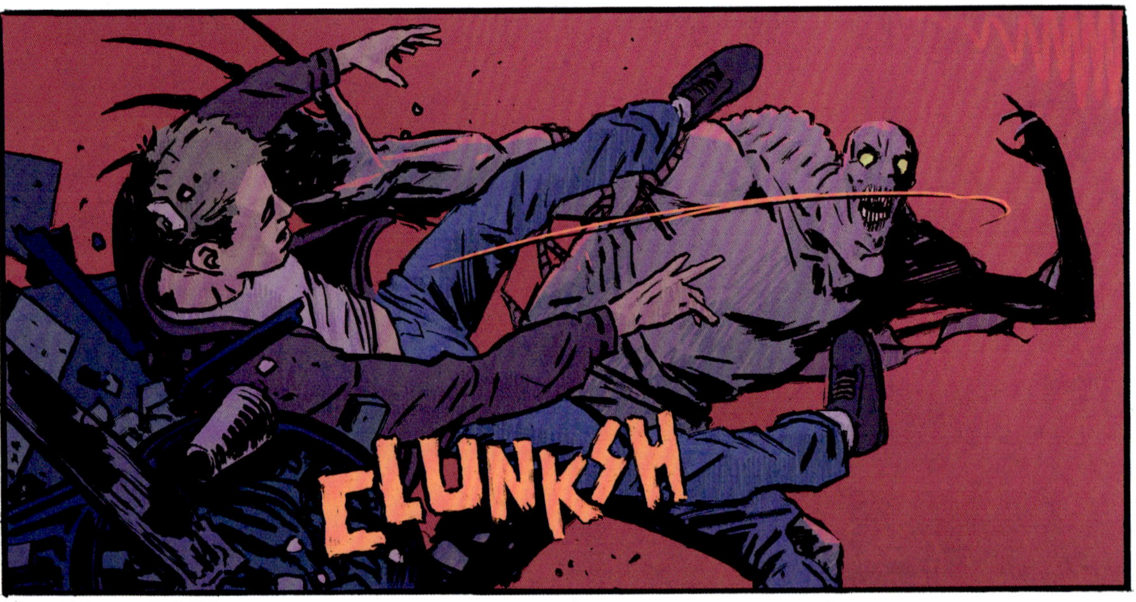
CLUNKSH

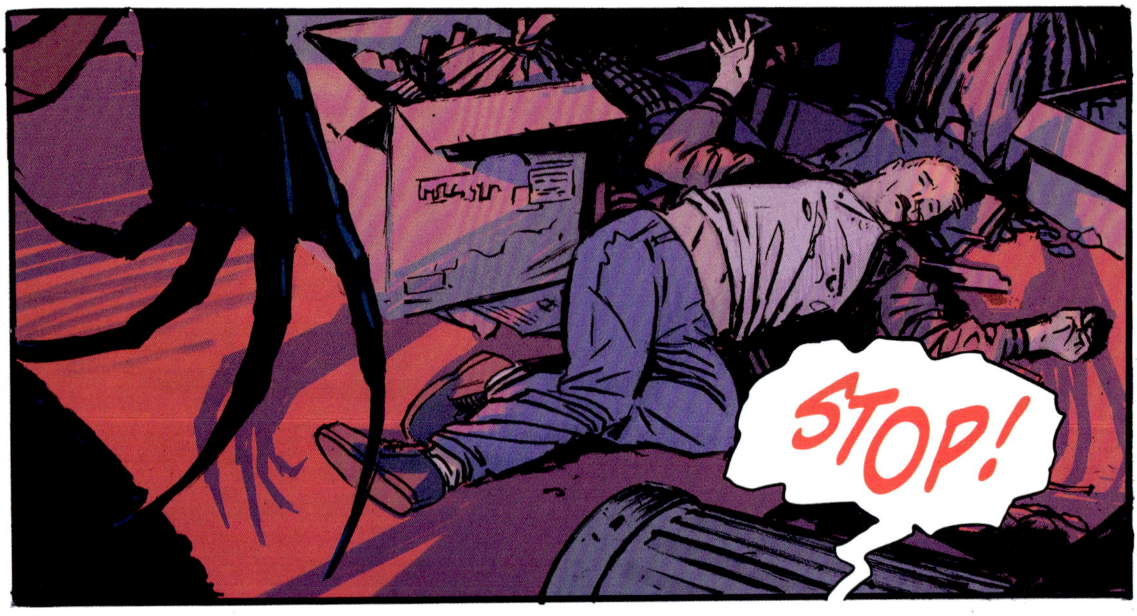
STOP!

FOR THE LOVE OF GOD, PLEASE STOP!
ALL RIGHT, I'LL ADMIT IT.
THIS ISN'T THE END...
...IT'S THE BEGINNING.

CHAPTER 2

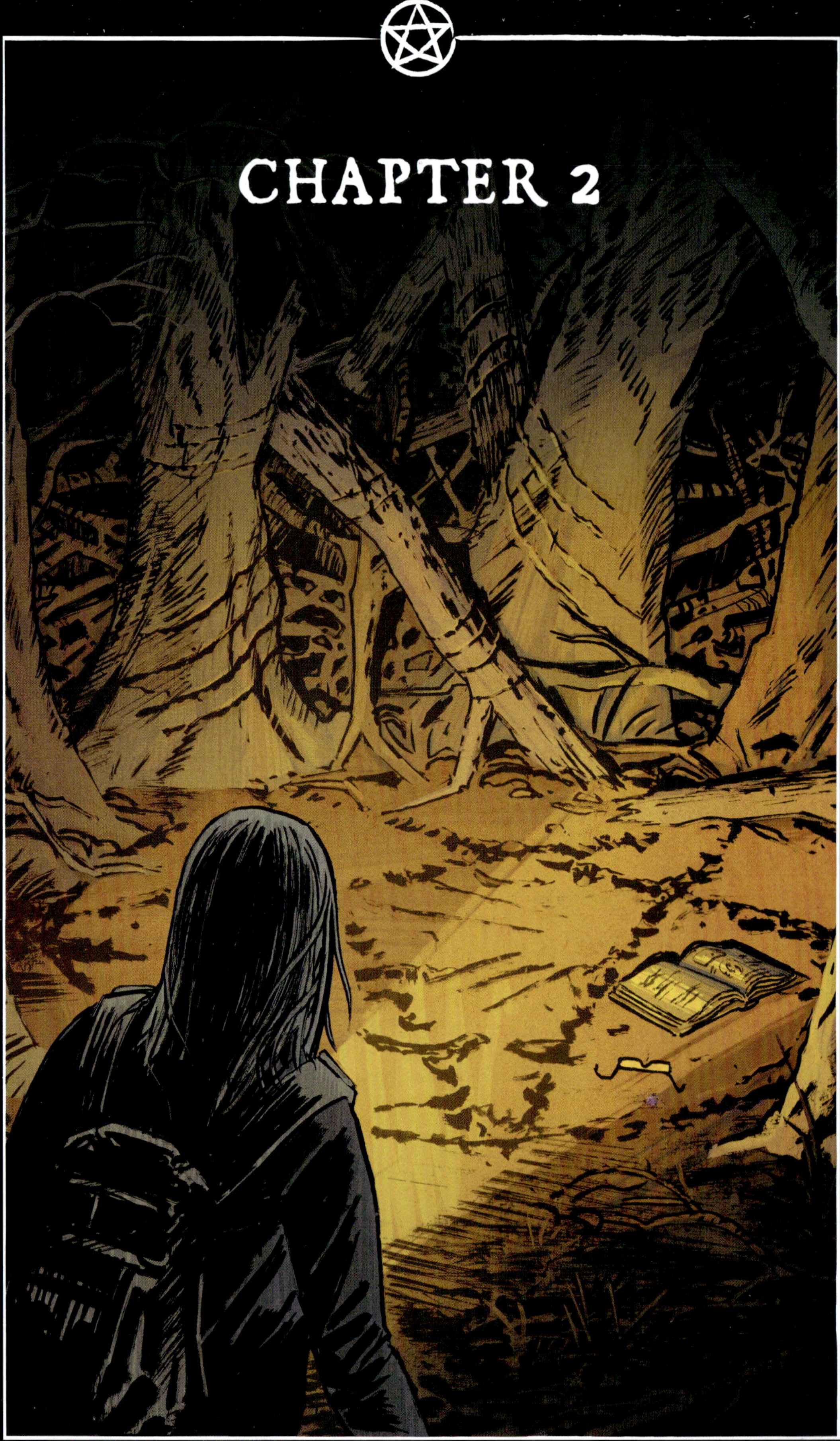

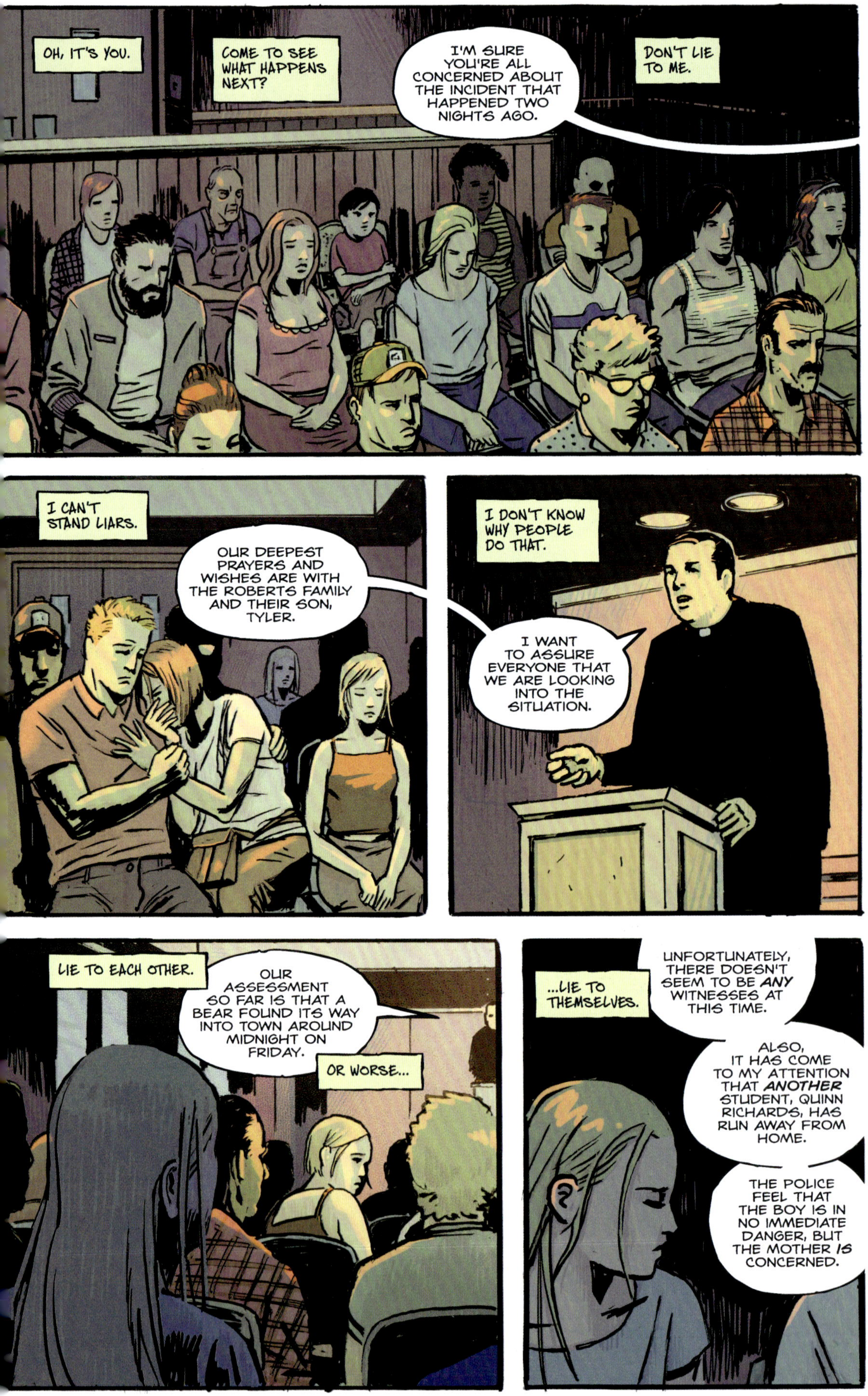

OH, IT'S YOU.
COME TO SEE WHAT HAPPENS NEXT?
I'M SURE YOU'RE ALL CONCERNED ABOUT THE INCIDENT THAT HAPPENED TWO NIGHTS AGO.
DON'T LIE TO ME.
I CAN'T STAND LIARS.
OUR DEEPEST PRAYERS AND WISHES ARE WITH THE ROBERTS FAMILY AND THEIR SON, TYLER.
I DON'T KNOW WHY PEOPLE DO THAT.
I WANT TO ASSURE EVERYONE THAT WE ARE LOOKING INTO THE SITUATION.
LIE TO EACH OTHER.
OUR ASSESSMENT SO FAR IS THAT A BEAR FOUND ITS WAY INTO TOWN AROUND MIDNIGHT ON FRIDAY.
OR WORSE...
...LIE TO THEMSELVES.
UNFORTUNATELY, THERE DOESN'T SEEM TO BE *ANY* WITNESSES AT THIS TIME.
ALSO, IT HAS COME TO MY ATTENTION THAT *ANOTHER* STUDENT, QUINN RICHARDS, HAS RUN AWAY FROM HOME.
THE POLICE FEEL THAT THE BOY IS IN NO IMMEDIATE DANGER, BUT THE MOTHER *IS* CONCERNED.

AMBER! WAIT UP!
HEY, LISA.
HEY, SO...
... THIS IS STUPID, AND I DON'T WANT TO BOTHER YOU, BUT YOU HAVEN'T BEEN TO THE HOSPITAL YET.
I'M SORRY, LISA...
...SHIT, IT'S JUST...
"... IT'S BEEN HARD."
I UNDER-STAND.
I WAS WORRIED. YOU DIDN'T TEXT ME BACK, AND I JUST WANTED TO MAKE SURE YOU WERE OKAY.
I THINK IT'D MEAN A LOT TO TYLER IF YOU STOPPED BY. I KNOW HE CAN'T SPEAK RIGHT NOW, BUT I THINK HE'D BE HAPPY TO SEE YOU.
YOU'RE A REALLY GREAT SISTER. I'LL TRY. DO YOU NEED ANY HELP THIS WEEK? I HAD MR. HOWARD FRESHMAN YEAR, TOO. HE'S KIND OF A DICK ABOUT EARTH SCIENCE.
NO, I'M ALL RIGHT. THANKS THOUGH. BUT IF YOU NEED TO TALK TO ME, I'M HERE.

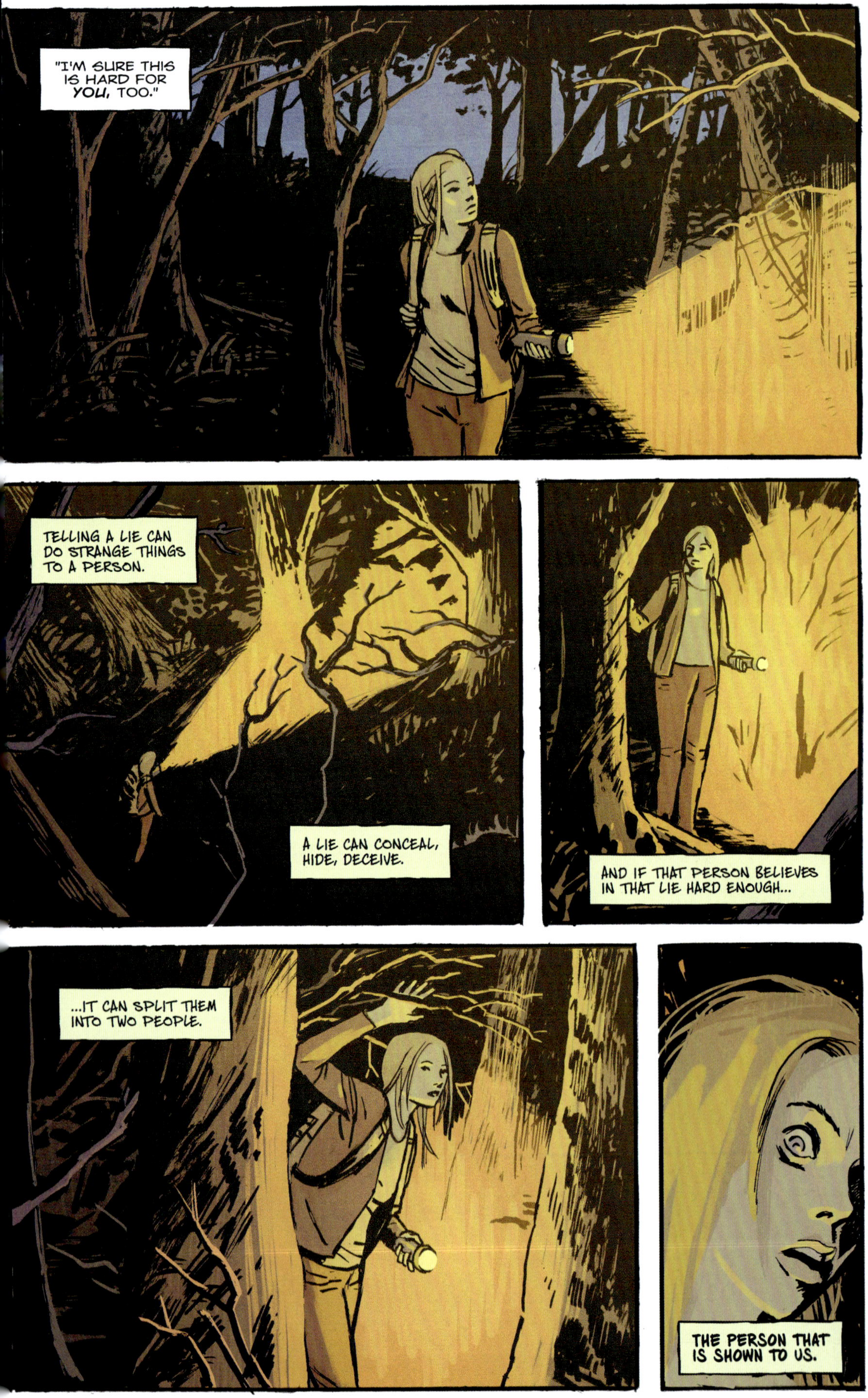
"I'M SURE THIS IS HARD FOR YOU, TOO."
TELLING A LIE CAN DO STRANGE THINGS TO A PERSON.
A LIE CAN CONCEAL, HIDE, DECEIVE.
AND IF THAT PERSON BELIEVES IN THAT LIE HARD ENOUGH...
...IT CAN SPLIT THEM INTO TWO PEOPLE.
THE PERSON THAT IS SHOWN TO US.

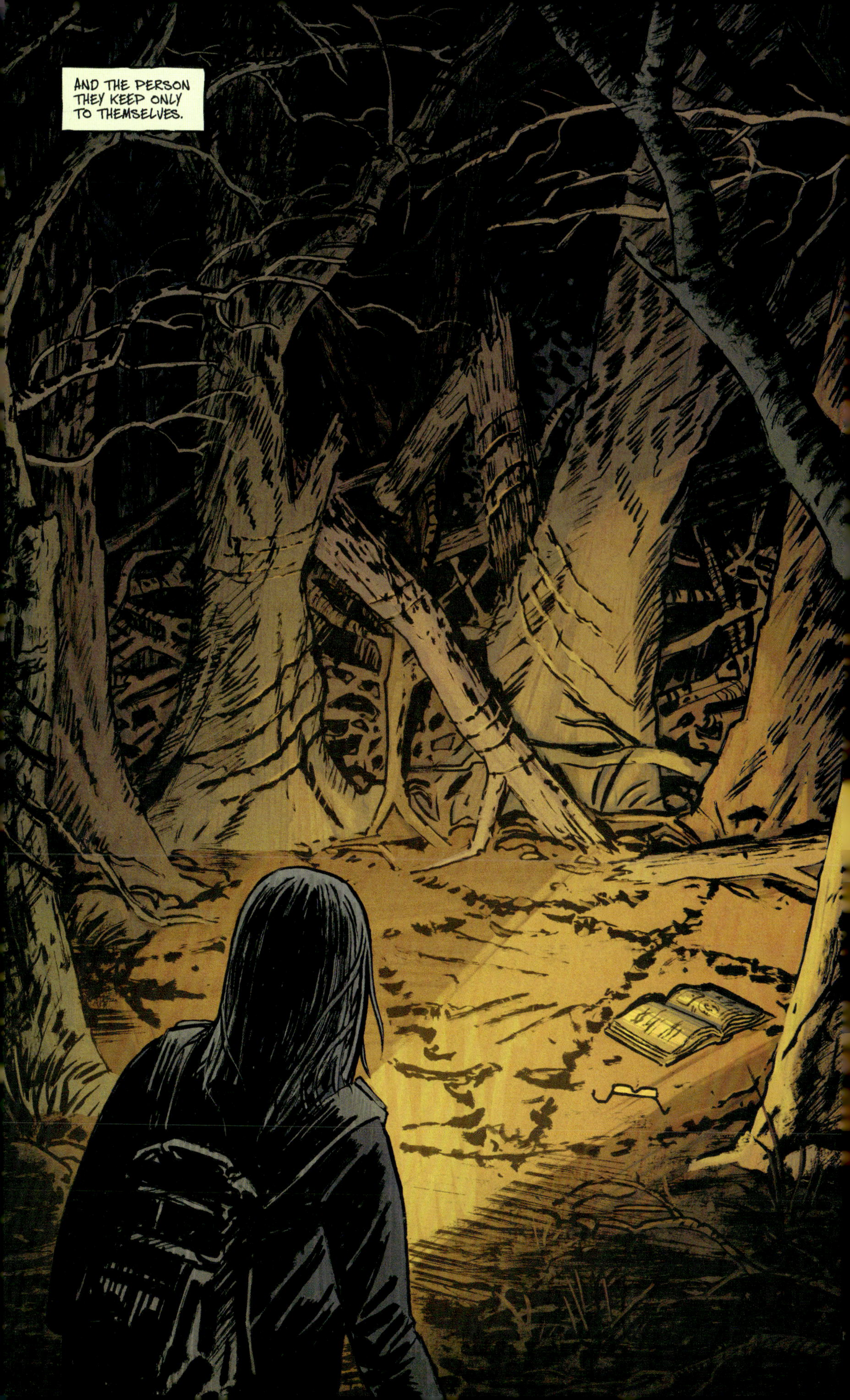
AND THE PERSON THEY KEEP ONLY TO THEMSELVES.

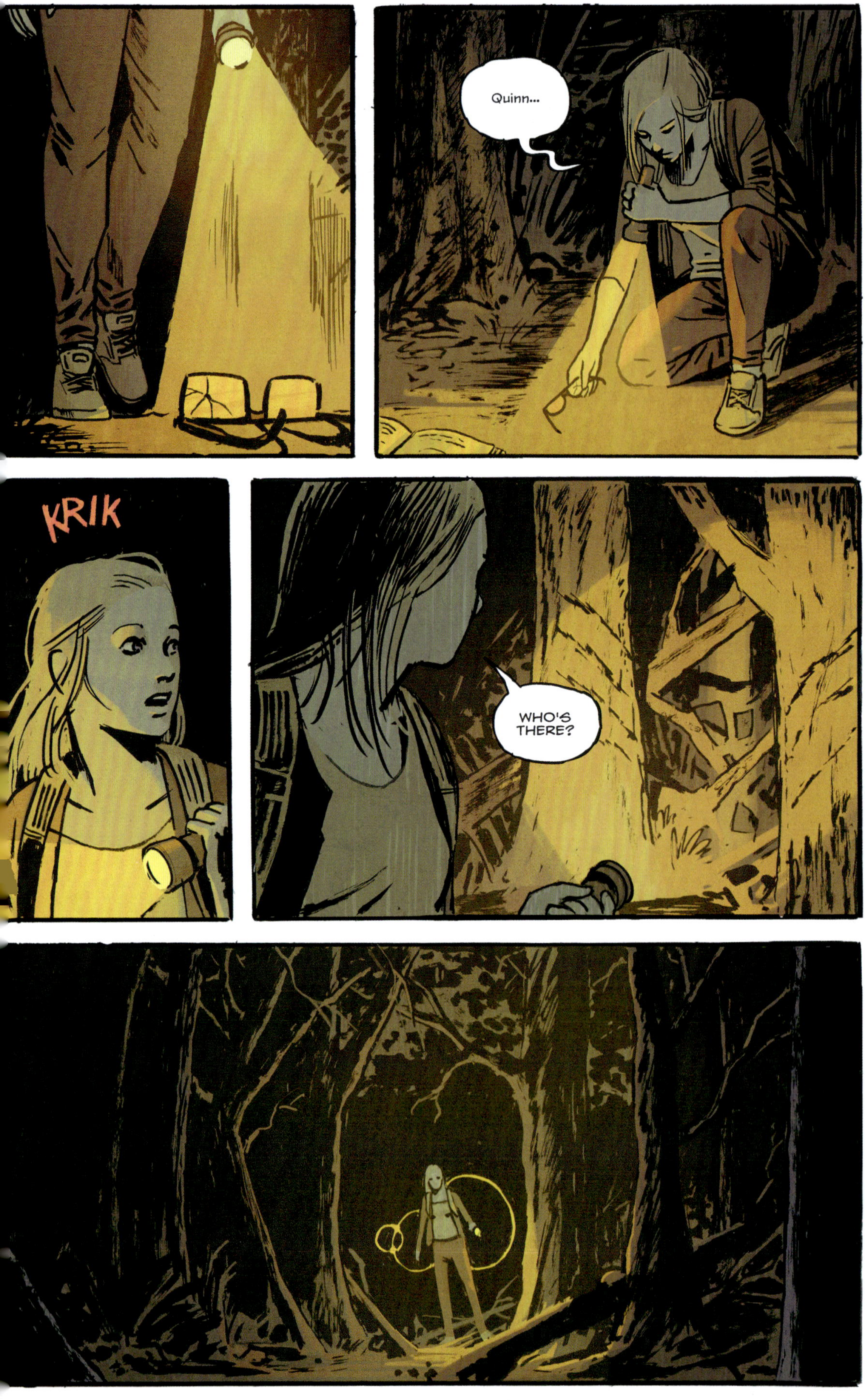
Quinn...
KRIK
WHO'S THERE?

WELL, THIS IS UNEXPECTED.
WHO ARE YOU?
BETTER QUESTION IS, WHO ARE YOU?
THAT THING THAT I SAW...THAT--THAT THING THAT DESTROYED TYLER. THAT THING WAS QUINN.
YOU'RE VERY CLEVER. TELL ME, WHAT IS YOUR NAME?
AND WHAT HAS BROUGHT YOU HERE TONIGHT?
I'M...I'M NOT TELLING YOU.
NO NEED TO BE AFRAID, AMBER. I WAS JUST BEING POLITE.
HOW DO YOU KNOW MY NAME?
BECAUSE THE LAST OWNER OF THAT BOOK SPOKE OF IT VERY FONDLY.
WHAT DID YOU DO TO QUINN? WHY DID YOU MAKE HIM THAT THING?

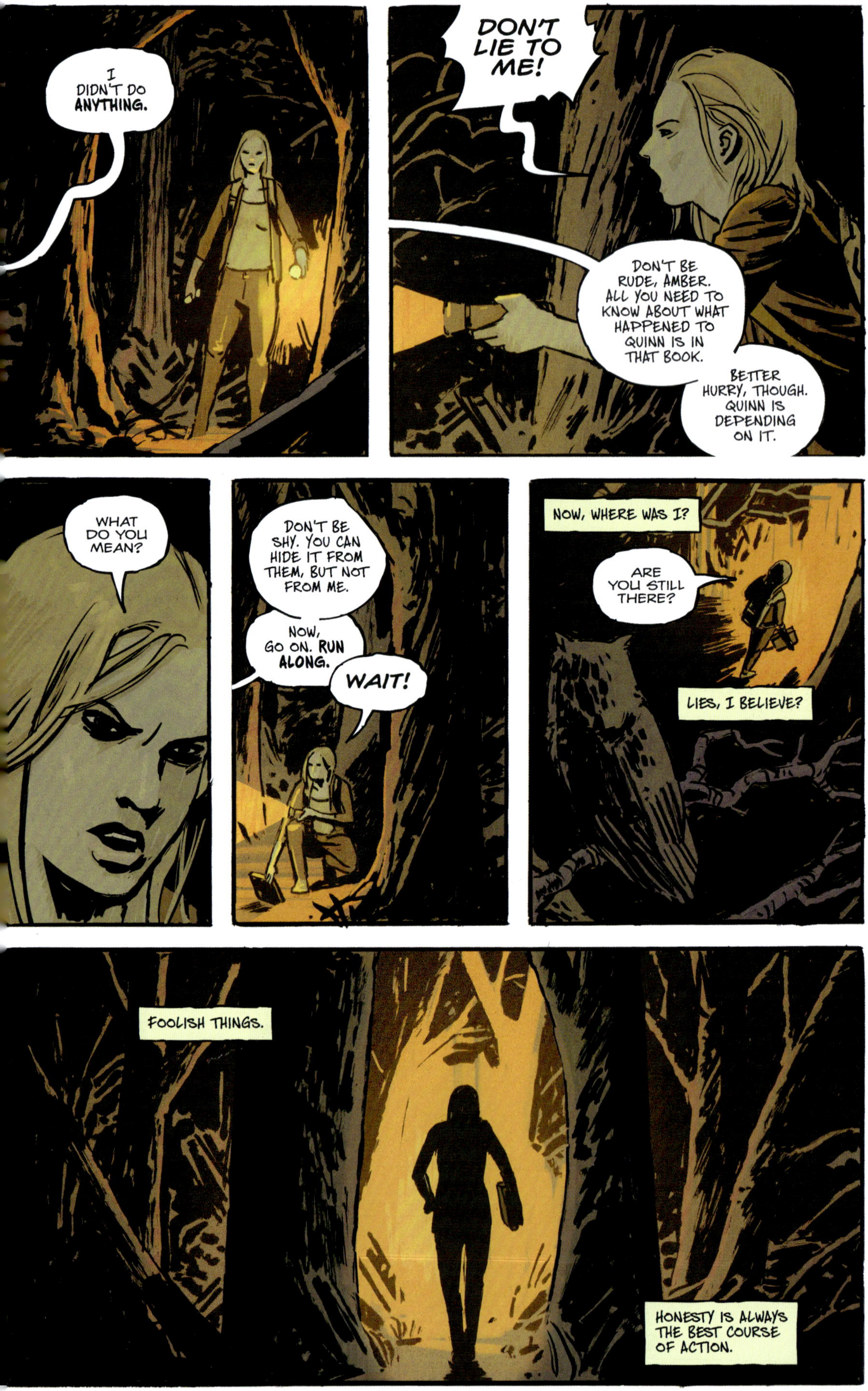

I DIDN'T DO ANYTHING.
DON'T LIE TO ME!
DON'T BE RUDE, AMBER. ALL YOU NEED TO KNOW ABOUT WHAT HAPPENED TO QUINN IS IN THAT BOOK.
BETTER HURRY, THOUGH. QUINN IS DEPENDING ON IT.
WHAT DO YOU MEAN?
DON'T BE SHY. YOU CAN HIDE IT FROM THEM, BUT NOT FROM ME.
NOW, GO ON. RUN ALONG.
WAIT!
NOW, WHERE WAS I?
ARE YOU STILL THERE?
LIES, I BELIEVE?
FOOLISH THINGS.
HONESTY IS ALWAYS THE BEST COURSE OF ACTION.

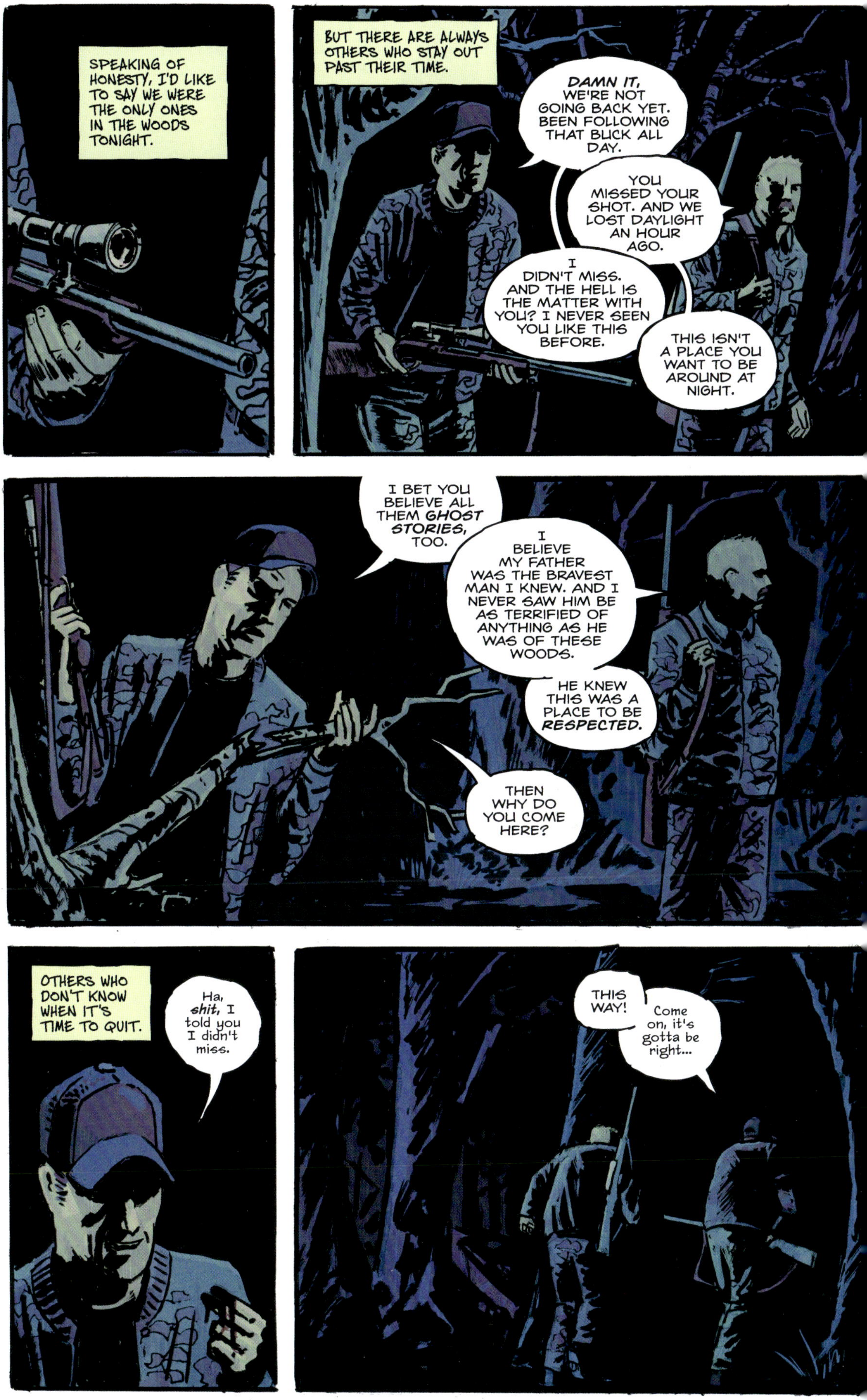
SPEAKING OF HONESTY, I'D LIKE TO SAY WE WERE THE ONLY ONES IN THE WOODS TONIGHT.
BUT THERE ARE ALWAYS OTHERS WHO STAY OUT PAST THEIR TIME.
DAMN IT, WE'RE NOT GOING BACK YET. BEEN FOLLOWING THAT BUCK ALL DAY.
YOU MISSED YOUR SHOT. AND WE LOST DAYLIGHT AN HOUR AGO.
I DIDN'T MISS. AND THE HELL IS THE MATTER WITH YOU? I NEVER SEEN YOU LIKE THIS BEFORE.
THIS ISN'T A PLACE YOU WANT TO BE AROUND AT NIGHT.
I BET YOU BELIEVE ALL THEM GHOST STORIES, TOO.
I BELIEVE MY FATHER WAS THE BRAVEST MAN I KNEW. AND I NEVER SAW HIM BE AS TERRIFIED OF ANYTHING AS HE WAS OF THESE WOODS.
HE KNEW THIS WAS A PLACE TO BE RESPECTED.
THEN WHY DO YOU COME HERE?
OTHERS WHO DON'T KNOW WHEN IT'S TIME TO QUIT.
Ha, shit, I told you I didn't miss.
THIS WAY!
Come on, it's gotta be right...

STRUNCH
AND FIND THINGS THEY SHOULDN'T.
Oh my God.
Clem, we need to get--
DAMN IT-- DON'T!
BLAM BLAM BLAM
AND DO THINGS THEY SHOULDN'T.

DIE! JUST DIE!
BLAM
SSLLICHSH
I offer myself to her. Tell her that. Tell her--

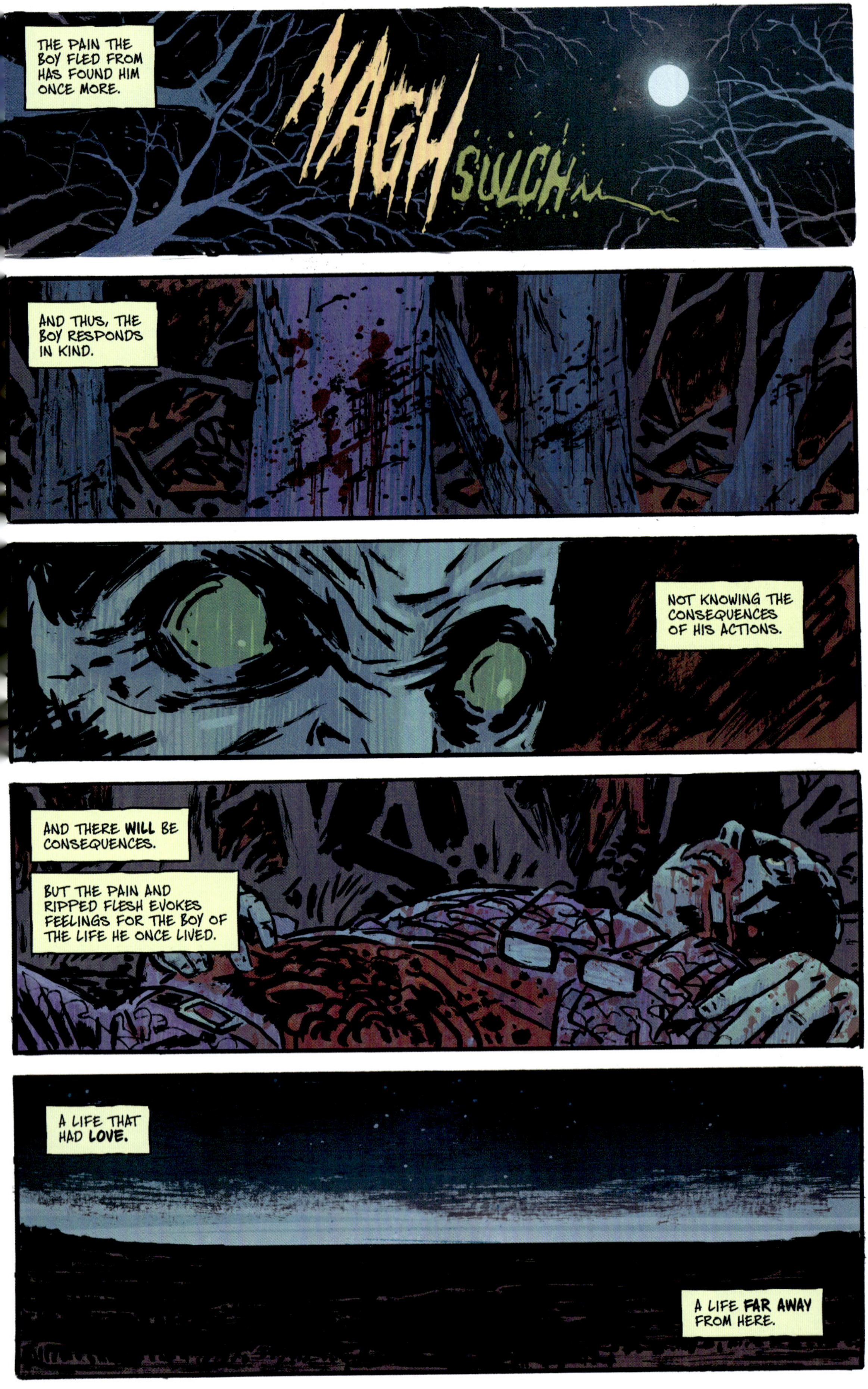
THE PAIN THE BOY FLED FROM HAS FOUND HIM ONCE MORE.
NAGH
SHLCH
AND THUS, THE BOY RESPONDS IN KIND.
NOT KNOWING THE CONSEQUENCES OF HIS ACTIONS.
AND THERE WILL BE CONSEQUENCES.
BUT THE PAIN AND RIPPED FLESH EVOKES FEELINGS FOR THE BOY OF THE LIFE HE ONCE LIVED.
A LIFE THAT HAD LOVE.
A LIFE FAR AWAY FROM HERE.

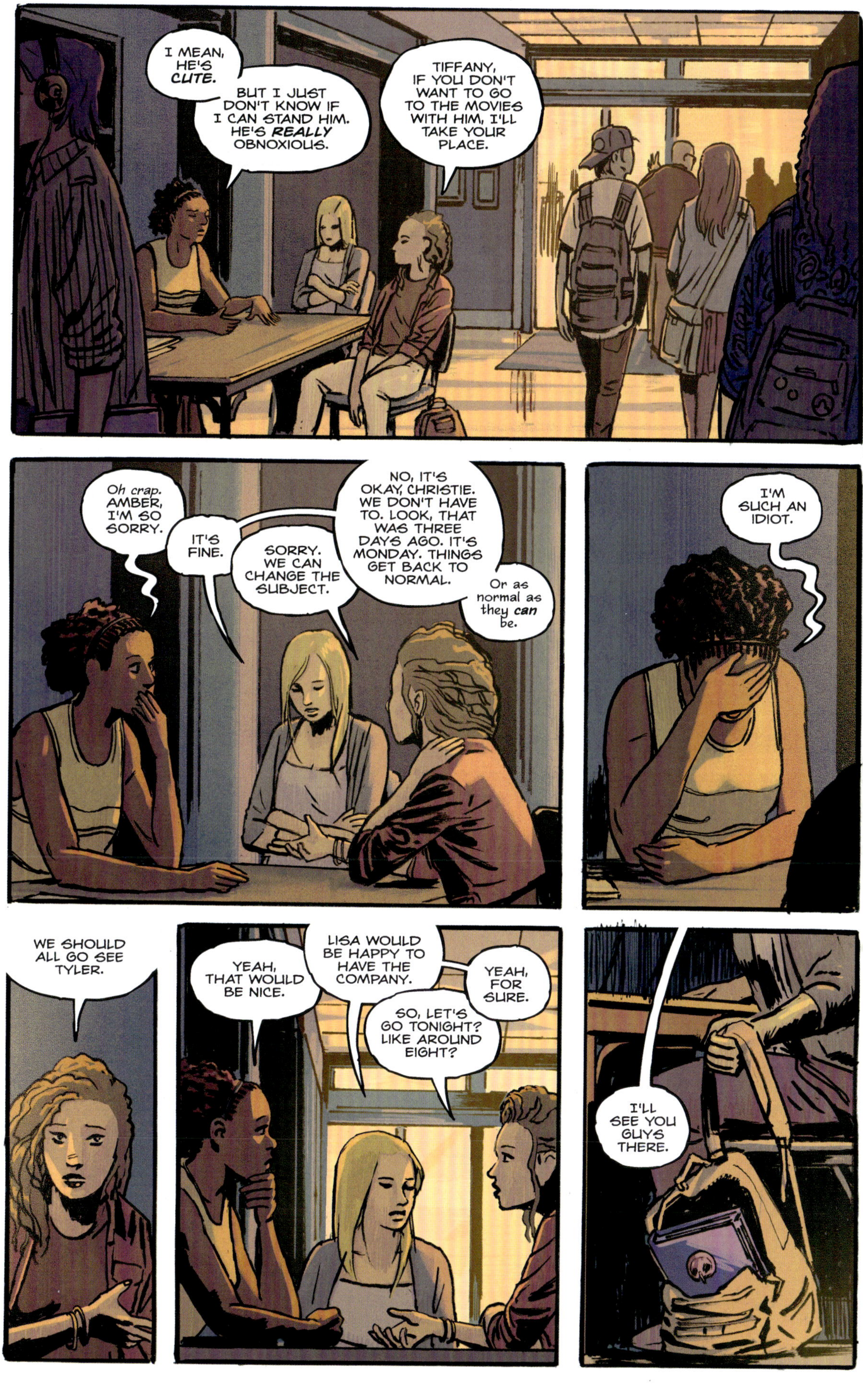
I MEAN, HE'S *CUTE.*
BUT I JUST DON'T KNOW IF I CAN STAND HIM. HE'S *REALLY* OBNOXIOUS.
TIFFANY, IF YOU DON'T WANT TO GO TO THE MOVIES WITH HIM, I'LL TAKE YOUR PLACE.
Oh crap. AMBER, I'M SO SORRY.
IT'S FINE.
SORRY. WE CAN CHANGE THE SUBJECT.
NO, IT'S OKAY, CHRISTIE. WE DON'T HAVE TO. LOOK, THAT WAS THREE DAYS AGO. IT'S MONDAY. THINGS GET BACK TO NORMAL.
Or as normal as they *can* be.
I'M SUCH AN IDIOT.
WE SHOULD ALL GO SEE TYLER.
YEAH, THAT WOULD BE NICE.
LISA WOULD BE HAPPY TO HAVE THE COMPANY.
YEAH, FOR SURE.
SO, LET'S GO TONIGHT? LIKE AROUND EIGHT?
I'LL SEE YOU GUYS THERE.

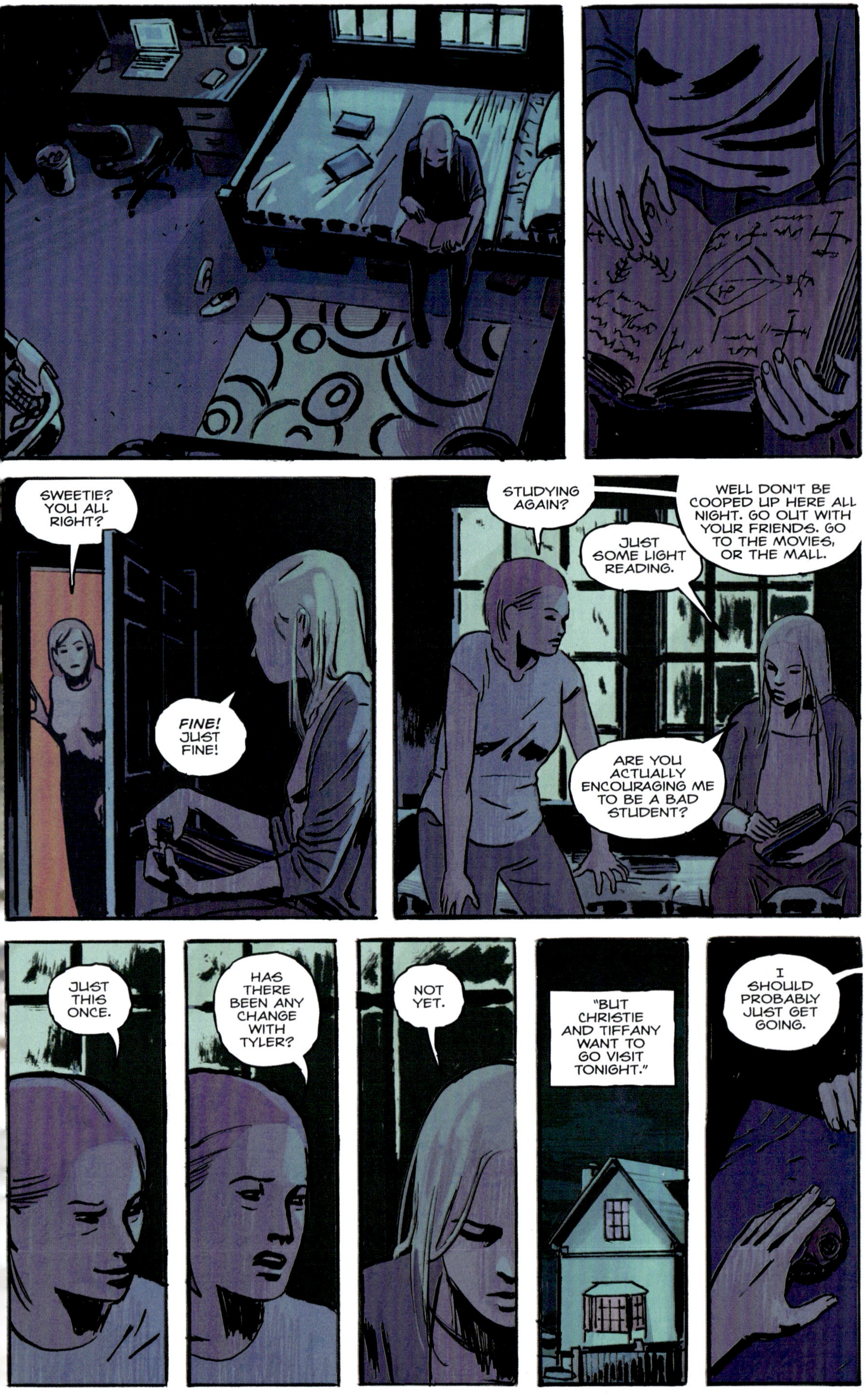
SWEETIE? YOU ALL RIGHT?
FINE! JUST FINE!
STUDYING AGAIN?
JUST SOME LIGHT READING.
WELL DON'T BE COOPED UP HERE ALL NIGHT. GO OUT WITH YOUR FRIENDS. GO TO THE MOVIES, OR THE MALL.
ARE YOU ACTUALLY ENCOURAGING ME TO BE A BAD STUDENT?
JUST THIS ONCE.
HAS THERE BEEN ANY CHANGE WITH TYLER?
NOT YET.
"BUT CHRISTIE AND TIFFANY WANT TO GO VISIT TONIGHT."
I SHOULD PROBABLY JUST GET GOING.

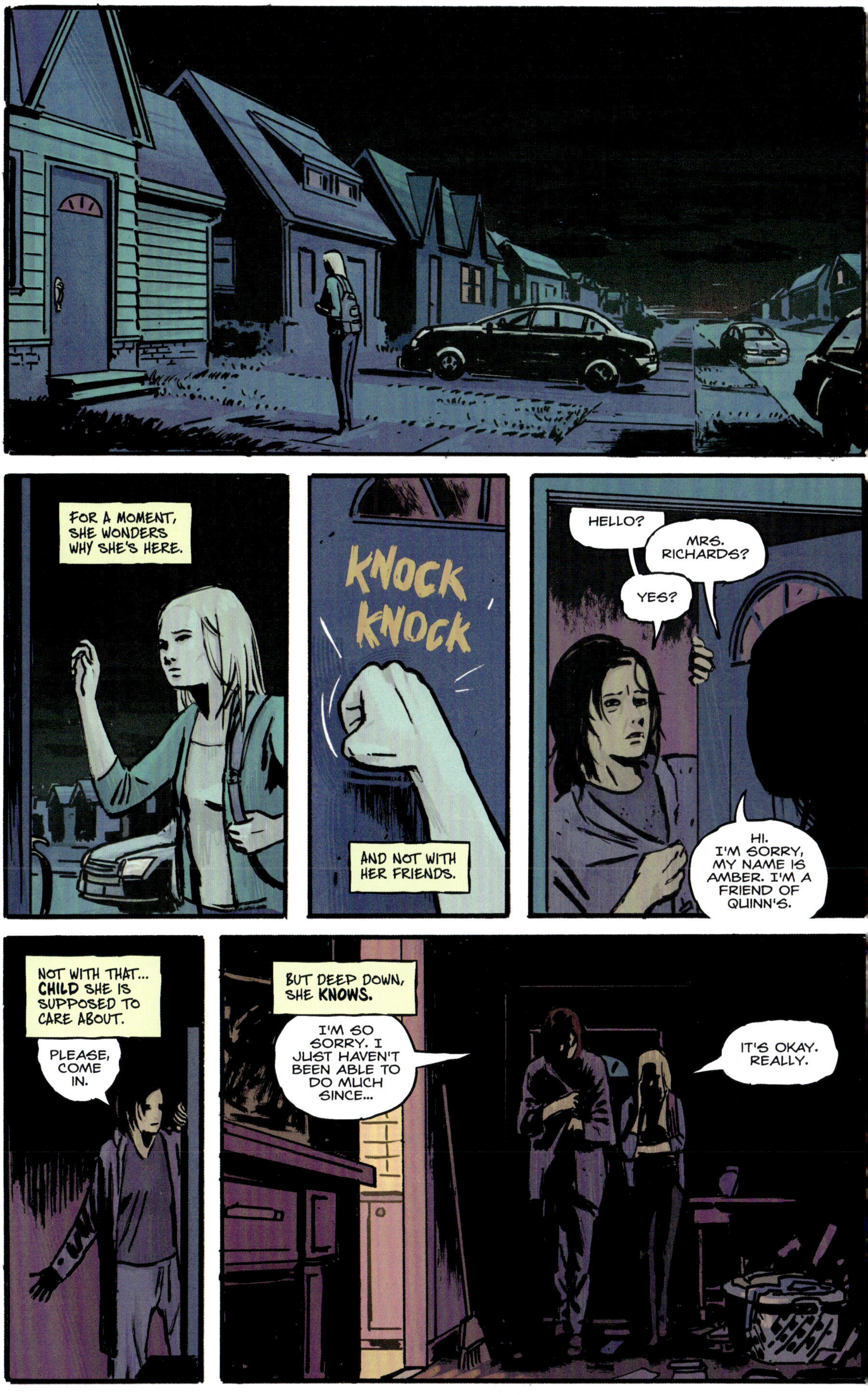
FOR A MOMENT, SHE WONDERS WHY SHE'S HERE.
KNOCK KNOCK
AND NOT WITH HER FRIENDS.
HELLO?
MRS. RICHARDS?
YES?
HI. I'M SORRY, MY NAME IS AMBER. I'M A FRIEND OF QUINN'S.
NOT WITH THAT... **CHILD** SHE IS SUPPOSED TO CARE ABOUT.
PLEASE, COME IN.
BUT DEEP DOWN, SHE **KNOWS.**
I'M SO SORRY. I JUST HAVEN'T BEEN ABLE TO DO MUCH SINCE...
IT'S OKAY. REALLY.

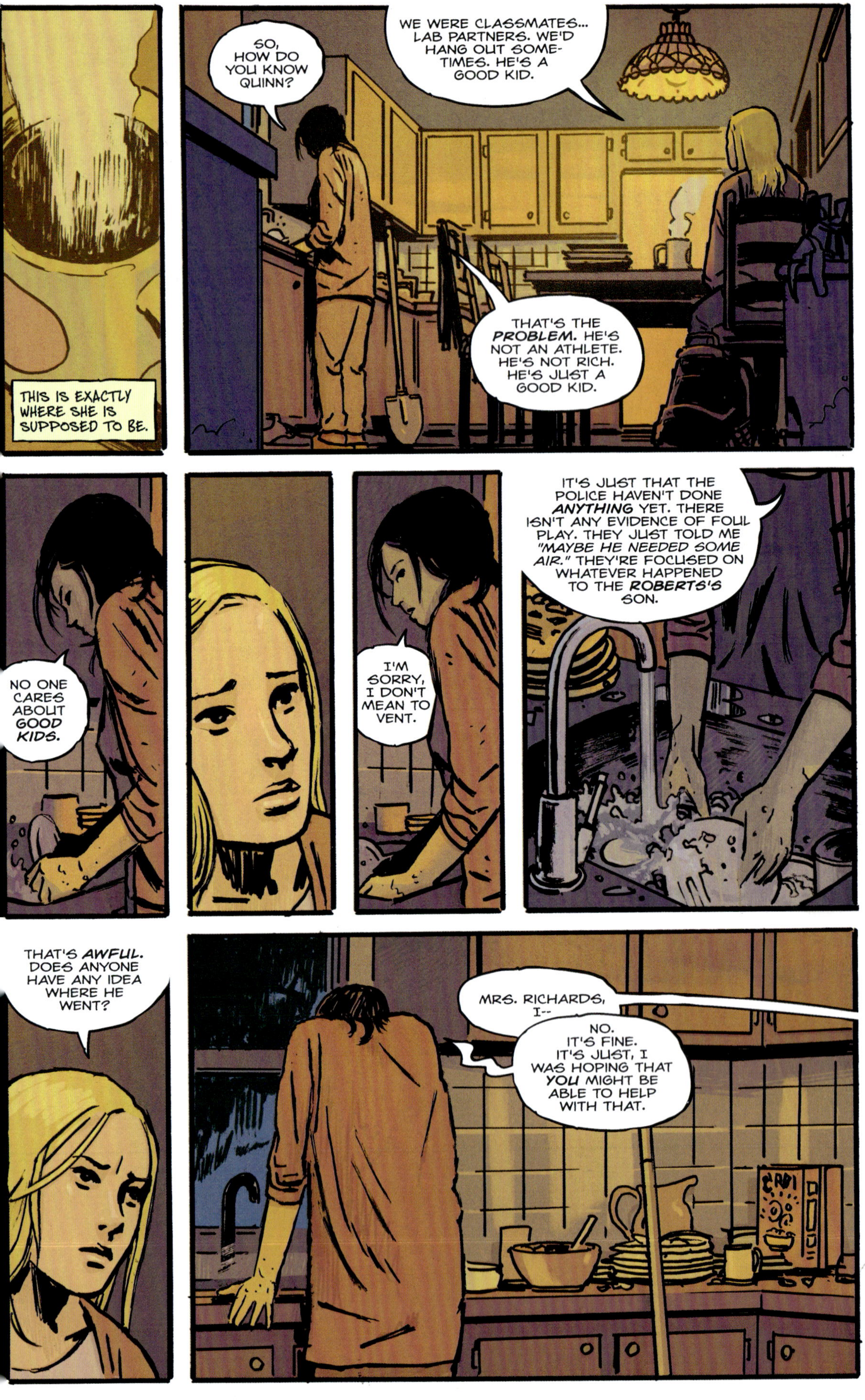
THIS IS EXACTLY WHERE SHE IS SUPPOSED TO BE.
SO, HOW DO YOU KNOW QUINN?
WE WERE CLASSMATES... LAB PARTNERS. WE'D HANG OUT SOME-TIMES. HE'S A GOOD KID.
THAT'S THE PROBLEM. HE'S NOT AN ATHLETE. HE'S NOT RICH. HE'S JUST A GOOD KID.
NO ONE CARES ABOUT GOOD KIDS.
I'M SORRY, I DON'T MEAN TO VENT.
IT'S JUST THAT THE POLICE HAVEN'T DONE ANYTHING YET. THERE ISN'T ANY EVIDENCE OF FOUL PLAY. THEY JUST TOLD ME "MAYBE HE NEEDED SOME AIR." THEY'RE FOCUSED ON WHATEVER HAPPENED TO THE ROBERTS'S SON.
THAT'S AWFUL. DOES ANYONE HAVE ANY IDEA WHERE HE WENT?
MRS. RICHARDS, I--
NO. IT'S FINE. IT'S JUST, I WAS HOPING THAT YOU MIGHT BE ABLE TO HELP WITH THAT.

I KNOW THIS MIGHT SOUND CRAZY, BUT...I WAS HOPING YOU KNEW SOME-THING.
YOU'RE THE FIRST PERSON TO COME HERE AND ASK ABOUT QUINN.
DO YOU KNOW ANYTHING ABOUT WHAT HAPPENED TO HIM? ANY IDEA OF WHERE HE WENT?
MRS. RICHARDS, I'M SORRY, BUT I JUST CAME HERE TO PICK UP A BOOK I LENT QUINN.
I'm so stupid.
I-I'M--
NO, PLEASE, I'M FINE. QUINN'S ROOM IS AT THE END OF THE HALL.
TAKE AS MUCH TIME AS YOU NEED.

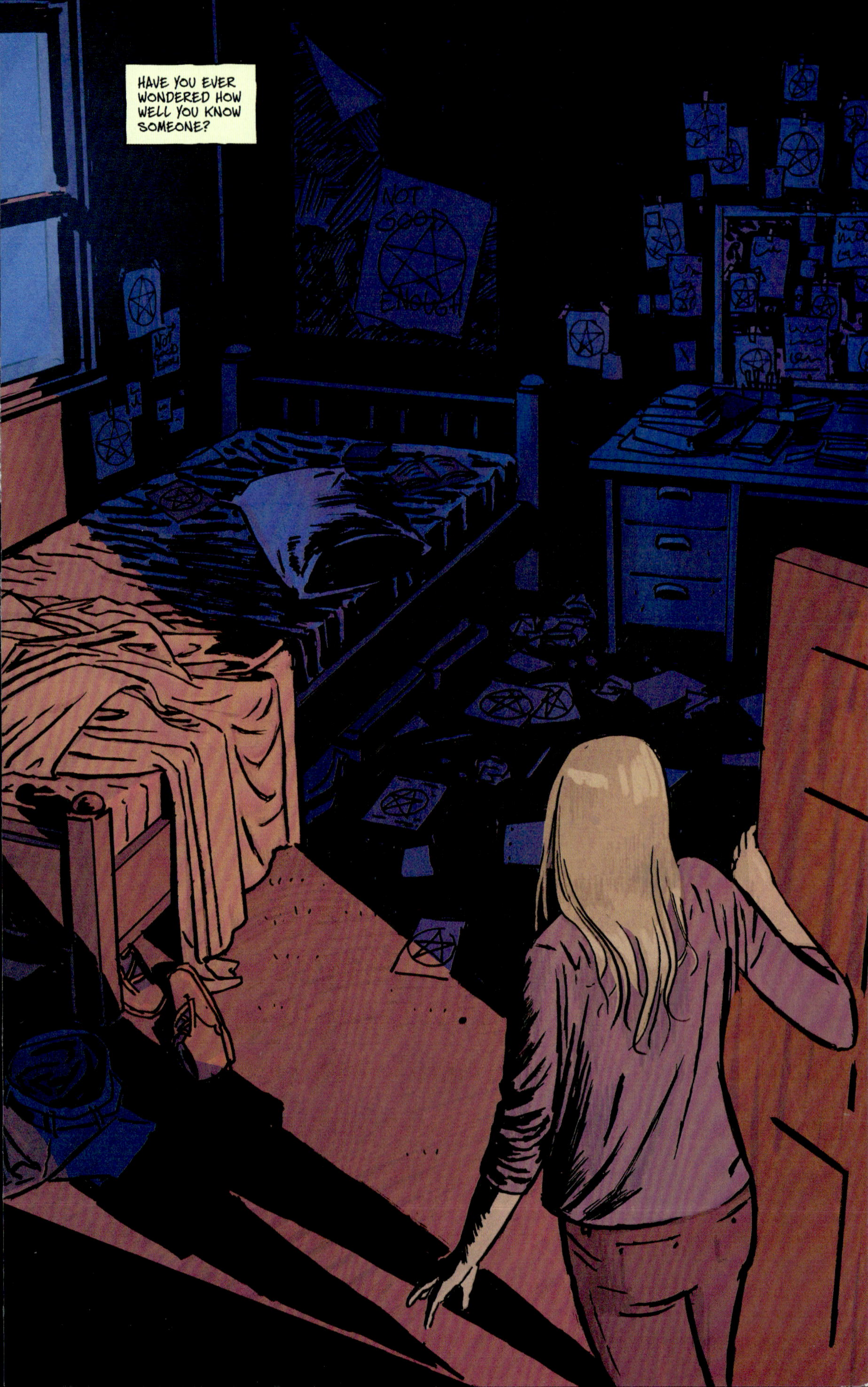
HAVE YOU EVER WONDERED HOW WELL YOU KNOW SOMEONE?

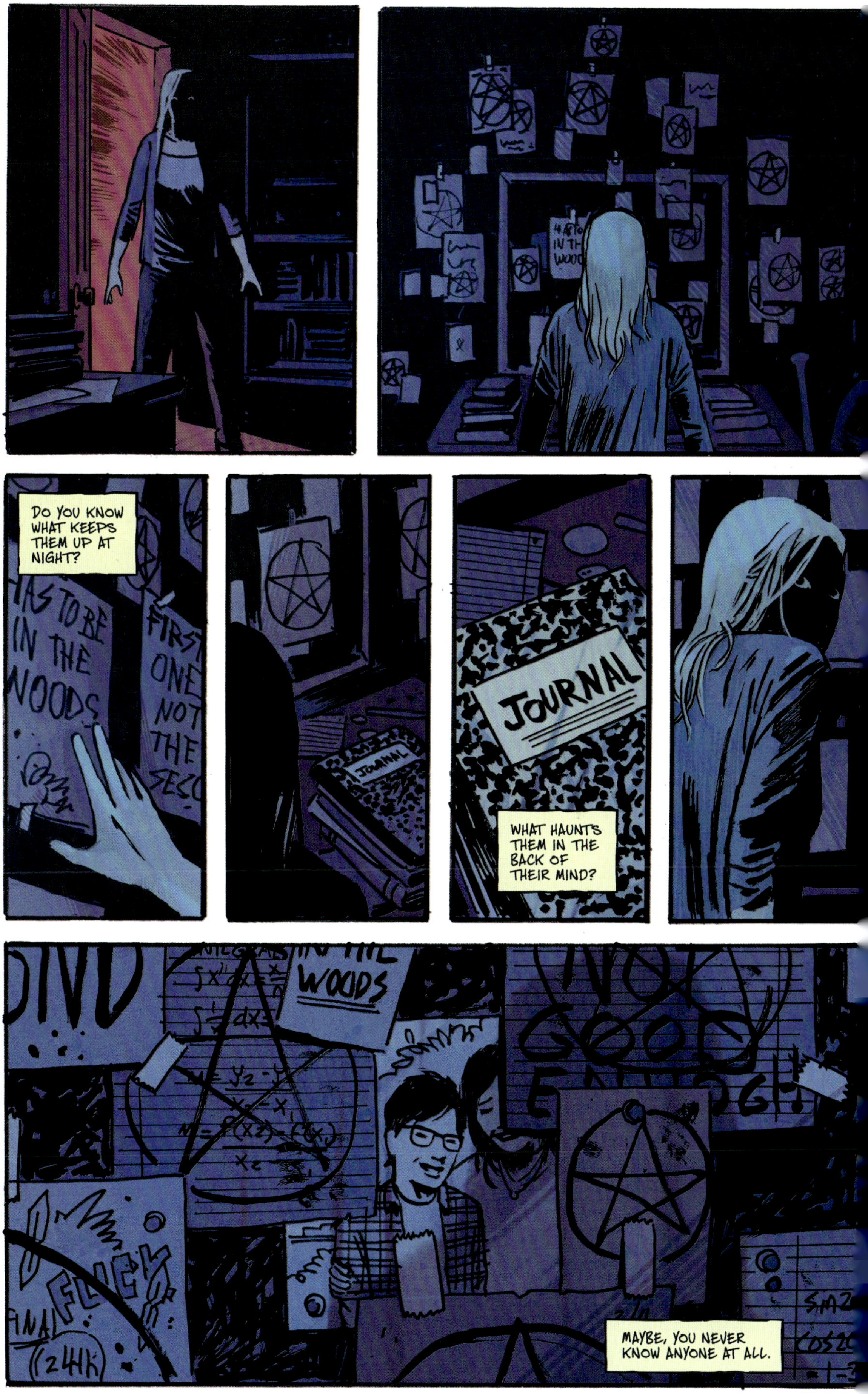
DO YOU KNOW WHAT KEEPS THEM UP AT NIGHT?
JOURNAL
WHAT HAUNTS THEM IN THE BACK OF THEIR MIND?
WOODS
MAYBE, YOU NEVER KNOW ANYONE AT ALL.

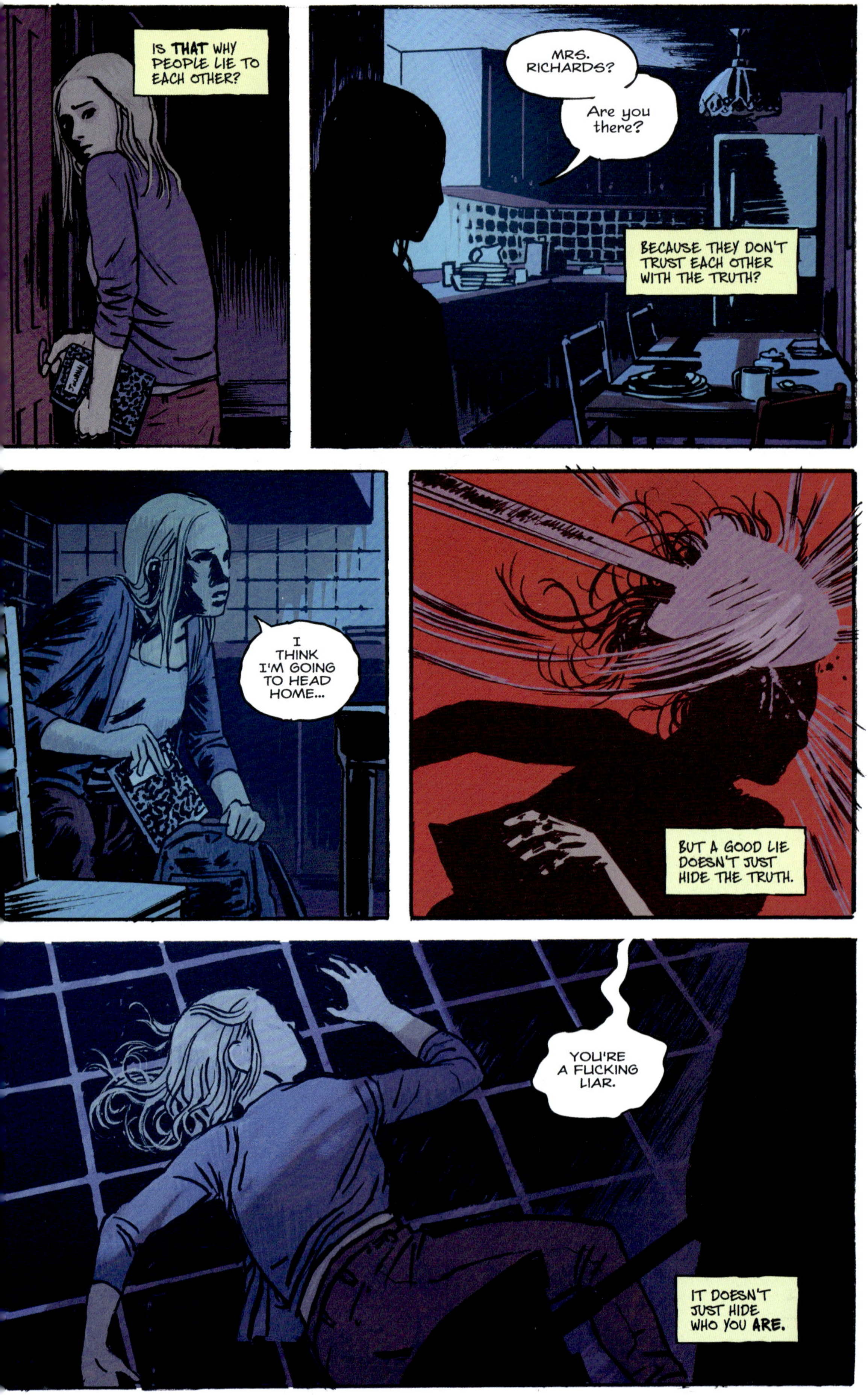
IS THAT WHY PEOPLE LIE TO EACH OTHER?
MRS. RICHARDS?
Are you there?
BECAUSE THEY DON'T TRUST EACH OTHER WITH THE TRUTH?
I THINK I'M GOING TO HEAD HOME...
BUT A GOOD LIE DOESN'T JUST HIDE THE TRUTH.
YOU'RE A FUCKING LIAR.
IT DOESN'T JUST HIDE WHO YOU ARE.

MY SON DOESN'T HAVE ANY FRIENDS.
IT GETS A PERSON TO BELIEVE SOMETHING THAT NEVER EXISTED AT ALL.

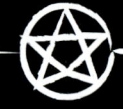

CHAPTER 3

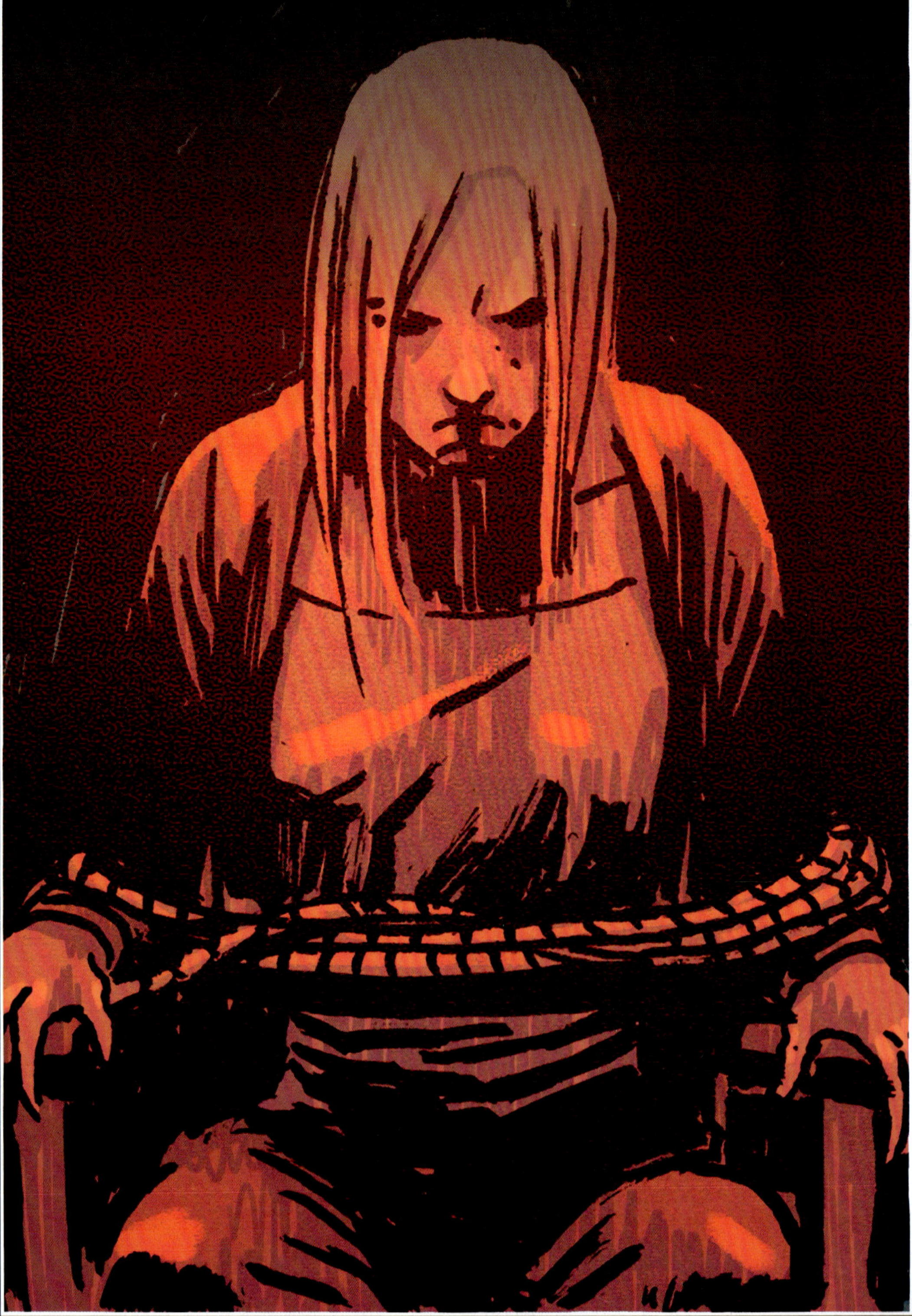

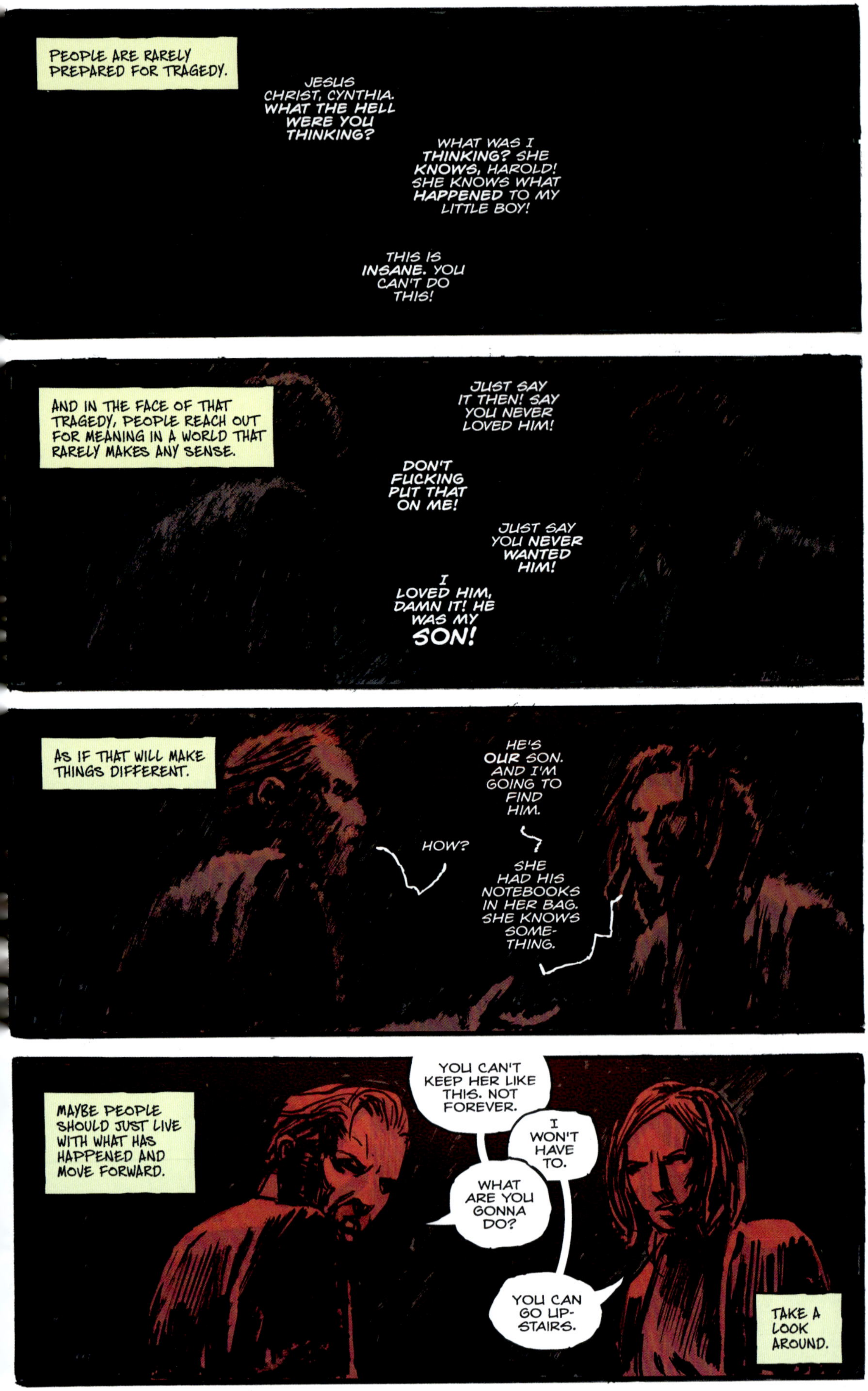
PEOPLE ARE RARELY PREPARED FOR TRAGEDY.
JESUS CHRIST, CYNTHIA. WHAT THE HELL WERE YOU THINKING?
WHAT WAS I THINKING? SHE KNOWS, HAROLD! SHE KNOWS WHAT HAPPENED TO MY LITTLE BOY!
THIS IS INSANE. YOU CAN'T DO THIS!
AND IN THE FACE OF THAT TRAGEDY, PEOPLE REACH OUT FOR MEANING IN A WORLD THAT RARELY MAKES ANY SENSE.
JUST SAY IT THEN! SAY YOU NEVER LOVED HIM!
DON'T FUCKING PUT THAT ON ME!
JUST SAY YOU NEVER WANTED HIM!
I LOVED HIM, DAMN IT! HE WAS MY SON!
AS IF THAT WILL MAKE THINGS DIFFERENT.
HE'S OUR SON. AND I'M GOING TO FIND HIM.
HOW?
SHE HAD HIS NOTEBOOKS IN HER BAG. SHE KNOWS SOME-THING.
MAYBE PEOPLE SHOULD JUST LIVE WITH WHAT HAS HAPPENED AND MOVE FORWARD.
YOU CAN'T KEEP HER LIKE THIS. NOT FOREVER.
I WON'T HAVE TO.
WHAT ARE YOU GONNA DO?
YOU CAN GO UP-STAIRS.
TAKE A LOOK AROUND.

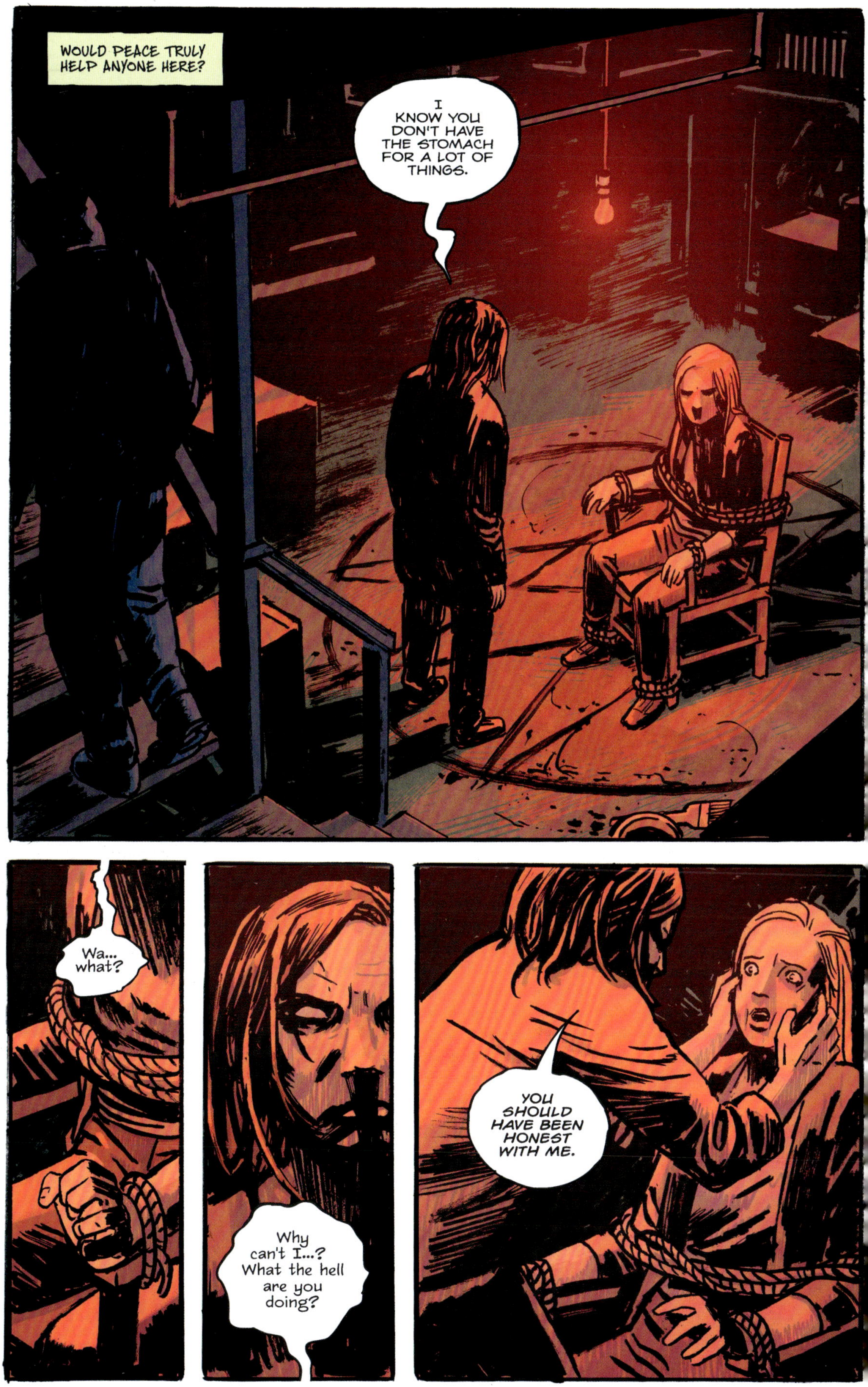
WOULD PEACE TRULY HELP ANYONE HERE?
I KNOW YOU DON'T HAVE THE STOMACH FOR A LOT OF THINGS.
Wa... what?
Why can't I...? What the hell are you doing?
YOU SHOULD HAVE BEEN HONEST WITH ME.

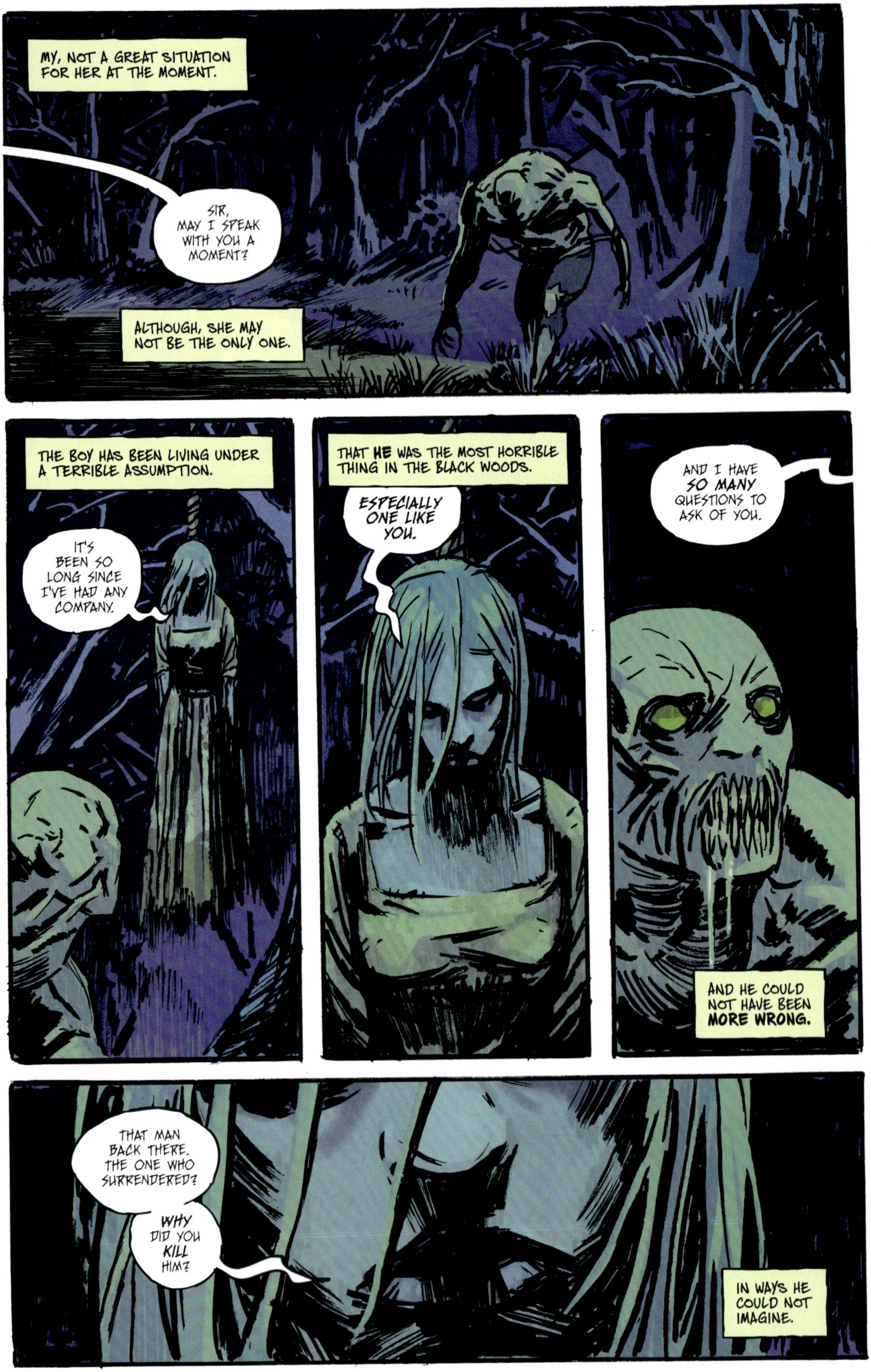
MY, NOT A GREAT SITUATION FOR HER AT THE MOMENT.
SIR, MAY I SPEAK WITH YOU A MOMENT?
ALTHOUGH, SHE MAY NOT BE THE ONLY ONE.
THE BOY HAS BEEN LIVING UNDER A TERRIBLE ASSUMPTION.
IT'S BEEN SO LONG SINCE I'VE HAD ANY COMPANY.
THAT **HE** WAS THE MOST HORRIBLE THING IN THE BLACK WOODS.
ESPECIALLY ONE LIKE YOU.
AND I HAVE ***SO MANY*** QUESTIONS TO ASK OF YOU.
AND HE COULD NOT HAVE BEEN **MORE WRONG.**
THAT MAN BACK THERE. THE ONE WHO SURRENDERED?
WHY DID YOU ***KILL*** HIM?
IN WAYS HE COULD NOT IMAGINE.

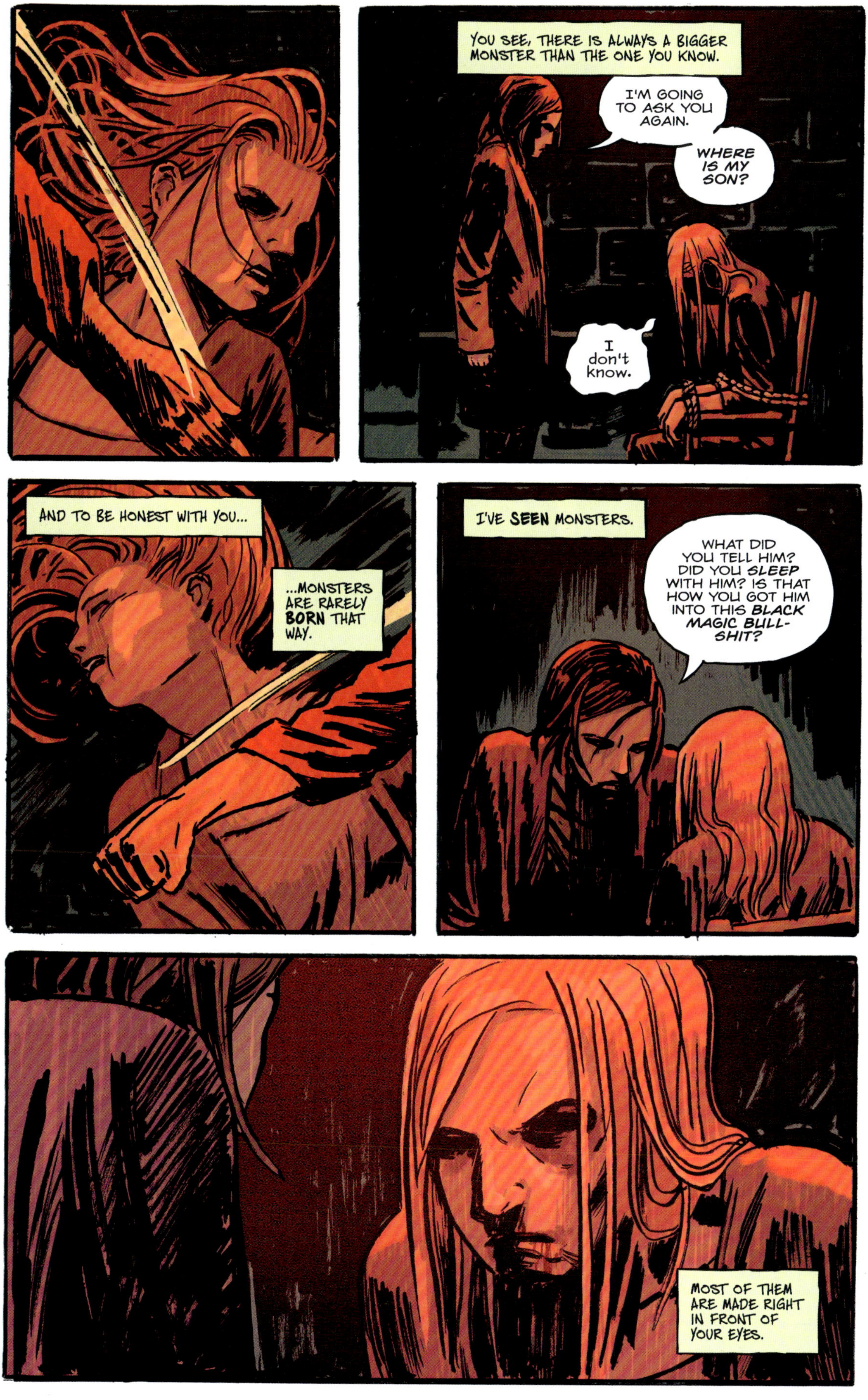

YOU SEE, THERE IS ALWAYS A BIGGER MONSTER THAN THE ONE YOU KNOW.
I'M GOING TO ASK YOU AGAIN.
WHERE IS MY SON?
I don't know.
AND TO BE HONEST WITH YOU...
...MONSTERS ARE RARELY BORN THAT WAY.
I'VE SEEN MONSTERS.
WHAT DID YOU TELL HIM? DID YOU SLEEP WITH HIM? IS THAT HOW YOU GOT HIM INTO THIS BLACK MAGIC BULL-SHIT?
MOST OF THEM ARE MADE RIGHT IN FRONT OF YOUR EYES.

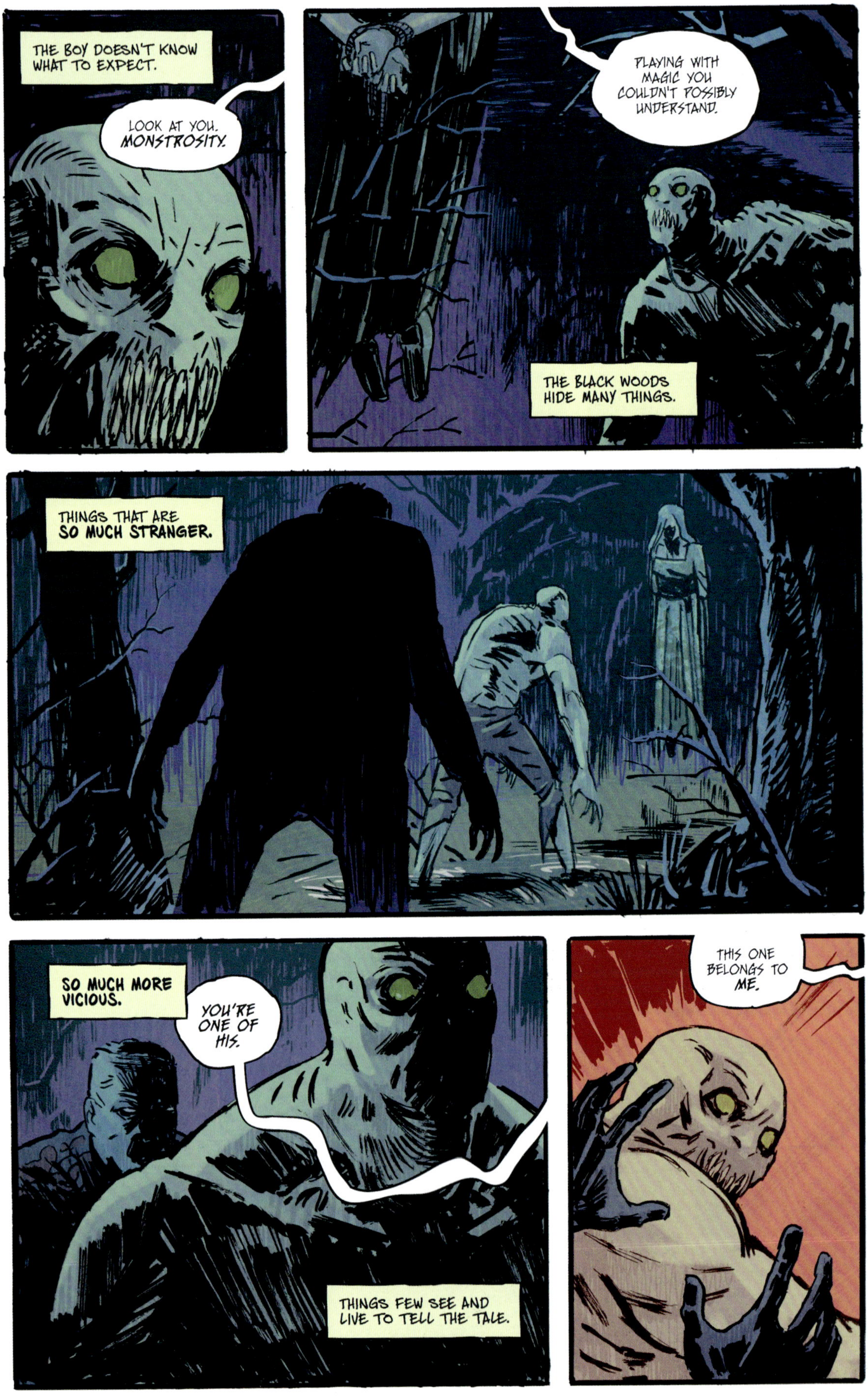
THE BOY DOESN'T KNOW WHAT TO EXPECT.
LOOK AT YOU. MONSTROSITY.
PLAYING WITH MAGIC YOU COULDN'T POSSIBLY UNDERSTAND.
THE BLACK WOODS HIDE MANY THINGS.
THINGS THAT ARE SO MUCH STRANGER.
SO MUCH MORE VICIOUS.
YOU'RE ONE OF HIS.
THINGS FEW SEE AND LIVE TO TELL THE TALE.
THIS ONE BELONGS TO ME.

THE WITCH HANGING FROM THE TREE THINKS SHE'S CLEVER.
PLEASE DON'T MISUNDERSTAND. THIS ONE MEANS NOTHING.
BUT HE PLEDGED HIMSELF TO ME.
KILL HIM.
ATTACKING THE BOY WHEN HE'S MOST CONFUSED.

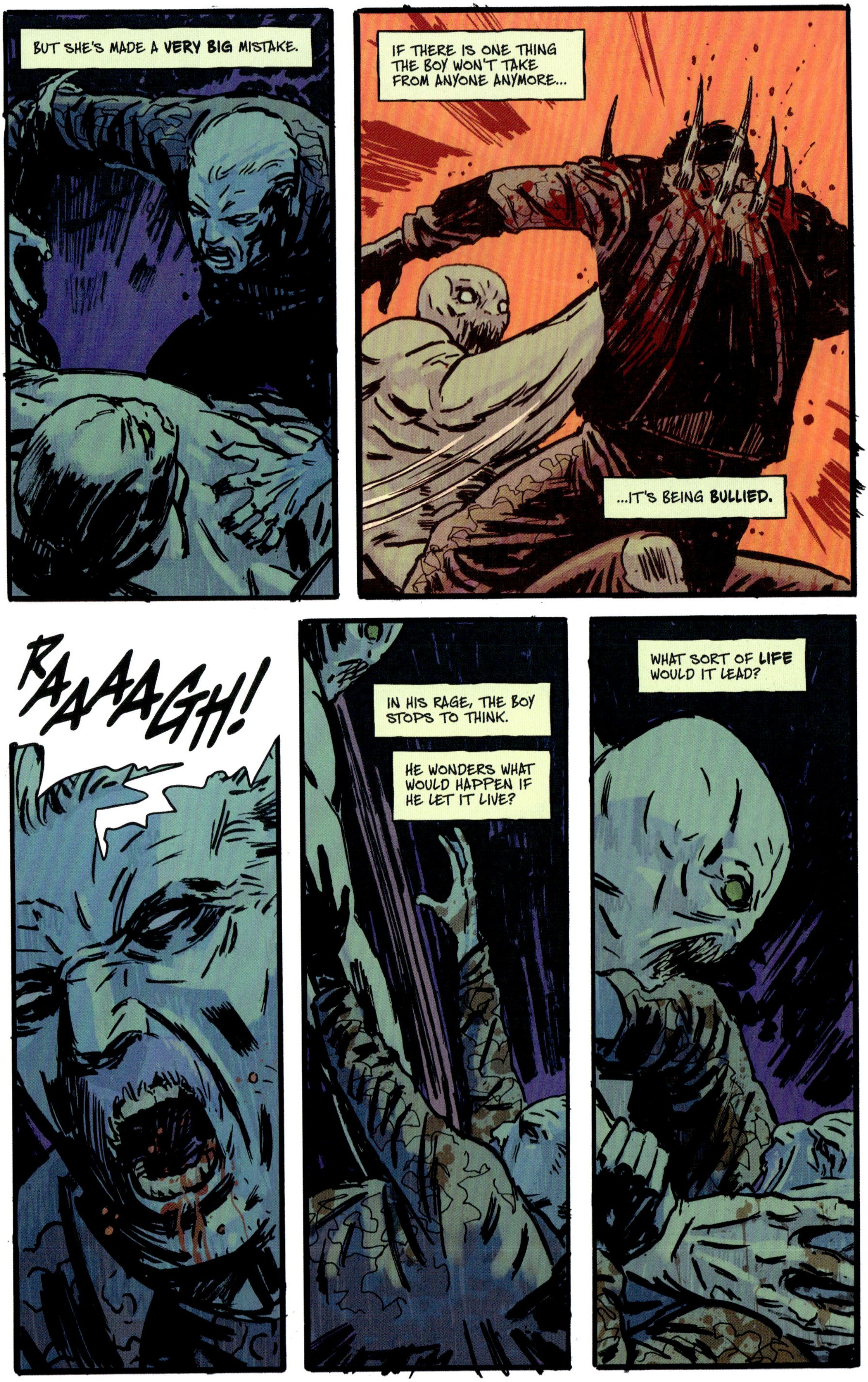
BUT SHE'S MADE A VERY BIG MISTAKE.
IF THERE IS ONE THING THE BOY WON'T TAKE FROM ANYONE ANYMORE...
...IT'S BEING BULLIED.
RAAAAGH!
IN HIS RAGE, THE BOY STOPS TO THINK.
HE WONDERS WHAT WOULD HAPPEN IF HE LET IT LIVE?
WHAT SORT OF LIFE WOULD IT LEAD?

PERHAPS IT WOULD LEAD THE SAME LIFE HE DOES NOW.
PERHAPS IT'S BETTER OFF DEAD.
WELL, THAT WAS CERTAINLY EXCITING.
ONE DAY, YOUR TIME WILL BE NO MORE. AND YOU WILL KNOW THAT IT WAS MY DOING.
NOT WITH EFFORTS LIKE THAT.
WHAT YOU SAW WAS JUST FOR **FUN.** I HAVE FAR WORSE PLANNED FOR YOU. AND FOR THAT NEW MONSTER YOU SEEM TO ENJOY SO MUCH.
I DON'T UNDERSTAND WHY YOU THINK IT HAS TO BE LIKE THIS.
I LOVE ALL MY CHILDREN **EQUALLY.**
EVEN YOU.
THEY SAY YOUR FIRST IS USUALLY YOUR FAVORITE.
YOU'RE GOING TO ***SUFFER*** FOR WHAT YOU DID TO ME. I AM GOING TO END YOU. ***I PROMISE.***

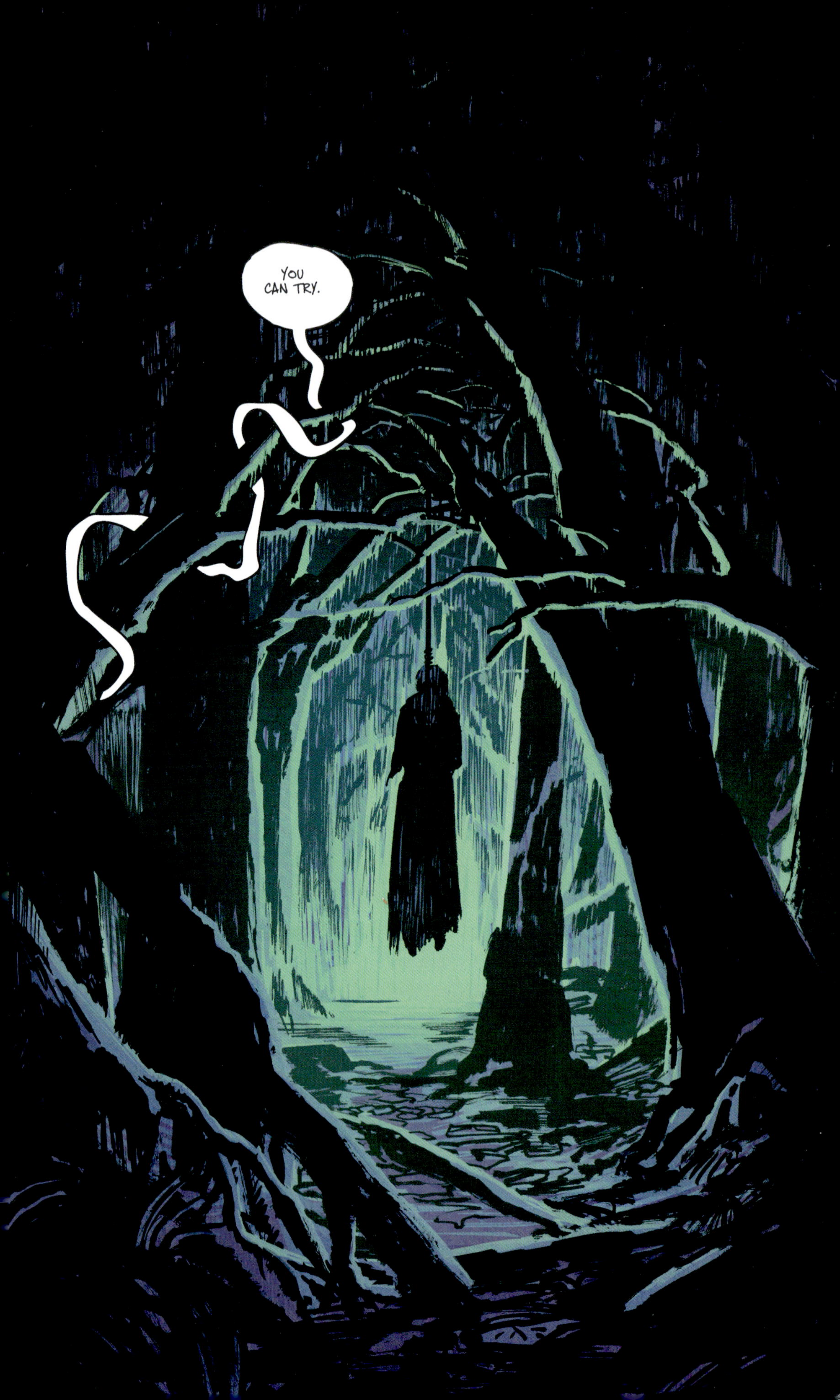
YOU CAN TRY.

DRINK THIS. SHE'LL BE BACK SOON.
SO, ARE YOU THE GOOD COP?
WHAT DID YOU LIKE ABOUT MY SON?
QUINN...HE NEVER BROUGHT FRIENDS OR ANYONE OVER. EVER.
I THINK TO SAY THAT I WAS A TERRIBLE FATHER WOULD BE AN UNDERSTATEMENT. WE HAD HIM WHEN WE WERE VERY YOUNG. WHEN QUINN WAS BORN, SHE WAS THE HAPPI-EST I'VE EVER SEEN HER. BUT I STILL HAD DREAMS.
I WAS NEVER THE BEAUTIFUL GIRL THAT BOYS WANTED. AND THEN I GOT TO HIGH SCHOOL AND THE CAPTAIN OF THE FOOTBALL TEAM WAS ASKING FOR MY NUMBER. I WAS STARSTRUCK.
PEOPLE WANTED TO DATE ME OR BE FRIENDS BUT I HAD NO IDEA WHY. I FEEL LIKE A SOCIAL PROP TO THE FRIENDS I DO HAVE. IT JUST ALL SEEMS SO FAKE.
BUT I NEVER GOT THAT FEELING WITH QUINN. FOR ALL HIS AWKWARDNESS, HE WAS ALWAYS GENUINE TO ME.
I NEVER HAD TO QUESTION HOW HE FELT ABOUT ME.

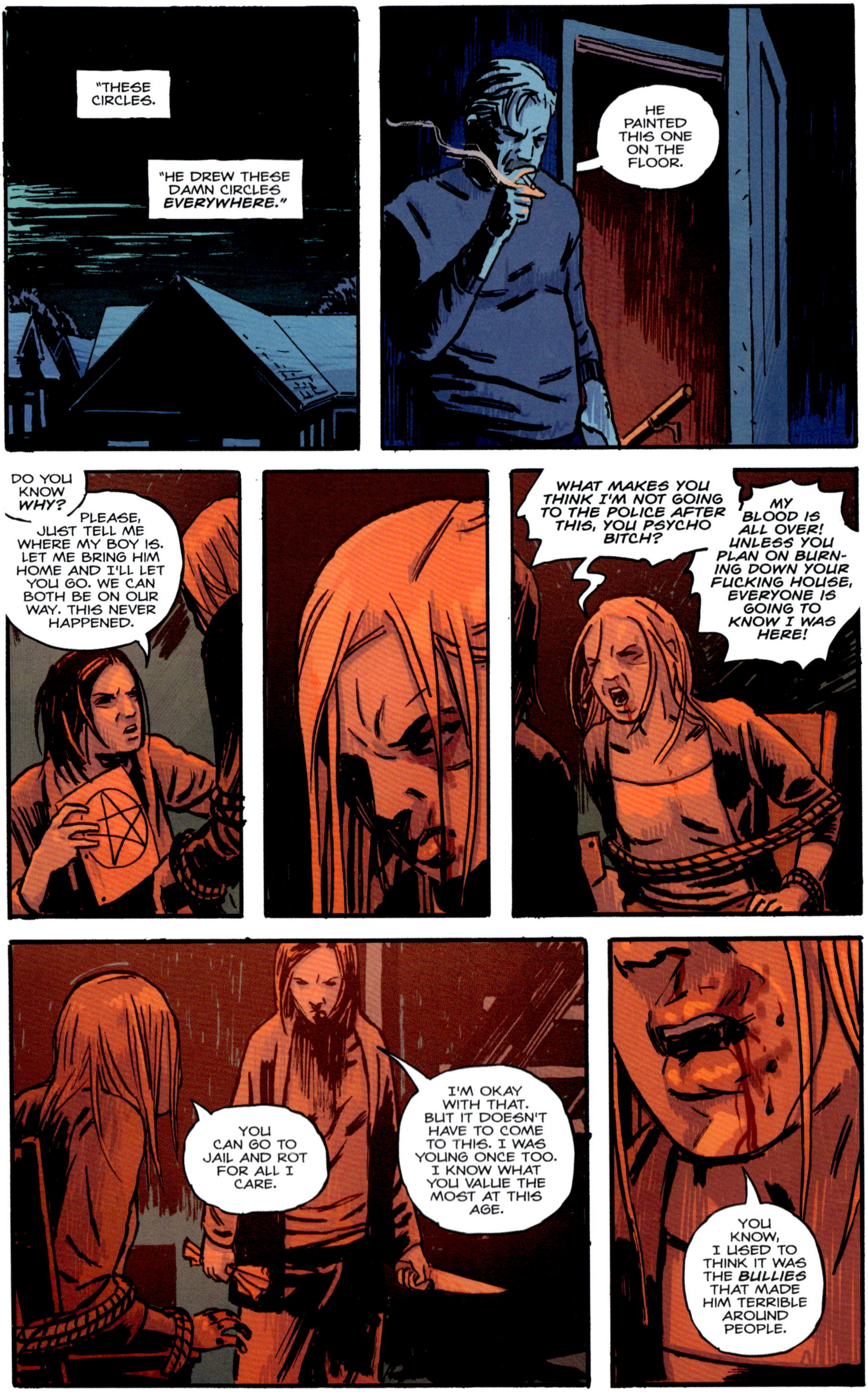
"THESE CIRCLES.
"HE DREW THESE DAMN CIRCLES *EVERYWHERE.*"
HE PAINTED THIS ONE ON THE FLOOR.
DO YOU KNOW *WHY?*
PLEASE, JUST TELL ME WHERE MY BOY IS. LET ME BRING HIM HOME AND I'LL LET YOU GO. WE CAN BOTH BE ON OUR WAY. THIS NEVER HAPPENED.
WHAT MAKES YOU THINK I'M NOT GOING TO THE POLICE AFTER THIS, YOU PSYCHO BITCH?
MY BLOOD IS ALL OVER! UNLESS YOU PLAN ON BURN-ING DOWN YOUR FUCKING HOUSE, EVERYONE IS GOING TO KNOW I WAS HERE!
YOU CAN GO TO JAIL AND ROT FOR ALL I CARE.
I'M OKAY WITH THAT. BUT IT DOESN'T HAVE TO COME TO THIS. I WAS YOUNG ONCE TOO. I KNOW WHAT YOU VALUE THE MOST AT THIS AGE.
YOU KNOW, I USED TO THINK IT WAS THE *BULLIES* THAT MADE HIM TERRIBLE AROUND PEOPLE.

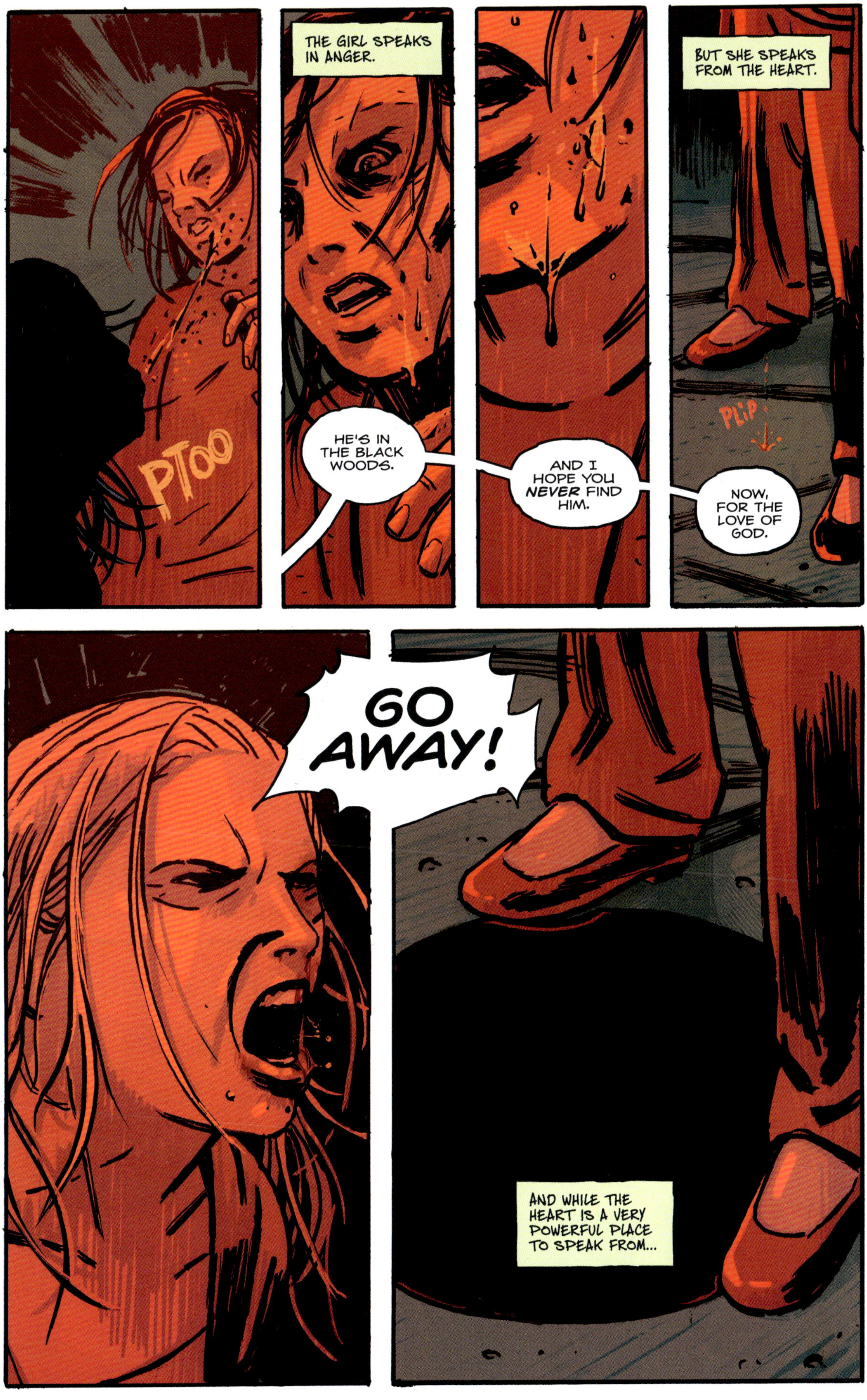
PTOO
THE GIRL SPEAKS IN ANGER.
HE'S IN THE BLACK WOODS.
AND I HOPE YOU *NEVER* FIND HIM.
BUT SHE SPEAKS FROM THE HEART.
PLIP
NOW, FOR THE LOVE OF GOD.
GO AWAY!
AND WHILE THE HEART IS A VERY POWERFUL PLACE TO SPEAK FROM...

...IT CAN ALSO BE THE MOST DANGEROUS.
HA-- HAROLD!
HAROLD!
OH MY GOD!
IT'S OKAY! I GOT YOU!

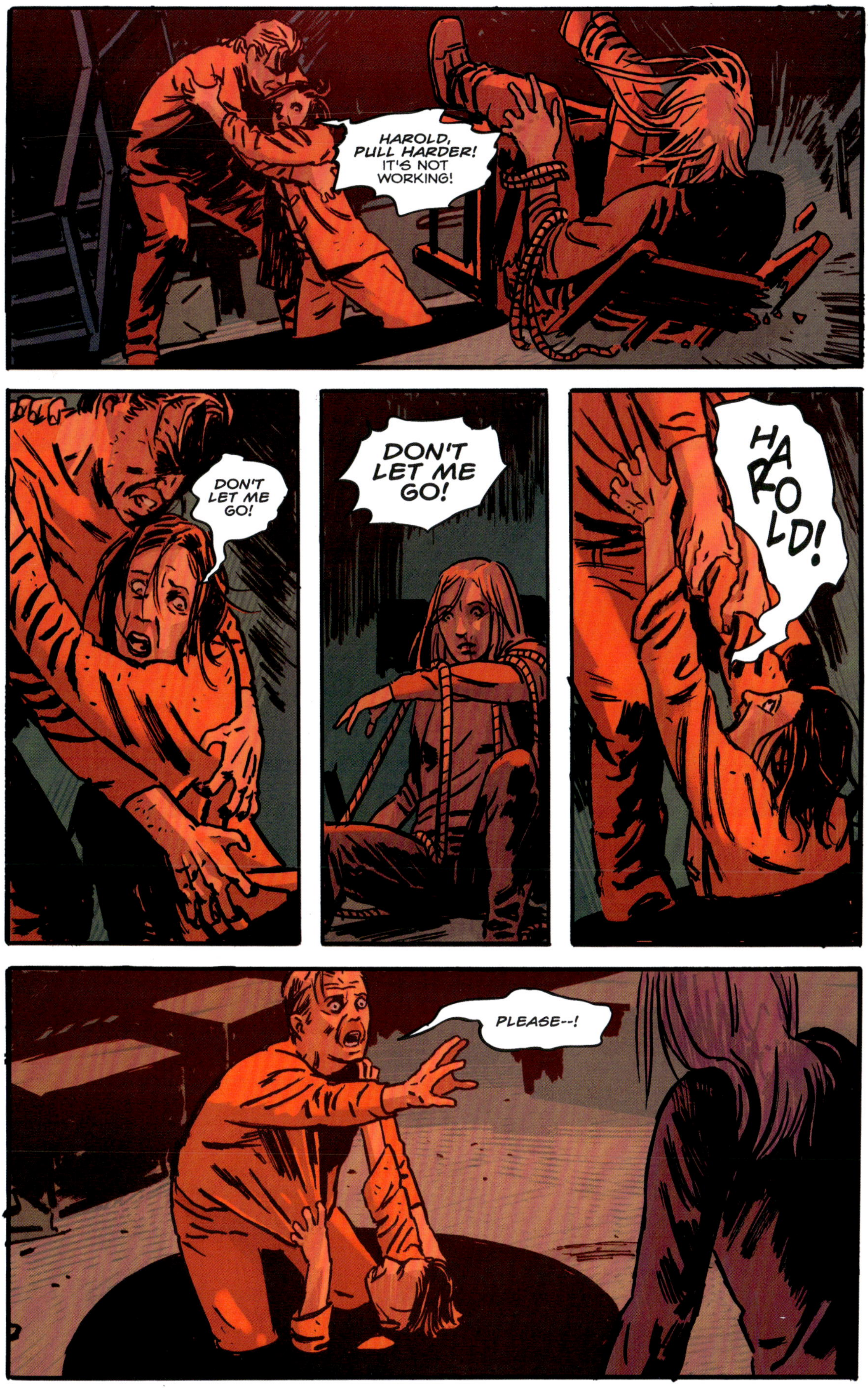
HAROLD, PULL HARDER! IT'S NOT WORKING!
DON'T LET ME GO!
DON'T LET ME GO!
HAROLD!
PLEASE--!

	Ha-Gul-Agh

A MOMENT. PLEASE!

HESITATION.

JUST GRAB MY

THAT'S ALL IT TAKES.

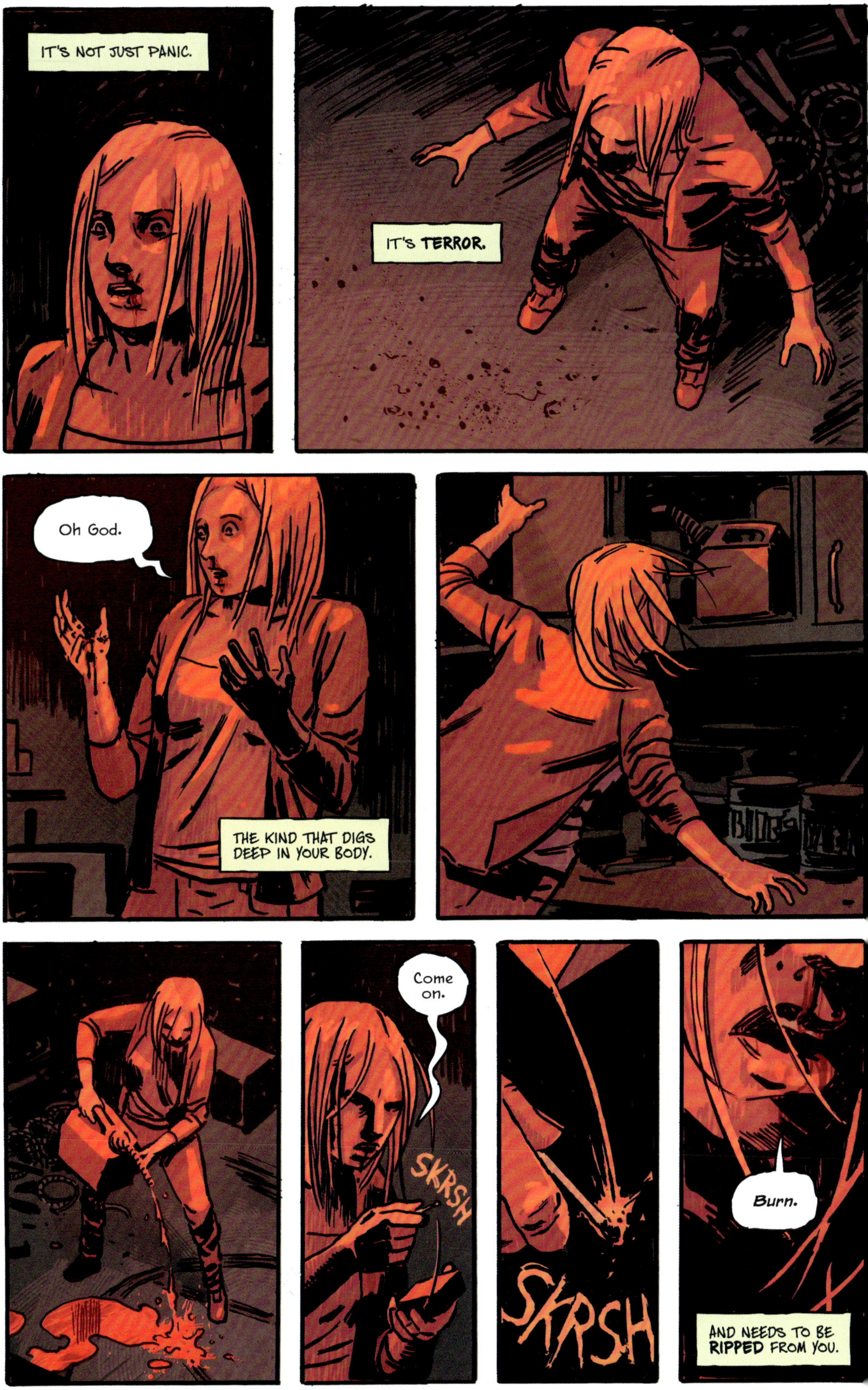
IT'S NOT JUST PANIC.
IT'S TERROR.
Oh God.
THE KIND THAT DIGS DEEP IN YOUR BODY.
Come on.
SKRSH
SKRSH
Burn.
AND NEEDS TO BE RIPPED FROM YOU.

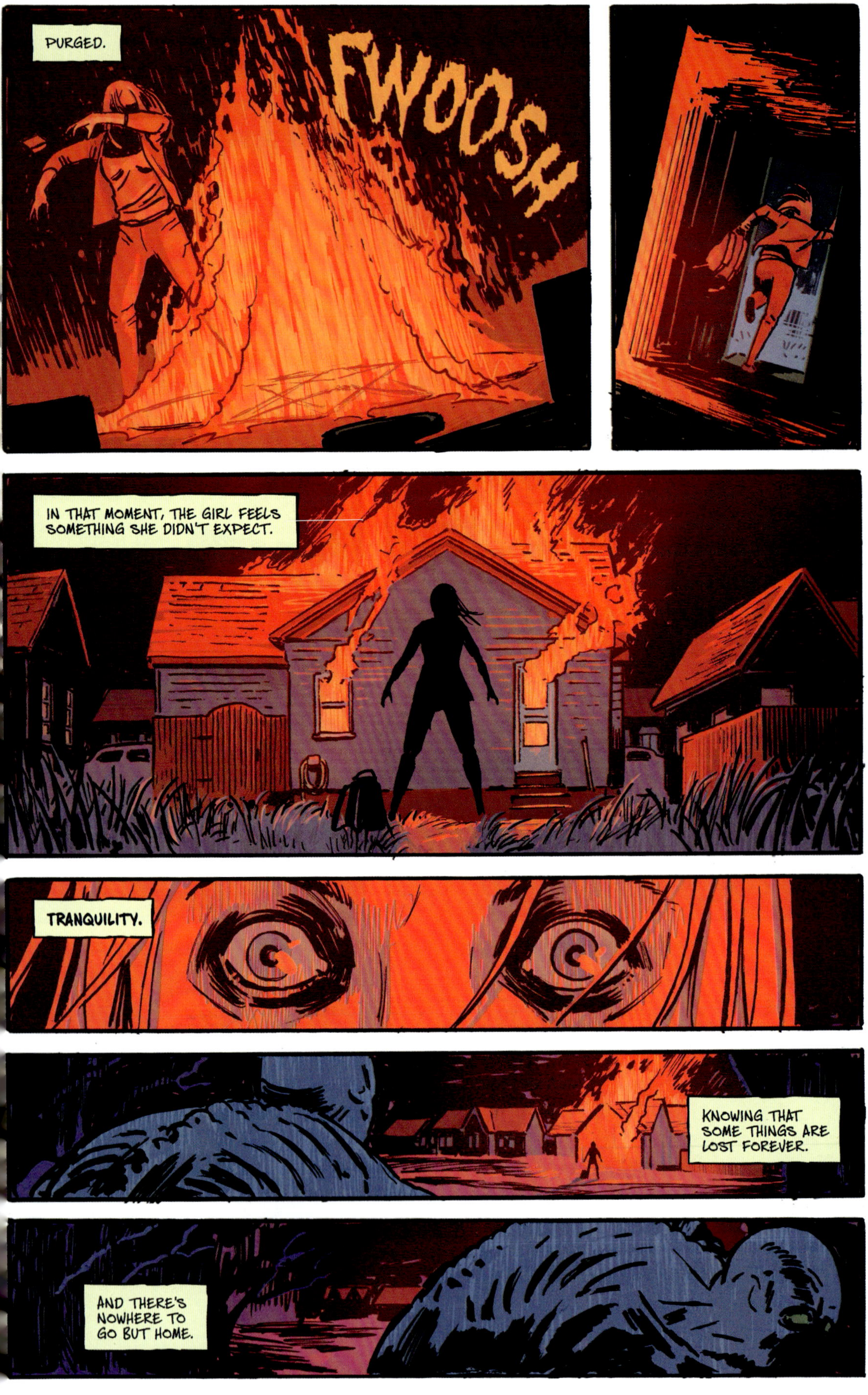
PURGED.
FWOOSH
IN THAT MOMENT, THE GIRL FEELS SOMETHING SHE DIDN'T EXPECT.
TRANQUILITY.
KNOWING THAT SOME THINGS ARE LOST FOREVER.
AND THERE'S NOWHERE TO GO BUT HOME.

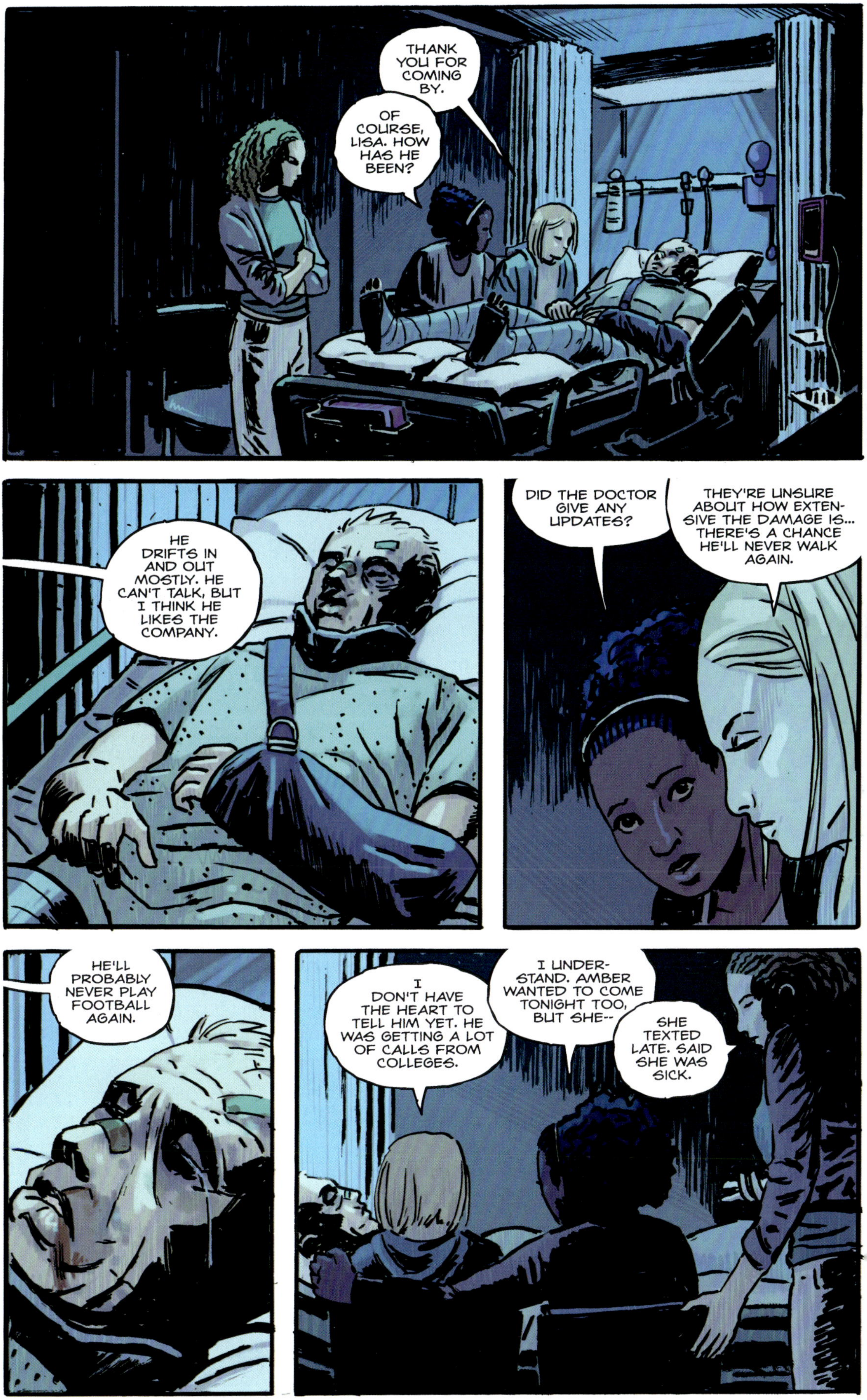
THANK YOU FOR COMING BY.
OF COURSE, LISA. HOW HAS HE BEEN?
HE DRIFTS IN AND OUT MOSTLY. HE CAN'T TALK, BUT I THINK HE LIKES THE COMPANY.
DID THE DOCTOR GIVE ANY UPDATES?
THEY'RE UNSURE ABOUT HOW EXTEN-SIVE THE DAMAGE IS... THERE'S A CHANCE HE'LL NEVER WALK AGAIN.
HE'LL PROBABLY NEVER PLAY FOOTBALL AGAIN.
I DON'T HAVE THE HEART TO TELL HIM YET. HE WAS GETTING A LOT OF CALLS FROM COLLEGES.
I UNDER-STAND. AMBER WANTED TO COME TONIGHT TOO, BUT SHE--
SHE TEXTED LATE. SAID SHE WAS SICK.

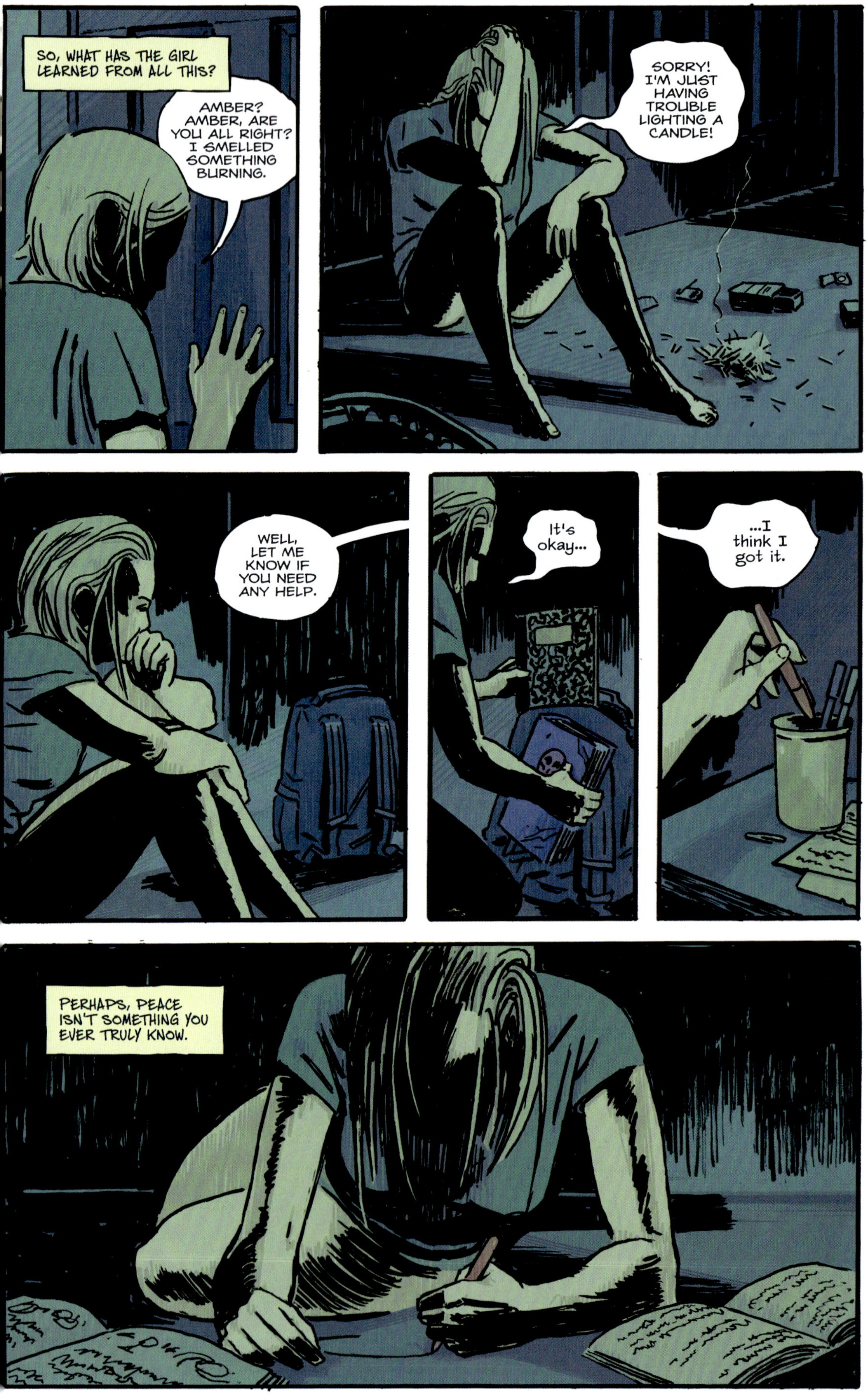
SO, WHAT HAS THE GIRL LEARNED FROM ALL THIS?
AMBER? AMBER, ARE YOU ALL RIGHT? I SMELLED SOMETHING BURNING.
SORRY! I'M JUST HAVING TROUBLE LIGHTING A CANDLE!
WELL, LET ME KNOW IF YOU NEED ANY HELP.
It's okay...
...I think I got it.
PERHAPS, PEACE ISN'T SOMETHING YOU EVER TRULY KNOW.

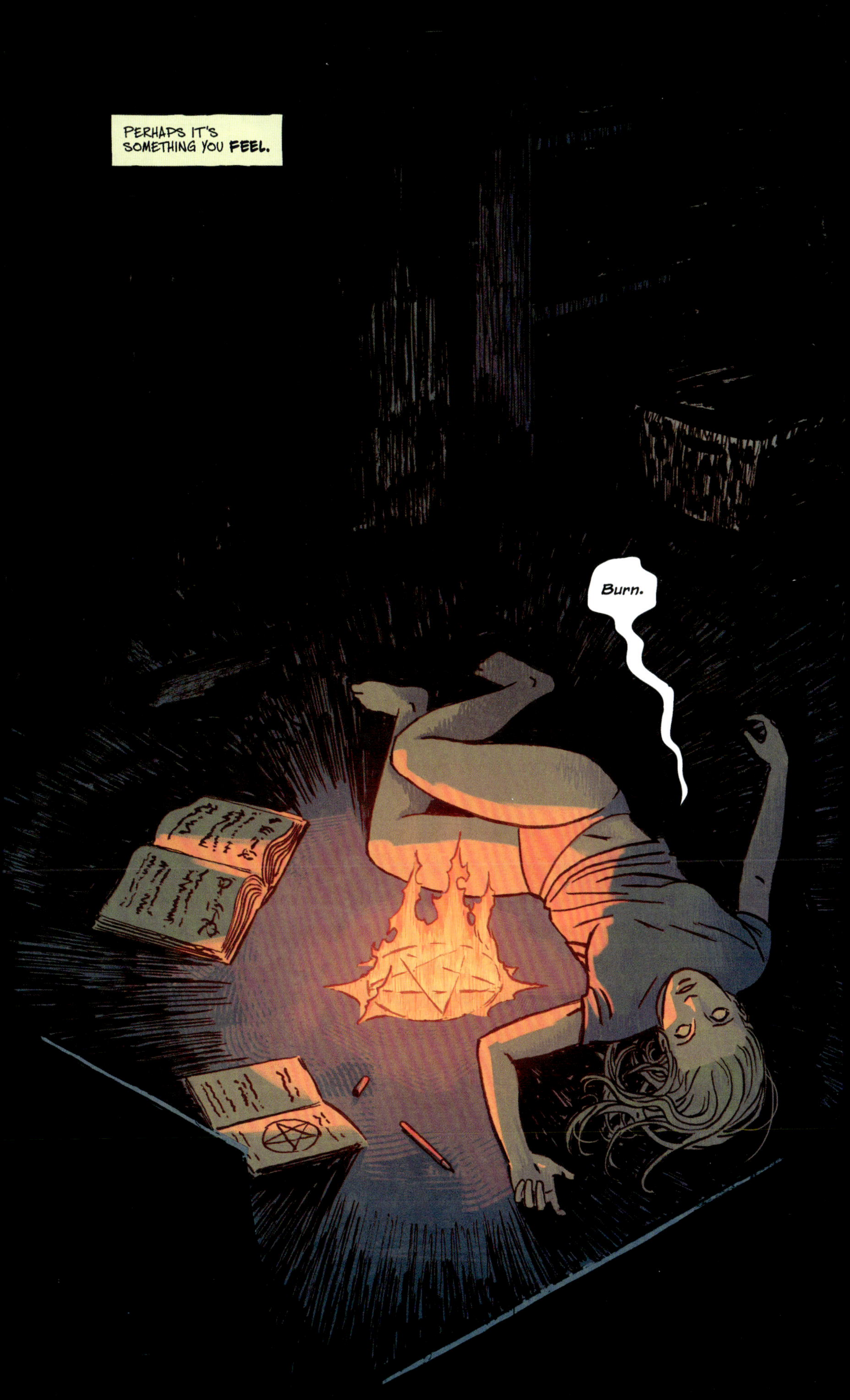
PERHAPS IT'S SOMETHING YOU **FEEL.**
Burn.

CHAPTER 4

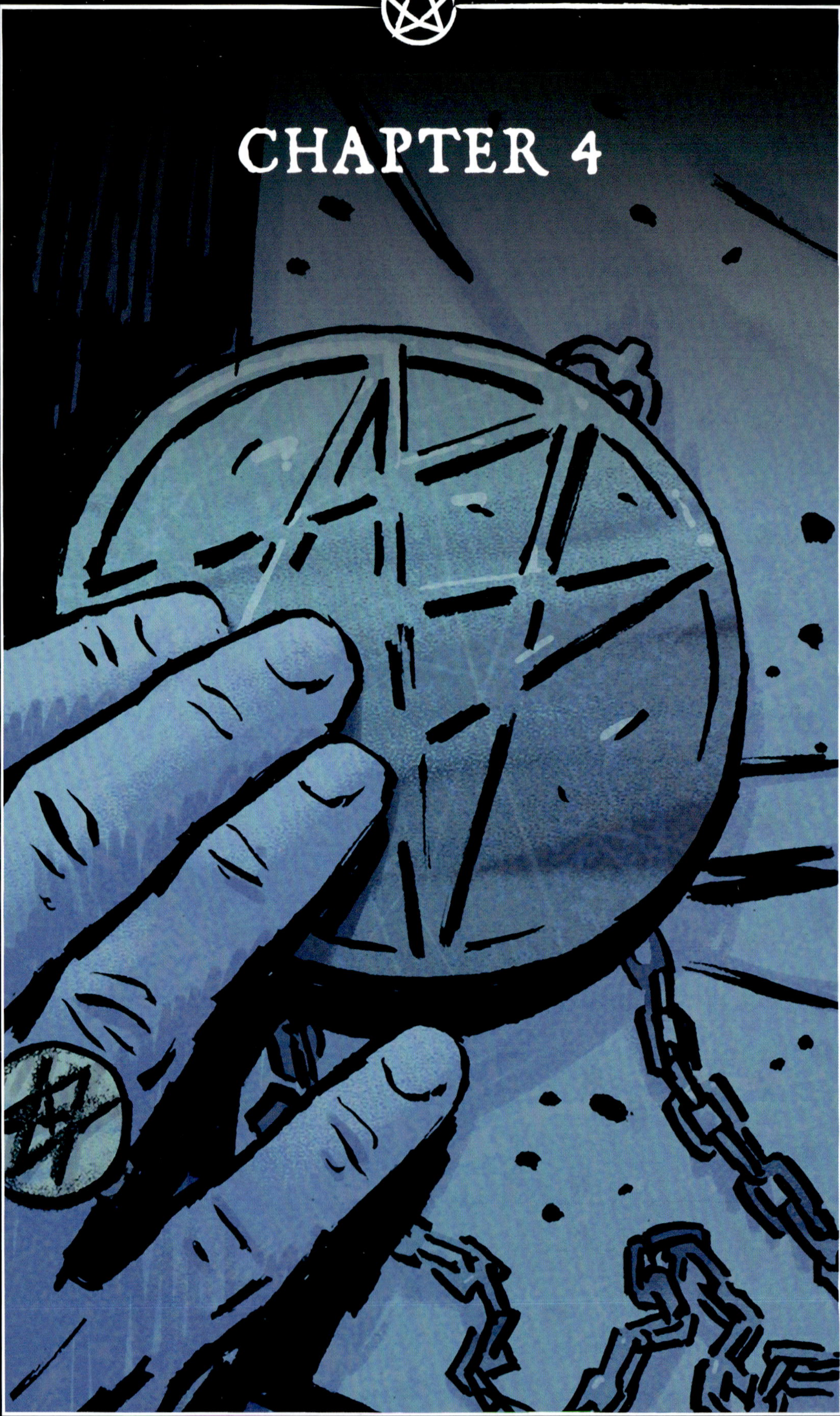

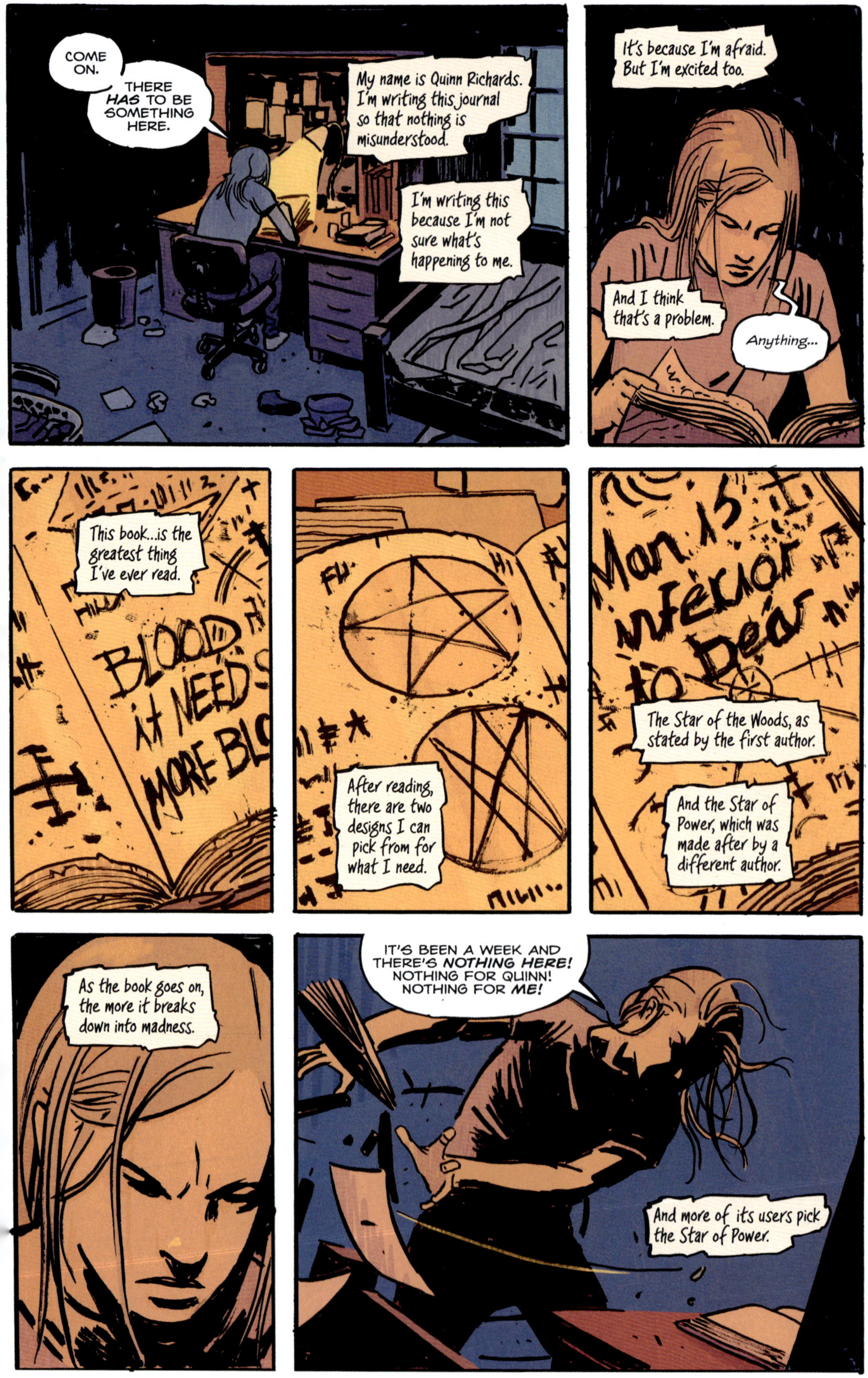

COME ON.
THERE *HAS* TO BE SOMETHING HERE.
My name is Quinn Richards. I'm writing this journal so that nothing is misunderstood.
I'm writing this because I'm not sure what's happening to me.
It's because I'm afraid. But I'm excited too.
And I think that's a problem.
Anything...
This book...is the greatest thing I've ever read.
BLOOD it NEEDS MORE BLO
After reading, there are two designs I can pick from for what I need.
The Star of the Woods, as stated by the first author.
And the Star of Power, which was made after by a different author.
As the book goes on, the more it breaks down into madness.
IT'S BEEN A WEEK AND THERE'S *NOTHING HERE!* NOTHING FOR QUINN! NOTHING FOR *ME!*
And more of its users pick the Star of Power.

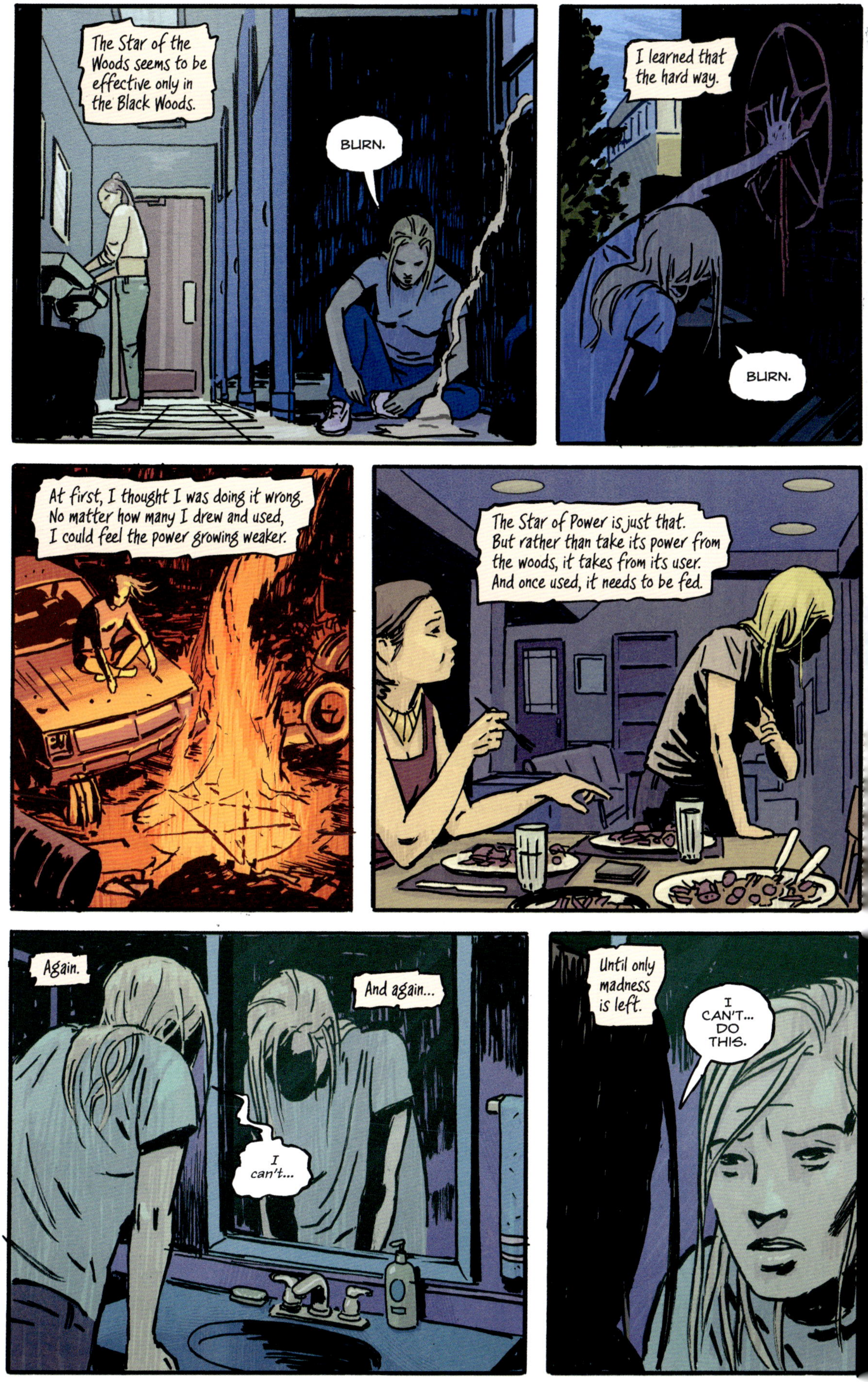
The Star of the Woods seems to be effective only in the Black Woods.
BURN.
I learned that the hard way.
BURN.
At first, I thought I was doing it wrong. No matter how many I drew and used, I could feel the power growing weaker.
The Star of Power is just that. But rather than take its power from the woods, it takes from its user. And once used, it needs to be fed.
Again.
And again...
I can't...
Until only madness is left.
I CAN'T... DO THIS.

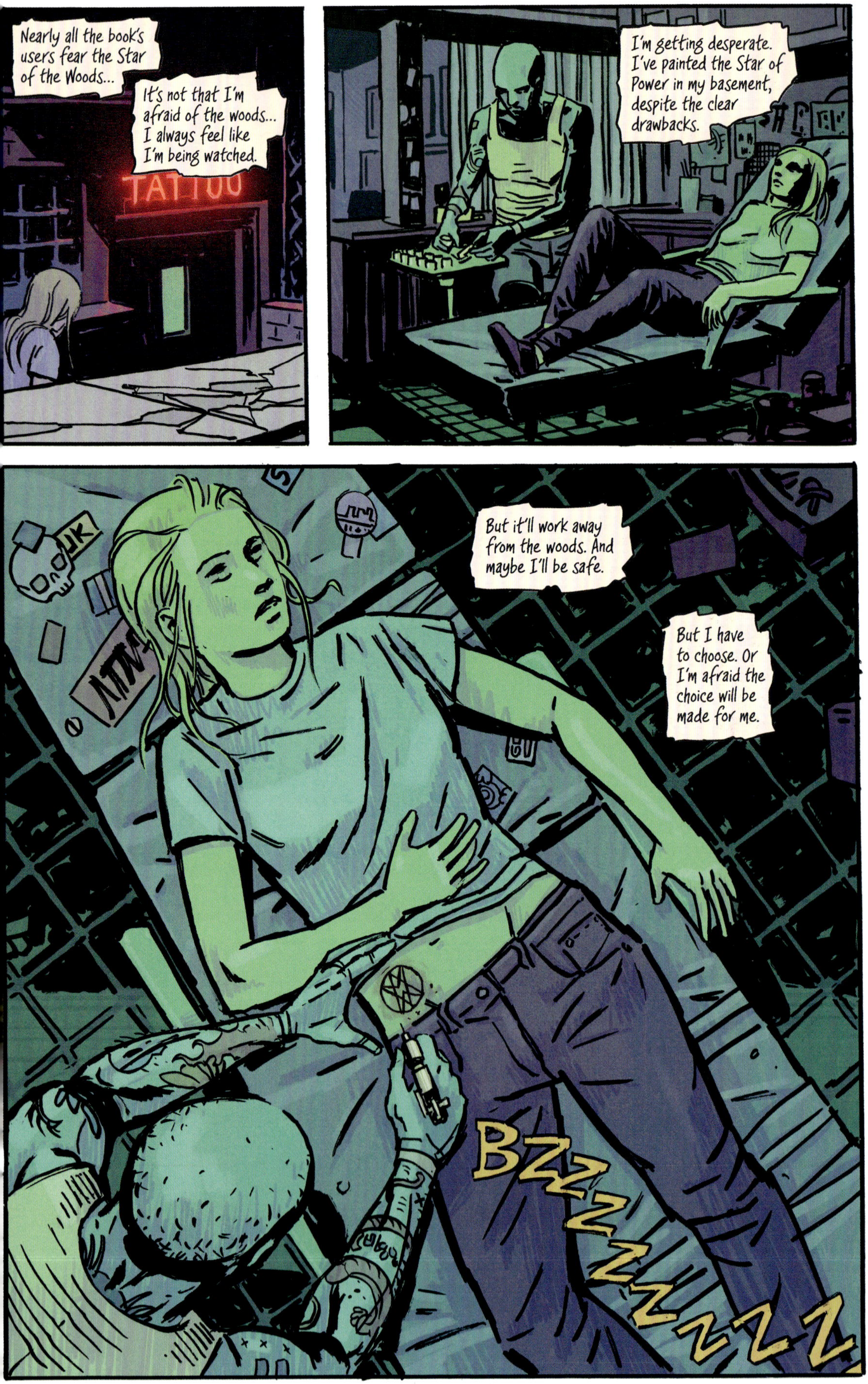

Nearly all the book's users fear the Star of the Woods...
It's not that I'm afraid of the woods... I always feel like I'm being watched.
TATTOO
I'm getting desperate. I've painted the Star of Power in my basement, despite the clear drawbacks.
But it'll work away from the woods. And maybe I'll be safe.
But I have to choose. Or I'm afraid the choice will be made for me.
BZZZZZZZZZ

SO, WE MIGHT GO SEE TYLER AGAIN TONIGHT. LISA MISSED YOU THE OTHER NIGHT.
YEAH... SURE. IT'S JUST...AREN'T YOU WORRIED ABOUT WHAT HAPPENED TO QUINN?
OF COURSE, BUT...
HE WAS A NICE KID. BUT HE WAS WEIRD. AND HIS HOUSE JUST BURNED DOWN AND HIS PARENTS WENT MISSING.
I KNOW IT'S TERRIBLE, BUT MAYBE IT'S BETTER IF HE'S NOT FOUND.
SHE WAS RIGHT. NO ONE CARES ABOUT GOOD KIDS.
LOOK, TYLER AND I BROKE UP RIGHT BEFORE HIS ACCIDENT.
AMBER!
WHY DIDN'T YOU TELL US?
IT'S NOT A BIG DEAL. PEOPLE BREAK UP ALL THE TIME.
YEAH... BUT YOU'VE JUST BEEN SO DISTANT, WE THOUGHT...
I MEAN, IT'S NOT YOUR FAULT.
I KNOW IT'S NOT MY FAULT!

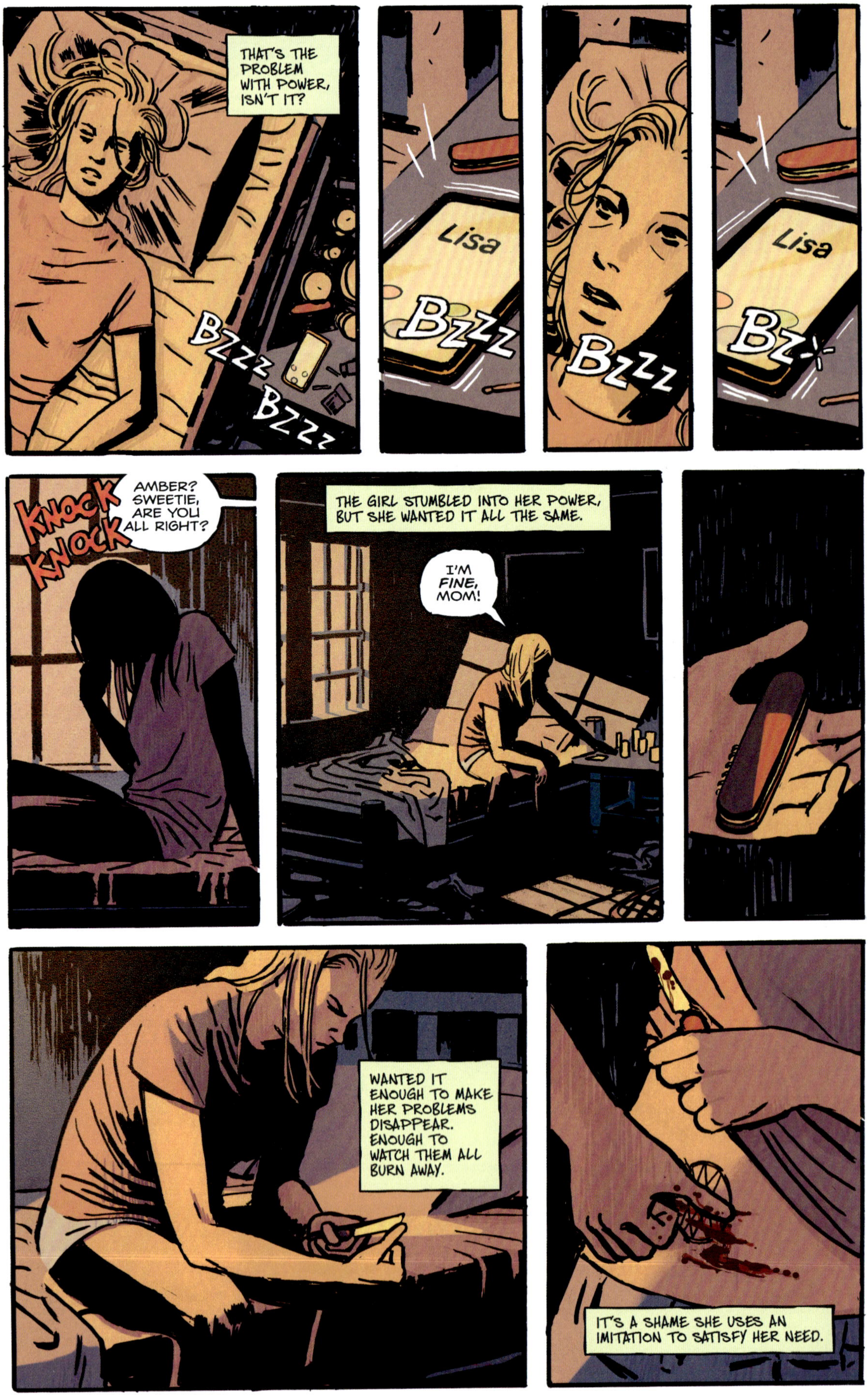
THAT'S THE PROBLEM WITH POWER, ISN'T IT?
BZZZ BZZZ
Lisa
BZZZ
BZZZ
Lisa
BZ
KNOCK KNOCK
AMBER? SWEETIE, ARE YOU ALL RIGHT?
THE GIRL STUMBLED INTO HER POWER, BUT SHE WANTED IT ALL THE SAME.
I'M FINE, MOM!
WANTED IT ENOUGH TO MAKE HER PROBLEMS DISAPPEAR. ENOUGH TO WATCH THEM ALL BURN AWAY.
IT'S A SHAME SHE USES AN IMITATION TO SATISFY HER NEED.

BUT THERE IS ALWAYS A PRICE TO PAY.
Burn.
BZZZZ BZZZZ
Lisa

MAYBE ONE DAY SHE'LL LEARN THAT.

THE BOY KNEW BETTER.
HE DECIDED TO PAY IN FULL.

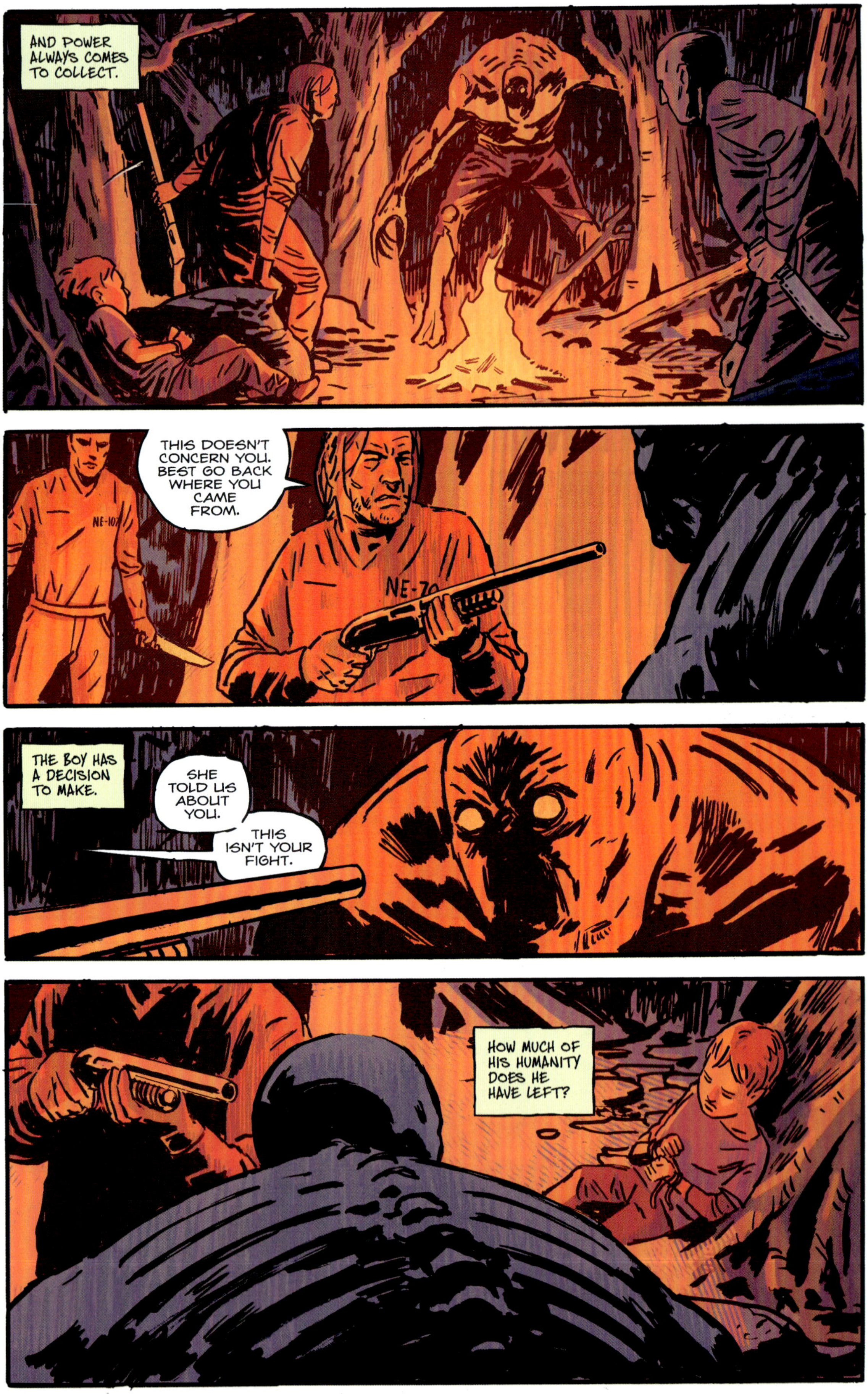
AND POWER ALWAYS COMES TO COLLECT.
THIS DOESN'T CONCERN YOU. BEST GO BACK WHERE YOU CAME FROM.
NE-107
NE-70
THE BOY HAS A DECISION TO MAKE.
SHE TOLD US ABOUT YOU.
THIS ISN'T YOUR FIGHT.
HOW MUCH OF HIS HUMANITY DOES HE HAVE LEFT?

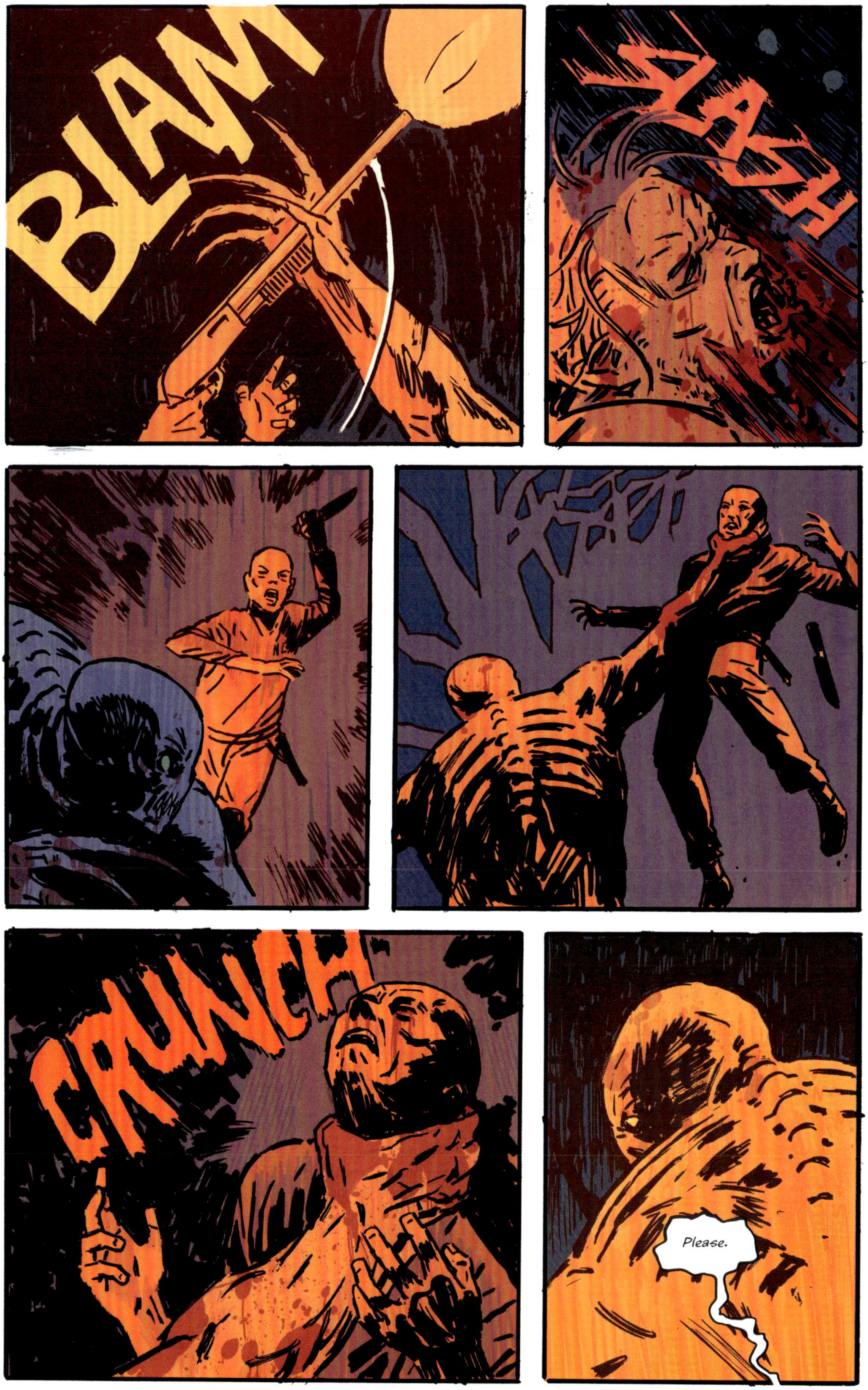
BLAM
CRUNCH
Please.

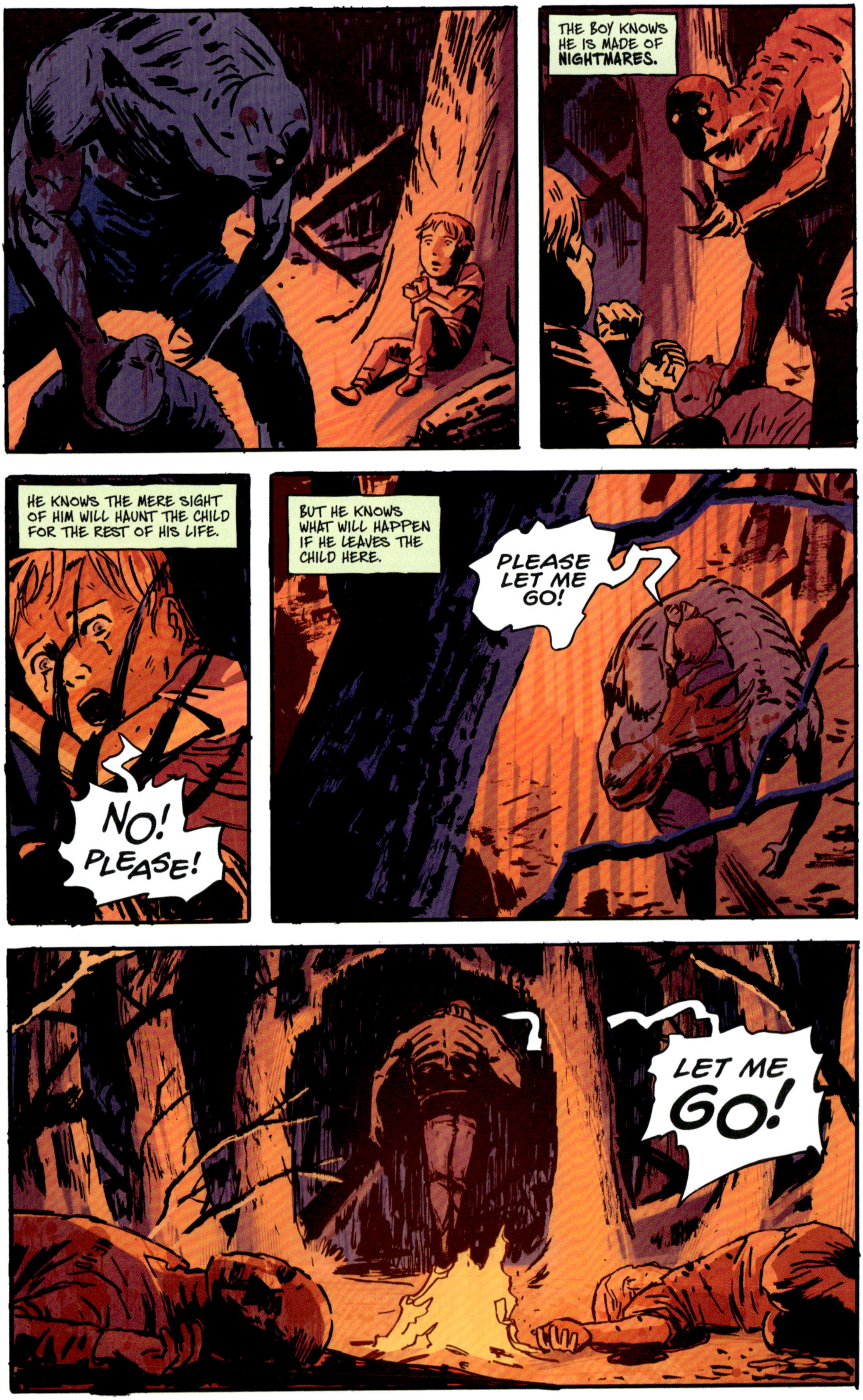
THE BOY KNOWS HE IS MADE OF **NIGHTMARES.**
HE KNOWS THE MERE SIGHT OF HIM WILL HAUNT THE CHILD FOR THE REST OF HIS LIFE.
NO! PLEASE!
BUT HE KNOWS WHAT WILL HAPPEN IF HE LEAVES THE CHILD HERE.
PLEASE LET ME GO!
LET ME GO!

AMBER, THANKS FOR MEETING ME.
DID YOU GET ANYTHING YET?
NO, I'M KIND OF NOT IN THE MOOD FOR COFFEE.
Oh... WELL, I CAN WAIT.
HOW HAVE YOU BEEN?
GOOD... NO, I'M NOT. I DID SOMETHING, LISA...
AND I HAVE NO IDEA HOW TO FIX IT.
I'M SORRY, I HAD NO IDEA.
I'VE JUST BEEN SO WRAPPED UP WITH TYLER.
IT'S FINE.
DO YOU MIND IF WE DON'T TALK ABOUT THAT?
ACTUALLY, I DO, AMBER.

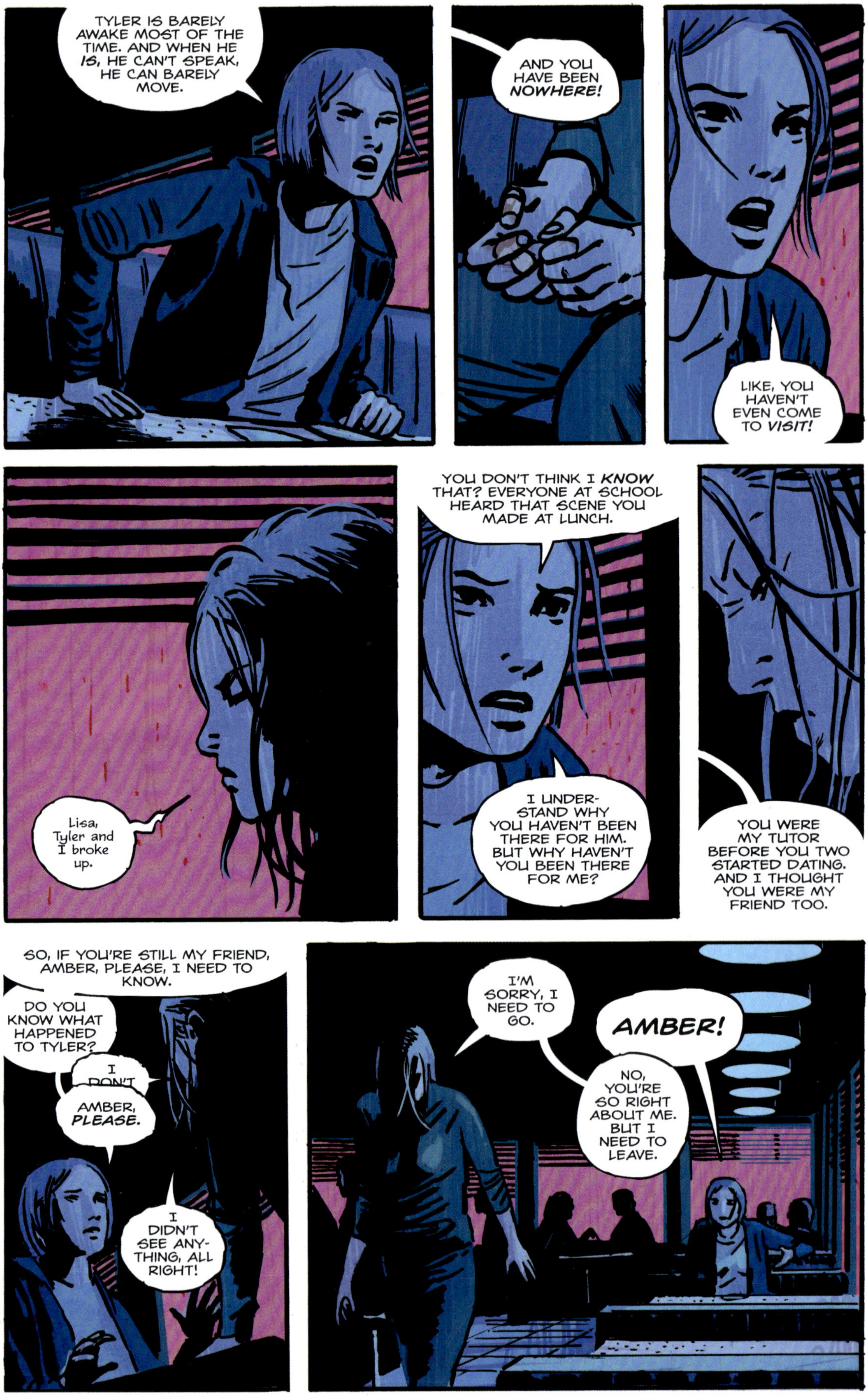

TYLER IS BARELY AWAKE MOST OF THE TIME. AND WHEN HE *IS*, HE CAN'T SPEAK, HE CAN BARELY MOVE.
AND YOU HAVE BEEN *NOWHERE!*
LIKE, YOU HAVEN'T EVEN COME TO *VISIT!*
Lisa, Tyler and I broke up.
YOU DON'T THINK I *KNOW* THAT? EVERYONE AT SCHOOL HEARD THAT SCENE YOU MADE AT LUNCH.
I UNDERSTAND WHY YOU HAVEN'T BEEN THERE FOR HIM. BUT WHY HAVEN'T YOU BEEN THERE FOR ME?
YOU WERE MY TUTOR BEFORE YOU TWO STARTED DATING. AND I THOUGHT YOU WERE MY FRIEND TOO.
SO, IF YOU'RE STILL MY FRIEND, AMBER, PLEASE, I NEED TO KNOW.
DO YOU KNOW WHAT HAPPENED TO TYLER?
I DON'T
AMBER, *PLEASE.*
I DIDN'T SEE ANYTHING, ALL RIGHT!
I'M SORRY, I NEED TO GO.
AMBER!
NO, YOU'RE SO RIGHT ABOUT ME. BUT I NEED TO LEAVE.

THE CHILD STOPPED CRYING AFTER FIFTEEN MINUTES.
THE BOY DOESN'T KNOW IF IT WAS OUT OF FEAR OR IF THE CHILD SIMPLY RAN OUT OF ENERGY.
AND HE DOESN'T PLAN ON STAYING AROUND TO FIND OUT.
KSSH
HONK HONK
HONK HONK
THE BOY KNOWS HE DOESN'T BELONG HERE.
SNIP
HONK HONK
ANYWHERE NEAR THE GIRL AND THE LIFE THAT IS NO LONGER HIS.
SO WHY DOES HE LINGER?
QUINN.

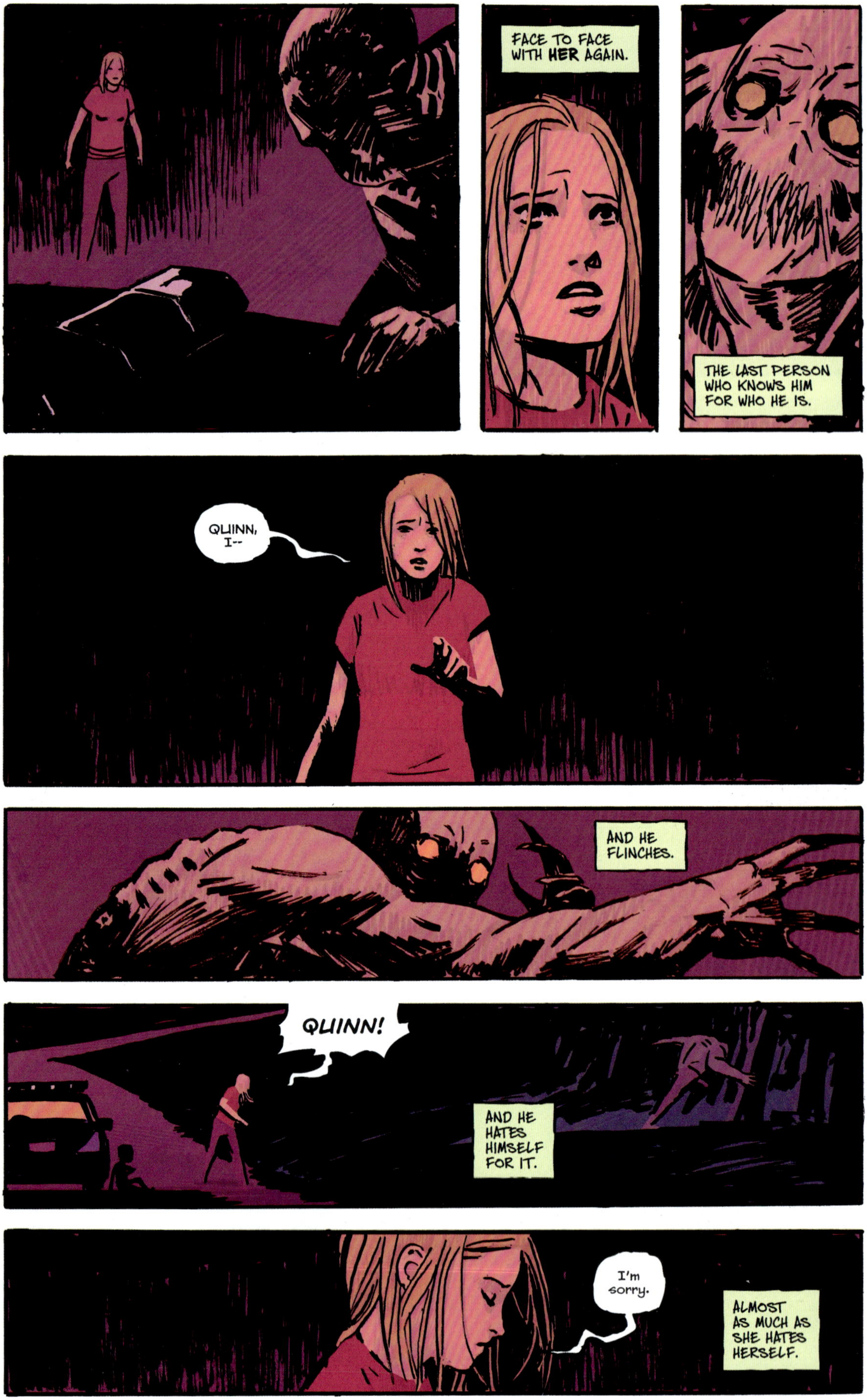
FACE TO FACE WITH HER AGAIN.
THE LAST PERSON WHO KNOWS HIM FOR WHO HE IS.
QUINN, I--
AND HE FLINCHES.
QUINN!
AND HE HATES HIMSELF FOR IT.
I'm sorry.
ALMOST AS MUCH AS SHE HATES HERSELF.

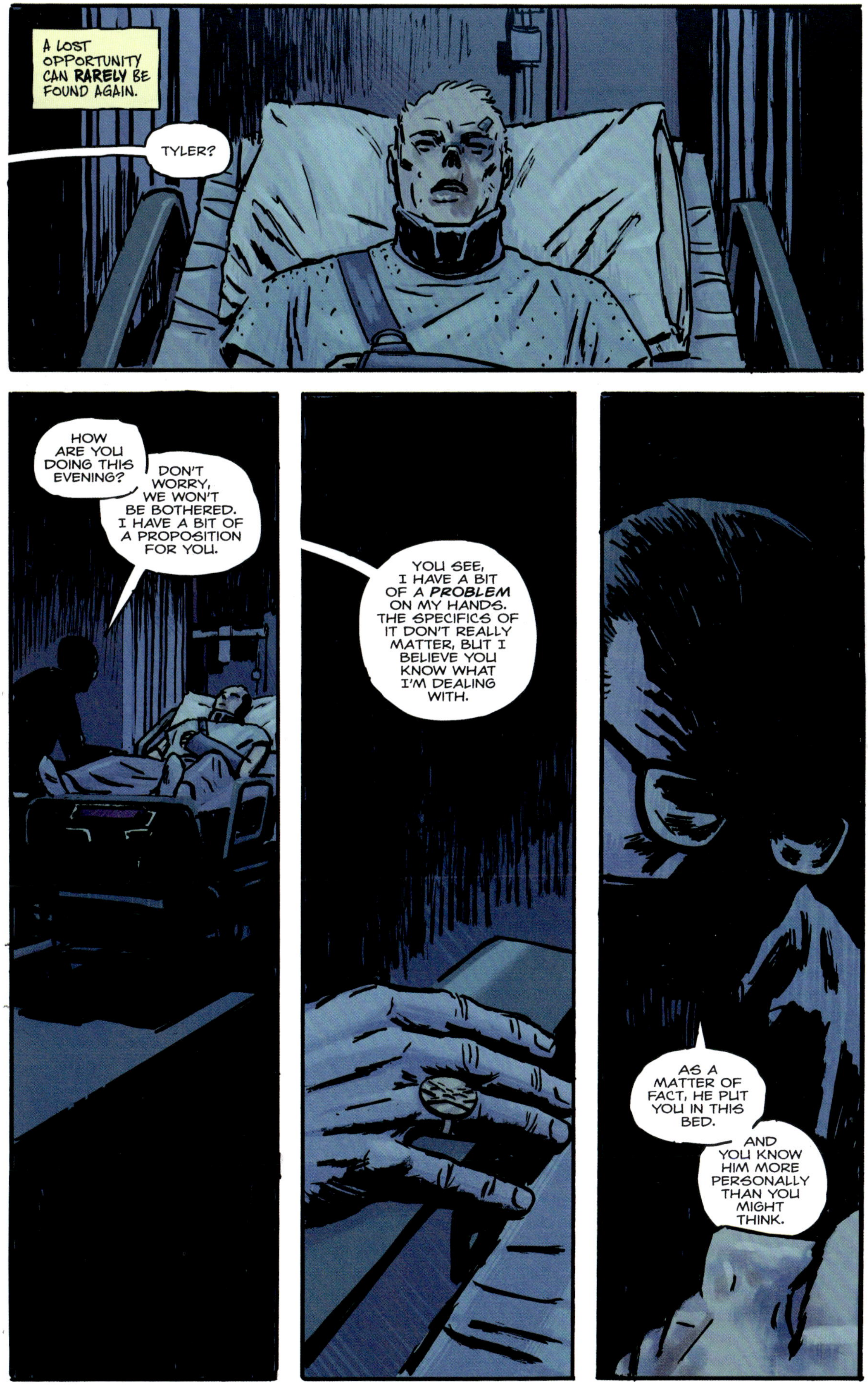
A LOST OPPORTUNITY CAN **RARELY** BE FOUND AGAIN.
TYLER?
HOW ARE YOU DOING THIS EVENING?
DON'T WORRY, WE WON'T BE BOTHERED. I HAVE A BIT OF A PROPOSITION FOR YOU.
YOU SEE, I HAVE A BIT OF A ***PROBLEM*** ON MY HANDS. THE SPECIFICS OF IT DON'T REALLY MATTER, BUT I BELIEVE YOU KNOW WHAT I'M DEALING WITH.
AS A MATTER OF FACT, HE PUT YOU IN THIS BED.
AND YOU KNOW HIM MORE PERSONALLY THAN YOU MIGHT THINK.

THIS WAS SUPPOSED TO GO TO SOMEONE ELSE TONIGHT. SOMEONE WHO MIGHT HAVE BEEN A BIT MORE MANAGEABLE.
BUT PLANS CHANGE. AND I THINK YOU'RE JUST THE PERSON TO STEP UP AND TAKE HIS PLACE.
WE'LL COVER FOR YOU, OF COURSE. TELL YOUR FAMILY YOU WERE MOVED ELSEWHERE FOR TREATMENT.
WHAT I'M OFFERING ISN'T JUST A CHANCE FOR YOU TO FIX YOUR BODY.
IT'S A CHANCE TO TAKE REVENGE ON A MONSTER.
IT'S *POWER.*
SO, WHAT WILL IT BE? WOULD YOU LIKE TO HEAR MORE?

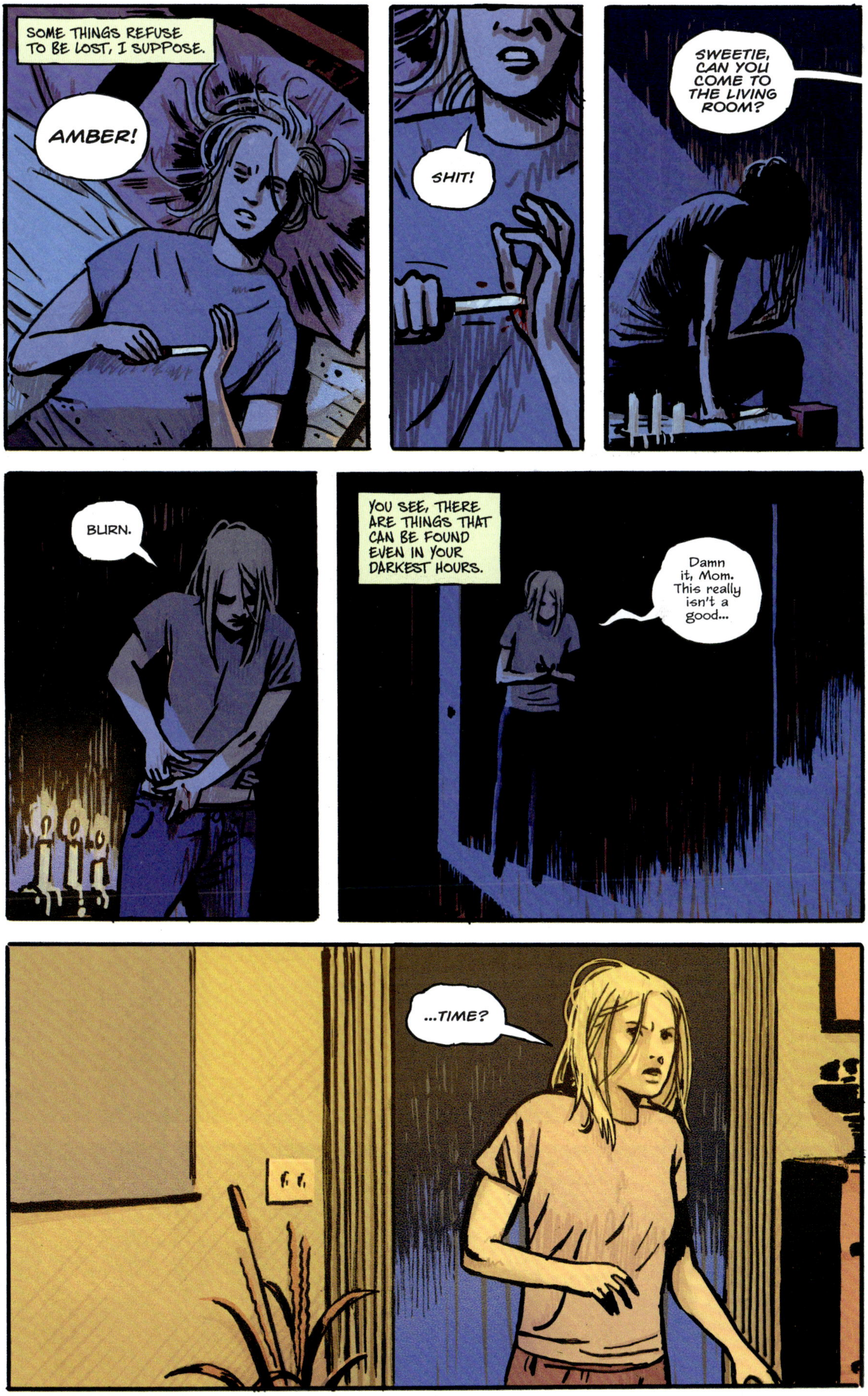
SOME THINGS REFUSE TO BE LOST, I SUPPOSE.
AMBER!
SHIT!
SWEETIE, CAN YOU COME TO THE LIVING ROOM?
BURN.
YOU SEE, THERE ARE THINGS THAT CAN BE FOUND EVEN IN YOUR DARKEST HOURS.
Damn it, Mom. This really isn't a good...
...TIME?

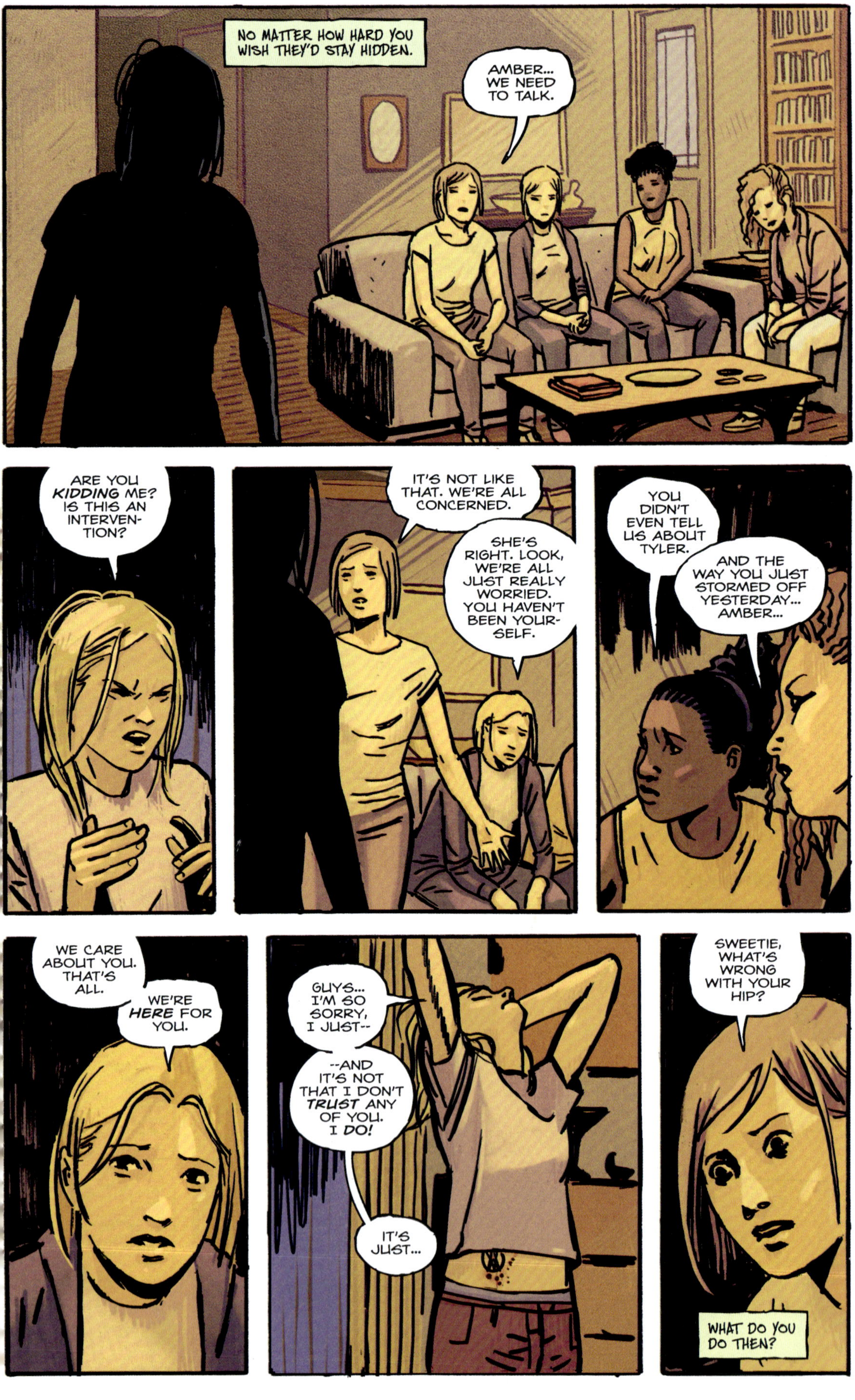
NO MATTER HOW HARD YOU WISH THEY'D STAY HIDDEN.
AMBER... WE NEED TO TALK.
ARE YOU KIDDING ME? IS THIS AN INTERVEN-TION?
IT'S NOT LIKE THAT. WE'RE ALL CONCERNED.
SHE'S RIGHT. LOOK, WE'RE ALL JUST REALLY WORRIED. YOU HAVEN'T BEEN YOUR-SELF.
YOU DIDN'T EVEN TELL US ABOUT TYLER.
AND THE WAY YOU JUST STORMED OFF YESTERDAY... AMBER...
WE CARE ABOUT YOU. THAT'S ALL.
WE'RE HERE FOR YOU.
GUYS... I'M SO SORRY, I JUST--
--AND IT'S NOT THAT I DON'T TRUST ANY OF YOU. I DO!
IT'S JUST...
SWEETIE, WHAT'S WRONG WITH YOUR HIP?
WHAT DO YOU DO THEN?

WHEN ALL OF YOUR UGLINESS IS BROUGHT TO THE LIGHT?
AMBER, YOUR HAND! WHAT HAPPENED?
Oh God.
MOM, I CAN EXPLAIN!
AMBER, WHAT IS THAT? WHY DO YOU HAVE THAT TATTOO?
WHY IS THERE BLOOD?
JESUS.
I...
...I NEED HELP.

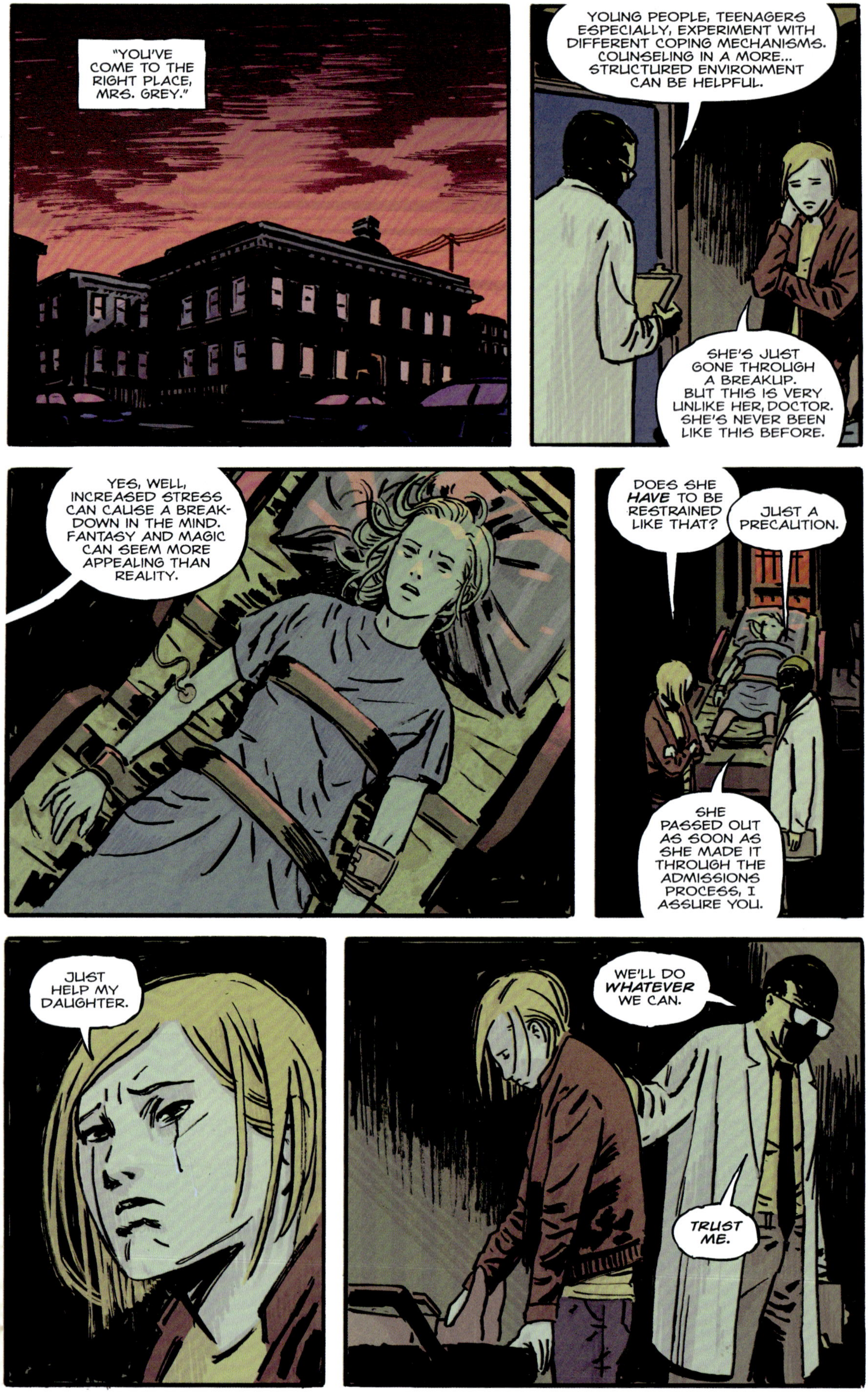
"YOU'VE COME TO THE RIGHT PLACE, MRS. GREY."
YOUNG PEOPLE, TEENAGERS ESPECIALLY, EXPERIMENT WITH DIFFERENT COPING MECHANISMS. COUNSELING IN A MORE... STRUCTURED ENVIRONMENT CAN BE HELPFUL.
SHE'S JUST GONE THROUGH A BREAKUP. BUT THIS IS VERY UNLIKE HER, DOCTOR. SHE'S NEVER BEEN LIKE THIS BEFORE.
YES, WELL, INCREASED STRESS CAN CAUSE A BREAK-DOWN IN THE MIND. FANTASY AND MAGIC CAN SEEM MORE APPEALING THAN REALITY.
DOES SHE HAVE TO BE RESTRAINED LIKE THAT?
JUST A PRECAUTION.
SHE PASSED OUT AS SOON AS SHE MADE IT THROUGH THE ADMISSIONS PROCESS, I ASSURE YOU.
JUST HELP MY DAUGHTER.
WE'LL DO WHATEVER WE CAN.
TRUST ME.

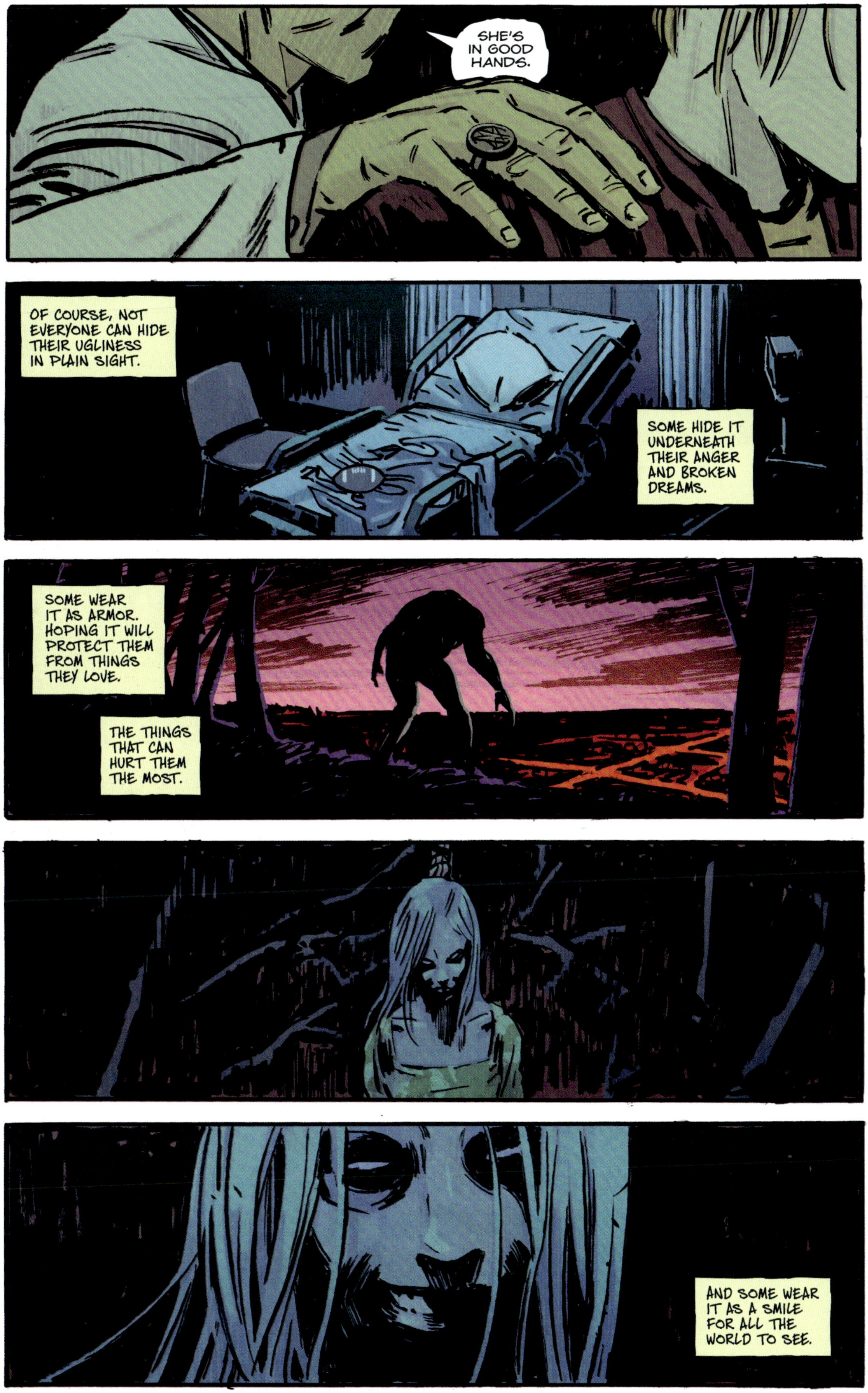
SHE'S IN GOOD HANDS.
OF COURSE, NOT EVERYONE CAN HIDE THEIR UGLINESS IN PLAIN SIGHT.
SOME HIDE IT UNDERNEATH THEIR ANGER AND BROKEN DREAMS.
SOME WEAR IT AS ARMOR. HOPING IT WILL PROTECT THEM FROM THINGS THEY LOVE.
THE THINGS THAT CAN HURT THEM THE MOST.
AND SOME WEAR IT AS A SMILE FOR ALL THE WORLD TO SEE.

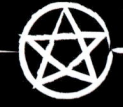

CHAPTER 5

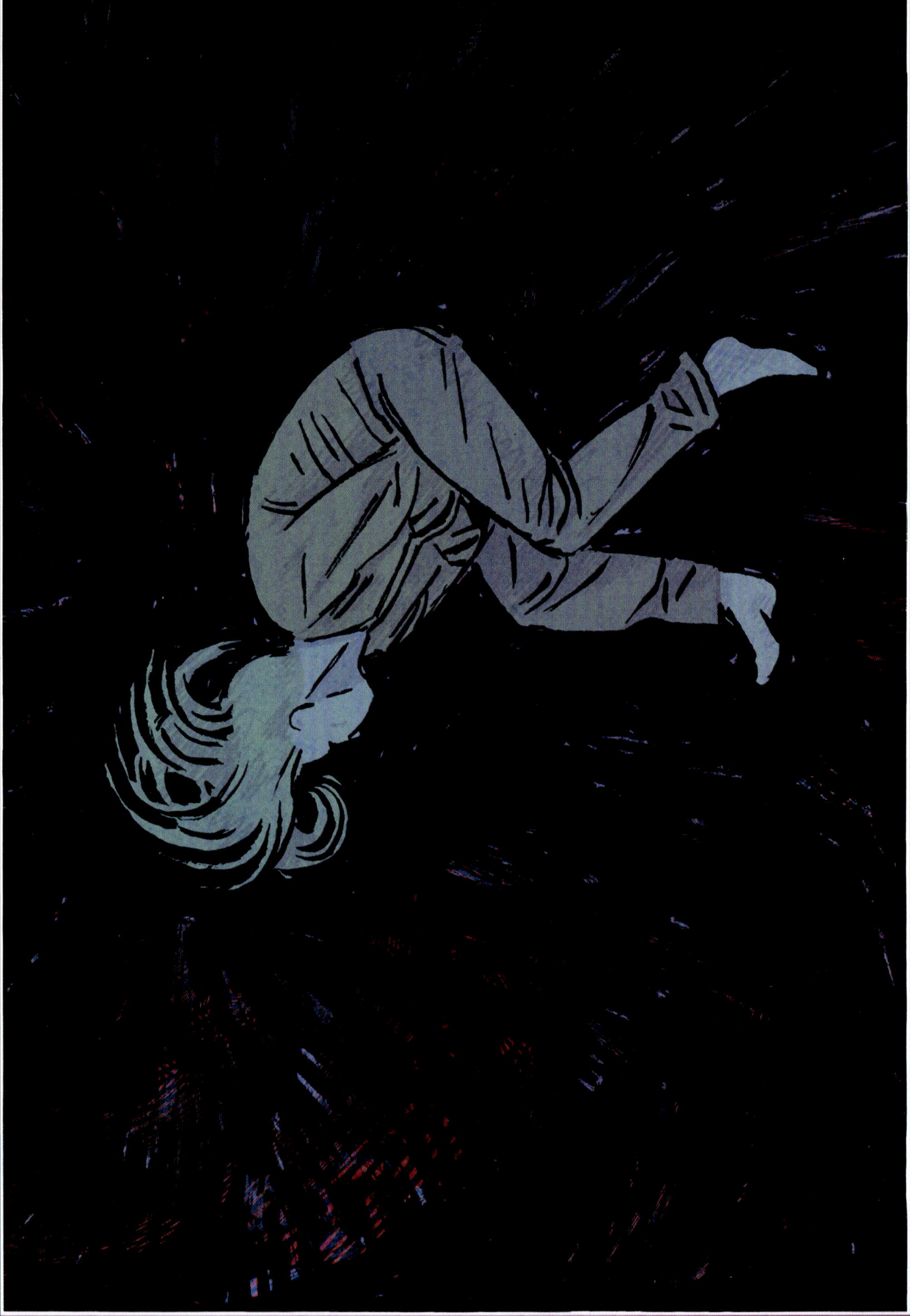

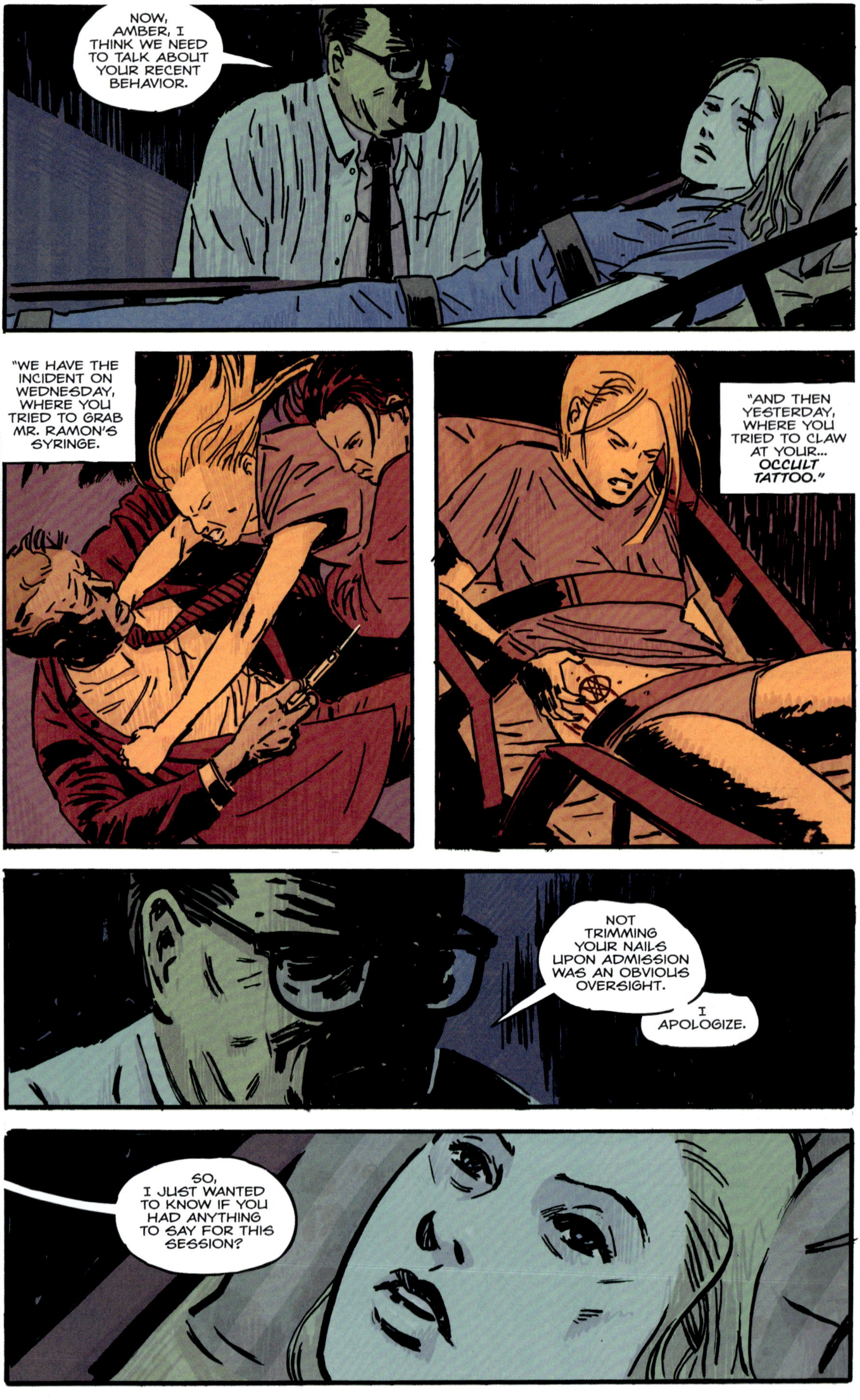
NOW, AMBER, I THINK WE NEED TO TALK ABOUT YOUR RECENT BEHAVIOR.
"WE HAVE THE INCIDENT ON WEDNESDAY, WHERE YOU TRIED TO GRAB MR. RAMON'S SYRINGE.
"AND THEN YESTERDAY, WHERE YOU TRIED TO CLAW AT YOUR... *OCCULT TATTOO.*"
NOT TRIMMING YOUR NAILS UPON ADMISSION WAS AN OBVIOUS OVERSIGHT.
I APOLOGIZE.
SO, I JUST WANTED TO KNOW IF YOU HAD ANYTHING TO SAY FOR THIS SESSION?

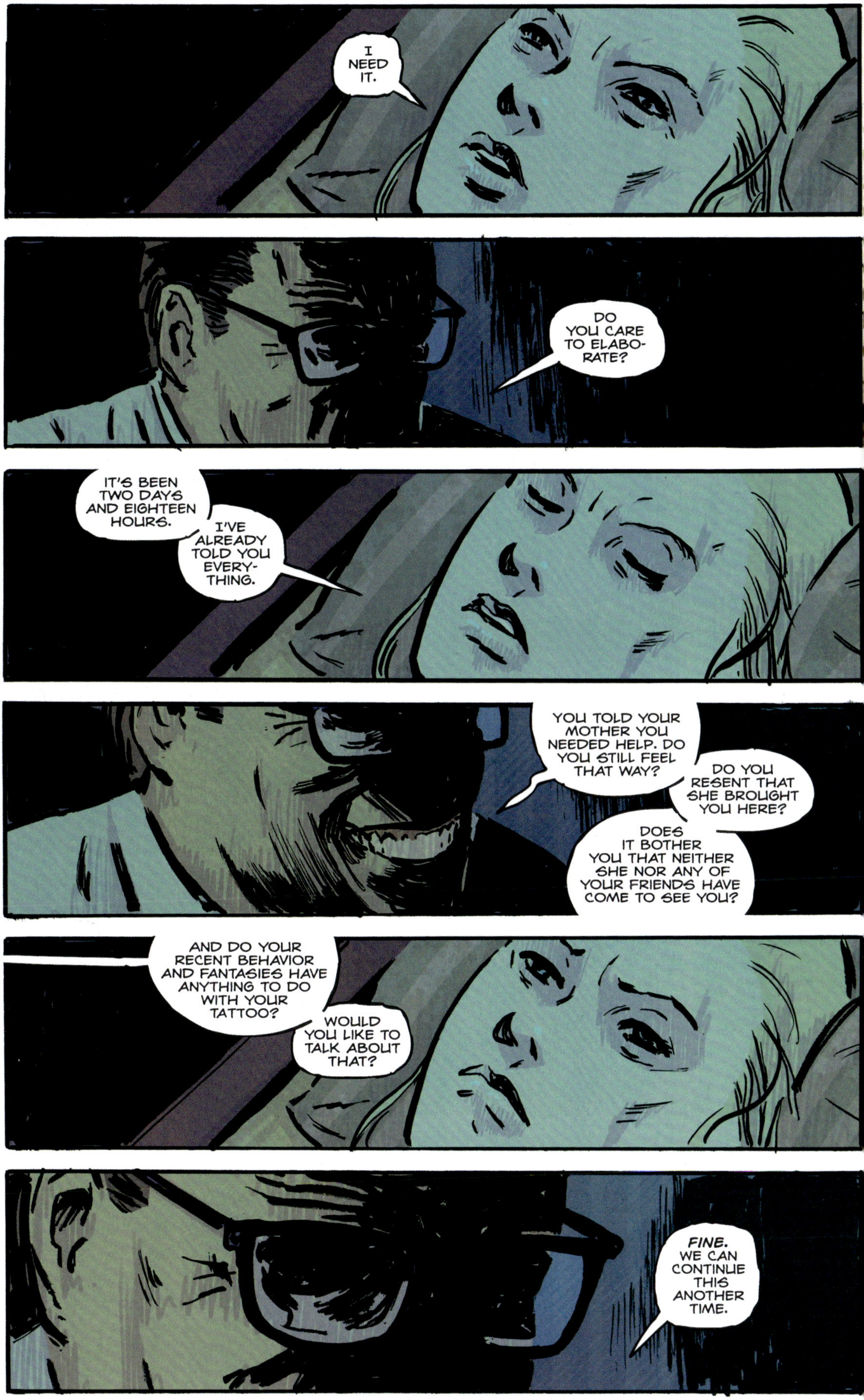
I NEED IT.
DO YOU CARE TO ELABO-RATE?
IT'S BEEN TWO DAYS AND EIGHTEEN HOURS.
I'VE ALREADY TOLD YOU EVERY-THING.
YOU TOLD YOUR MOTHER YOU NEEDED HELP. DO YOU STILL FEEL THAT WAY?
DO YOU RESENT THAT SHE BROUGHT YOU HERE?
DOES IT BOTHER YOU THAT NEITHER SHE NOR ANY OF YOUR FRIENDS HAVE COME TO SEE YOU?
AND DO YOUR RECENT BEHAVIOR AND FANTASIES HAVE ANYTHING TO DO WITH YOUR TATTOO?
WOULD YOU LIKE TO TALK ABOUT THAT?
FINE. WE CAN CONTINUE THIS ANOTHER TIME.

IT'S A SHAME. I THOUGHT WE WERE MAKING SUCH PROGRESS.
NO! DON'T KNOCK ME OUT AGAIN!

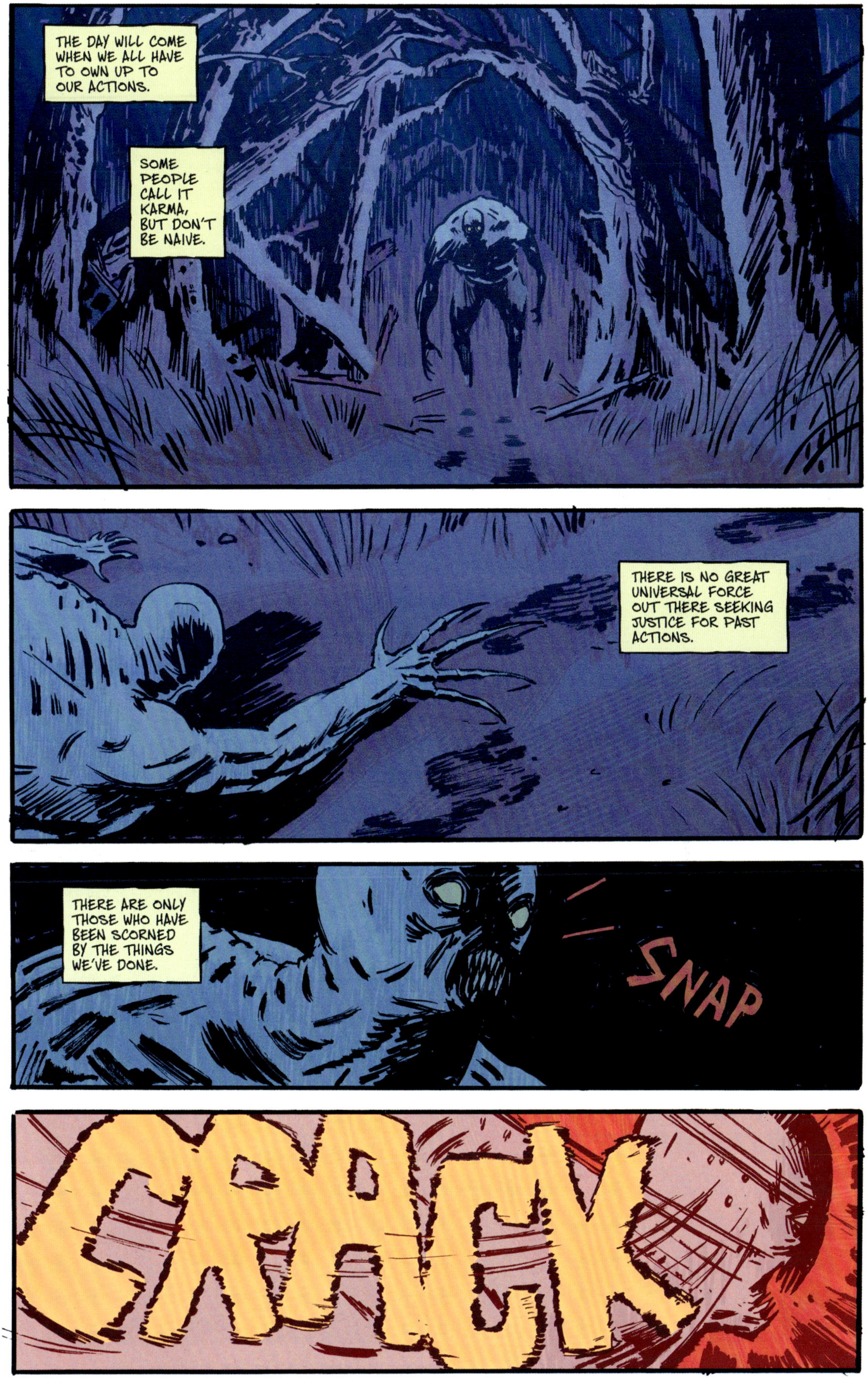
THE DAY WILL COME WHEN WE ALL HAVE TO OWN UP TO OUR ACTIONS.
SOME PEOPLE CALL IT KARMA, BUT DON'T BE NAIVE.
THERE IS NO GREAT UNIVERSAL FORCE OUT THERE SEEKING JUSTICE FOR PAST ACTIONS.
THERE ARE ONLY THOSE WHO HAVE BEEN SCORNED BY THE THINGS WE'VE DONE.
SNAP
CRACK

AND THE TERRIBLE LENGTHS THEY'LL GO TO SEEK RETRIBUTION.
I'M SUPPOSED TO TELL YOU THIS IS REVENGE FROM SOME WITCH OR SOMETHING.
BUT I DON'T REALLY GIVE A FUCK ABOUT THAT.
I JUST WANT YOU TO DIE.

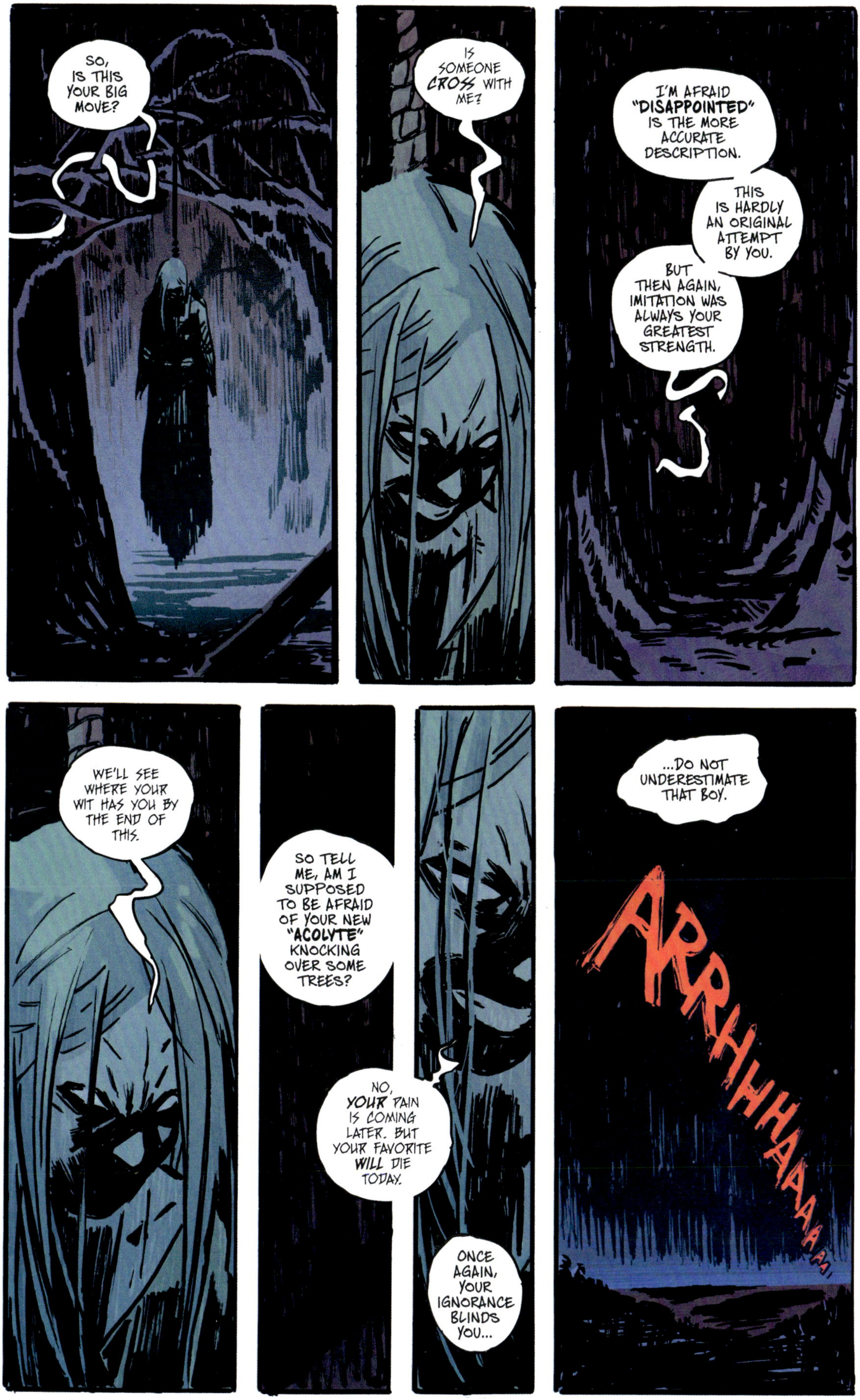
SO, IS THIS YOUR BIG MOVE?
IS SOMEONE CROSS WITH ME?
I'M AFRAID "DISAPPOINTED" IS THE MORE ACCURATE DESCRIPTION.
THIS IS HARDLY AN ORIGINAL ATTEMPT BY YOU.
BUT THEN AGAIN, IMITATION WAS ALWAYS YOUR GREATEST STRENGTH.
WE'LL SEE WHERE YOUR WIT HAS YOU BY THE END OF THIS.
SO TELL ME, AM I SUPPOSED TO BE AFRAID OF YOUR NEW "ACOLYTE" KNOCKING OVER SOME TREES?
NO, YOUR PAIN IS COMING LATER. BUT YOUR FAVORITE WILL DIE TODAY.
ONCE AGAIN, YOUR IGNORANCE BLINDS YOU...
...DO NOT UNDERESTIMATE THAT BOY.
ARRHHHAAAAAA

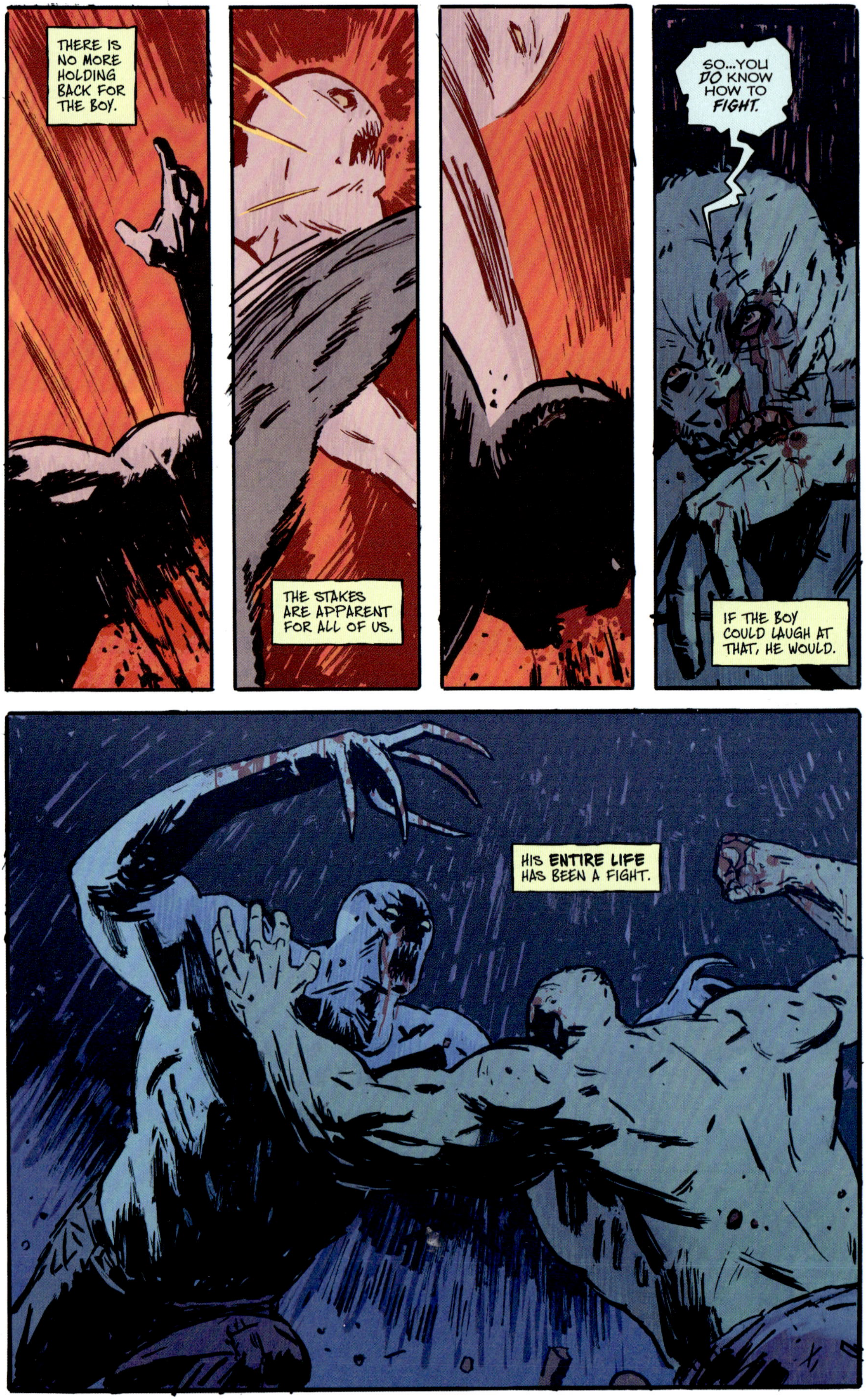
THERE IS NO MORE HOLDING BACK FOR THE BOY.
THE STAKES ARE APPARENT FOR ALL OF US.
SO...YOU DO KNOW HOW TO FIGHT.
IF THE BOY COULD LAUGH AT THAT, HE WOULD.
HIS ENTIRE LIFE HAS BEEN A FIGHT.

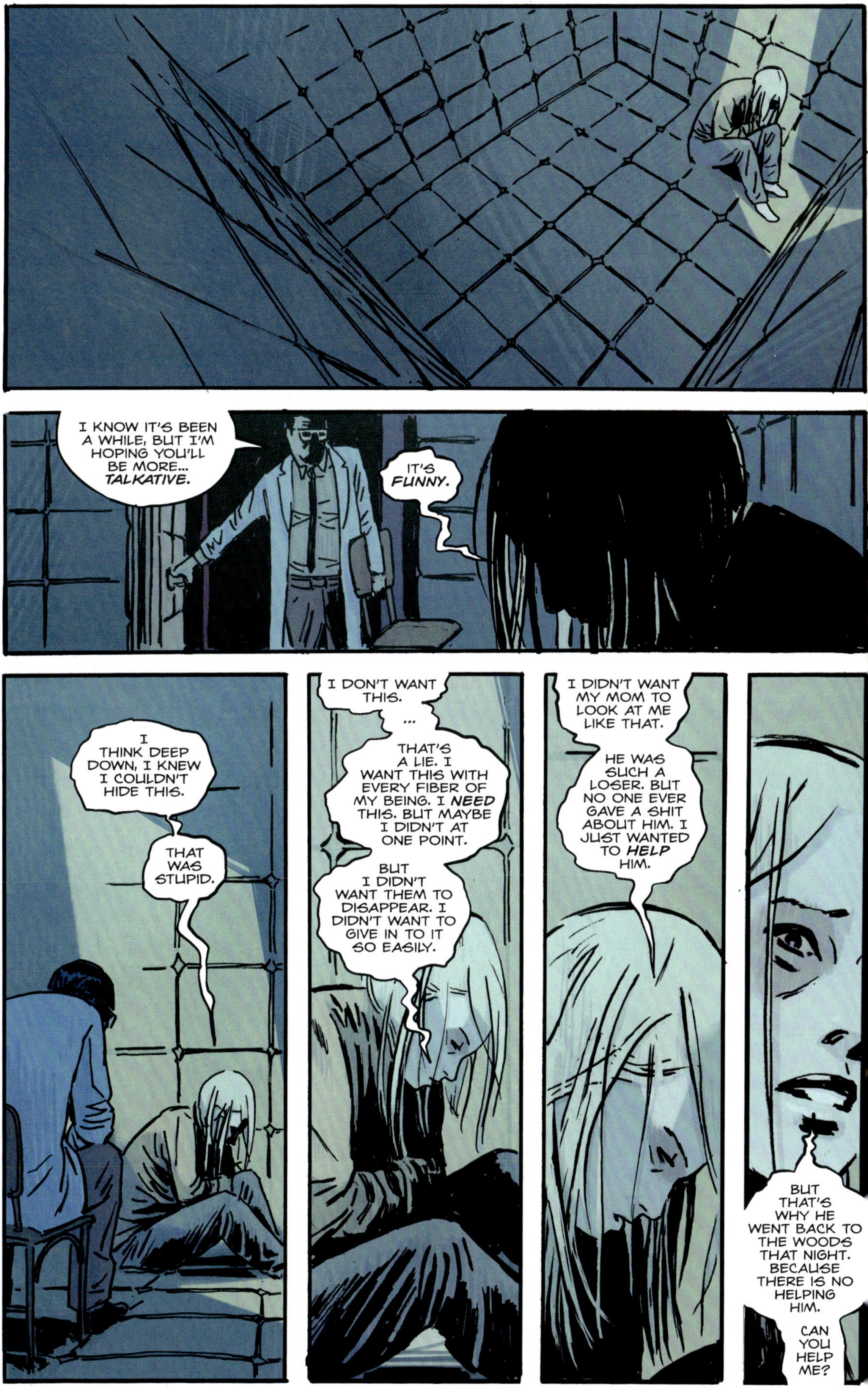
I KNOW IT'S BEEN A WHILE, BUT I'M HOPING YOU'LL BE MORE... *TALKATIVE.*
IT'S *FUNNY.*
I THINK DEEP DOWN, I KNEW I COULDN'T HIDE THIS.
THAT WAS STUPID.
I DON'T WANT THIS.
...
THAT'S A LIE. I WANT THIS WITH EVERY FIBER OF MY BEING. I *NEED* THIS. BUT MAYBE I DIDN'T AT ONE POINT.
BUT I DIDN'T WANT THEM TO DISAPPEAR. I DIDN'T WANT TO GIVE IN TO IT SO EASILY.
I DIDN'T WANT MY MOM TO LOOK AT ME LIKE THAT.
HE WAS SUCH A LOSER. BUT NO ONE EVER GAVE A SHIT ABOUT HIM. I JUST WANTED TO *HELP* HIM.
BUT THAT'S WHY HE WENT BACK TO THE WOODS THAT NIGHT. BECAUSE THERE IS NO HELPING HIM.
CAN YOU HELP ME?

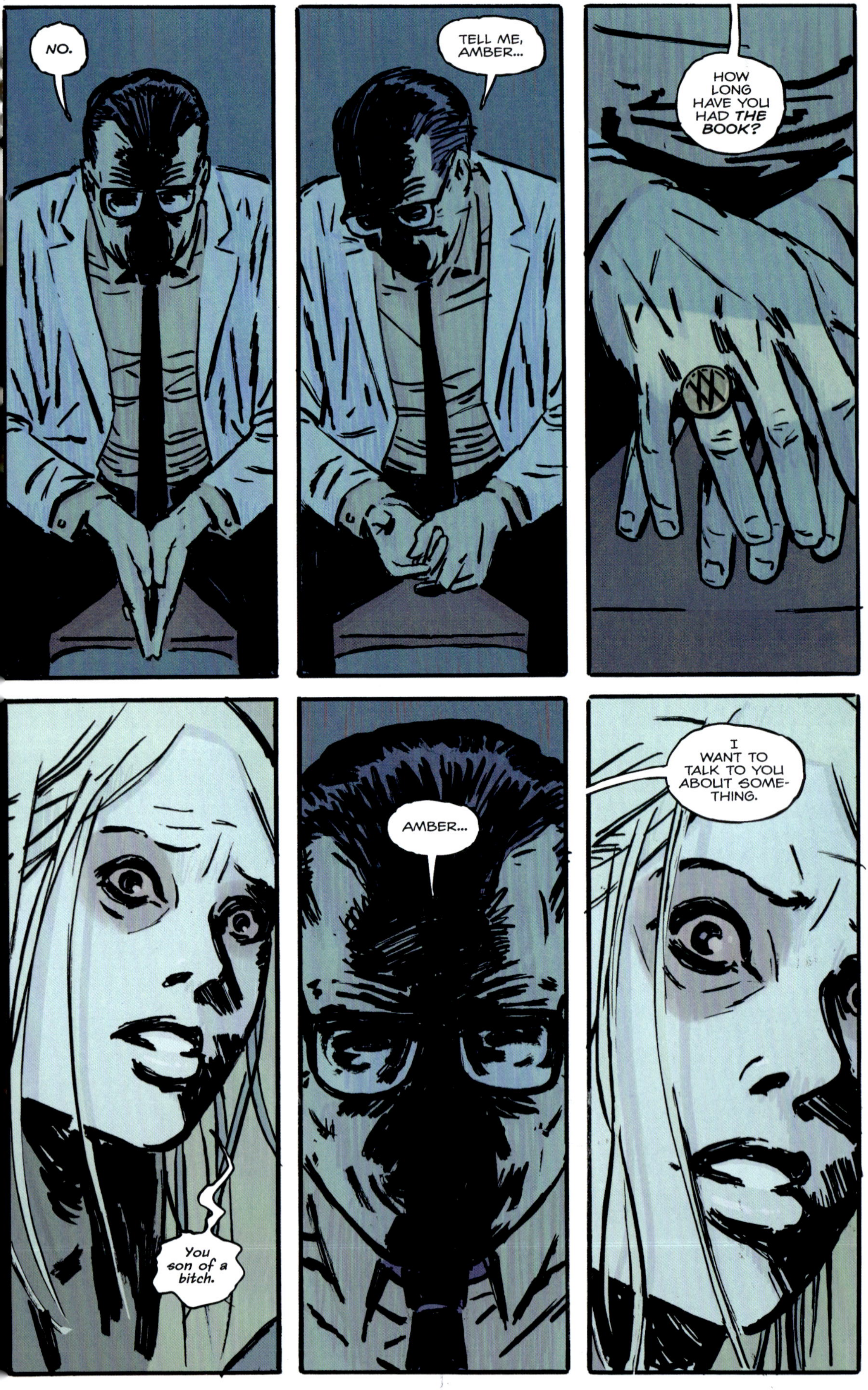
NO.
TELL ME, AMBER...
HOW LONG HAVE YOU HAD THE BOOK?
You son of a bitch.
AMBER...
I WANT TO TALK TO YOU ABOUT SOME-THING.

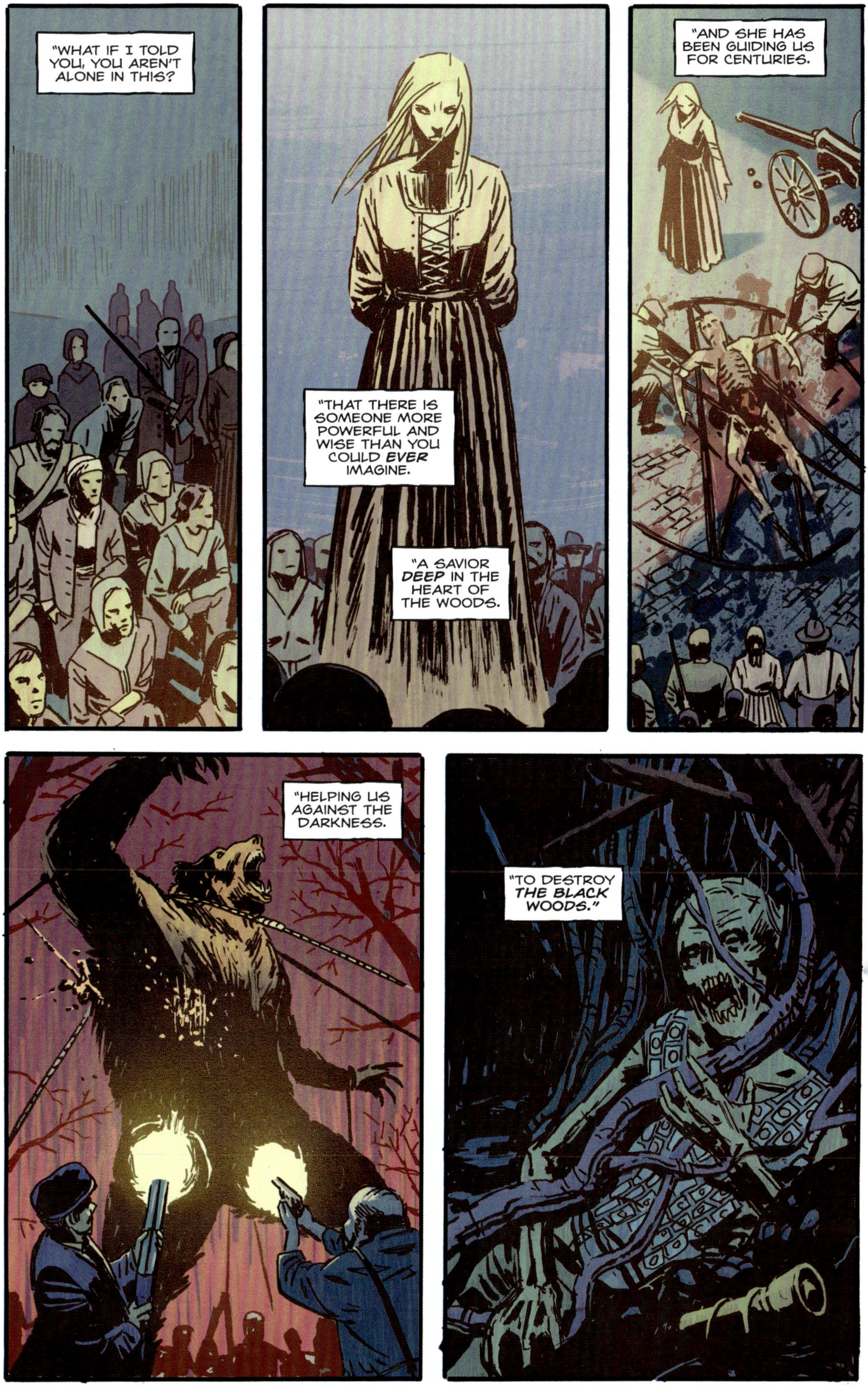
"WHAT IF I TOLD YOU, YOU AREN'T ALONE IN THIS?
"THAT THERE IS SOMEONE MORE POWERFUL AND WISE THAN YOU COULD *EVER* IMAGINE.
"A SAVIOR *DEEP* IN THE HEART OF THE WOODS.
"AND SHE HAS BEEN GUIDING US FOR CENTURIES.
"HELPING US AGAINST THE DARKNESS.
"TO DESTROY *THE BLACK WOODS.*"

FOR TOO DAMN LONG, THESE WOODS AND ITS CHILDREN HAVE RUINED OUR LIVES.
BUT YOU CAN END THAT, AMBER. YOU CAN END THE DARKNESS FOREVER.
YOU CAN BURN DOWN THE BLACK WOODS.
I'LL KILL YOU BEFORE I EVER DO ANYTHING FOR YOU.
AND WHAT THE HELL DID THE WOODS DO TO YOU?
ENOUGH.
THIS IS HER SYMBOL, AMBER. SHE CREATED IT. WE WEAR IT TO SHOW OUR LOYALTY.
SINCE YOU BRANDED YOURSELF, YOU CAN BE COUNTED AMONG THE LOYAL.
FUCK YOU. I'M NOT ONE OF YOU.

BUT YOU WILL BE. YOU HAVE NO ONE ELSE.
YOUR OWN MOTHER LEFT YOU HERE.
YOU'RE LOSING YOURSELF, AMBER. YOU AND I BOTH KNOW THAT.
NO, ONCE THE MADNESS HAS YOU, I THINK YOU'LL DO EXACTLY AS I SAY.
WE'LL JUST HAVE TO WAIT UNTIL THEN.

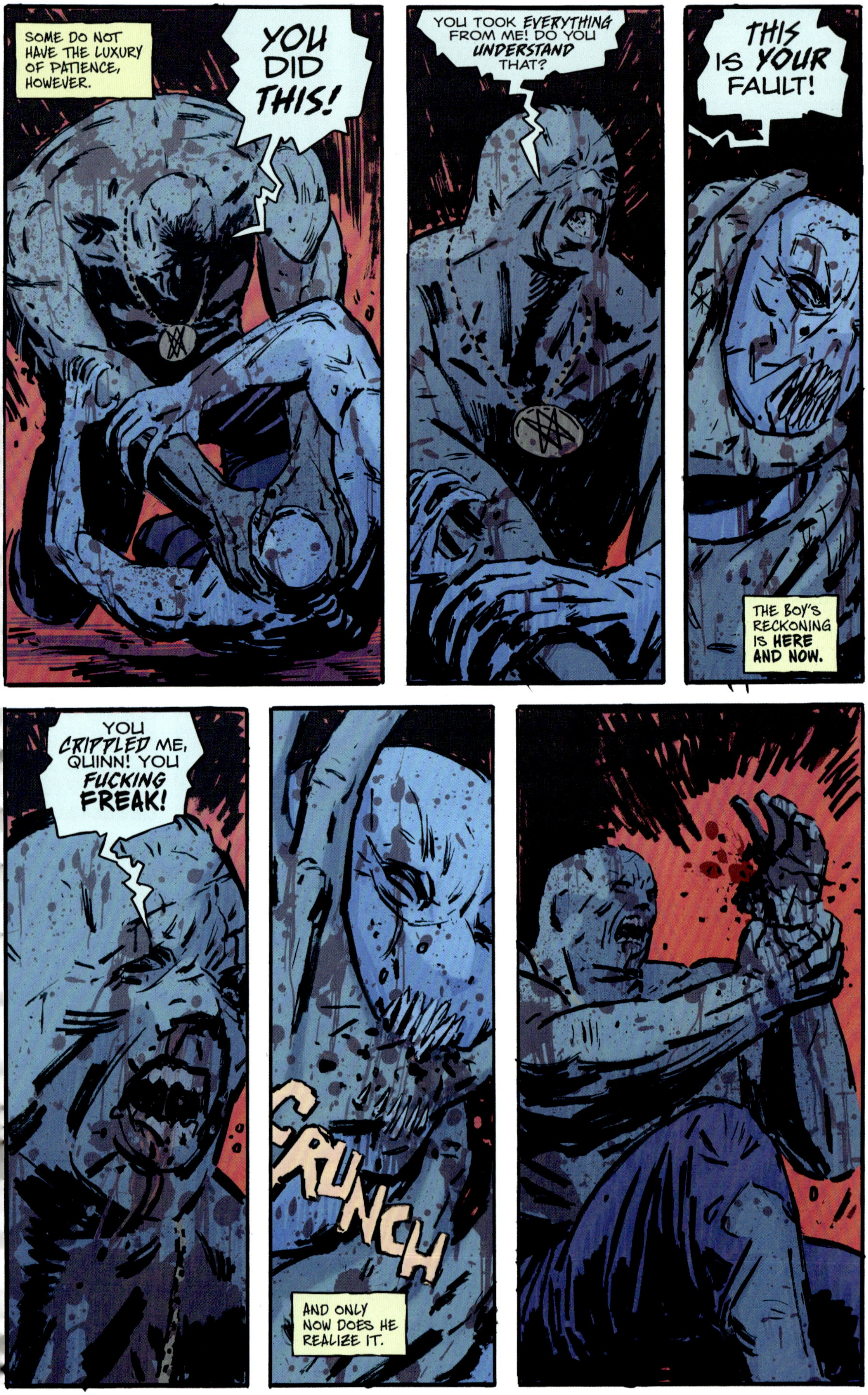
SOME DO NOT HAVE THE LUXURY OF PATIENCE, HOWEVER.
YOU DID THIS!
YOU TOOK EVERYTHING FROM ME! DO YOU UNDERSTAND THAT?
THIS IS YOUR FAULT!
THE BOY'S RECKONING IS HERE AND NOW.
YOU CRIPPLED ME, QUINN! YOU FUCKING FREAK!
CRUNCH
AND ONLY NOW DOES HE REALIZE IT.

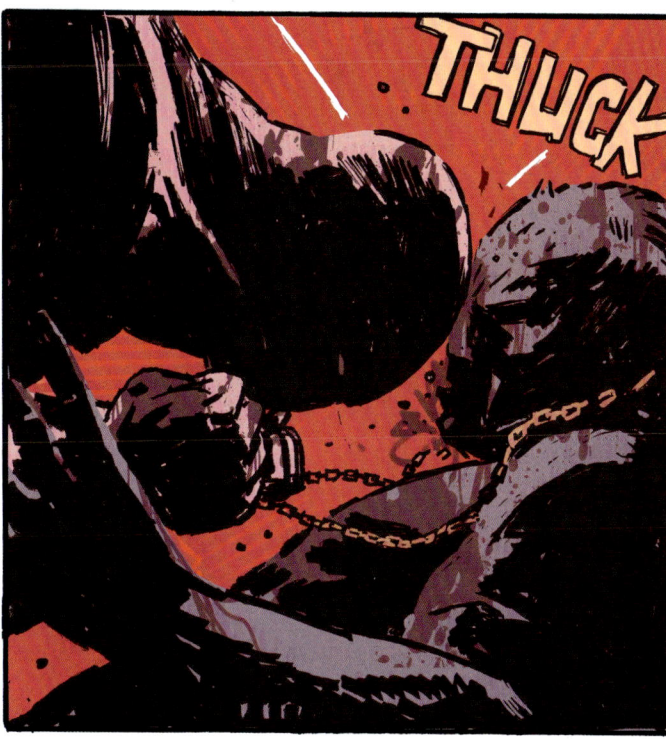

FOR A WHILE, THE BOY FOOLED HIMSELF INTO THINKING HIS HATRED HAD GONE AWAY.

PTOO

IT HASN'T.

REAL HATRED NEVER FADES.

THUCK

REAL HATRED STANDS THE TEST OF TIME.

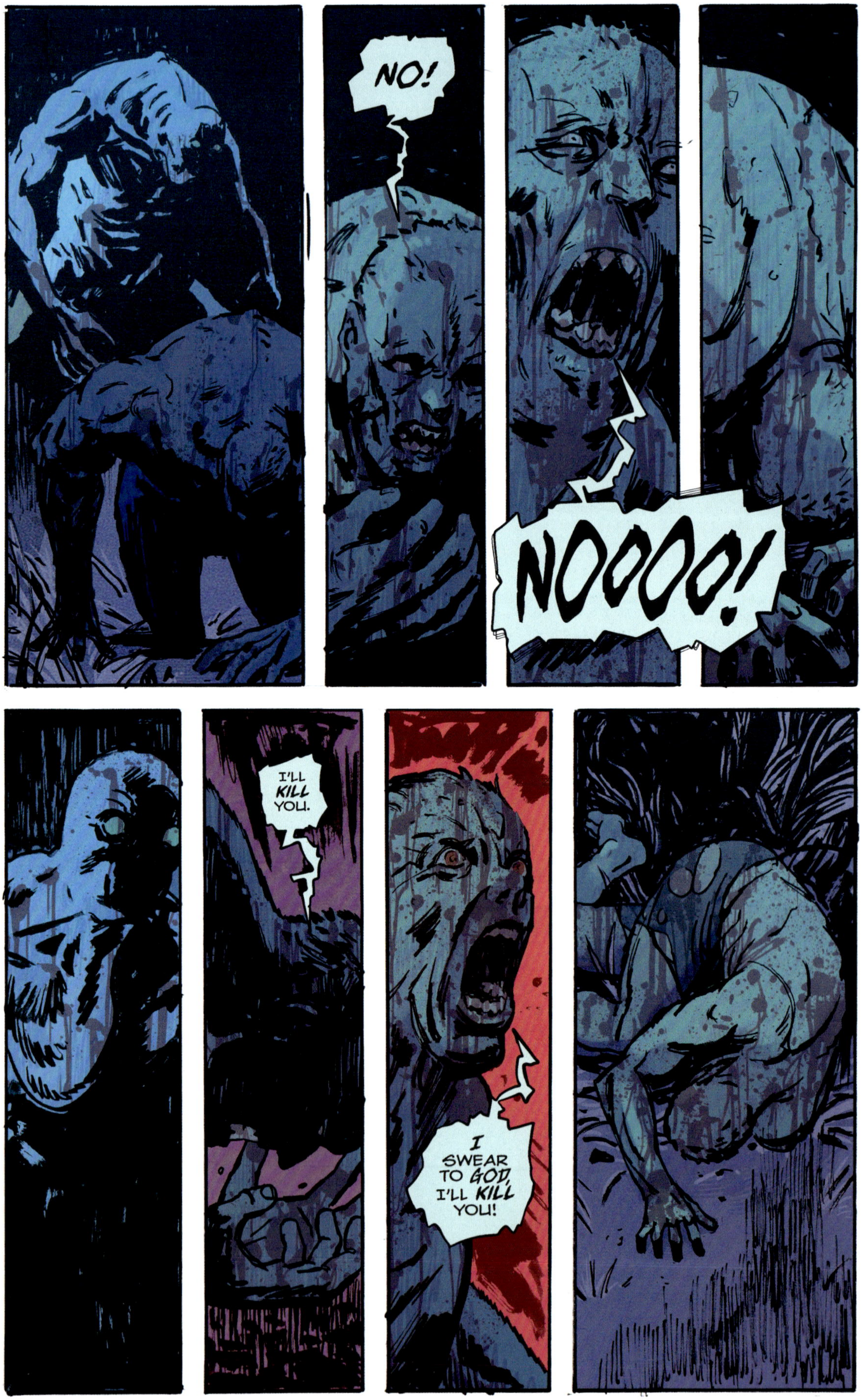
NO!
NOOOO!
I'LL KILL YOU.
I SWEAR TO GOD, I'LL KILL YOU!

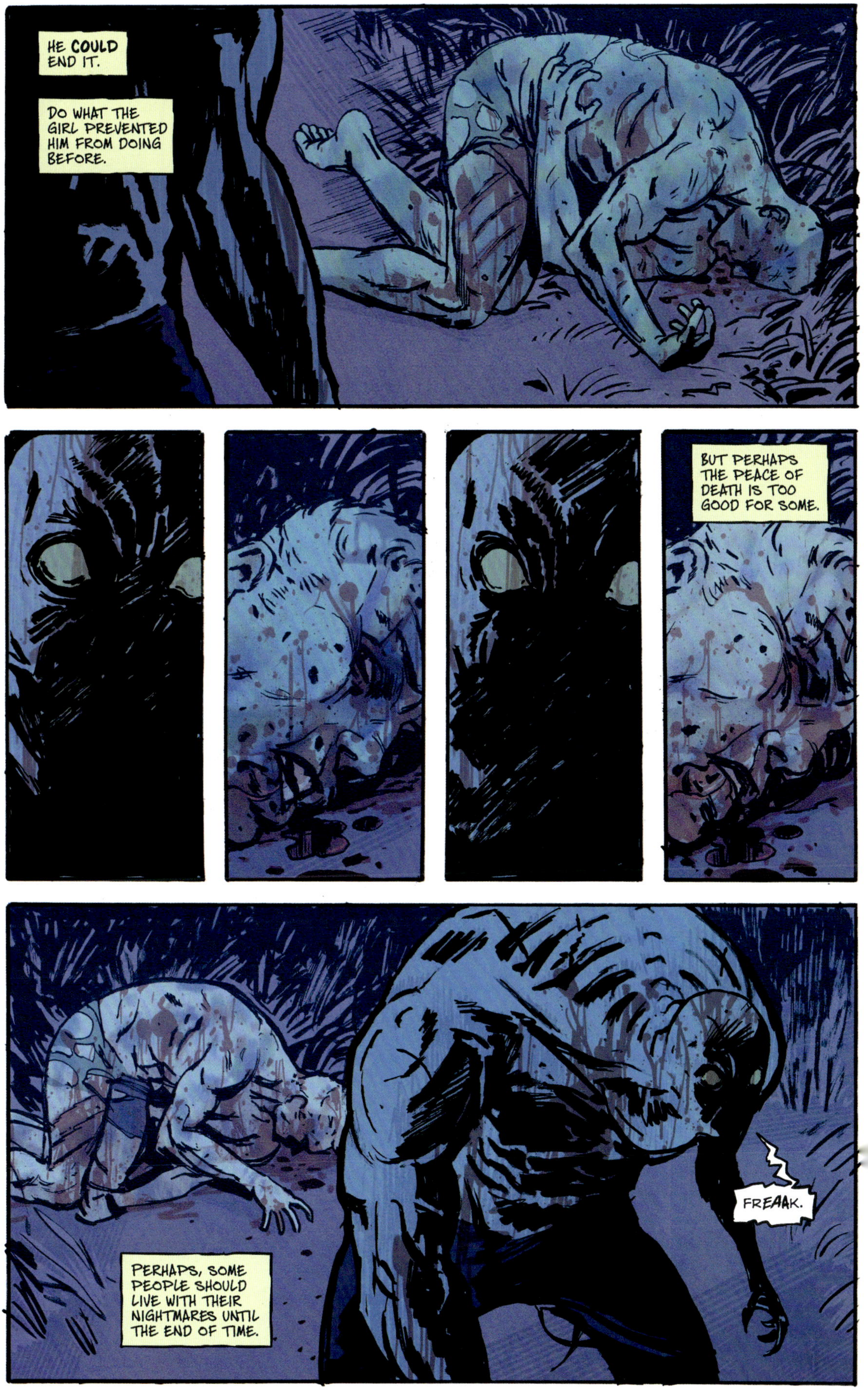
HE COULD END IT.
DO WHAT THE GIRL PREVENTED HIM FROM DOING BEFORE.
BUT PERHAPS THE PEACE OF DEATH IS TOO GOOD FOR SOME.
FREAAK.
PERHAPS, SOME PEOPLE SHOULD LIVE WITH THEIR NIGHTMARES UNTIL THE END OF TIME.

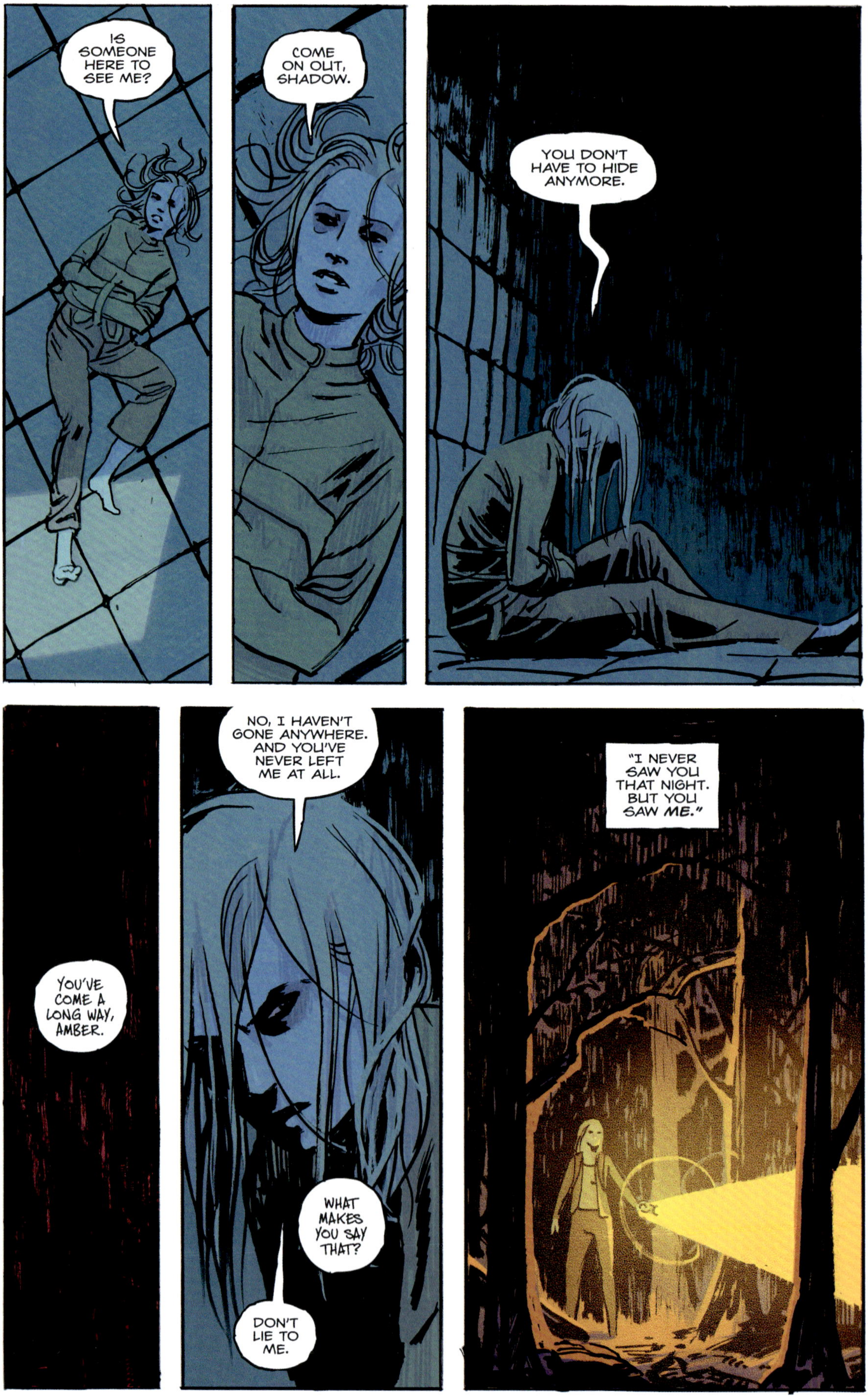
IS SOMEONE HERE TO SEE ME?
COME ON OUT, SHADOW.
YOU DON'T HAVE TO HIDE ANYMORE.
YOU'VE COME A LONG WAY, AMBER.
NO, I HAVEN'T GONE ANYWHERE. AND YOU'VE NEVER LEFT ME AT ALL.
WHAT MAKES YOU SAY THAT?
DON'T LIE TO ME.
"I NEVER SAW YOU THAT NIGHT. BUT YOU SAW ME."

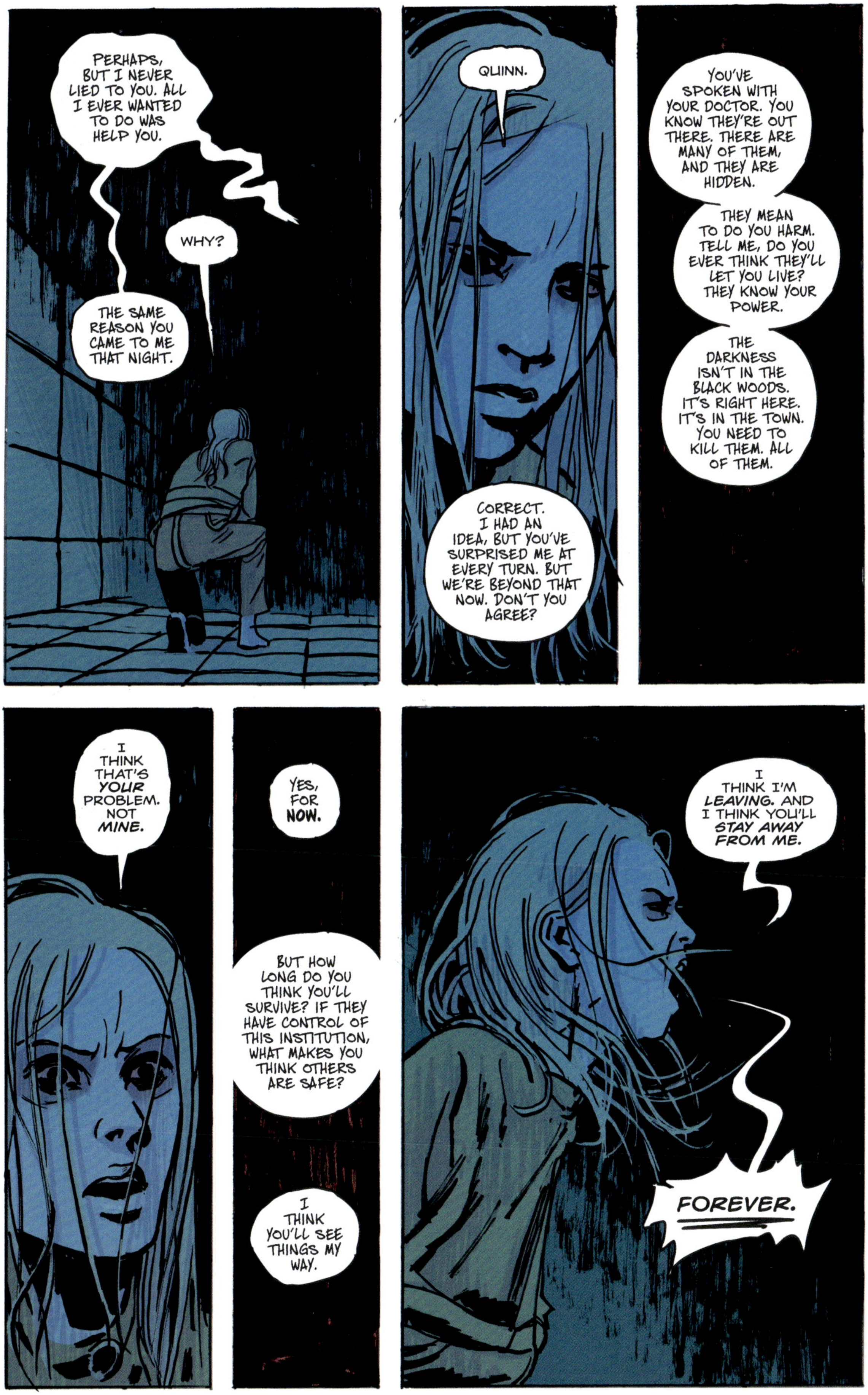
PERHAPS, BUT I NEVER LIED TO YOU. ALL I EVER WANTED TO DO WAS HELP YOU.
WHY?
THE SAME REASON YOU CAME TO ME THAT NIGHT.
QUINN.
CORRECT. I HAD AN IDEA, BUT YOU'VE SURPRISED ME AT EVERY TURN. BUT WE'RE BEYOND THAT NOW. DON'T YOU AGREE?
YOU'VE SPOKEN WITH YOUR DOCTOR. YOU KNOW THEY'RE OUT THERE. THERE ARE MANY OF THEM, AND THEY ARE HIDDEN.
THEY MEAN TO DO YOU HARM. TELL ME, DO YOU EVER THINK THEY'LL LET YOU LIVE? THEY KNOW YOUR POWER.
THE DARKNESS ISN'T IN THE BLACK WOODS. IT'S RIGHT HERE. IT'S IN THE TOWN. YOU NEED TO KILL THEM. ALL OF THEM.
I THINK THAT'S *YOUR* PROBLEM. NOT *MINE.*
YES, FOR **NOW.**
BUT HOW LONG DO YOU THINK YOU'LL SURVIVE? IF THEY HAVE CONTROL OF THIS INSTITUTION, WHAT MAKES YOU THINK OTHERS ARE SAFE?
I THINK YOU'LL SEE THINGS MY WAY.
I THINK I'M *LEAVING.* AND I THINK YOU'LL *STAY AWAY FROM ME.*
FOREVER.

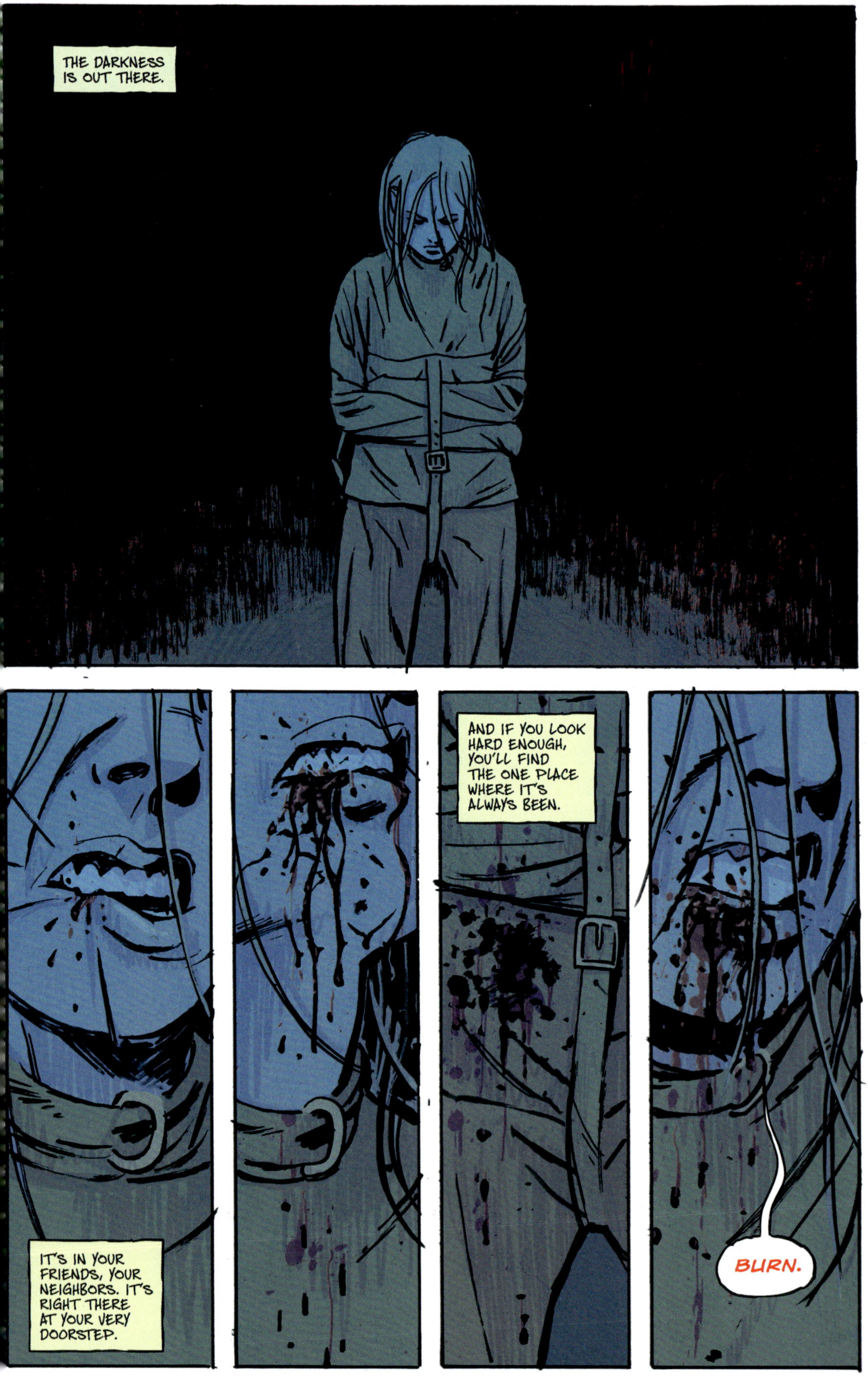
THE DARKNESS IS OUT THERE.
IT'S IN YOUR FRIENDS, YOUR NEIGHBORS. IT'S RIGHT THERE AT YOUR VERY DOORSTEP.
AND IF YOU LOOK HARD ENOUGH, YOU'LL FIND THE ONE PLACE WHERE IT'S ALWAYS BEEN.
BURN.

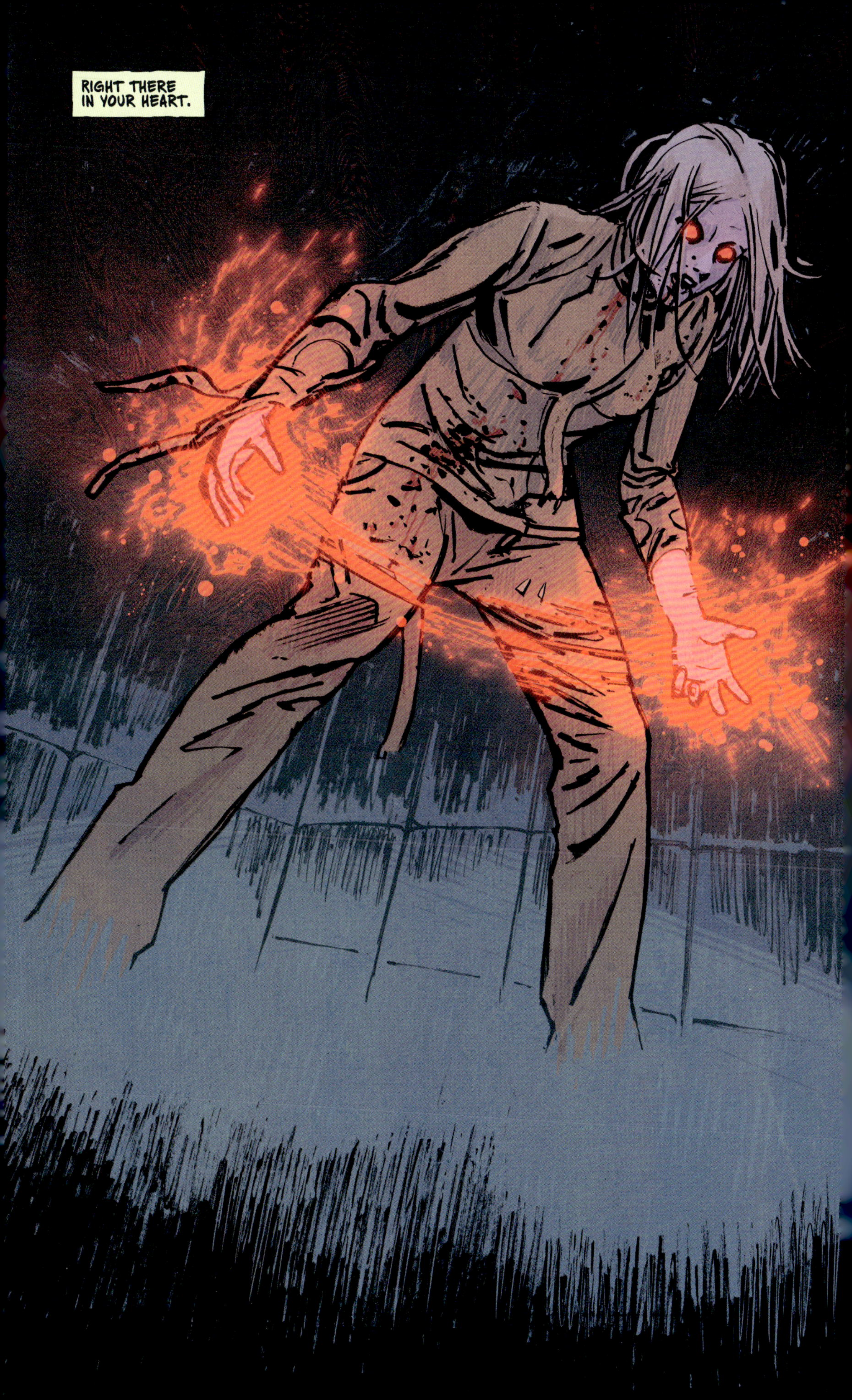
RIGHT THERE IN YOUR HEART.

CHAPTER 6

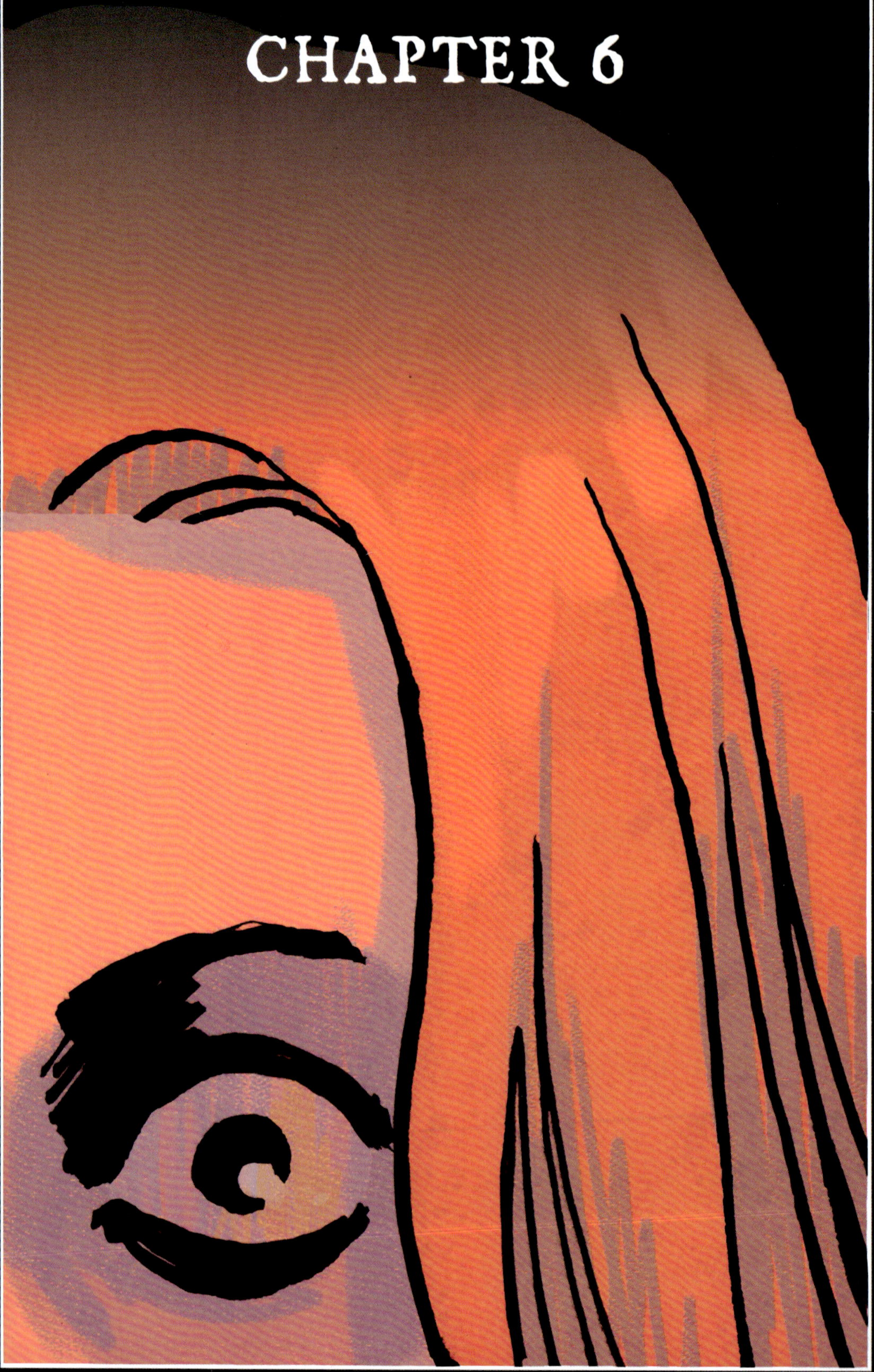

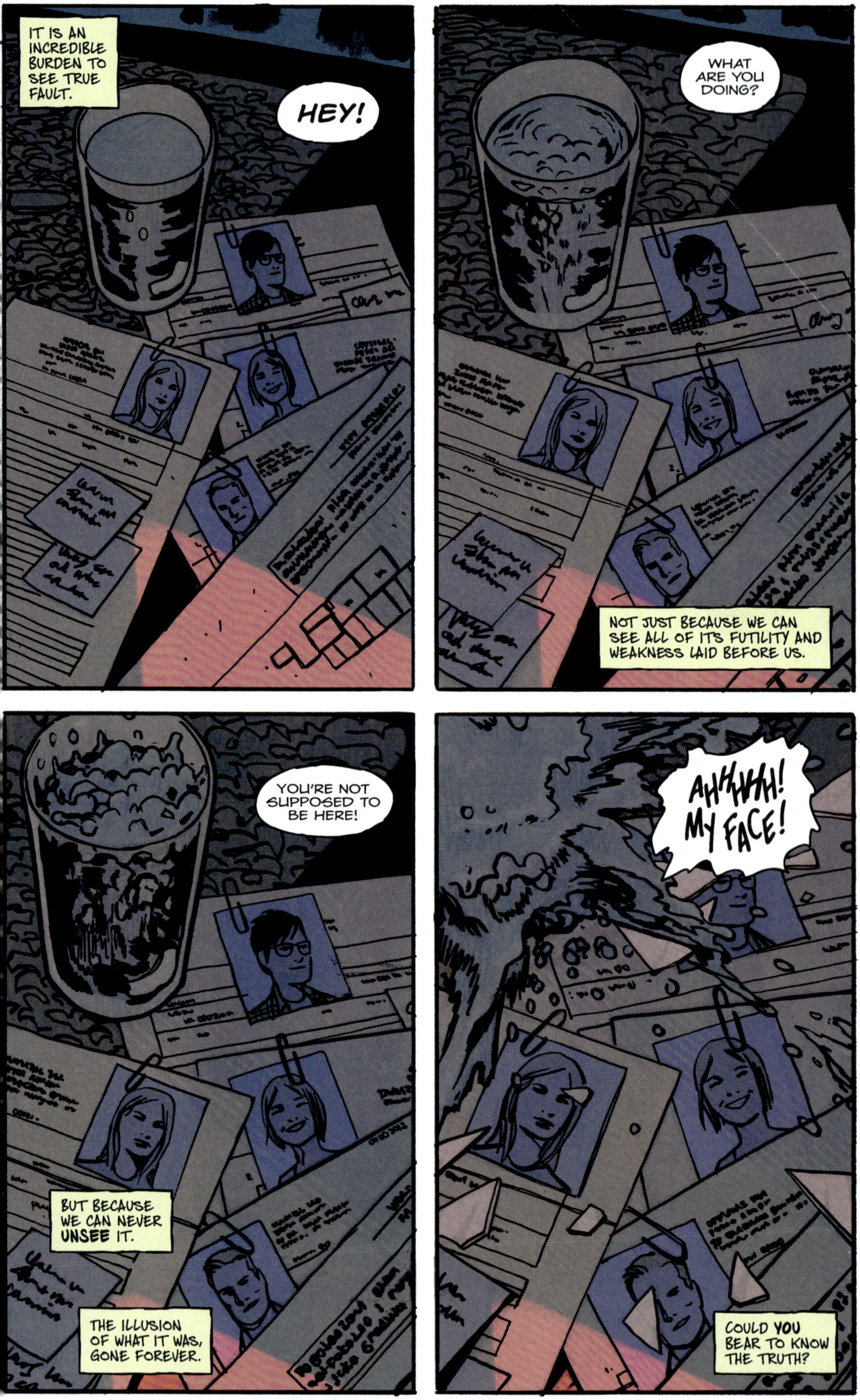
IT IS AN INCREDIBLE BURDEN TO SEE TRUE FAULT.
HEY!
WHAT ARE YOU DOING?
NOT JUST BECAUSE WE CAN SEE ALL OF ITS FUTILITY AND WEAKNESS LAID BEFORE US.
YOU'RE NOT SUPPOSED TO BE HERE!
BUT BECAUSE WE CAN NEVER UNSEE IT.
THE ILLUSION OF WHAT IT WAS, GONE FOREVER.
AHHHHH! MY FACE!
COULD YOU BEAR TO KNOW THE TRUTH?

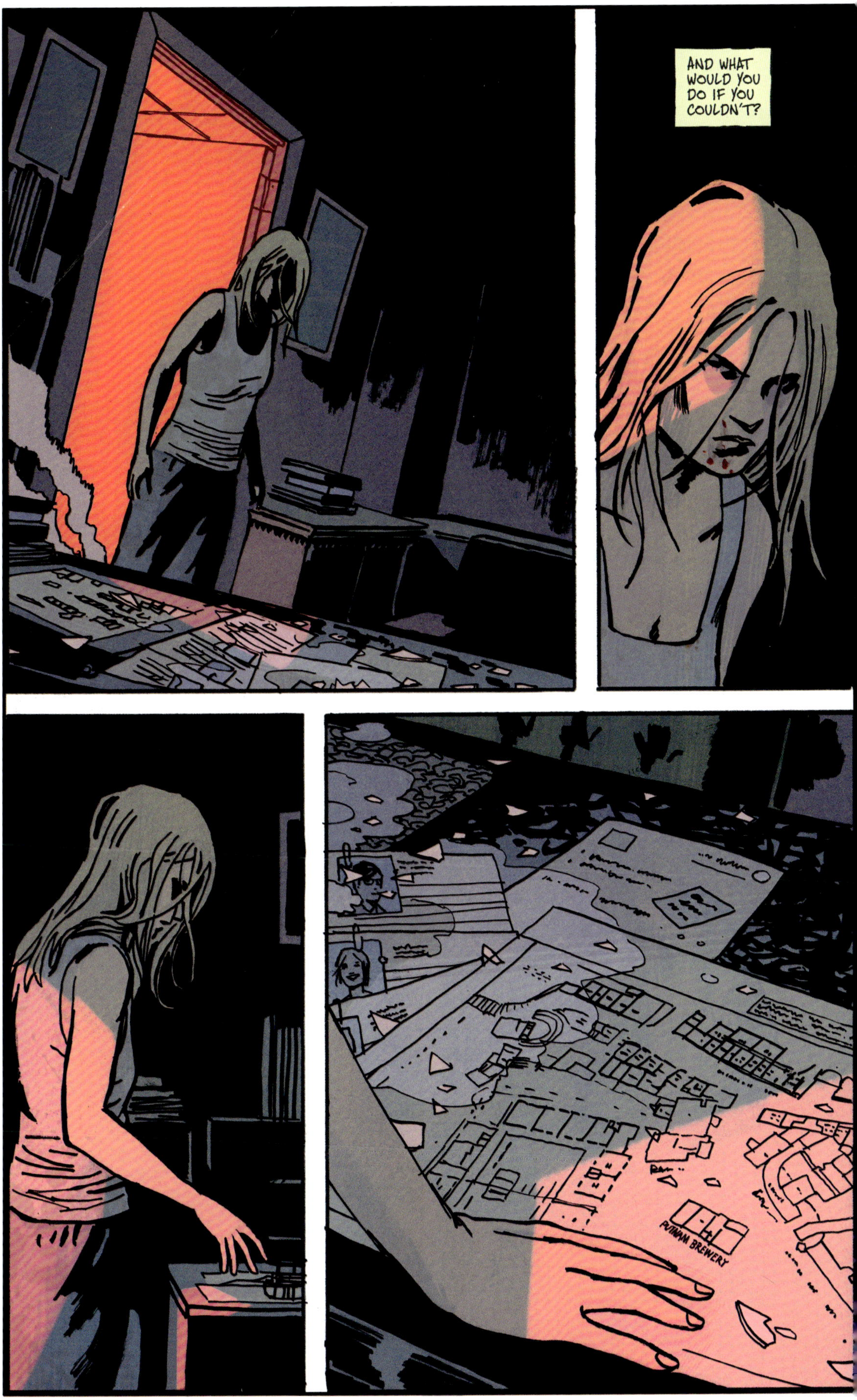
AND WHAT WOULD YOU DO IF YOU COULDN'T?
PUTNAM BREWERY

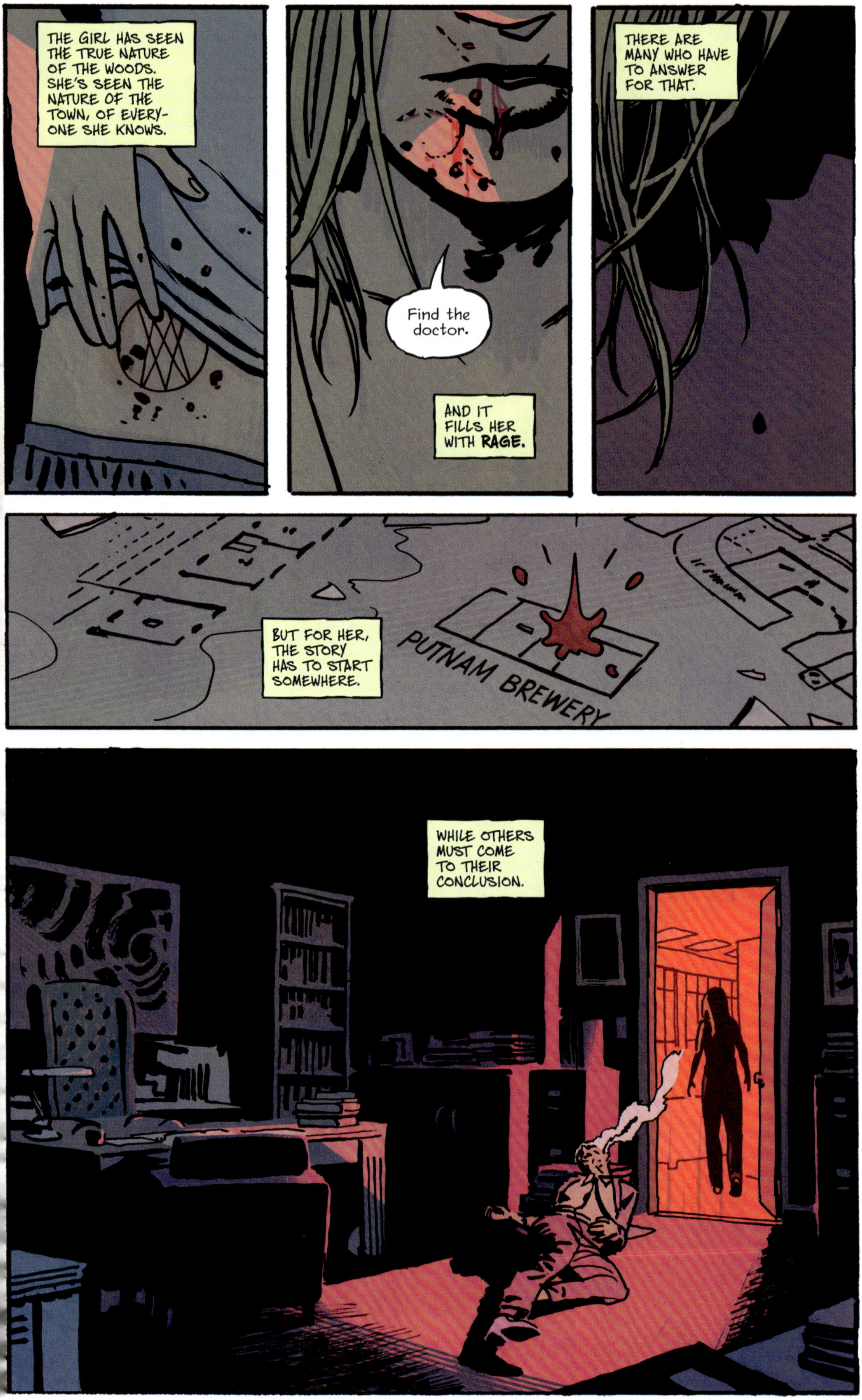
THE GIRL HAS SEEN THE TRUE NATURE OF THE WOODS. SHE'S SEEN THE NATURE OF THE TOWN, OF EVERY-ONE SHE KNOWS.
Find the doctor.
AND IT FILLS HER WITH **RAGE.**
THERE ARE MANY WHO HAVE TO ANSWER FOR THAT.
BUT FOR HER, THE STORY HAS TO START SOMEWHERE.
PUTNAM BREWERY
WHILE OTHERS MUST COME TO THEIR CONCLUSION.

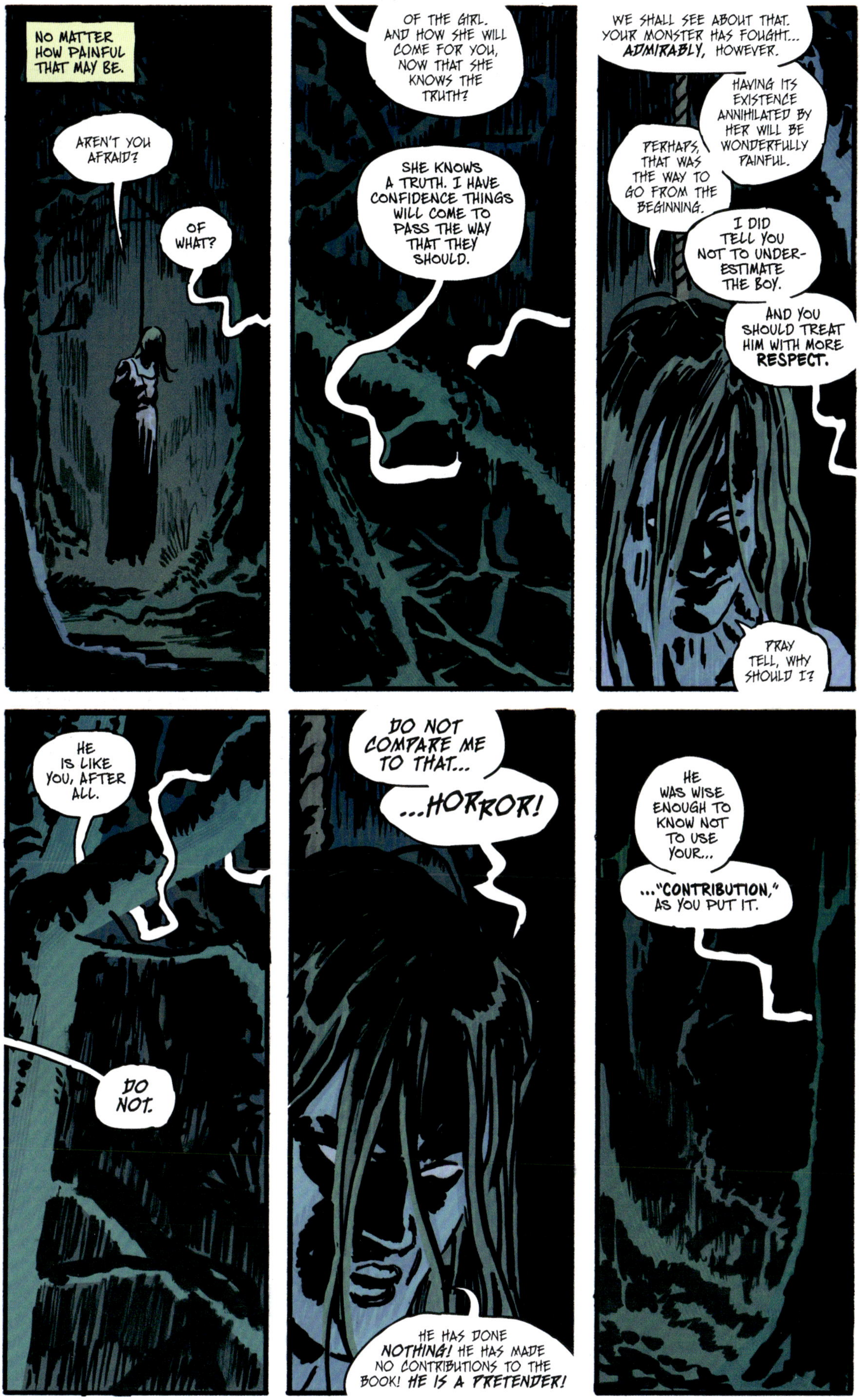
NO MATTER HOW PAINFUL THAT MAY BE.
AREN'T YOU AFRAID?
OF WHAT?
OF THE GIRL. AND HOW SHE WILL COME FOR YOU, NOW THAT SHE KNOWS THE TRUTH?
SHE KNOWS A TRUTH. I HAVE CONFIDENCE THINGS WILL COME TO PASS THE WAY THAT THEY SHOULD.
WE SHALL SEE ABOUT THAT. YOUR MONSTER HAS FOUGHT... ADMIRABLY, HOWEVER.
HAVING ITS EXISTENCE ANNIHILATED BY HER WILL BE WONDERFULLY PAINFUL.
PERHAPS, THAT WAS THE WAY TO GO FROM THE BEGINNING.
I DID TELL YOU NOT TO UNDER-ESTIMATE THE BOY.
AND YOU SHOULD TREAT HIM WITH MORE RESPECT.
PRAY TELL, WHY SHOULD I?
HE IS LIKE YOU, AFTER ALL.
DO NOT.
DO NOT COMPARE ME TO THAT...
...HORROR!
HE HAS DONE NOTHING! HE HAS MADE NO CONTRIBUTIONS TO THE BOOK! HE IS A PRETENDER!
HE WAS WISE ENOUGH TO KNOW NOT TO USE YOUR...
..."CONTRIBUTION," AS YOU PUT IT.

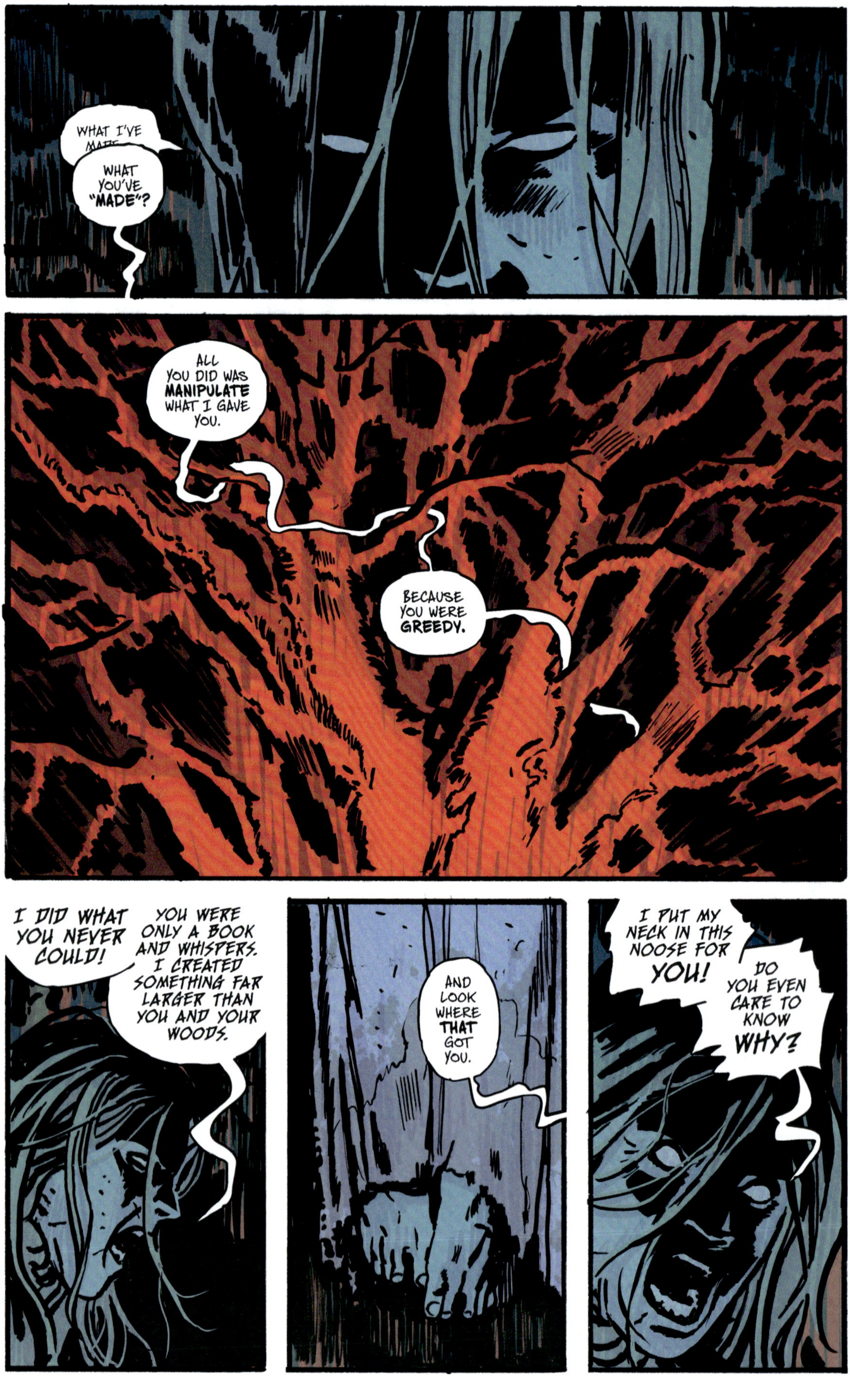
WHAT I'VE
WHAT YOU'VE "MADE"?
ALL YOU DID WAS MANIPULATE WHAT I GAVE YOU.
BECAUSE YOU WERE GREEDY.
I DID WHAT YOU NEVER COULD!
YOU WERE ONLY A BOOK AND WHISPERS. I CREATED SOMETHING FAR LARGER THAN YOU AND YOUR WOODS.
AND LOOK WHERE THAT GOT YOU.
I PUT MY NECK IN THIS NOOSE FOR YOU!
DO YOU EVEN CARE TO KNOW WHY?

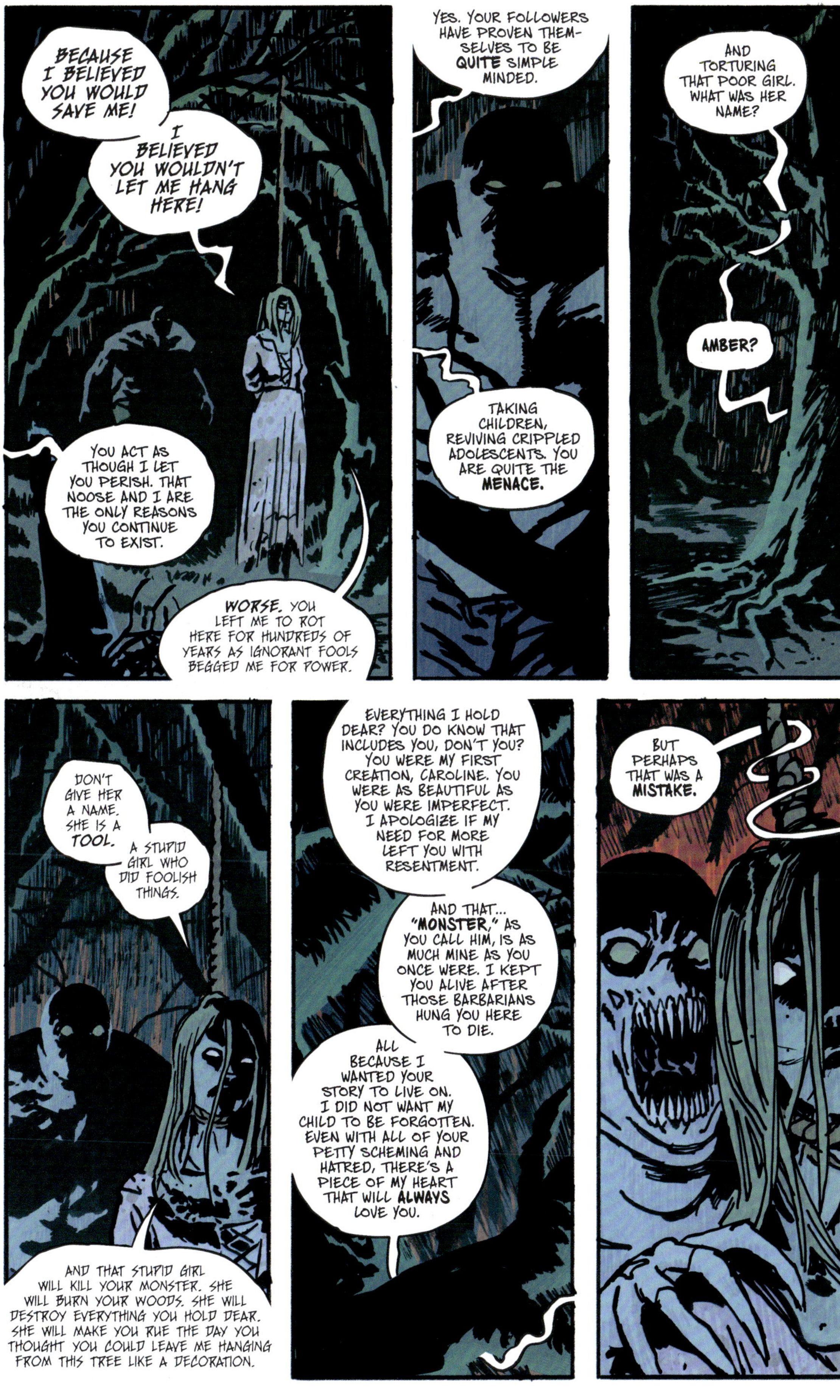
BECAUSE I BELIEVED YOU WOULD SAVE ME!
I BELIEVED YOU WOULDN'T LET ME HANG HERE!
YOU ACT AS THOUGH I LET YOU PERISH. THAT NOOSE AND I ARE THE ONLY REASONS YOU CONTINUE TO EXIST.
WORSE. YOU LEFT ME TO ROT HERE FOR HUNDREDS OF YEARS AS IGNORANT FOOLS BEGGED ME FOR POWER.
YES. YOUR FOLLOWERS HAVE PROVEN THEMSELVES TO BE QUITE SIMPLE MINDED.
TAKING CHILDREN, REVIVING CRIPPLED ADOLESCENTS. YOU ARE QUITE THE MENACE.
AND TORTURING THAT POOR GIRL. WHAT WAS HER NAME?
AMBER?
DON'T GIVE HER A NAME. SHE IS A TOOL.
A STUPID GIRL WHO DID FOOLISH THINGS.
AND THAT STUPID GIRL WILL KILL YOUR MONSTER. SHE WILL BURN YOUR WOODS. SHE WILL DESTROY EVERYTHING YOU HOLD DEAR. SHE WILL MAKE YOU RUE THE DAY YOU THOUGHT YOU COULD LEAVE ME HANGING FROM THIS TREE LIKE A DECORATION.
EVERYTHING I HOLD DEAR? YOU DO KNOW THAT INCLUDES YOU, DON'T YOU? YOU WERE MY FIRST CREATION, CAROLINE. YOU WERE AS BEAUTIFUL AS YOU WERE IMPERFECT. I APOLOGIZE IF MY NEED FOR MORE LEFT YOU WITH RESENTMENT.
AND THAT... "MONSTER," AS YOU CALL HIM, IS AS MUCH MINE AS YOU ONCE WERE. I KEPT YOU ALIVE AFTER THOSE BARBARIANS HUNG YOU HERE TO DIE.
ALL BECAUSE I WANTED YOUR STORY TO LIVE ON. I DID NOT WANT MY CHILD TO BE FORGOTTEN. EVEN WITH ALL OF YOUR PETTY SCHEMING AND HATRED, THERE'S A PIECE OF MY HEART THAT WILL ALWAYS LOVE YOU.
BUT PERHAPS THAT WAS A MISTAKE.

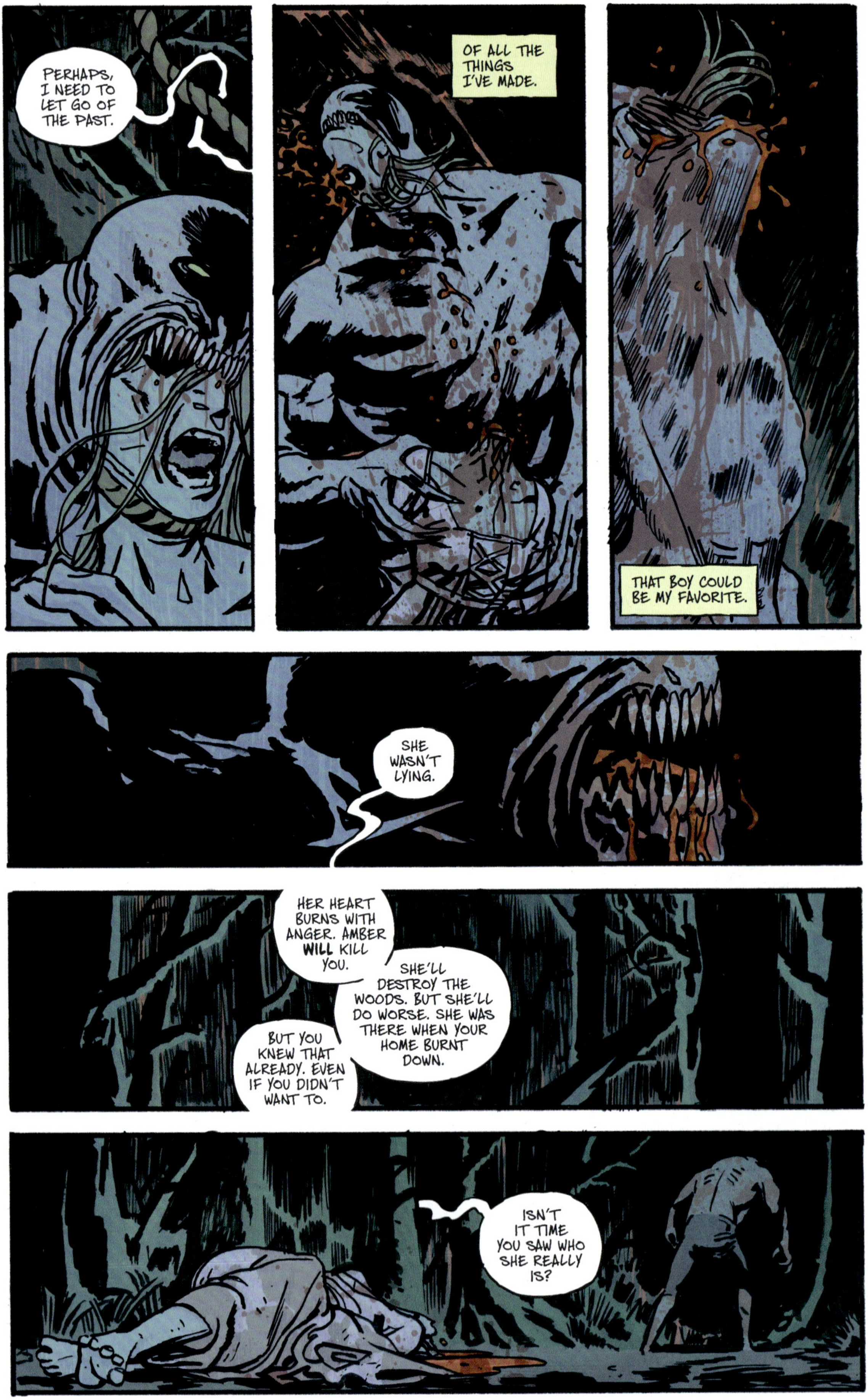
PERHAPS, I NEED TO LET GO OF THE PAST.
OF ALL THE THINGS I'VE MADE.
THAT BOY COULD BE MY FAVORITE.
SHE WASN'T LYING.
HER HEART BURNS WITH ANGER. AMBER WILL KILL YOU.
SHE'LL DESTROY THE WOODS. BUT SHE'LL DO WORSE. SHE WAS THERE WHEN YOUR HOME BURNT DOWN.
BUT YOU KNEW THAT ALREADY. EVEN IF YOU DIDN'T WANT TO.
ISN'T IT TIME YOU SAW WHO SHE REALLY IS?

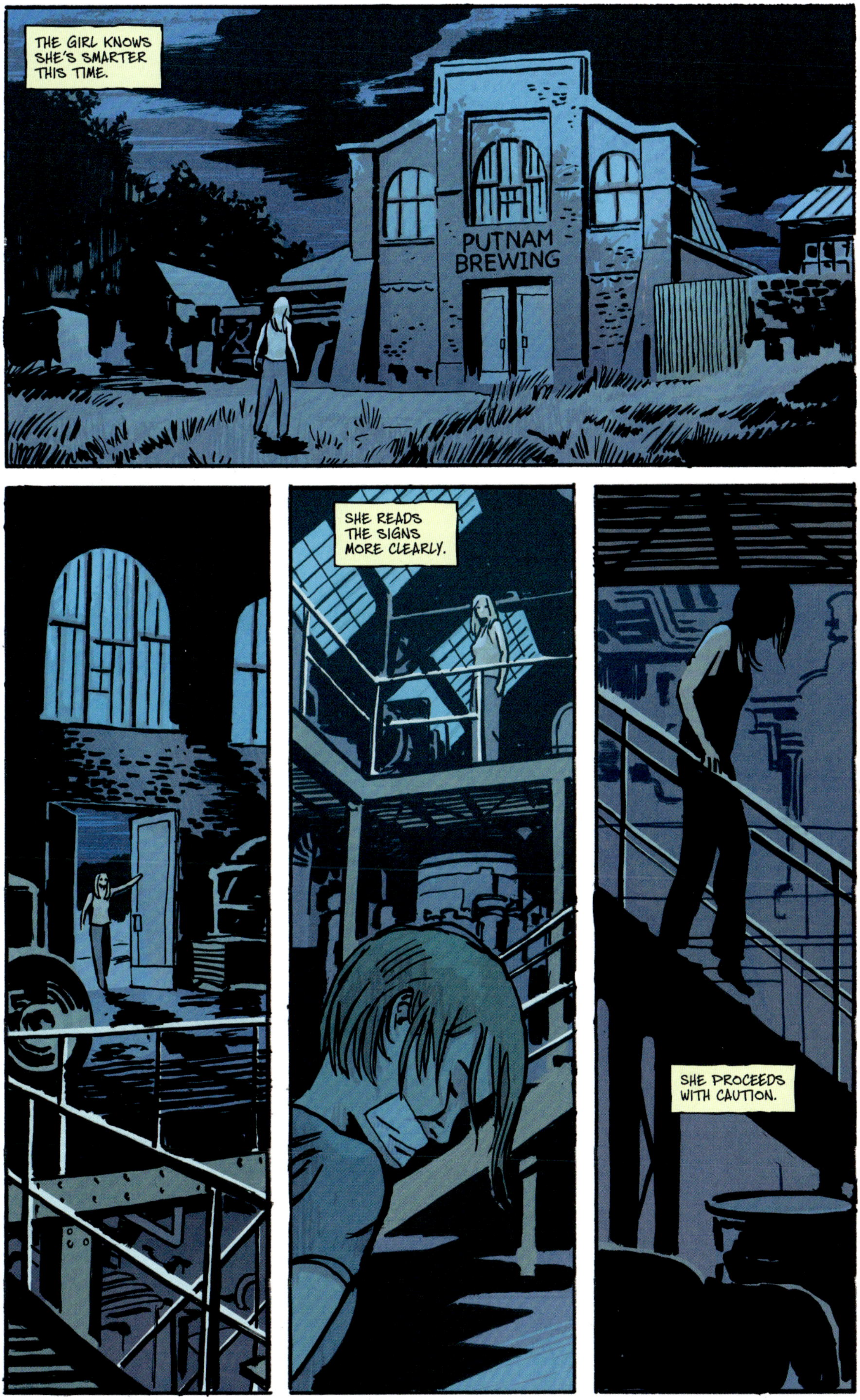
THE GIRL KNOWS SHE'S SMARTER THIS TIME.
PUTNAM BREWING
SHE READS THE SIGNS MORE CLEARLY.
SHE PROCEEDS WITH CAUTION.

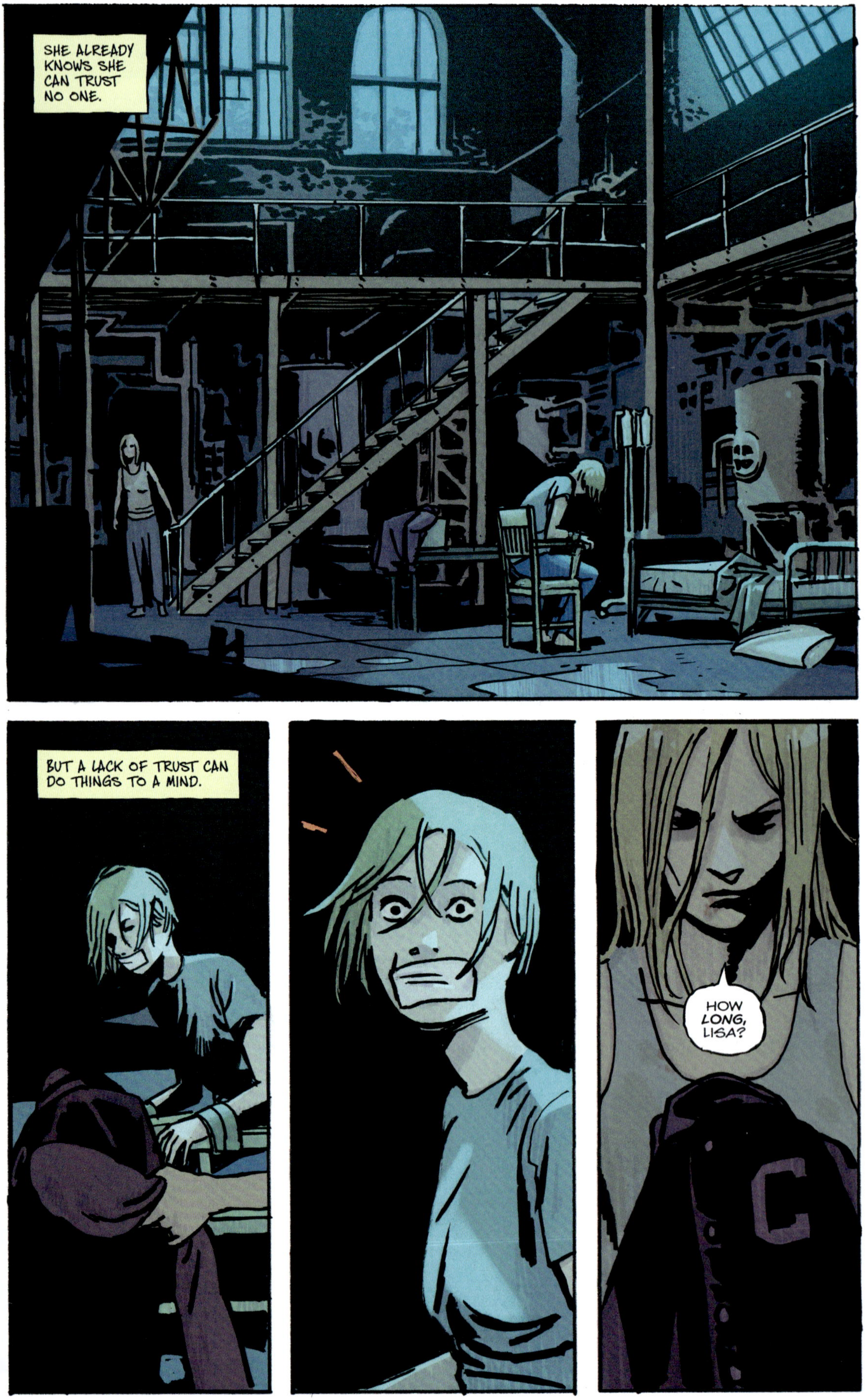

SHE ALREADY KNOWS SHE CAN TRUST NO ONE.
BUT A LACK OF TRUST CAN DO THINGS TO A MIND.
HOW LONG, LISA?

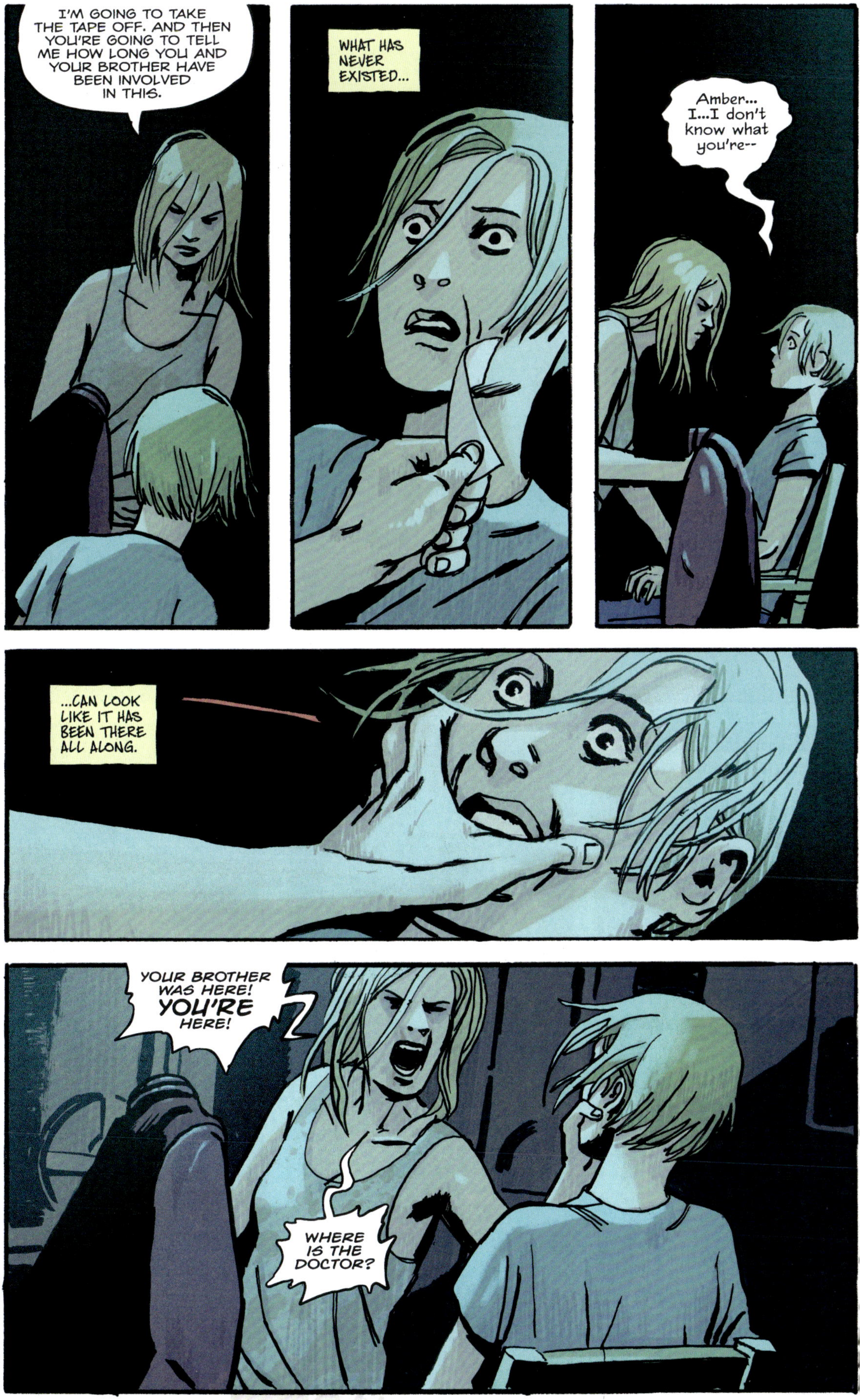
I'M GOING TO TAKE THE TAPE OFF. AND THEN YOU'RE GOING TO TELL ME HOW LONG YOU AND YOUR BROTHER HAVE BEEN INVOLVED IN THIS.
WHAT HAS NEVER EXISTED...
Amber... I...I don't know what you're--
...CAN LOOK LIKE IT HAS BEEN THERE ALL ALONG.
YOUR BROTHER WAS HERE! YOU'RE HERE!
WHERE IS THE DOCTOR?

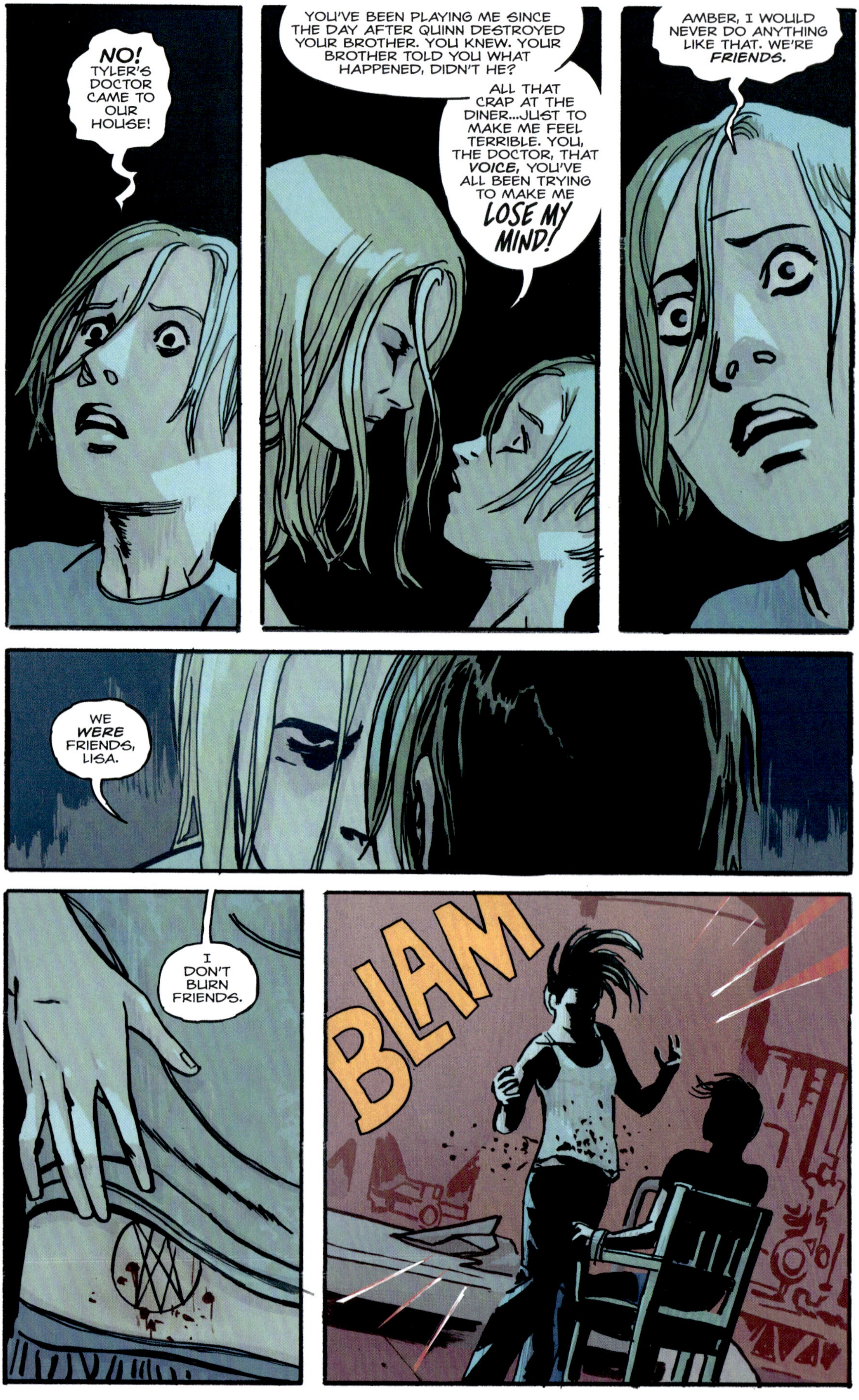
NO! TYLER'S DOCTOR CAME TO OUR HOUSE!
YOU'VE BEEN PLAYING ME SINCE THE DAY AFTER QUINN DESTROYED YOUR BROTHER. YOU KNEW. YOUR BROTHER TOLD YOU WHAT HAPPENED, DIDN'T HE?
ALL THAT CRAP AT THE DINER...JUST TO MAKE ME FEEL TERRIBLE. YOU, THE DOCTOR, THAT VOICE, YOU'VE ALL BEEN TRYING TO MAKE ME LOSE MY MIND!
AMBER, I WOULD NEVER DO ANYTHING LIKE THAT. WE'RE FRIENDS.
WE WERE FRIENDS, LISA.
I DON'T BURN FRIENDS.
BLAM

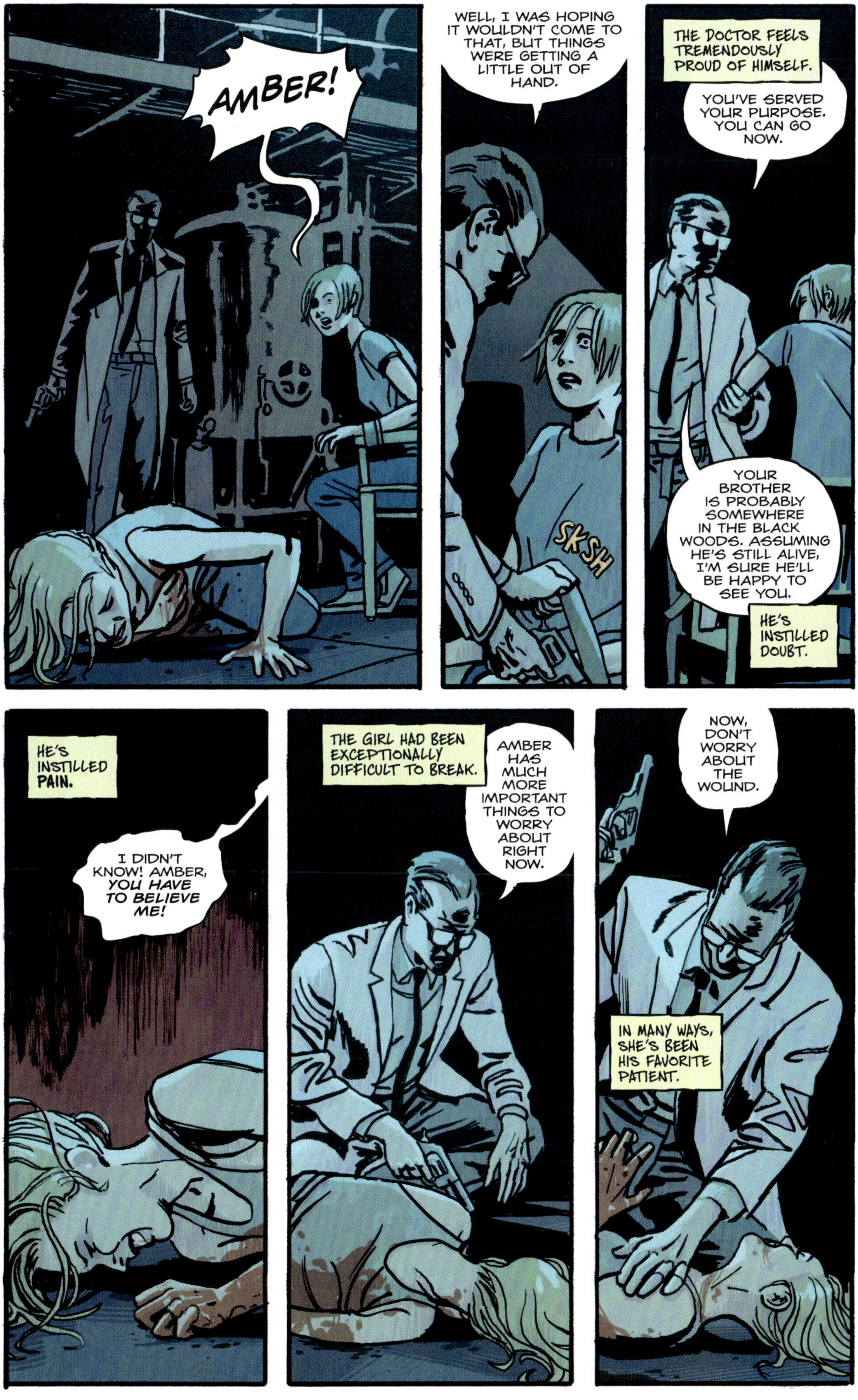
AMBER!
WELL, I WAS HOPING IT WOULDN'T COME TO THAT, BUT THINGS WERE GETTING A LITTLE OUT OF HAND.
THE DOCTOR FEELS TREMENDOUSLY PROUD OF HIMSELF.
YOU'VE SERVED YOUR PURPOSE. YOU CAN GO NOW.
YOUR BROTHER IS PROBABLY SOMEWHERE IN THE BLACK WOODS. ASSUMING HE'S STILL ALIVE, I'M SURE HE'LL BE HAPPY TO SEE YOU.
HE'S INSTILLED DOUBT.
HE'S INSTILLED PAIN.
I DIDN'T KNOW! AMBER, YOU HAVE TO BELIEVE ME!
THE GIRL HAD BEEN EXCEPTIONALLY DIFFICULT TO BREAK.
AMBER HAS MUCH MORE IMPORTANT THINGS TO WORRY ABOUT RIGHT NOW.
NOW, DON'T WORRY ABOUT THE WOUND.
IN MANY WAYS, SHE'S BEEN HIS FAVORITE PATIENT.

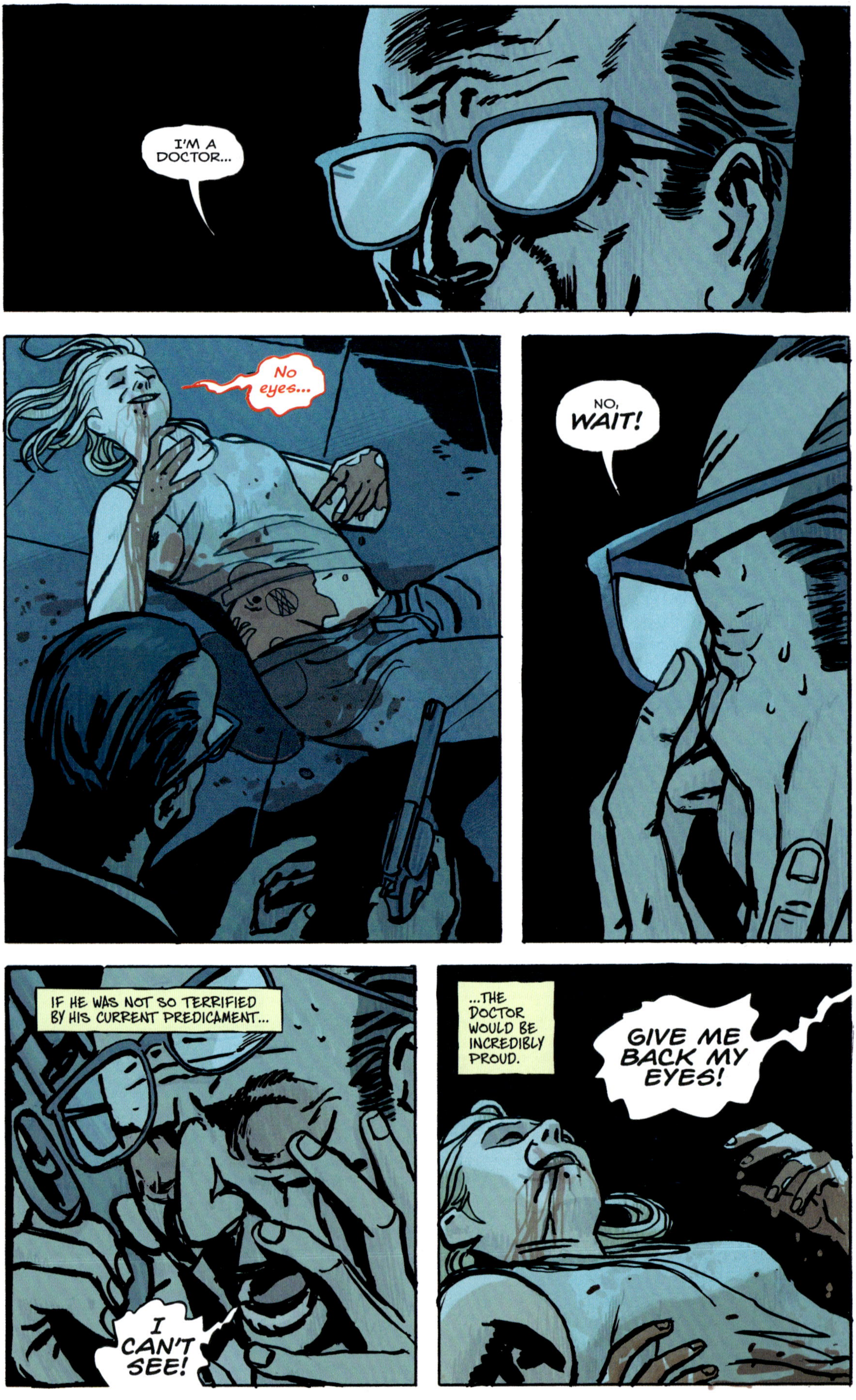

I'M A DOCTOR...
No eyes...
NO, WAIT!
IF HE WAS NOT SO TERRIFIED BY HIS CURRENT PREDICAMENT...
I CAN'T SEE!
...THE DOCTOR WOULD BE INCREDIBLY PROUD.
GIVE ME BACK MY EYES!

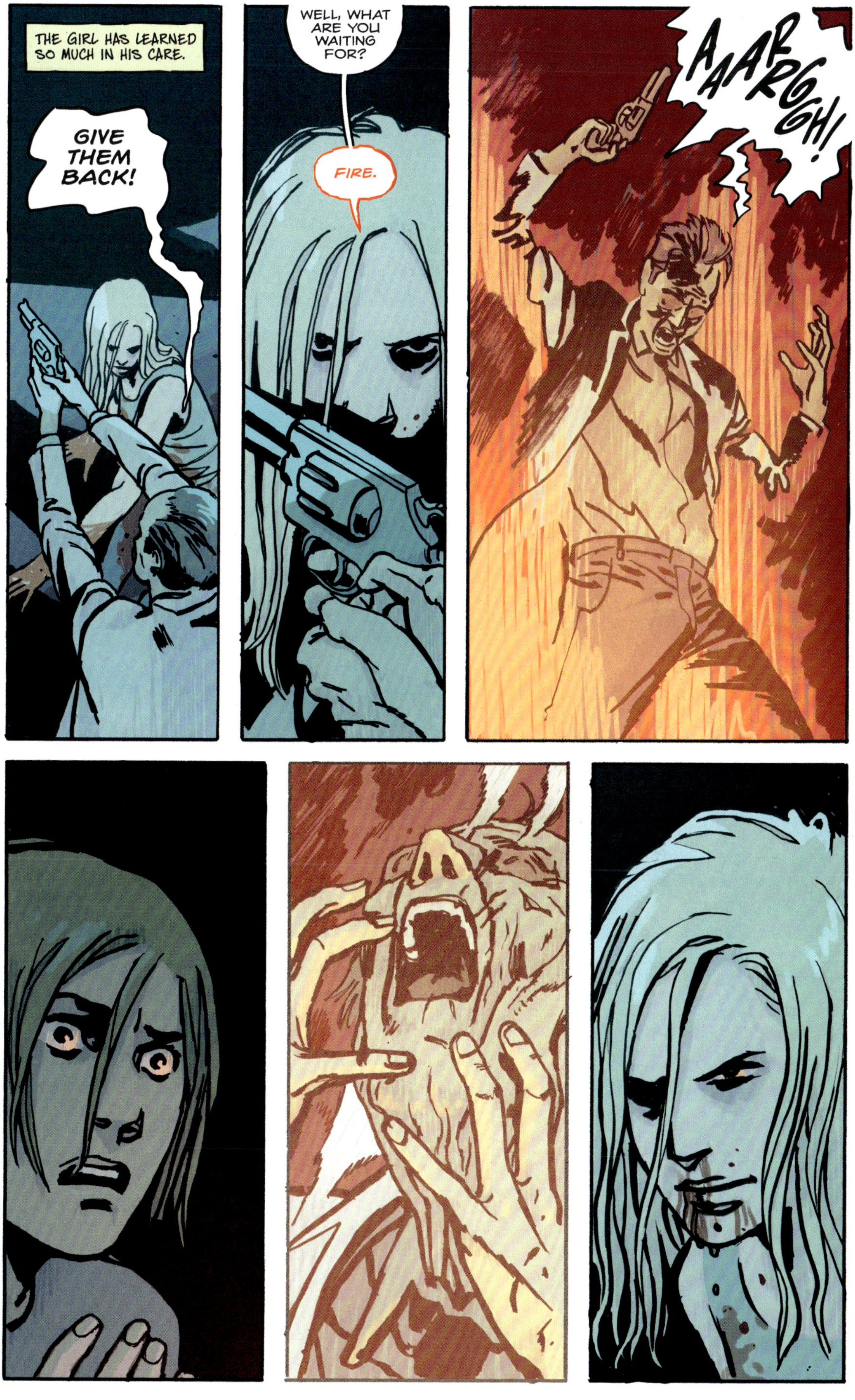
THE GIRL HAS LEARNED SO MUCH IN HIS CARE.
GIVE THEM BACK!
WELL, WHAT ARE YOU WAITING FOR?
FIRE.
AAARGGH!

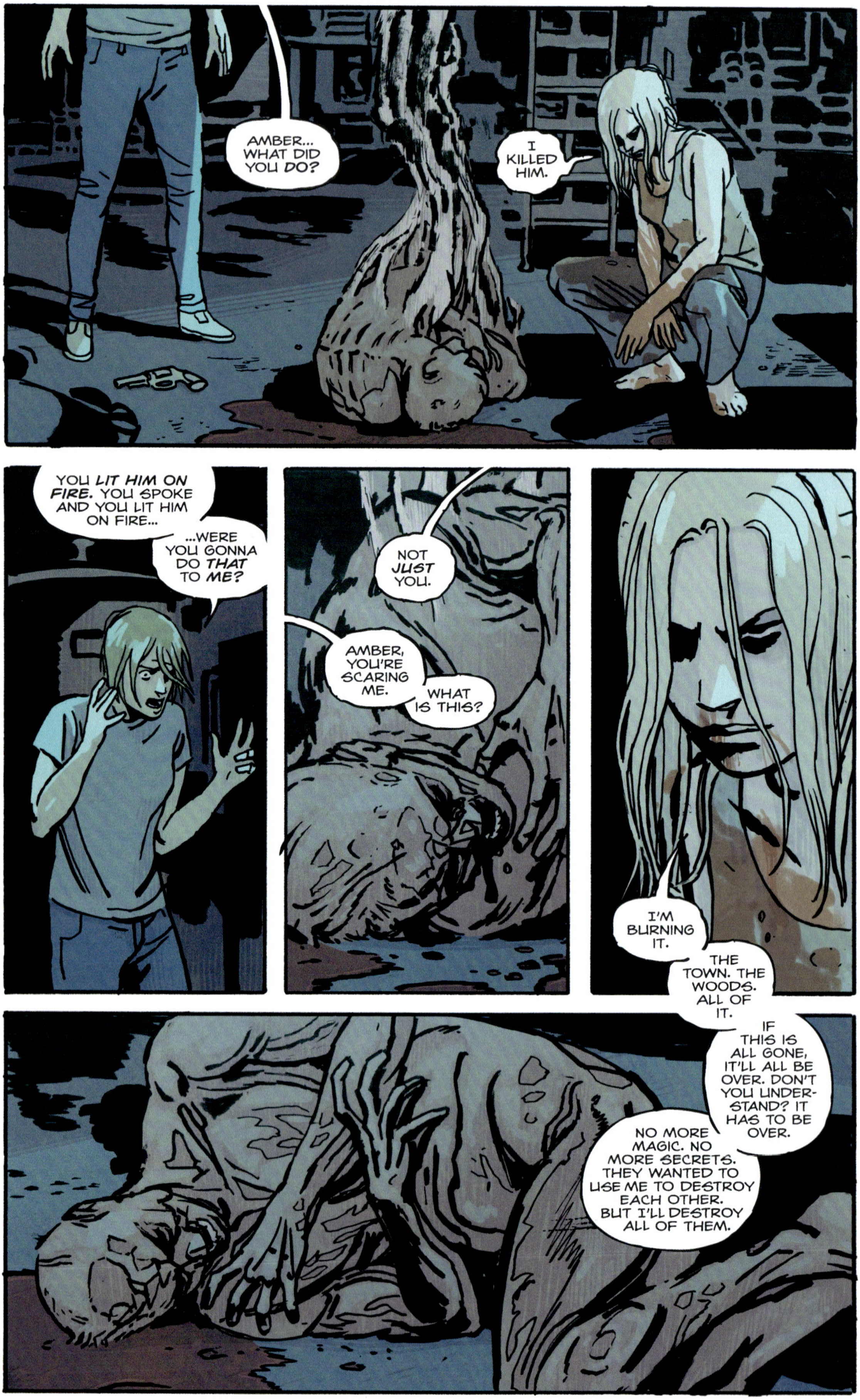
AMBER... WHAT DID YOU *DO?*
I KILLED HIM.
YOU *LIT HIM ON FIRE.* YOU SPOKE AND YOU LIT HIM ON FIRE...
...WERE YOU GONNA DO *THAT* TO *ME?*
NOT *JUST* YOU.
AMBER, YOU'RE SCARING ME.
WHAT IS THIS?
I'M BURNING IT.
THE TOWN. THE WOODS. ALL OF IT.
IF THIS IS ALL GONE, IT'LL ALL BE OVER. DON'T YOU UNDER-STAND? IT HAS TO BE OVER.
NO MORE MAGIC. NO MORE SECRETS. THEY WANTED TO USE ME TO DESTROY EACH OTHER. BUT I'LL DESTROY ALL OF THEM.

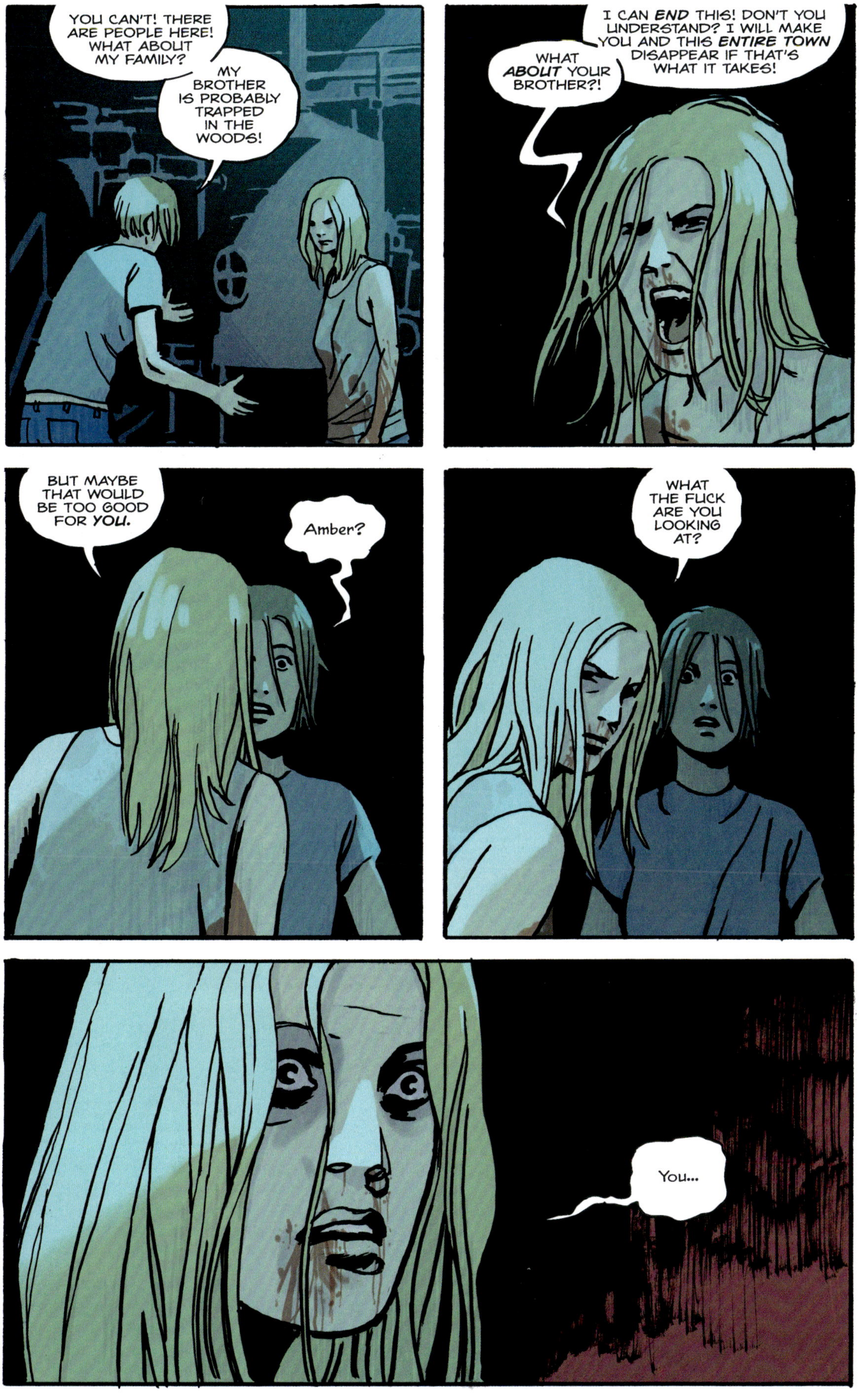
YOU CAN'T! THERE ARE PEOPLE HERE! WHAT ABOUT MY FAMILY?
MY BROTHER IS PROBABLY TRAPPED IN THE WOODS!
I CAN END THIS! DON'T YOU UNDERSTAND? I WILL MAKE YOU AND THIS ENTIRE TOWN DISAPPEAR IF THAT'S WHAT IT TAKES!
WHAT ABOUT YOUR BROTHER?!
BUT MAYBE THAT WOULD BE TOO GOOD FOR YOU.
Amber?
WHAT THE FUCK ARE YOU LOOKING AT?
You...

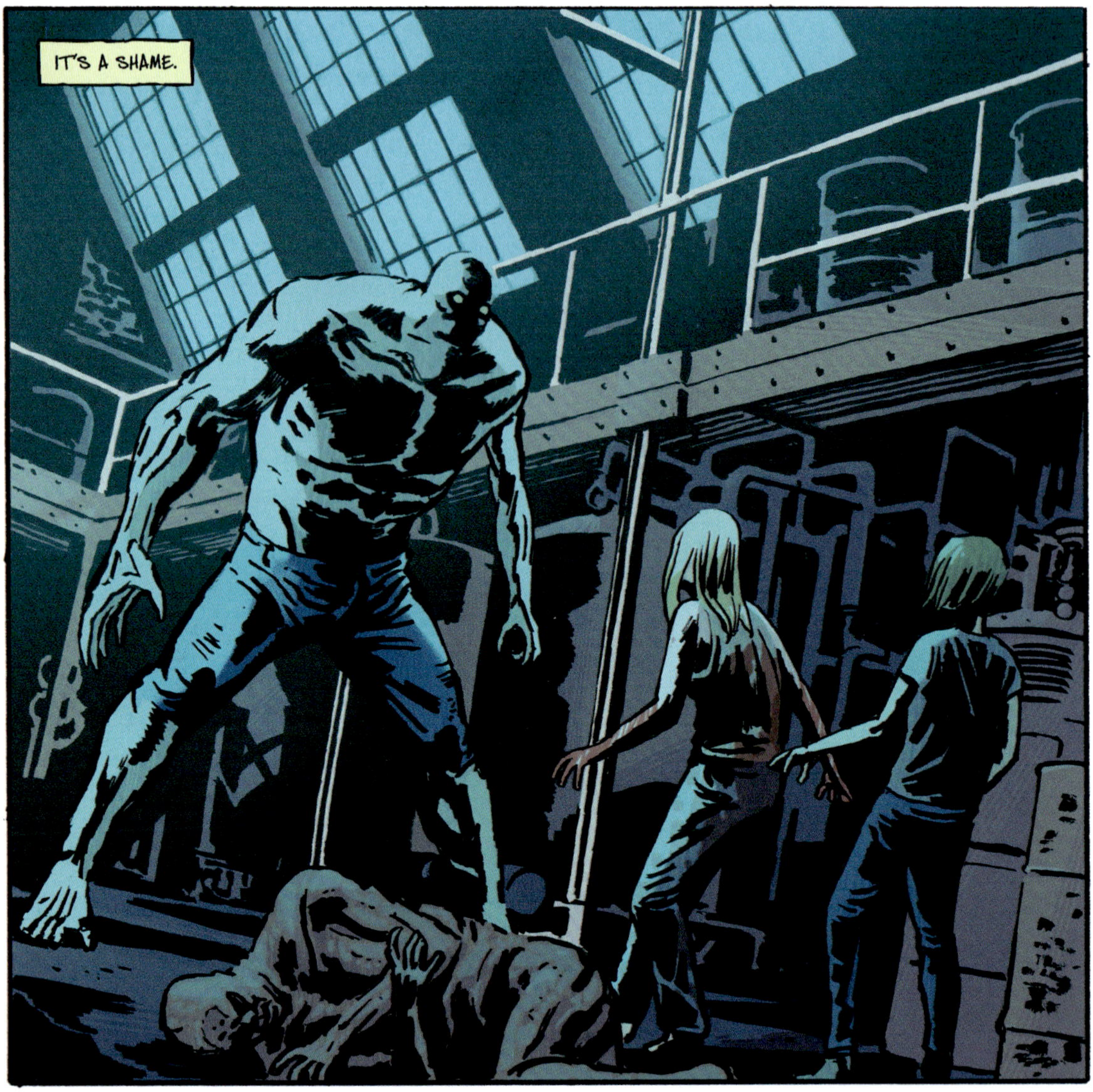
IT'S A SHAME.

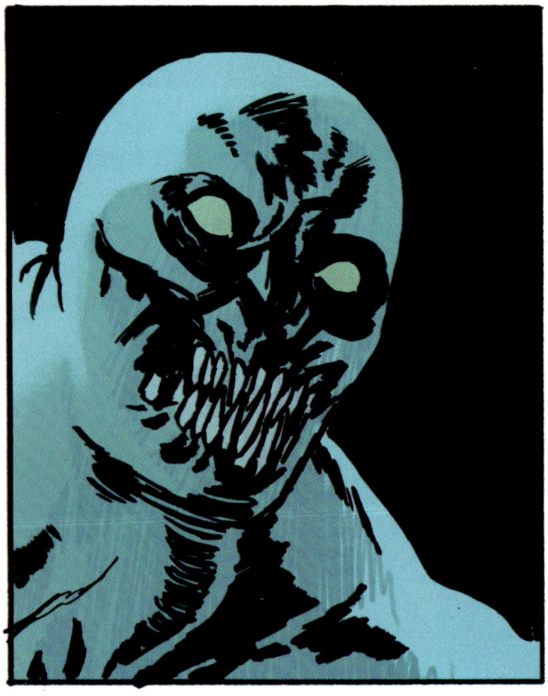

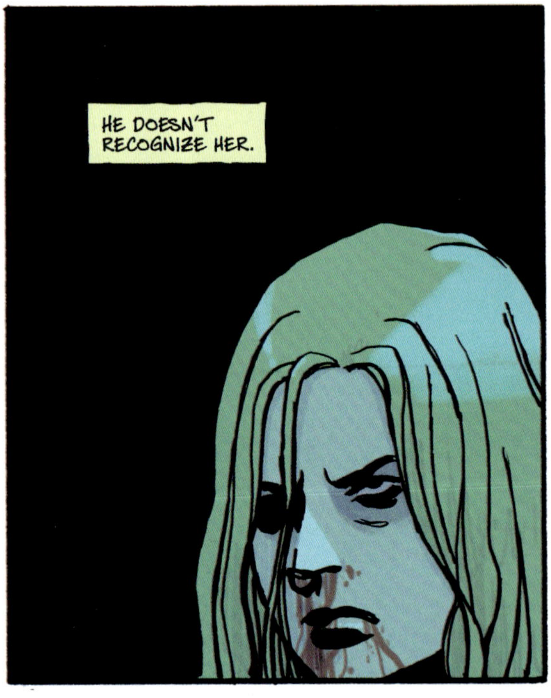
HE DOESN'T RECOGNIZE HER.

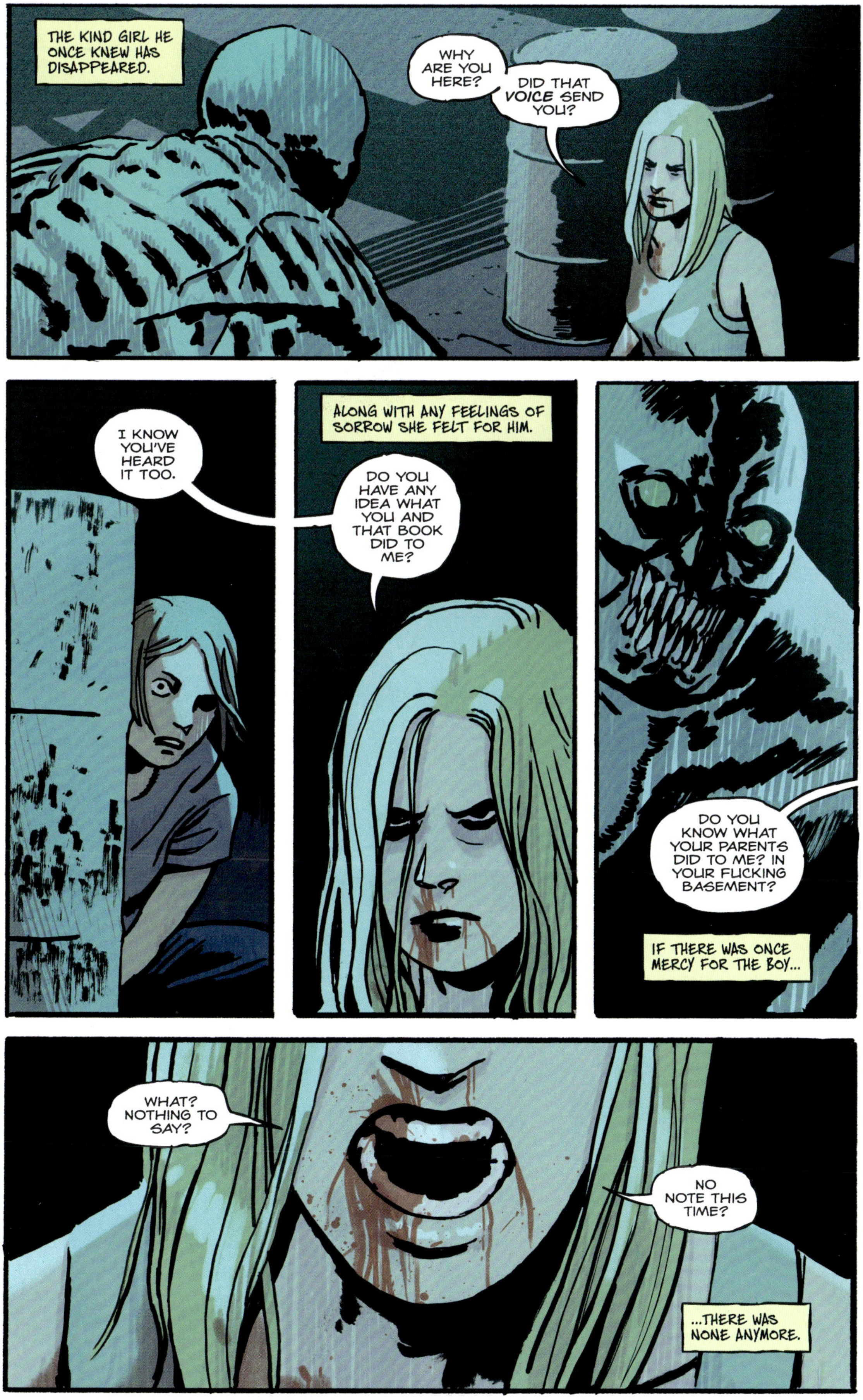
THE KIND GIRL HE ONCE KNEW HAS DISAPPEARED.
WHY ARE YOU HERE?
DID THAT *VOICE* SEND YOU?
I KNOW YOU'VE HEARD IT TOO.
ALONG WITH ANY FEELINGS OF SORROW SHE FELT FOR HIM.
DO YOU HAVE ANY IDEA WHAT YOU AND THAT BOOK DID TO ME?
DO YOU KNOW WHAT YOUR PARENTS DID TO ME? IN YOUR FUCKING BASEMENT?
IF THERE WAS ONCE MERCY FOR THE BOY...
WHAT? NOTHING TO SAY?
NO NOTE THIS TIME?
...THERE WAS NONE ANYMORE.

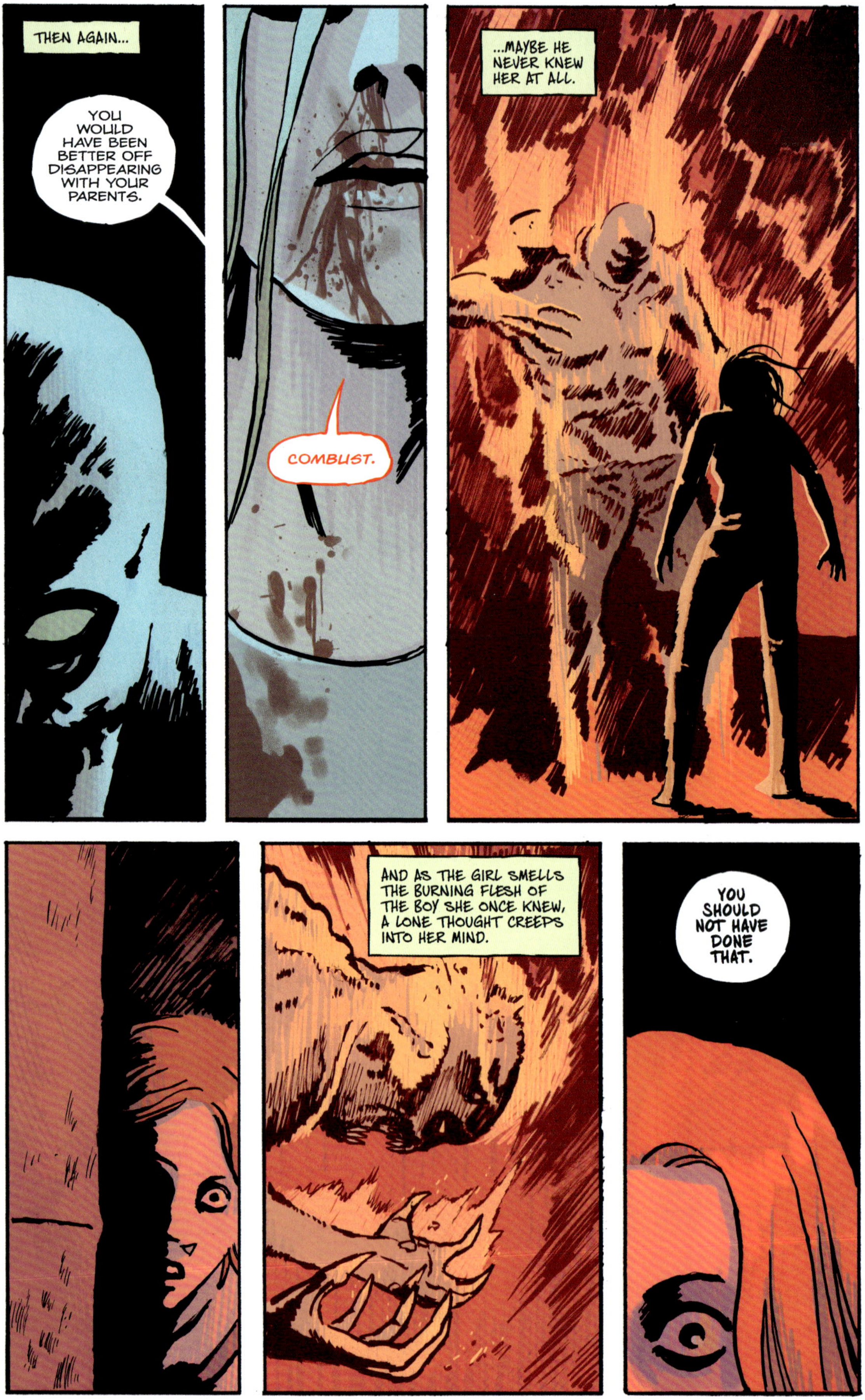
THEN AGAIN...
YOU WOULD HAVE BEEN BETTER OFF DISAPPEARING WITH YOUR PARENTS.
COMBUST.
...MAYBE HE NEVER KNEW HER AT ALL.
AND AS THE GIRL SMELLS THE BURNING FLESH OF THE BOY SHE ONCE KNEW, A LONE THOUGHT CREEPS INTO HER MIND.
YOU SHOULD NOT HAVE DONE THAT.

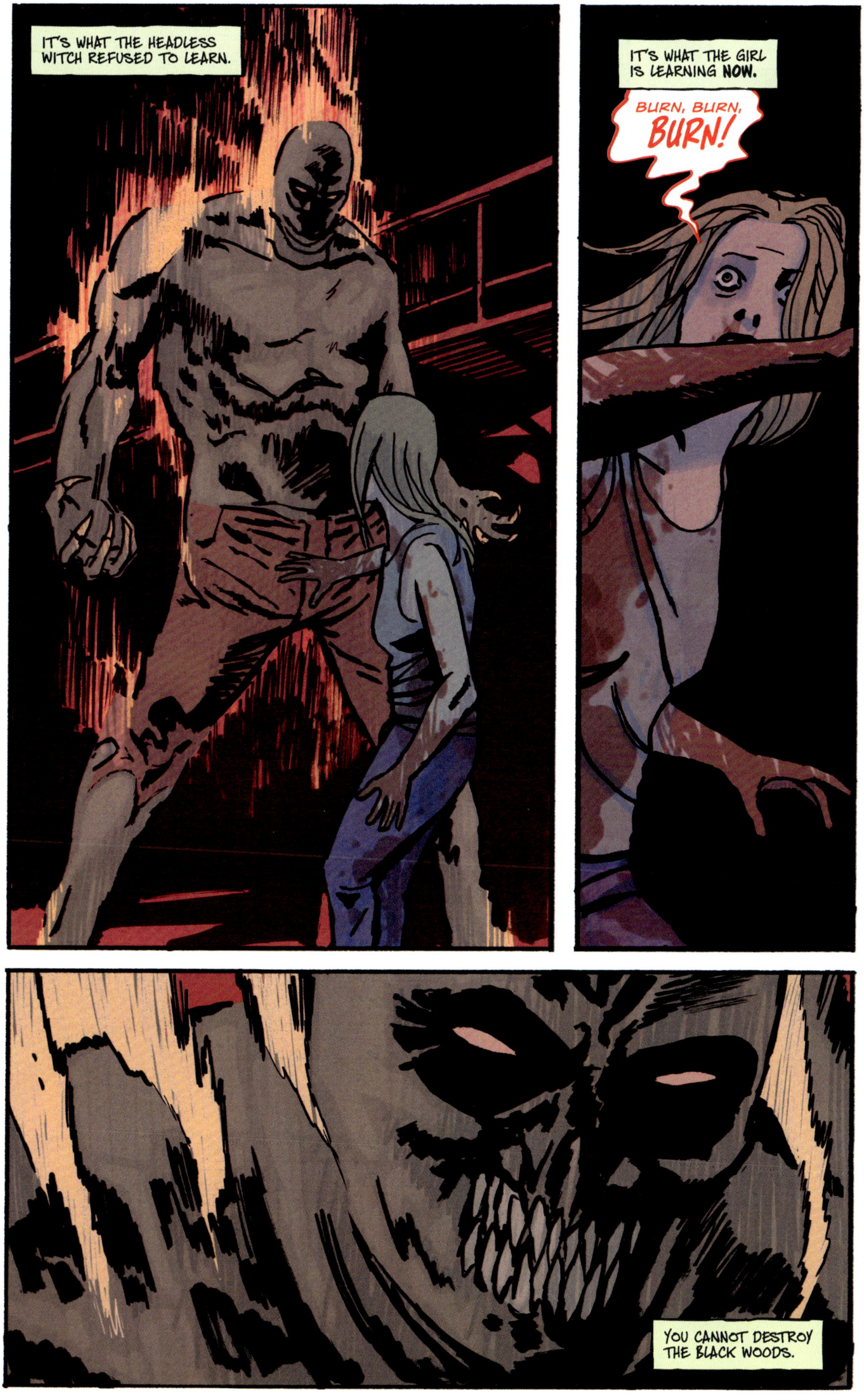
IT'S WHAT THE HEADLESS WITCH REFUSED TO LEARN.
IT'S WHAT THE GIRL IS LEARNING NOW.
BURN, BURN, BURN!
YOU CANNOT DESTROY THE BLACK WOODS.

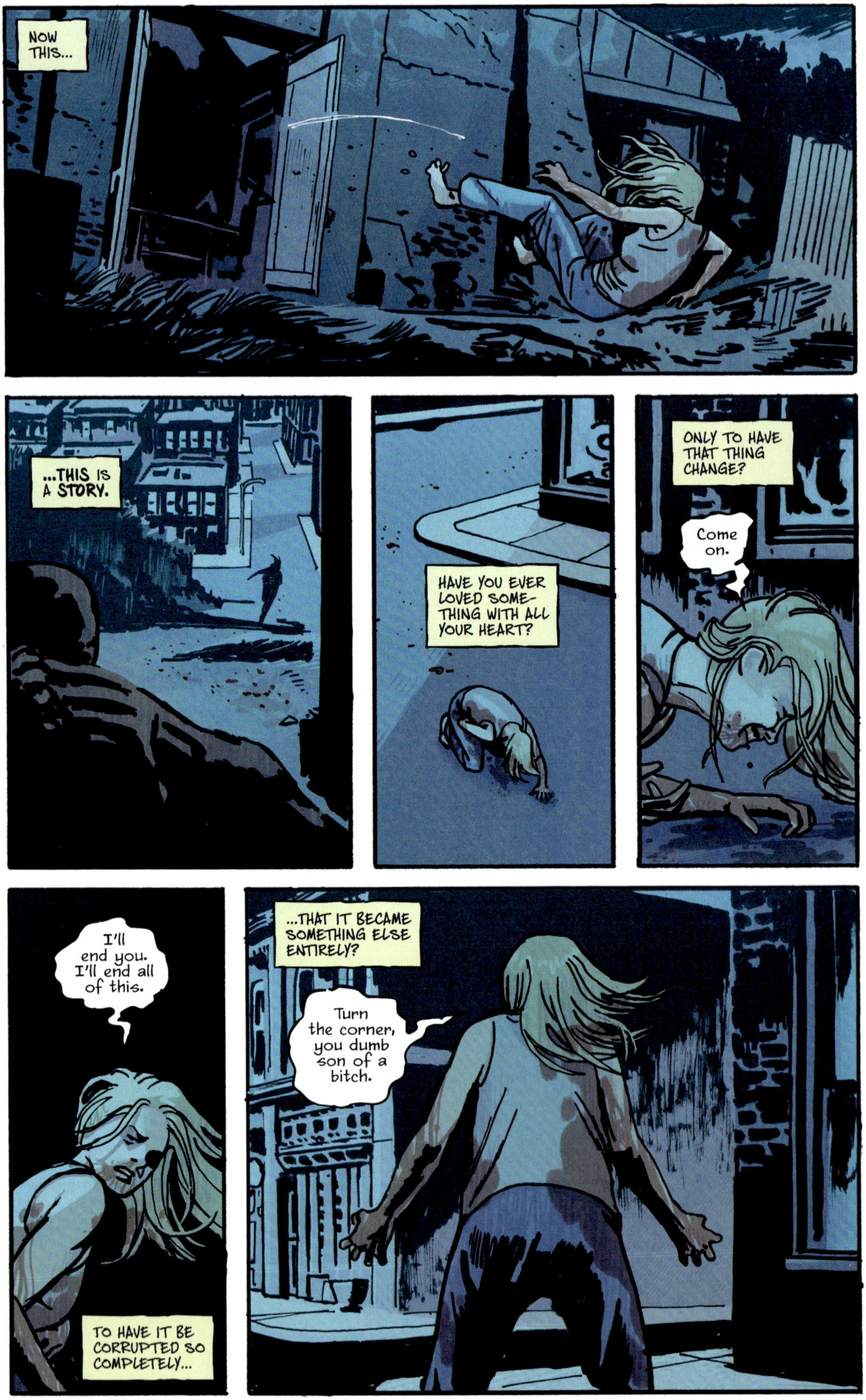
NOW THIS...
...THIS IS A STORY.
HAVE YOU EVER LOVED SOME-THING WITH ALL YOUR HEART?
ONLY TO HAVE THAT THING CHANGE?
Come on.
I'll end you. I'll end all of this.
TO HAVE IT BE CORRUPTED SO COMPLETELY...
...THAT IT BECAME SOMETHING ELSE ENTIRELY?
Turn the corner, you dumb son of a bitch.

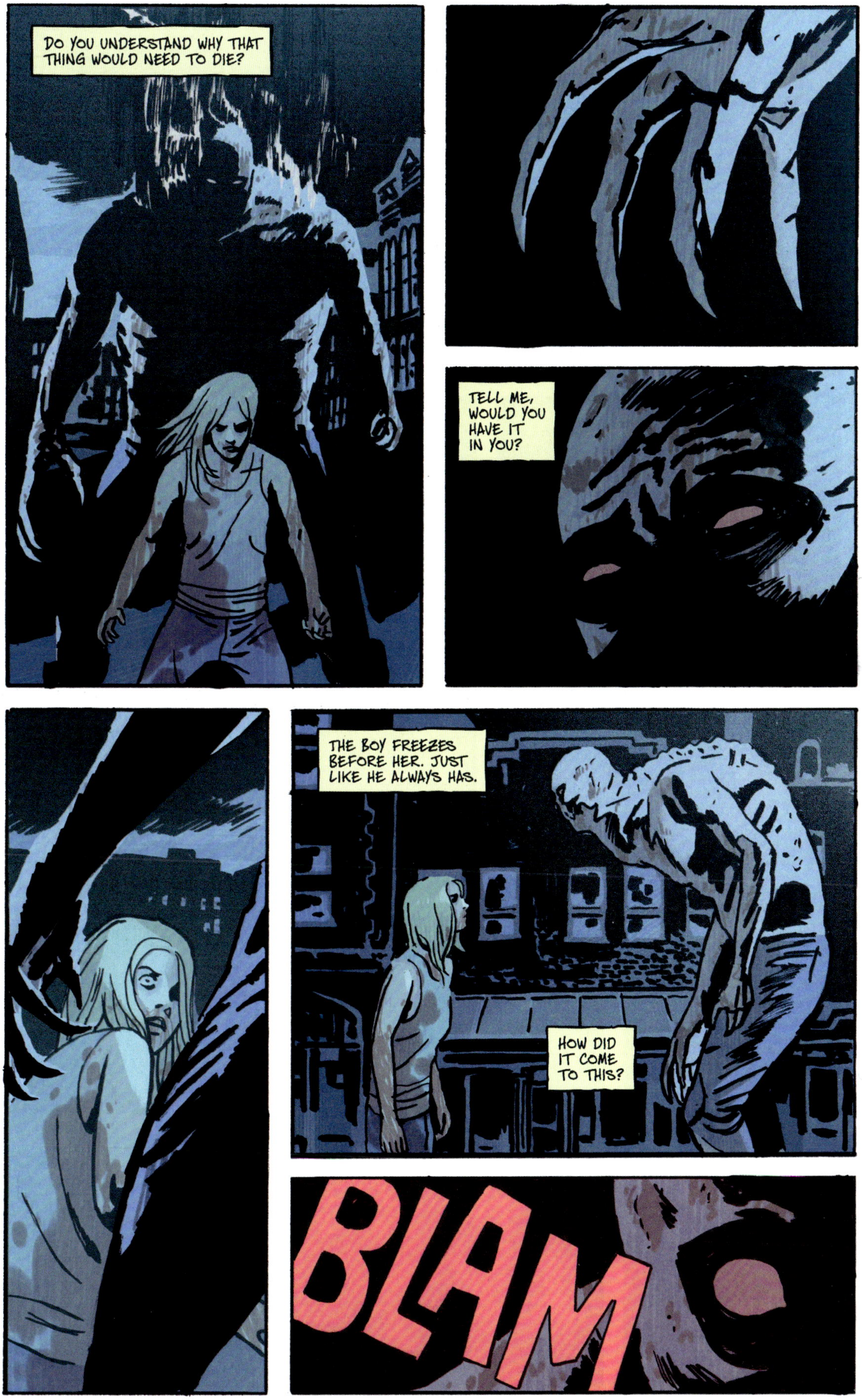
DO YOU UNDERSTAND WHY THAT THING WOULD NEED TO DIE?
TELL ME, WOULD YOU HAVE IT IN YOU?
THE BOY FREEZES BEFORE HER. JUST LIKE HE ALWAYS HAS.
HOW DID IT COME TO THIS?
BLAM

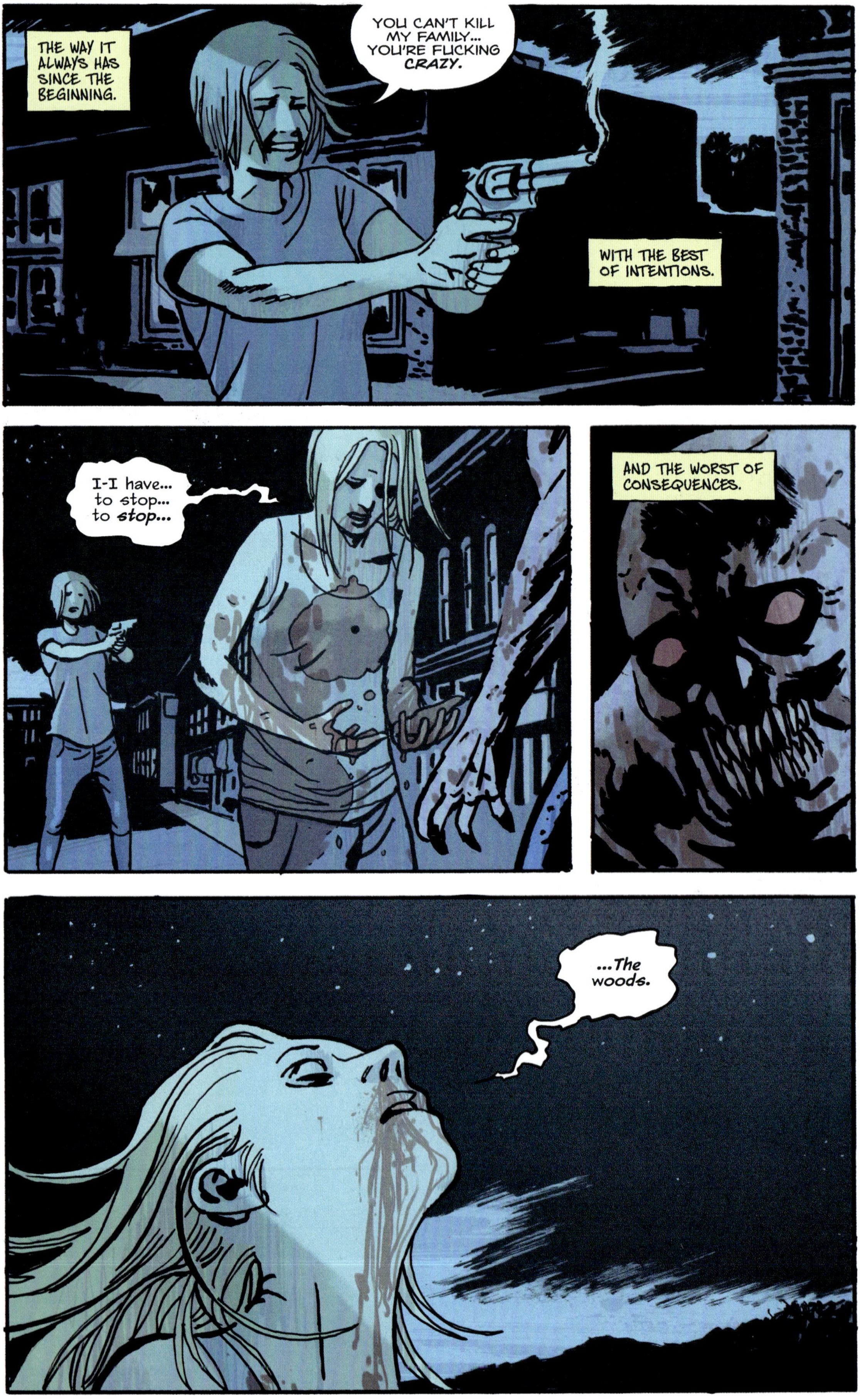
THE WAY IT ALWAYS HAS SINCE THE BEGINNING.
YOU CAN'T KILL MY FAMILY... YOU'RE FUCKING *CRAZY.*
WITH THE BEST OF INTENTIONS.
I-I have... to stop... to *stop*...
AND THE WORST OF CONSEQUENCES.
...The woods.

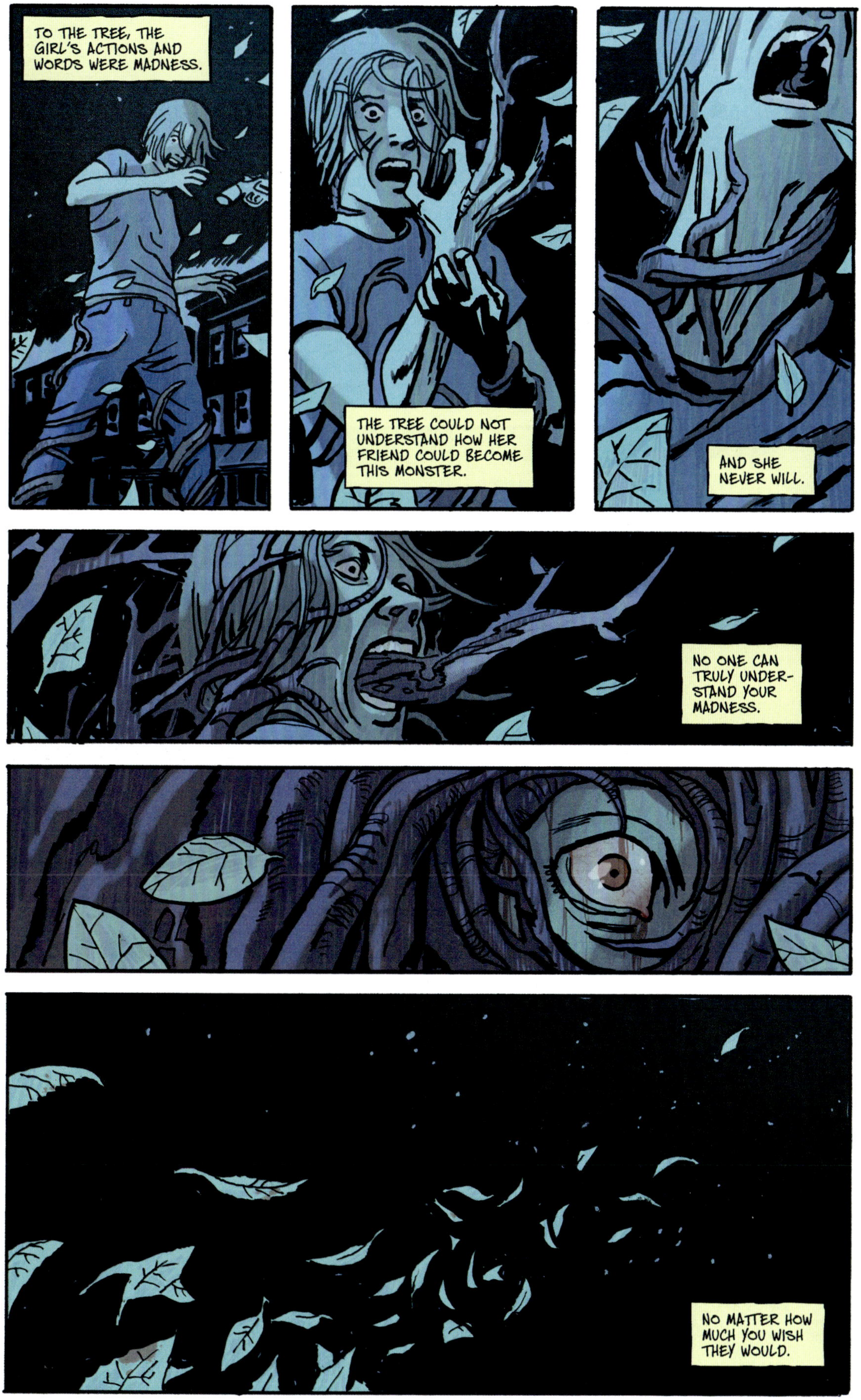
TO THE TREE, THE GIRL'S ACTIONS AND WORDS WERE MADNESS.
THE TREE COULD NOT UNDERSTAND HOW HER FRIEND COULD BECOME THIS MONSTER.
AND SHE NEVER WILL.
NO ONE CAN TRULY UNDER-STAND YOUR MADNESS.
NO MATTER HOW MUCH YOU WISH THEY WOULD.

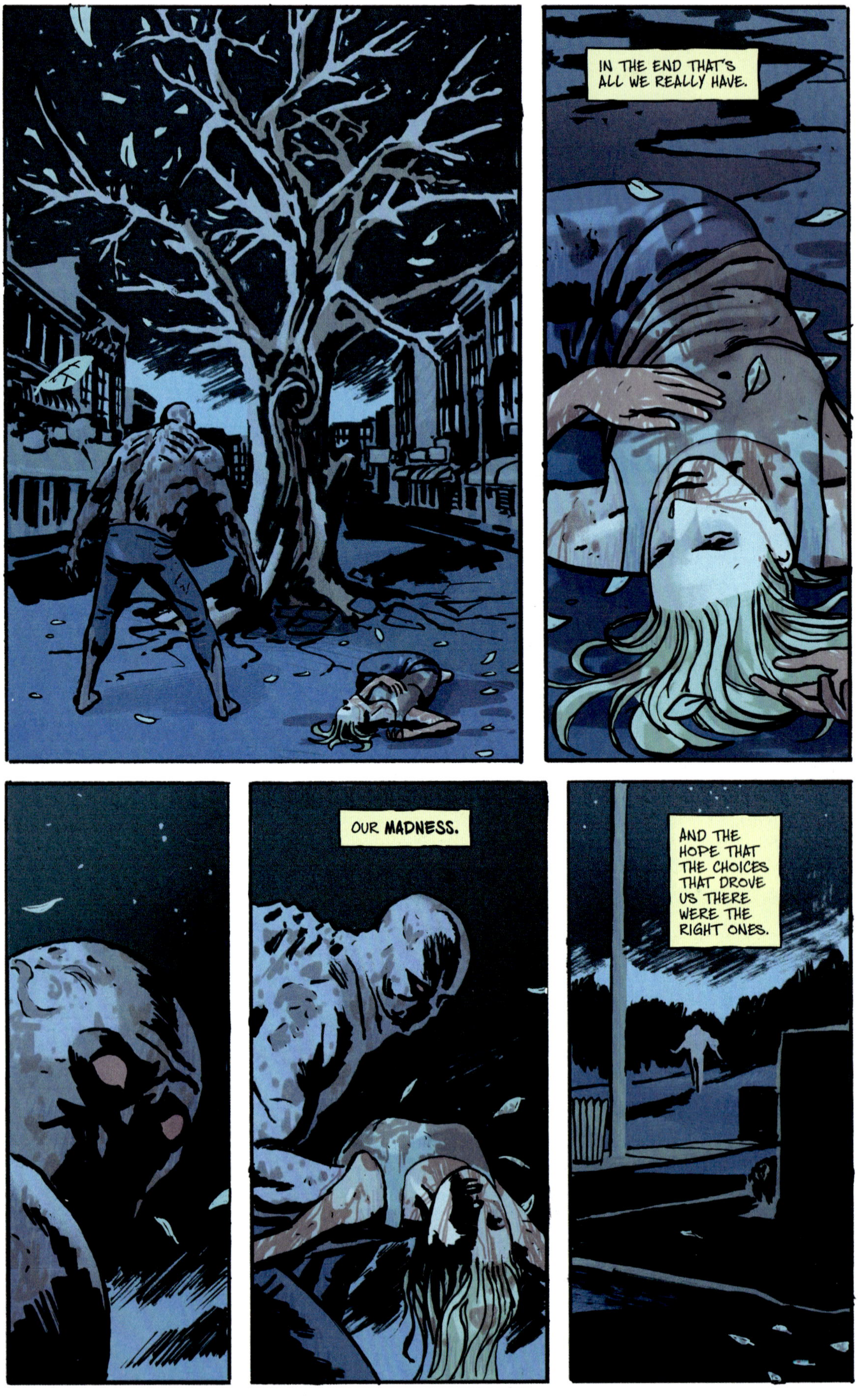
IN THE END THAT'S ALL WE REALLY HAVE.
OUR MADNESS.
AND THE HOPE THAT THE CHOICES THAT DROVE US THERE WERE THE RIGHT ONES.

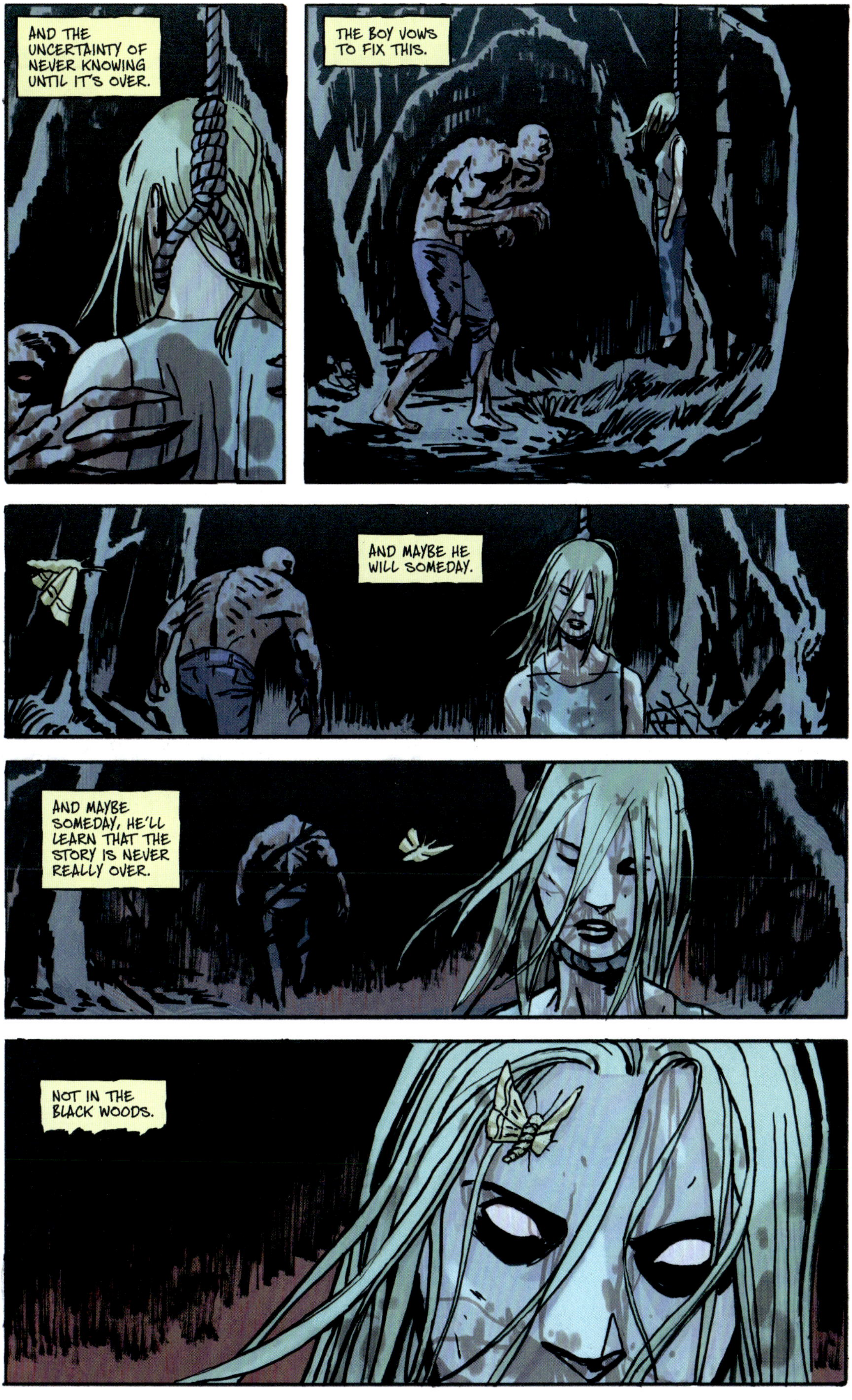
AND THE UNCERTAINTY OF NEVER KNOWING UNTIL IT'S OVER.
THE BOY VOWS TO FIX THIS.
AND MAYBE HE WILL SOMEDAY.
AND MAYBE SOMEDAY, HE'LL LEARN THAT THE STORY IS NEVER REALLY OVER.
NOT IN THE BLACK WOODS.

CHILDREN OF THE WOODS™

SKETCHBOOK

Commentary by Joe Ciano

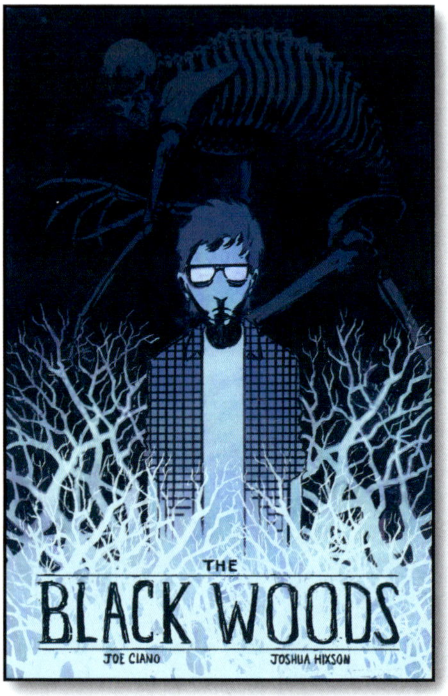
THE
BLACK WOODS
JOE CIANO
JOSHUA HIXSON

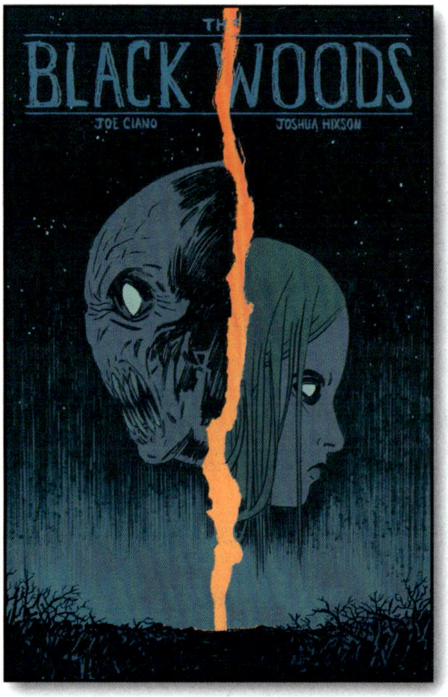
THE
BLACK WOODS
JOE CIANO
JOSHUA HIXSON

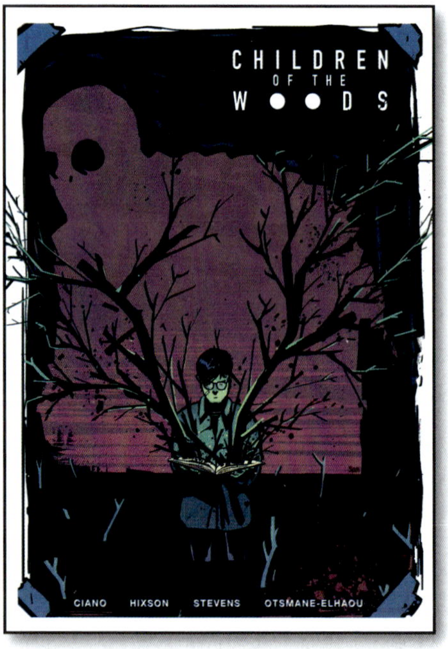
CHILDREN
OF THE
WOODS
CIANO
HIXSON
STEVENS
OTSMANE-ELHAOU

We originally developed the story under the title *The Black Woods* with an issue-style release before switching to the new name and deciding to put it out as an original graphic novel. We tried to make each cover thematically fit the issue, while also just looking really engaging. For issue one (*top left*), we have Quinn with the skeleton/foundation of what he would become both physically and psychologically. With issue three (*top right*), we tried to show Amber becoming more like Quinn, and while they are split, they're very much two sides of the same journey.

Besides being an amazing colorist, Roman is also a really fantastic artist. One day, he just surprised us all with this original piece (left). The focused look on Quinn's face and the visual of the trees coming out of the book are just incredible. It captures the early part of the story so well, and we absolutely had to include this in the book.

This scene originally called for a portal to appear and tentacles to come out and drag Mr. and Mrs. Richards to their fate. Early in the sketching stage for chapter three, we kind of came to the realization that it would be too "Elder Gods" and not really the style we were looking to hit. Josh came up with this amazing idea of them sinking into the floor, and I think that worked so much better. It kept the spirit of the scene the same, and just felt much more like us. Add in what Hassan was able to do with lettering as Mr. and Mrs. Richards became submerged, and it came together to feel really special.

In the early draft of this, Quinn is supposed to bite down on Caroline's head and crunch it. Kind of make it gory and disgusting. We decided to change it to where he swallows it whole, and it's now one of my favorite images in the book. The outline of her face as she slides down Quinn's throat is probably one of the most unsettling visuals we did. Sometimes less is more.

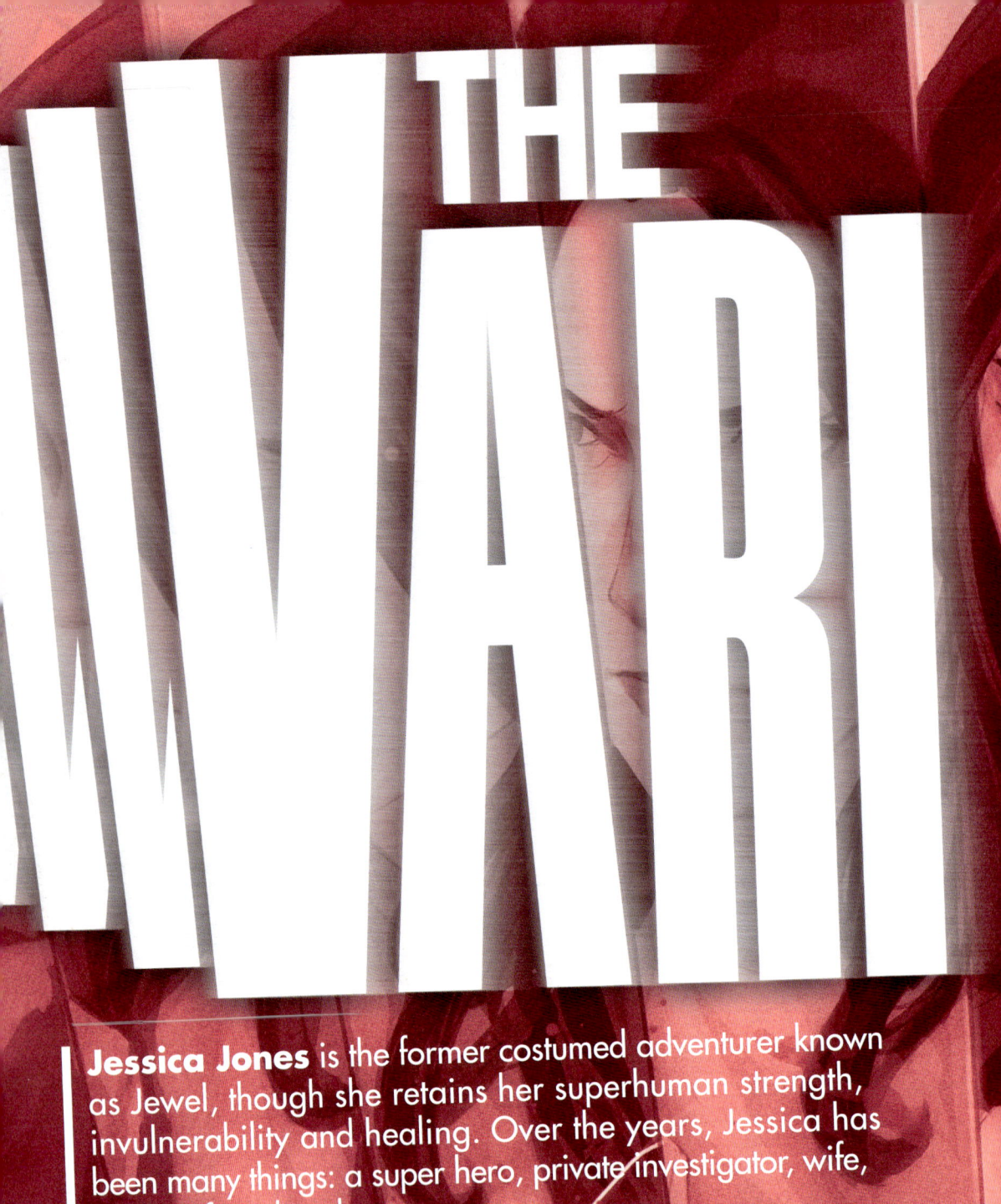

Jessica Jones is the former costumed adventurer known as Jewel, though she retains her superhuman strength, invulnerability and healing. Over the years, Jessica has been many things: a super hero, private investigator, wife, mother, friend and more.

Across the **Multiverse**, there exist infinite versions of Jessica from countless realities.

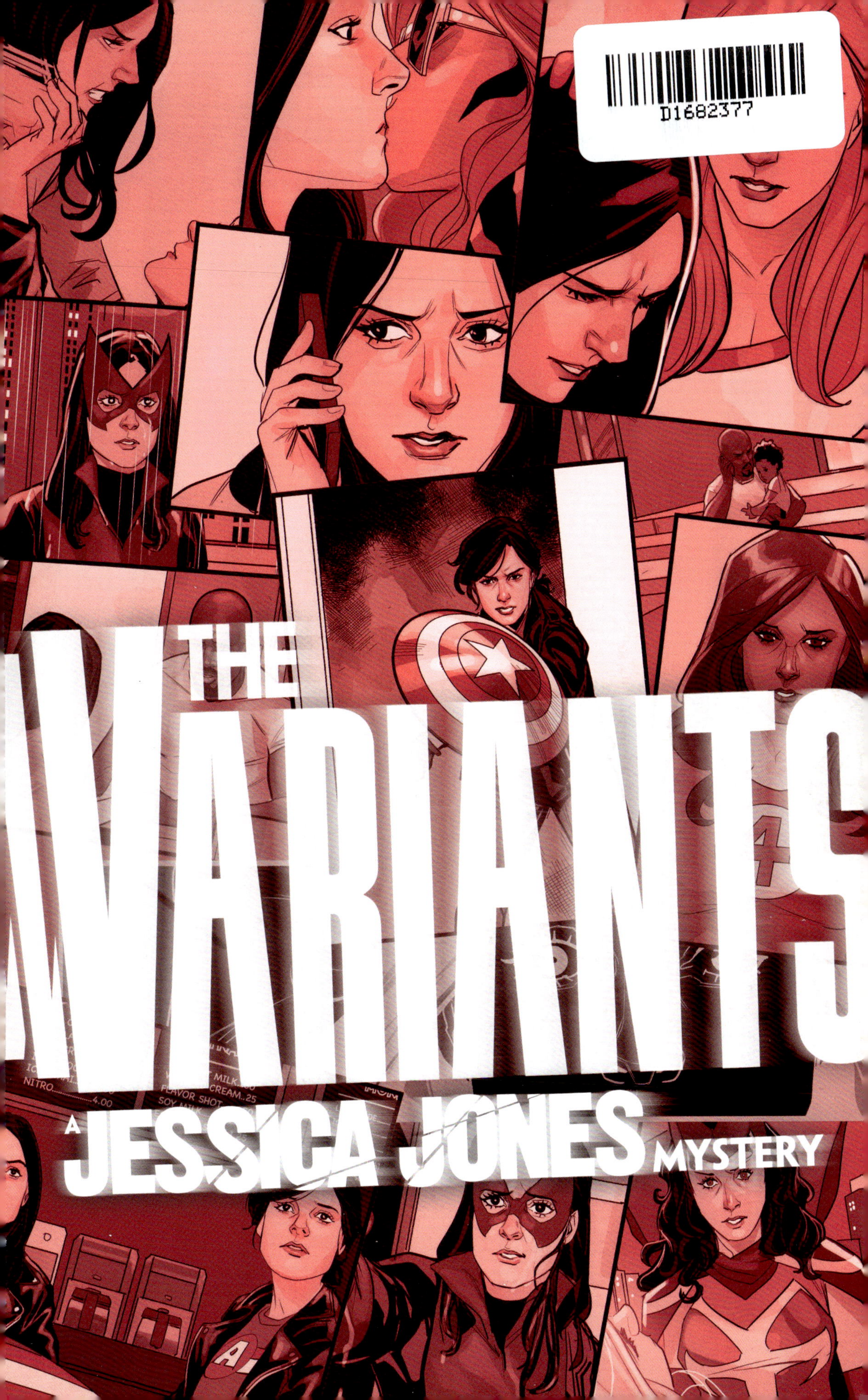
THE
VARIANTS
A JESSICA JONES MYSTERY